TALES FROM
JABBA'S PALACE

edited by
Kevin J. Anderson

D0001527

SPECTRA™

BANTAM
New York Toronto London Sydney Auckland

TALES FROM JABBA'S PALACE

A Bantam Spectra Book / January 1996

*SPECTRA and the portrayal of a boxed "s" are trademarks of Bantam
Books, a division of Random House, Inc.*

®, ™, © *1995 by Lucasfilm Ltd. All rights reserved. Used under
authorization.*
*Interior illustrations by Michael Manley, Aaron McClellan, Al
Williamson, and Lucasfilm Ltd. Courtesy of West End Games.*
Copyright © 1995 Lucasfilm Ltd.
Cover art by Stephen Youll.
Cover art copyright © 1995 by Lucasfilm Ltd.
*No part of this book may be reproduced or transmitted in any form or by
any means, electronic or mechanical, including photocopying, recording,
or by any information storage and retrieval system, without permission
in writing from the publisher.*
For information address: Bantam Books.

ISBN 0-553-56815-9

Published simultaneously in the United States and Canada

*Bantam Books are published by Bantam Books, a division of Random
House, Inc. Its trademark, consisting of the words "Bantam Books" and
the portrayal of a rooster, is Registered in U.S. Patent and Trademark
Office and in other countries. Marca Registrada. Bantam Books, 1540
Broadway, New York, New York 10036.*

PRINTED IN THE UNITED STATES OF AMERICA

OPM   17

WELCOME TO TATOOINE: ONE CRIMINAL KINGPIN, TWO SUNS, A HUNDRED ROGUES

MALAKILI—The professional monster trainer was transferred from the Circus Horrificus to care for Jabba's pet rancor. But the voracious carnivore was only the second most dangerous beast in the palace.

MELVOSH BLOOR—The academic came to study Jabba at his palace—and discovered a new meaning for "publish or perish."

OOLA THE DANCER—Despite the chain around her neck, her grace was her glory. As Jabba drooled and tugged upon her chain, she stood her ground —on the edge of eternity.

GARTOGG THE GAMORREAN—Dim-witted, friendless, the palace guard patrolled the ill-lit back hallways where nothing ever happened. Now he has a chance to solve a murder, make a name for himself, and make some new, if decidedly odd, friends.

BIB FORTUNA—Jabba's majordomo had big plans for himself—to overthrow the Hutt and take over his palace and his riches. But a traitor should be careful, for those involved in his plot may have plans of their own.

BOBA FETT—Famous as the galaxy's fiercest bounty hunter, he learned firsthand about the slow death faced by the unfortunates who landed in the Great Pit of Carkoon—and how mercy and vengeance are sometimes the same thing.

To SUE ROSTONI

*who has been more helpful than any of Jabba's min-
ions could have ever been, offering suggestions,
troubleshooting obstacles, and navigating me
through a forest of details that would have given
even a Hutt a headache!*

Acknowledgments

Thanks go to Lucy Wilson for being so enthusiastic about the idea of anthologies in the first place, Tom Dupree for his efforts at Bantam Books, and Bill Smith at West End Games for providing the foundations for so many of these stories. And, as always, Rebecca Moesta Anderson, for putting up with me at times when she probably should have just fed me to the rancor.

—KJA
October 1994

Contents

CONTENTS ✧ x

"If I told you half the things I've heard about this Jabba the Hutt, you'd probably short-circuit!"

—See-Threepio to Artoo-Detoo

Introduction

Jabba the Hutt has many enemies.

Called a "vile gangster" by some, Jabba's criminally gained wealth and power has placed him in a dangerous position in his guarded citadel under the twin suns of Tatooine. Though few openly covet Jabba's wealth, this does not stop them from plotting in secret.

The Lady Valarian, the female Whiphid owner of the Lucky Despot hotel and casino, is Jabba's chief rival. Hairy and tusk-faced, with a voracious appetite (some say literally) for males of her species, she keeps a low profile, planning in the long term.

Prefect Eugene Talmont, stationed in Mos Eisley, is the Imperial in charge of the Tatooine garrison. He hates his backwater assignment and hopes that by eliminating Jabba he can find a way out of the arid hole where he has landed.

Then there is the mysterious order of B'omarr monks, who originally built the enormous citadel for their solitude in the desert depths. The monks, wrapped in their ethereal concerns, seem oblivious to the fact that Jabba—and many other bandits in the decades before him—usurped their stone fortress. But no one can know what the quiet, uncommunicative monks are really thinking.

Jabba is always on his guard, but little does he suspect that his greatest nemesis will come in the form of a single Jedi Knight, who walks in alone from the desert . . .

Note: For the reader's convenience, all alien languages have been translated into Basic.

A Boy and His Monster:
The Rancor Keeper's Tale

by Kevin J. Anderson

Special Cargo

The unidentified ship tore through the brittle atmosphere of Tatooine with a finger of fire, trailing greasy black smoke. Waves of sound, sonic booms from the crashing ship, made an avalanche through the air.

Below, the Jawa sandcrawler continued its endless

path across the Dune Sea looking for forgotten scraps of abandoned metal, delicious salvage. By sheer luck the crawler stood only two dunes away when the plummeting ship struck the ocean of blind sand and spewed a funnel of dust that glittered like mica chips under the blazing twin suns.

The pilot of the corroded sandcrawler, Tteel Kkak, stared out the narrow window high up on the bridge deck, unable to believe the incredible fortune the luck of his ancestors had dropped in his lap. His crawler's year-long trek across the wastelands had been practically fruitless, and he would have been ashamed to return to his clan's hidden fortress bearing so little—but now a virgin ship lay within reach, unclaimed by other scavenging clans and unsullied by time.

The ancient reactor engines shoved the immense sandcrawler into motion. It ground over the shifting sands seeking purchase with wide treads in a straight line for the smoldering wreckage.

The ship lay in a crater of loose, blasted sands that might have cushioned the impact; some of the cargo should still be intact. The armored chambers and parts of the computer core might be salvageable. Or so Tteel Kkak hoped.

Jawas swarmed out of the sandcrawler toward the wreckage: the entire scavenging arm of the Kkak clan, little hooded creatures surrounded by a rank musty scent, chattering as they claimed their prize.

The front group of Jawas carried chemical fire-suppressant packs, which they sprayed on the hissing hot metal to minimize further damage. They did not look to see if anyone had survived the crash, because that was not their primary concern. In fact, living passengers or crew would only complicate the Kkak salvage claim. Those injured in such wrecks rarely survived Jawa first aid.

The Jawas used up two battery packs in the sputtering old laser cutters to cut their way through the hull into the armored bridge compartment. Dim light from emergency systems and the still-flickering glow from internally burning electronics components lit the abandoned stations.

Harsh chemical fumes and curling gray-blue smoke struck Tteel Kkak's sensitive nostrils—but underneath he could detect an undertone of metallic fear, the copper smells of blood splashed and burned. He knew he would find no one alive in the captain's chair. What he was not prepared for, though, was to find no bodies at all—just dark, wet arcs of sprayed blood, melted starbursts from blaster fire on the walls.

The other Jawas opened the main bulkhead doors and flowed in, chittering. Scout teams poured into the remains of the ship, spraying down smoldering sections and squirming through collapsed walls to find other treasures in the cargo hold.

Tteel Kkak directed one of the younger clan members to demonstrate his prowess by slicing into the main bridge computer to download the registry number and owner of the vessel, just in case there might be some large bounty, a reward for simply reporting the whereabouts of the hulk—after they had stripped it of all valuables, of course.

The young clan member—Tteel Kkak's third sister's fifth son by her primary mate—pulled out a scuffed, flatscreen reader with stripped raw wires dangling from the end. He used his rodentlike claws to peel back the access plate of the bridge panel and squealed as sparks flew when he connected the wires. He jammed the leads into other pickups, tapped into the dying energy in the ship's backup batteries, and called up the information in flickering green phosphor letters across the screen.

The captain of the ship had been a humanoid named Grizzid, and Tteel Kkak's fantasies diminished.

He had hoped for some well-known dignitary or VIP passenger.

This Grizzid person had departed from the Tarsunt system, another place Tteel Kkak had never heard of. Dismissing that, he directed his young assistant to find more important information—the cargo manifest.

When new letters scrolled up on the screen, the device flickered, and his young assistant had to slap it several times before it functioned again. The flat-screen scrolled up a dismayingly short list of contents. Tteel Kkak's thumping heart sank. One item, marked only as "special cargo," had been placed aboard by a Bothan trader named Grendu, a dealer in "rare antiquities," who requested that extreme precautions be taken. A heavily reinforced duranium cage filled most of the ship's cargo hold.

Tteel Kkak let pheromones of disappointment waft into the air, strong enough to overcome even the acrid burning smells. Unless that cage had been immensely strong indeed, this precious special cargo, whatever it was, had certainly been killed in the crash.

Just as that thought crossed his mind, though, he heard squeals of terror and pain—and a rumbling growl from within the wreck, basso and bone-jarring, deep enough to make the remnants of the ship vibrate.

Over half the Jawas wisely bolted through the opening in the hull, fleeing back to the safety of the sandcrawler; but Tteel Kkak was pilot and clan representative, and he was responsible for salvage. Though it seemed the smartest thing to do, he could not simply run from a loud, scary sound. He wanted to find out what this thing was. The "special cargo" might be valuable, after all.

He grabbed the arm of his young assistant, who sent up an unpleasant aroma of dark, ice-metal terror. As they charged down the sloping corridors, they were nearly bowled over by seven shrieking, retreating Jawas who squealed an incomprehensible mixture of words and an impossible-to-read scent that conveyed nothing more than nauseating fear.

Tteel Kkak saw long streaks of blood along the corridor, huge red-smeared footprints. The lights had burned out farther down the corridor, and the ship still clicked and settled as the fires cooled and the desert sun baked the outside. The loud, reverberating growl came again.

Tteel Kkak's young assistant tore away from his grip and joined the others running out of the ship. Alone now, Tteel Kkak proceeded slowly, cautiously. Chewed bones lay on the floor, as if something had stripped the flesh with scimitar fangs and discarded the leftovers like white sticks.

Ahead, a doorway to the lower cargo hold gaped like a skull's empty eyesocket. Outwardly bent bars crisscrossed the opening. The door had been ripped from its hinges—but not in the last few moments and not in the crash, as far as he could tell. This had happened some time earlier.

Within the shadows, something enormous moved, growled, lashed out. As far as Tteel Kkak could tell, the thing had broken out of its cage as the ship approached Tatooine and had gone back to its lair to finish devouring the rest of the crew. But when the unmanned ship had crashed, the thick walls had crumpled inward, trapping the thing in the same cage that had protected it from death in the impact.

Drawn by a deadly curiosity even greater than his fear, Tteel Kkak crept closer. He could smell the thing now: a thick, moist scent of violence and rotting meat. He saw the torn shreds of several Jawa cloaks. He sniffed the air, smelled sour Jawa blood.

He hesitated one step away from the opening— when suddenly a wide, many-clawed hand larger than

Tteel Kkak's entire body swept out in a rapid arc like a branched fork of lightning during sandwhirl season. Tteel Kkak stumbled backward and fell flat on his back. The monstrous clawed hand, the only part of the creature that could reach through the opening, swept across the air, seeming to tear space itself. Claws struck the corridor walls, *skreek*ing along the wall plates and leaving parallel white gashes.

Before the monster could slash again, Tteel Kkak leaped to his feet and scuttled up the sloping corridor to the opening in the bridge compartment. Before he had gotten halfway there, though, his mind began to reassess the situation, wondering how he could still get any profit from this wreck.

He knew only one being who might appropriately enjoy this hideous, dangerous creature: one who lived on the other side of the Dune Sea, in an ancient, brooding citadel that had stood for centuries.

Tteel Kkak would have to forfeit most of the salvage materials, but he did not want to deal with this monster. He hoped he could talk Jabba the Hutt into paying him a large finder's fee, at least.

The Care and Feeding of a Rancor

Malakili, professional monster trainer and beast handler, found himself unceremoniously transferred from the Circus Horrificus—a traveling show of alien monstrosities that wandered from system to system, aweing and frightening crowds of spectators. "Transferred" was the word imprinted on his contract file, but the truth was that Malakili had been purchased outright like a slave and then hustled off to this unpleasant scab of a desert planet.

As the Tatooine suns broiled down, Malakili already missed the dozens of bloodthirsty alien creatures he had tended for years. No one else understood exactly what he did. No one else knew how to tend the touchy and often excitable beasts on display. The circus performances would no doubt get very bloody as inexperienced handlers tried to do those things for which Malakili had become famous. The Circus Horrificus would fall on hard times without his services.

But as he disembarked from the private landspeeder outside the looming spires of a citadel high on the cliffs, Malakili began to grasp the importance and the power of this being called Jabba the Hutt.

The rock walls of the palace thrummed in the baking heat of double suns. At the base of one of the spires a spiked portcullis clattered upward, and two humanoid creatures stepped out of the shadows. One was clad in flowing black robes that accentuated the paleness of his pasty skin, bright eyes, and fanged mouth. A pair of long, thick tentacles hung from the back of the creature's head, one wrapped around his neck like a garrote: a Twi'lek, Malakili noted, one of the heartless creatures from the harsh planet Ryloth, who had a reputation for shifting sides as rapidly as a breeze shifted in the desert.

Beside the Twi'lek stood a scarred, grizzle-faced human, a Corellian from the looks of him, whose face was puckered with either pockmarks from a disease or the long-healed scar from a vicious blaster burn. The Corellian's hair was black except for a shock of pure white that streaked through it like a distress flare.

"You are Malakili," the Twi'lek said. It was not a question. "I am Bib Fortuna, and this is my associate, Bidlo Kwerve."

Kwerve nodded his head, but his emerald eyes remained fixed on Malakili as if nailed in place. Malakili flinched under his stare. Given other training, he thought, this Corellian could have become a good beast handler.

Malakili was muscular from a life of lifting heavy objects and wrestling strong creatures. His paunch had grown large from the good eating he enjoyed as the star of Circus Horrificus, his face was stretched and ugly, his eyes wide and round like full moons. But Malakili cared little for his personal appearance. He was out to impress no one. As long as the monsters held him in respect, he asked for nothing else.

"We are Jabba's lieutenants. We have summoned you," Bib Fortuna said.

"Why?" Malakili asked, his voice gruff, his fists planted squarely on his ample hips.

"We have a gift for Jabba," Fortuna continued. "A ship crashed in the desert carrying a special cargo, a creature that no one seems able to identify. Bidlo Kwerve here used eight gas grenades to stun the monster enough that we could transport it into one of the dungeons beneath the palace." The Twi'lek rubbed his clawed hands together. "It is our master's birthday tomorrow. He has been away on business, having recently purchased a cantina in Mos Eisley. But he will be back tomorrow, and we want to surprise him. Of course with a creature of this, er, bulk and temperament, we wanted it to come with its own keeper."

"But why me?" Malakili said. His words came out as displeased grunts. He was not accustomed to extended conversations. "I was happy with my old job."

"Yes," Bib Fortuna said, flashing a mouthful of needle-sharp teeth. "You spent seven seasons with the Circus Horrificus, training their specimens without being eaten. That's a record for them, you know."

"I know," Malakili said. "I liked the monsters."

Bib Fortuna clacked his claws together. "Then you'll *love* this one."

• • •

Bib Fortuna and Bidlo Kwerve stepped back into the dripping shadows of the lower dungeons as Malakili stared through the barred peephole into the pit. He was enthralled, enraptured by the mammoth beast.

It growled as it breathed. Its beady eyes flashed even in the darkness. It moved with a quick, liquid grace that many agile creatures half its size could not manage.

"Magnificent," Malakili said through puffy lips. He felt cool tears like lines of ice down his cheeks. He had never seen anything so beautiful in his life.

"Did I not tell you?" Bib Fortuna said.

"I think—" Malakili drew a deep breath, still awed and afraid to voice his suspicions. "I think this is a rancor. I have heard of them, but never dreamed that I would be lucky enough to see one in my lifetime."

"You're not just *seeing* this one," Bib Fortuna said. "He is yours. You must take care of him."

Malakili felt his heart swell with pride, and he beamed at Jabba's two lieutenants. "That I will do to the best of my ability," he said.

The bloated crimelord Jabba the Hutt knew everything, so it was impossible to keep a secret from him—even a supposedly secret birthday gift. Still, his two lieutenants—with Malakili standing behind them—acted as if they were presenting Jabba with a great honor as they congratulated him on his birthday.

"As our gift to you, great Jabba," Bib Fortuna said, "we have found a magnificent and exotic new pet for you—a vicious monster called a rancor. This is its keeper." He gestured behind him, extending wicked-looking claws toward Malakili, who still wore only a loincloth and draped black headdress. He had washed his bare chest and polished his paunch to be presentable for the first time he met his new master.

Jabba leaned forward, his large eyes blinking. A tongue as thick as a wet human thigh stroked a new layer of slime along his swollen lips. His dais slid forward, closer to the grilled opening.

Below, the rancor paced in its dank confinement, making sounds like tearing wet paper. Jabba's body rumbled with pleasure. Malakili saw both Bib Fortuna and Bidlo Kwerve visibly relax their tense shoulders as they saw that Jabba was pleased. Taking heart from this, Bidlo Kwerve stepped forward and spoke, the first time Malakili had heard words come from the scarred Corellian.

"I performed the actual capture, Master Jabba." His voice was high and raspy—rather whiny, Malakili thought. No wonder Bidlo Kwerve kept his mouth shut most of the time.

Jabba sat up quickly, a startled reaction. Bib Fortuna waved his hands frantically to exercise damage control. "Yes, Master, what Bidlo Kwerve says is true, but I performed all of the . . . administrative details. You know how difficult these things can be."

Jabba leaned forward again to stare at the rancor. He sighed with pleasure. Bib Fortuna explained the workings of the new trapdoor they had installed in front of the dais, anticipating how much amusement Jabba might get from dropping enemies into the rancor pit. Salacious Crumb, the loudmouth Kowakian lizard-monkey, laughed and jabbered at Jabba's shoulder, sometimes repeating words, other times making his own nonsensical sentences.

"I am most pleased," Jabba said.

Malakili pricked up his ears but kept his face impassive. He had learned how to speak the Hutt's dialect many years before because the most bloodthirsty audiences to which the Circus Horrificus played consisted of coldhearted Hutts watching other creatures in pain.

"I shall reward each of you greatly," Jabba said.

"One of you shall become my new majordomo, my right-hand man to assist me and to run the palace while I'm away. The other . . . shall have an even greater reward, one that history will remember."

Bib Fortuna bowed, and his head-tails lashed. He seemed tense, though Malakili could not understand why. Bidlo Kwerve looked satisfied and unconcerned. "Master," Fortuna said, "I shall be satisfied with the majordomo position. As Bidlo Kwerve has pointed out, he performed the greatest service to you. Please allow him to have the greater honor."

Bidlo Kwerve shot a suspicious glance at him, blinking his ice-green eyes. Jabba nodded. "Good," the Hutt said.

Kwerve stepped forward. The Corellian looked again at Bib Fortuna. "What did he say?" Now Malakili understood the twitching expressions on the Corellian's face. Bidlo Kwerve didn't understand Huttese!

Bib Fortuna gestured him forward as he himself stepped back. Kwerve raised his pocked chin in the air and stood in front of Jabba, awaiting his reward.

"You shall be the first victim I feed to my rancor," Jabba said. "I will watch your struggles and remember them for all time."

Salacious Crumb cackled maniacally. The group of Jabba's followers in the throne room snickered and watched. Bidlo Kwerve looked to Bib Fortuna, and it was clear he did not know what Jabba had said.

As the Corellian's face was turned aside, Jabba punched the button that released the trapdoor. The floor fell out from beneath Bidlo Kwerve.

In following years, everyone agreed that Bidlo Kwerve put up a spectacular fight. The Corellian had somehow managed to conceal a small holdout blaster in his body armor—which was strictly forbidden in Jabba's presence. But the rancor's sheer ferocity astonished the spectators even more as it devoured its first live meal since its capture on Tatooine.

Malakili watched the monster's victory and felt warm inside, like a proud father.

General Dentistry

Jabba took exceptional delight in his new pet over the next few months, devising various victims and combat situations for the monster.

Bib Fortuna rose in prominence in the crimelord's organization. Malakili, though, kept to the lower levels of the palace, talking with only the few denizens who also preferred the dank coolness and the anonymity of shadows to being in plain sight of Jabba or his minions.

In his prowls scavenging extra food for his pet, Malakili got to know Jabba's primary chef, Porcellus, rather well. The man was a talented food preparer who lived in constant fear that he would create something Jabba didn't like, at which point his life and his culinary skills would be forfeit. Malakili would toss slabs of fresh, dripping meat into the openings for the rancor, and the monster seemed gradually to accept him as its caretaker.

For those seeking Jabba's approval, it soon became a game to find new combatants for the rancor. At first Malakili took the challenges with pride and confidence, knowing that the coiled killing machine would snap up any prey—but gradually he became aware that Jabba did not esteem the rancor as Malakili did. The Hutt saw it as merely a diversion, and if some monster were found that could defeat the rancor, then Jabba would be just as pleased to have a new toy.

The Hutt had no compassion for the beautiful beast. He wanted only to test it and test it until it failed.

The rancor became injured for the first time when Jabba released three Caridan combat arachnids into the pit. The combat arachnids had twelve legs each and crimson body armor splotched with maroon, as tough as a thin layer of diamond sheeting. Their bodies were so covered with needle-sharp spines that it was difficult to tell where the spines ended and the sharp legs began. But the jaws were very obvious, jagged pistons three times the size of the bullet-shaped heads and driven with enough power to shear open the hull of an armored transport.

As the gates in the secondary cells were opened and the three angry combat arachnids rushed out with a thunder caused by three dozen legs, Malakili and the rancor—as if psychically connected—both reared back in surprise. Up above, Jabba's booming laugh, "Hoo-hoo-hoo," reverberated through the observation grille along with the cheers and catcalls from the simpering minions who crowded around to show their loyalty.

The rancor bent over and splayed its hands, blinked its small dark eyes, and let out a bellow of challenge. It waited for the attack.

The three combat arachnids surged forward seemingly in silence, but Malakili's ears hurt from a painful high-pitched throbbing, as if the arachnids communicated on some hypersonic level.

One arachnid ran directly beneath the rancor's legs. Moving too slowly to react to this unexpected tactic, the rancor swept the ground with its fistful of claws, but the combat arachnid escaped to the other side.

While the rancor was distracted, the other two

arachnids lunged at its leathery legs, slashing with spines. The rancor batted one creature away, knocking it against the wall with a crunch that split its armor plating open and speared the soft inner organs with broken shards.

But the rancor howled in pain and held up its hand. Malakili could see dark dribbling spots where two of the arachnid's long spines had thrust all the way through.

The second combat arachnid latched onto the back of the rancor's leg, where the taut muscles pulled like durasteel cables. The huge mandibles clamped down and ground together, chewing with all the mindless mechanical force the combat arachnid could apply.

Snarling, the rancor bent over and tried to use its shovellike hands to rip the mandibles free; when it could not break their grip, it pried at the head of the arachnid instead.

Finally, the third combat arachnid leaped onto the rancor's lumpy back from behind as the monster bent over. The third creature slashed with its sharp legs, stabbing with spines, tearing open a butcher's pattern in the rancor's hide.

With a squeal of confusion and betrayed pain, the rancor reared up, stumbled backward, and slammed itself into the stone blocks of the wall. The rancor rammed backward again and again, shattering the hard plating of the arachnid clinging to its back until the thing lay in a jumble of twitching sharp legs on the debris-strewn flagstone floor.

The last surviving arachnid continued to chew on the sinewy leg. Finally, as if numb with pain and unable to think clearly, the rancor grabbed the powerful mandibles and tore the monster's head completely off, ripping the body away and lifting it up so that it dangled a few strings of bright red ganglia out of its neck socket. The head remained clamped to the rancor's leg, still chewing in a reflex action.

With no other outlet for his rage, the rancor hefted the spiny, armored body of the combat arachnid into his sword-filled mouth and bit down, crushing through the spiny pincushion of the arachnid's carcass. Bright vermilion ooze spurted out of the rancor's mouth from the ruptured, bloated abdomen—but it was mixed with another color of ichor as well, the blood of the rancor. Its mouth had been flayed, ripped to shreds by chomping down on the dead carcass of its last enemy.

Malakili began to mumble in dismay. The rancor was hurt; it bled from many different wounds. As it continued to gnash reflexively on the brittle, spiked arachnid in its mouth, the rancor tore free the still-fastened head on its leg, yanking away a bloody gobbet of its own flesh as it did so.

Malakili wanted to react, wanted to rush in and help the rancor in its pain—but he didn't dare. The monster was in such a blind frenzy that it would not know the difference between friend and enemy. Malakili bit down on his knuckle, trying to decide what to do as the rancor stood bleeding and thrashing.

Suddenly, with a hollow thumping sound, four grenade canisters dropped down into the pit, spewing heavily drugged gas into the chamber. Impenetrable metal sheets dropped over the windows, sealing the ventilation shafts to keep the knockout gas inside until the rancor could be sufficiently stunned.

He heard a step behind him and turned to see Gonar, one of the other skulking humans who seemed at a loss whether to spend more time hanging around Malakili and watching the rancor or remaining upstairs in the throne room so he could earn points with Jabba.

"Jabba wants to get the shells of those combat

arachnids," Gonar said, nodding like a marionette. His nose was turned up and flat, like a Gamorrean's, and his hair hung in greasy reddish curls as if he styled it with fresh blood.

Dazed, Malakili held a hand to his paunch, about to be sick. "What?"

"The carapaces," Gonar said. "Very hard and jewel-like. Combat arachnids are raised for their chitin as well as their fighting abilities. Didn't you know?"

Finally, after the rancor had slumped into unconsciousness, the sleeping gas was pumped out and the large access doors raised up, their bottoms jagged like teeth, as Jabba's crew of Gamorrean guards stumped in to haul away the broken remains of the arachnids.

Malakili pushed past them and rushed forward to the grunting, snoring hulk of his pet monster. The Gamorrean guards used a hydraulic winch to open the rancor's gigantic jaws, prying the fang-filled maw apart so they could remove the armored carcass of the combat arachnid.

The guards were not terribly bright, in Malakili's opinion, and they did not think before they acted. They exercised no care whatsoever as they tore free the dead insectlike creature, ripping the gashes in the rancor's mouth even wider.

Malakili shouted at them, charging forward and looking even more fearsome than his pet monster. The Gamorreans snorted in alarm, without a clue as to what they had done wrong; but Gamorrean guards were accustomed to not understanding, so they did not argue as they grabbed the jeweled carcasses and hauled them away.

Malakili ordered Gonar to fetch several large drums of a medicated salve kept in the infirmary of Jabba's palace, and soon the red-haired human came inside rolling one of the drums. Gonar popped it open, letting a vile chemical smell rise into the confined chamber of the rancor pen.

Malakili already felt dizzy, not just from the chemical smell, but from residual sleeping gas that clung to the dank air, as well as nausea from his disgust at seeing what had happened to the rancor. Taking handfuls of the wet, stringy goop, Malakili slathered the raw wounds in the rancor's hide. He looked around and found the flat, gnawed scapula of one of the rancor's previous meals and used the shoulder blade as a trowel to lay the disinfectant substance lovingly across the gashes.

Gonar assisted him reluctantly, afraid to come too close to the monster and yet wanting to. With the major exterior injuries tended to, Malakili turned to the ruined mess of the monster's mouth. He sent Gonar running for a pair of tongs, which he used to grasp the shards of diamond-hard chitin still wedged like broken glass between the rancor's fangs. He stood directly inside the rancor's mouth, yanking and tugging as he extricated the jammed pieces.

Gonar trembled watching him, but Malakili had no time to worry about such things. The rancor was in pain. If these shards remained stuck in its jaws, the wounds would become infected, and the monster would be even more ornery.

A foul stench rose from the rancor's throat as its stuttering snores grew quieter. Malakili found the shattered stumps of two rotten teeth that must have snapped off in some other battle. Malakili grasped these too and tugged them out. The stumps came loose more easily than he expected, but the rancor's mouth was so full of fangs that it seemed to grow two for every one it lost.

The monster stirred, and its beady black eyes blinked. Its nostrils flared as it heaved in a deep breath. Malakili leaped out of the way just as the jaws snapped shut.

"It's awake!" Gonar shrieked, and fled through the low door. The dose of the sleeping gas had worn off with alarming swiftness.

Malakili fell backward as the rancor lurched to its feet. It swayed unsteadily for a moment. Malakili considered that this might be his last chance to bolt for the door.

The rancor reared up and spread its claw-laden hands. It snorted and glared down at him, still in obvious agony.

Malakili froze, looking up at the monster. If he ran, that would draw its attention, and he would instantly be eaten. A part of him prayed that the rancor would recognize him and not kill him.

The rancor grunted again, then bent low to sniff the medicinal salve on its torn legs. It raised its humongous hand to its flattened nostrils and sniffed again, looking at where the wounds from the combat arachnid's spines had been salved and bandaged. The rancor grunted at Malakili, then looked around the floor of its den as if searching for something.

Malakili continued to stare, frozen in awe and terror. Sweat poured off his grimy skin. His heart hammered like colliding starships in his chest.

But then the rancor found what it was looking for: the long femur from a food beast. Still looking sidelong at the human in its pen, the rancor picked up the bloody bone and squatted down in its cage, gnawing nonchalantly, though his mouth must still have been in great pain.

Malakili stood there for a long, long time before he finally, quietly left.

A Game of Fetch

Malakili didn't bother to ask if he could take the rancor outside of the palace, where the monster could romp in the desert vastness, stretch its sinewy legs, and enjoy the freedom of open air. He figured no one would argue with him if he was accompanied by multiple tons of fangs and claws.

Malakili had been around vicious animals enough to know that the thing they wanted most in life, the thing simmering behind their small, ultrafocused minds as they paced in the pens they had grown to hate was the simple wish to *get out, get out, Get Out!*

Malakili waited until the hottest part of a Tatooine afternoon, after both suns had reached their peaks. At this time Jabba and his pandering minions took a siesta as their only defense against the smothering heat.

From the main garage levels, he took a one-person sandskimmer and parked it outside one of the huge weighted doors at the base of the citadel. This door had been opened exactly once, when Bidlo Kwerve and Bib Fortuna had hauled the stunned rancor into its pen and then sealed the door again with locks from the inside and outside. But Malakili used small explosive charges to blow the locks off the outside. The metal locks vaporized into silver steam. The echoing thump of the charges sent small scuttling things dashing to hide in shadowy cracks.

Malakili stood listening as a drowsy hot silence fell back over the palace, then he slipped inside to the dungeon levels. He stood outside the rancor cage, holding a small but powerful vibroblade specifically tuned to metal frequencies. The blade could chop through the thick locks inside the external door; it would take longer than small charges, but he didn't want the explosions to upset the rancor.

Gonar, the scrawny, high-strung human clinger, appeared out of the shadows. Malakili didn't like the way the young man always pestered him, watched him, followed him. "What are you going to do?" Gonar said. His greasy curls of red hair looked as if they had been anointed with fresh oil and his sallow face looked like spoiled milk.

"We're going to go out for a jaunt," Malakili said. "A game of fetch."

Gonar's eyes ratcheted open like huge cargo doors. "You're crazy. You're letting the rancor loose?"

Malakili chuckled. He was feeling very good about this entire excursion. He patted his rounded paunch. "I think we could both use the exercise, him and me."

He opened the cage door and ducked inside, clattering it shut behind him. Gonar gripped the bars and stared, but the young man would never dream of following Malakili into the monster's den while the rancor remained awake.

With the disturbance of its new visitor, the rancor rose to its feet and rumbled a low, liquid growl—but Malakili paid no attention. The rancor continued to look at him with cold and glittering eyes that showed an icy intelligence. But the monster had grown to tolerate Malakili's presence. In fact, the rancor seemed to enjoy the keeper's visits. Malakili had come to count on that.

In a blatant show of trust, Malakili waddled across the bone-littered floor of the den and walked directly between the rancor's knobby legs to get to the opposite wall where the slime-encrusted door had been sealed.

He bent down with his vibroblade and tuned the frequency and energy density higher as he chopped at the metal locks. Sparks and droplets of molten durasteel flew, but Malakili kept battering away until the locks lay severed.

The controls had been disconnected, but Malakili attached a new battery pack and hot-wired the circuit. With a screeching, ponderous sound, the heavy metal door labored upward, splitting open at the bottom and spilling a knifeblade of buttery sunlight into the dank pen. Hot breezes whipped in, stealing the cool dampness, until the door had groaned completely to the top, an open window to the freedom of the desert.

The rancor stood up, blinking its impenetrable eyes. It opened its arms, stretching out its heavily clawed hands as if worshiping the suns and the fresh air. The monster stood in amazement and confusion, glancing down at Malakili, not certain what was going on. Malakili motioned for it to go through the opening.

"It's okay," Malakili said in a soothing voice. "Go on, it's all right. We'll come back in a little while."

The rancor stepped out into the sunlight, flinched from the glare. Its shoulders hunched. Its shovel hands swung from side to side, scraping the floor of the pit—and then it stood up, strode out into the full light and heat, and bellowed a cry of sheer joy. Its fangs glittered in the double sunlight.

As if suddenly released from chains, the rancor broke into a loping run, stretching its legs, flailing its heavy hands from side to side to keep balance. The mottled green-tan hide seemed to vanish into the desert rocks.

Malakili watched the creature romp for several seconds, feeling his own delight, then he hopped onto the sandskimmer, fired up the popping, stuttering engine, and drifted after his pet monster.

The rancor sprang to the top of an outcropping of blistered lava rock. It tilted its head up and roared at the sky, raising huge claws, and then it jumped down again, picking its way along the rough, sloping cliff face.

Above, in the towers of Jabba's palace, emergency beacons flashed on. Malakili heard the distant, squeaking sounds of faraway guards shouting in alarm; but at the moment he didn't care. He would come back with the rancor. He would show that everything was all right.

When he flew too close to the rancor in the droning sandskimmer, the monster reflexively lashed sideways with its bony claws, as if Malakili were a bothersome insect. But Malakili swung around and flitted in front of the monster so that the rancor could identify him. The monster backed away, hung its head as if abashed at what it had tried to do, then continued out into the open sands.

The rancor loped across the hot, cracked ground, leaping over outcroppings in ecstasy. It ran far from Jabba's palace, but it was not fleeing—it just loved its freedom.

Malakili's chest swelled with joy, though he was ashamed at his own emotional weakness. Tears traced cool patterns on his cheeks. This was probably one of the most remarkable days in his life.

The rancor sprinted for a line of red-tan crags striped with strata that showed the rugged geological past of Tatooine. The broken mountains fanned out, cracked with numerous canyons like razor-blade jaws, rocky narrows cut sharply by ancient torrents of forgotten water. Seeing the shade and the rugged stair-like rocks to climb, the rancor put on a burst of speed toward the shadowy canyons.

Malakili punched the accelerator of the sandskimmer—but instead of providing additional speed, the small vehicle popped and coughed like a sick man spitting up a bubble of blood. The sandskimmer dropped under Malakili's weight. He clutched the handles, and his hands were suddenly greasy with sweat.

Jabba's palace loomed behind him in the distance, a brooding citadel like a stern father watching over those who had disobeyed.

Oblivious, the rancor dashed into one of the near canyons and vanished into the shadows.

"Wait!" Malakili shouted, his voice sucked dry like moisture in the desert sun. He wrestled with the sandskimmer as it angled toward the powdery sands and sharp knuckles of rock. Somehow, the vehicle remained aloft, puttering and staggering through the air until it reached the rocky wall of the ridge. He concentrated so heavily on keeping the skimmer in the air that he had lost track of which of the numerous side canyons the rancor had entered.

Malakili moaned as the skimmer finally crashed to the ground, tumbling him into sharp broken scree. He picked himself up from the stinging rocks and gazed toward the welcoming shade of the side canyons. The desert heat from the double suns screamed down at him.

He staggered across the broken ground, leaving the sandskimmer behind. He finally made his way into the dusty alluvial fan at the canyon's mouth, stepping over flattened clay and into the darker shade. Every step sent a crisp tinkling sound of broken rock as dry pebbles skittered against each other. Otherwise the world was incredibly silent.

He didn't know what to do. He couldn't walk all the way back to Jabba's palace, although he might try it in the dimness of the night. Despite his own peril, Malakili's main concern now was for finding the rancor. If he had lost the monster, Jabba would find a long series of imaginative and unspeakably painful tortures for him. It would be better to just lie down and bake to death in the desert sun.

But he couldn't believe that the rancor would abandon him so blithely. They had been through too much together.

He picked his way over the ancient riverbed for about an hour, looking for the rancor's tracks, but he saw nothing, heard nothing, only a few pattering rocks from high above.

At last, up ahead, came a surprisingly soft skitter of stones underfoot. A large lumbering shadow disappeared into a small split in the wall, a miniature canyon with sharp overhangs and time-smoothed rock faces.

Malakili picked up speed, hoping to find the rancor so that at least they could face the future together. "Hello!" he said. His feet crunched on the dry pebbles as he waddled forward. "Here, boy!"

But as he rounded the corner, a screaming demon leaped out in front of him—man-sized, but with a face wrapped in bandages, mouth covered by sand filter, and eyes peering through a pair of gleaming metal tubes.

Sand People! Tusken Raiders.

The demon held a long, sharp gaffi stick in his hands like a quarter staff. Its hooked end bounced up and down as the Raider bellowed a challenge.

Malakili staggered back and then recognized two other Sand People astride enormous woolly banthas, mammoth-sized beasts with curved tusks around their ears. The two mounted Tuskens squawked, and the banthas responded as if telepathically, charging toward him.

The unmounted Tusken leaped down from the rock and swung at Malakili with his hooked gaffi stick.

Malakili was unarmed. He lumbered backward, but knew he could not escape. He reached down, grabbed a rock, and threw it at his attacker, but the projectile went wide.

Huffing and snorting, the banthas stampeded

toward him. Malakili fell onto the sharp rocks, and he knew the monsters were going to trample him. He would be crushed to a pulp within seconds.

Then, with an echoing roar that split loose rocks from the cliff face, the rancor leaped down from an overhang high above. Reaching out with its claws, the monster crashed into the lead bantha, tackling it to the ground.

The bantha snorted and reared, but it didn't understand what had just happened. The rancor used his powerful claws and durasteel-strong muscles to grab the tusks on both sides of the bantha's head, twisting it as if turning a wheel on a bulkhead door. The bantha's head wrenched sideways, and its spine gave a hollow, wet crack as its neck snapped.

In a single follow-through motion, the rancor swept its claws sideways and tore open the Tusken Raider that had been knocked from the bantha.

The second rider wailed a challenge, thrashed his own gaffi stick in the air, and charged directly at the rancor. The bantha kept its head down, curved tusks forward like a battering ram—but the rancor flitted sideways with deceptively easy speed and snatched the Tusken from the bantha's back. It raised the victim to its cavernous mouth and stuffed the Tusken in, chomping down with vise jaws of razor fangs, swallowing the attacker in only two gulps.

With its rider gone, the bantha went wild, as if crazed. The rancor scooped up an enormous broken sandstone boulder that had fallen from the cliffs above in ages past.

Malakili staggered to his feet. The first Tusken Raider had turned his bandaged face to stare at the battle between rancor and bantha, forgetting his human victim. Watching the rancor, Malakili felt the fury from his pet monster. He saw the Tusken who had attacked him, who had swung a gaffi stick at him.

Malakili picked up a much smaller boulder, but one still deadly enough.

The bantha reared up and tried to butt the rancor, but the rancor hefted the sandstone boulder. It brought the stone crashing down on the mammoth beast's shaggy head, snapping the tusks like brittle straws and caving in the creature's thick skull. The bantha grunted. Momentum carried it forward until it slumped in a tumbled heap to the canyon floor.

As the last Tusken Raider heard a sound beside him, he whirled, bringing his gaffi stick up just as Malakili struck with the smaller boulder, crushing his attacker's swathed head. The Tusken Raider fell to the rocks, thick bandages soaking up the spreading flower of bright blood.

Malakili's heart pounded as he looked at the carnage. The rancor let out a ululating bellow of triumph and looked at Malakili with something like contented satisfaction. Then the monster squatted over the bloody carcass of the slain bantha and began to feed.

Later, Malakili clung to the dry knobby skin of the rancor's neck as the monster trotted across the sands in the desert twilight. It knew where its home was and arrowed straight toward the underbelly of Jabba's palace. As it ran hunched over, puffs of sand drifted into the purpling night.

The rancor had gorged itself, and blood spattered the monster's chest. It seemed to consider Malakili strange for not devouring the Tusken Raider he had killed, but Malakili had no appetite.

Already he was wondering how he would explain everything to Jabba the Hutt.

Lunchtime Beneath the Jaws

It turned out that Jabba didn't particularly care that Malakili had taken the rancor out for a romp in the wastelands—he was furious, however, that he had missed its titanic battle with the two banthas.

Malakili beamed with a paternal pride as he extolled his monster's bravery and viciousness, but Bib Fortuna whispered a different suggestion into Jabba's ear. The Hutt lurched upright on his dais with a belch of delight. Wouldn't it make a magnificent duel to pit the rancor against a *krayt dragon*?

The legendary desert dragons of Tatooine were huge and rare and instilled more fear than any other creature in this sector of the galaxy. None had ever been captured alive before, but Jabba's incentive—one hundred thousand credits guaranteed to anyone who could bring in a live, unharmed specimen—was enough to ensure the most ambitious efforts. Even the great bounty hunter Boba Fett vowed to remain at Jabba's palace as he considered the best way to tackle the challenge.

Malakili was convinced that someone would succeed, and he looked upon the threatened battle with great dread. Though he was proud of his rancor's abilities, he knew how awesome the krayt dragons were.

Jabba planned to build a special amphitheater out in the bowl of desert sands visible from his tallest towers, where the krayt dragon and the rancor would face off and tear each other apart. Even if the rancor managed to defeat the incredible dragon, Malakili suspected the battle itself would wound the rancor grievously, perhaps mortally.

He couldn't allow that.

Down in the lower levels of the dungeons, Malakili wheeled a heavily laden cart stacked high with dripping stacks of meat, sawed bones, and leftovers from the slaughterhouse connected to Jabba's kitchens. Porcellus, Jabba's chef, had set aside choice morsels as treats for the rancor, as well as a sandwich of sliced, marinated meat for Malakili's own lunch.

Malakili got along well with the skittish cook, passing along whatever gossip he managed to hear in the lower levels, though he had to listen to the chef's ever-increasing fears that Jabba would soon tire of his culinary abilities and feed him to the rancor.

With a sigh, Malakili pushed the cart to the barred gate of the rancor pit. The wheels squeaked like a terrified bristling rodent in the dungeon levels. He swung open the gate, pulled the cart through, and fastened the door behind him.

The rancor stood up and watched him bring the mound of meat closer, running a stubby purplish tongue across the edges of its packed rows of teeth. Malakili nudged the meat in front of the rancor after removing his own white-wrapped sandwich from the top of the pile. The rancor used a hooked claw to sort through the lunch offerings until it selected a curved dewback rib studded with lumps of gristly meat.

Malakili unwrapped his sandwich and hunkered down on the rancor's bench-sized toe. Above him, the monster chewed on the long rib bone, gnawing and slurping. Malakili's black headdress protected him from the splattering gobbets of dripping juices that fell from the rancor's mouth, showering him and running down his own bare back.

As he ate, munching absently on his delicious sandwich, Malakili thought about his possibilities, the options—and his future.

It had been clear from the start that Jabba's main goal was to challenge the rancor until some greater opponent killed it. Jabba cared nothing for the monster, and neither did any of the others. Even greasy-haired Gonar was terrified of the monster, wanting to be around the rancor only for the prestige and the power it offered. The other spectators who hung around the dungeons had no attachment to the beast either—not the hairy Whiphid guard who poked his tusks against the bars of the cage, watching the bestial power of the rancor as if it reminded him of something from his home planet; not Lorindan, the nozzle-nosed spy who had no motives other than to find information he might sell to someone else.

No, Malakili was alone on Tatooine. He alone loved the monster, and it was up to him to see that his pet was protected. He would find some way to help the rancor escape—and himself along with it.

Malakili continued to chew on his sandwich, swallowing in a dry throat as plans began to form in his mind. Jabba was a powerful crimelord, yes, but he was not the only power on Tatooine. Jabba had many enemies, and Malakili had much information.

Perhaps he could find some way to buy freedom for his pet.

In the Monster's Lair

Near the center of the grubby city of Mos Eisley, a battered cargo hauler gathered dust. After landing one time too many, the *Lucky Despot* could no longer pass a single safety test, and so the hulk had remained where it sat, abandoned, until a group of misguided Arconan investors decided to convert it into a luxury hotel, hoping to take advantage of the extensive tourist trade on Tatooine.

Shortly after the entrepreneurs went bankrupt, the Lucky Despot hotel and casino was taken over by a new crimelord on Tatooine, an upstart rival to Jabba who had great dreams, modest capital, and a mean streak wider than her yawning, tooth-filled mouth.

The Lady Valarian lounged back in her contorted chair, relaxing in her plush office. She looked as suave as was possible for a horse-faced, tusk-mouthed, bristle-haired Whiphid female. As she spoke her smooth syllables, it seemed as if she were trying to purr—but to Malakili, it sounded like an overgorged gundark gargling with its own bodily fluids.

"I know you are from Jabba's palace," Lady Valarian said with a grunt deep in her throat. Her peglike tusks shoved forward from her underjaw as she leaned closer. She batted long eyelashes at him.

Malakili whiffed her heavy perfume that attempted to mask the rank, musky smell of Whiphid fur; he thought this was a worse odor than anything he had smelled in the cages at the Circus Horrificus.

"Yes, I am from Jabba's palace," Malakili said, stroking his black headdress, "but Jabba can't always provide everything I need. So I've come to you, Lady Valarian."

She hunched her shoulders and lifted her brutally ugly face. Her body trembled in what Malakili took to be an expression of mirth. "And how do you expect to pay for this favor you ask of me?"

"I know that Jabba is your enemy, Lady Valarian," Malakili said. "I know that you might wish to have full schematics of the palace. The B'omarr monks who built it have kept the layout secret. You might wish to learn some of the hidden entrances to the lower levels. You might wish to know some of Jabba's habits and weaknesses."

Lady Valarian snorted. "Don't you think I have my own operatives inside Jabba's palace?"

Malakili showed no expression, although he was terrified. "I said nothing about your operatives. I merely offered my own services. If you intend to challenge Jabba the Hutt, you must be very careful, indeed."

He hoped he had said the right words. He, who had

spent seven seasons taming the wildest creatures in the Circus Horrificus, now felt completely out of his depth in a plush room with a perfumed female who could squash him with a snap of her fingers.

"I'm not saying that I have any personal interest in doing harm to Jabba," she said. "In fact, he and I have a limited partnership. He owns a token percentage of the Lucky Despot. But, information is sometimes incalculably valuable, difficult to estimate its worth. It is unwise to dismiss an opportunity to increase one's knowledge." She raised a bristly eyebrow. "Would you care for a drink? Then you may tell me about this favor I can grant you."

Malakili nodded dumbly as she brought him one of Tatooine's most expensive beverages in a frosted glass: clear, chilled water with two ice cubes floating in it. Malakili sipped his drink, licked his lips as the cold liquid danced down his throat.

"I'll need a ship—a cargo ship with a specially reinforced cage chamber."

Lady Valarian widened her nostrils with a hefty sniff of curiosity. "A cage? What are you going to transport?"

"A live animal," Malakili said. "And myself. I intend to take Jabba's pet rancor with me. I need to find a deserted world, preferably lush, a jungle moon perhaps or a backwater forested planet where a resourceful person could eke out a living, and where a large creature could have his freedom and enough prey to hunt to his own satisfaction."

Lady Valarian growled in stuttering low bursts, which Malakili interpreted as delighted laughter. "You want to steal Jabba's rancor? That would be hilarious! Oh, this is too good to miss. Yes, yes, I will provide the ship you need. We can set the time and the date."

"As soon as possible," Malakili said.

Calmly, Lady Valarian waved a clawed hand across the glowing sheen of her antique desktop. "Yes, yes, as soon as possible. The most important thing, I think, will be to install a tiny spycam in Jabba's throne room —just so I can watch the expression on his bloated face when he finds out what's happened!"

Valarian tapped some unseen marker on her desk, and a melodious chime rang out. The door whisked open, and two heavily polished protocol droids marched in. "Yes, Lady Valarian?" they said in unison.

She directed one of the droids to take Malakili to another room where he would provide "certain information." The other she instructed to arrange for a ship, to find a suitable world according to Malakili's specifications, and to arrange all the details of the passage.

"My gratitude, Lady Valarian," Malakili said, stumbling over his words, still unable to believe that he had stepped down the irrevocable path.

Valarian chortled again as Malakili got up to follow the protocol droid into the corridor. "No, thank *you*," she said. "This is worth any number of investments." The door closed behind her while she was still chuckling.

Bad Timing

Malakili tried to remain calm and behave normally as he counted the days to the appointed hour of his rescue.

He watched with furtive eyes, suspecting spies in every shadow—but Jabba and his followers above in the throne room seemed oblivious to Malakili's actions. Jabba was caught up in the troublesome details of running his new cantina, and he also boasted that his bounty hunters would shortly bring him a krayt dragon—which meant that the Hutt limited the violent challenges upon the rancor, not wishing the monster to be injured before its titanic battle. The most recent fresh and kicking meal the rancor had devoured was a mere Twi'lek dancing girl, which the rancor savored, consuming her in three delicate bites rather than the customary one large gulp.

Malakili tried to relax, hoping that perhaps his plan would come off smoothly after all. But, as he was wheeling the meat-laden cart of the rancor's lunch to the cell gate, pallid-faced Gonar stepped out of the shadows with an idiotic, devilish grin.

"I know about you, Malakili!" Gonar said in a hushed, hoarse whisper. "I know about you and the Lady Valarian."

Malakili stopped the cart and turned slowly, trying to keep from showing his shock—but he had never been good at hiding his emotions. "And just what do you know about me and Valarian?" he asked.

"I know you're spying for her. You were traced going into Mos Eisley, into the Lucky Despot. I know you saw her in her private chambers. I don't know what your game is, but I know that Jabba won't like it."

Malakili couldn't hide. His eyes flitted from side to side. Inside the cage the rancor sensed his keeper's alarm and let out a low growl. "What do you want?" Malakili said.

Gonar heaved a relieved sigh, as if pleased that he wasn't going to have to argue any more. He swiped a greasy strand of hair out of his eyes. "*I* want to take care of the rancor," he said. "I've been around him as much as you have. He should be *my* pet."

Gonar flicked his eyes toward the cage. "Either you flee now and leave me to take care of the monster," he said, "or I'll report you to Jabba, and he will kill you, and I will still claim the rancor as my reward.

Either way, I get what I want. The exact manner is up to you."

"You don't leave me much choice," Malakili said, whimpering.

"No," Gonar said, drawing himself up, puffed with his own triumph. "No, I don't leave you much choice."

Malakili grabbed a heavy femur from the rancor's lunch pile. Without pause, he swung the blood-wet bone with all the strength behind his bulging muscles. He brought the knobbed club smack against Gonar's forehead. His skull crushed like a soap bubble. The young red-haired man slumped to the floor. His last sound was merely a squeak of surprise.

Inside its cage the rancor stirred and made a rumbling, hungry noise. This had not been as difficult as killing the Tusken Raider out in the canyon, Malakili thought, but it seemed more satisfying somehow. More of a personal triumph.

He picked up Gonar's limp body. It seemed to have acquired a dozen more joints from the way his arms and legs and spine flopped in all directions.

Just as Malakili was hauling the body onto the cart, he heard thumping footsteps and a clank of armor as one of Jabba's plodding, not-too-bright Gamorrean guards came around the corner carrying another dead body on his shoulder. He blinked his porcine eyes and curled his lower lip to push protruding fangs out. The guard shoved his helmet down against the horns on his head and squinted at the scene with Malakili and the fresh body.

"What this?" the guard asked, using one of the few Basic phrases it knew.

Malakili stared at him, holding the body of a man he had just murdered. The bloodied club still lay on top of the pile. He couldn't possibly make up a good explanation. "I'm feeding the rancor. What does it look like I'm doing?"

The Gamorrean stared at the dead body along with the butchered remains from the kitchen. He grunted and nodded again. "Need help?"

"No," Malakili said. "No, I'm doing just fine." He looked meaningfully into the dimness of the rancor's cage and at the Gamorrean's burden. "You want to unload him, too?"

"No! Evidence of crime!"

The Gamorrean waddled off humming to itself, unchallenged by life and delighted to be doing his tedious job to the best of his ability.

That day the rancor enjoyed its lunch even more than usual.

The pickup from Lady Valarian was scheduled for just after dawn, before Jabba and his minions could rouse themselves from the lethargy brought upon them by wild parties all through the night.

As far as Malakili could tell, no one had mentioned the disappearance of Gonar, but other clingers had taken the young man's place as standby observers during feeding time and training: each one in awe of the beast, each one wanting to share a bit of its power just by being close to it.

Malakili went inside the rancor cage and made sure the locks on the heavy outside door had been freshly cut so that the escape would be easy once Valarian's ship arrived.

He looked at his chronometer, double-checking, counting down. Less than an hour to go. His heart pounded.

The rancor was tense and restless in its cage. It knew something was up, and it made questioning, snorting

noises every time Malakili came within view of the outside doors.

"Just a little while longer, my pet," Malakili said.
"Then we can both be free of this place."

Above, he heard only the dull silence and the
drowsy sounds as Jabba and the others slept, even the
scantily clad new human wench whom he kept
chained to the dais.

Malakili heard footsteps skittering about like spiders
above, those few who remained awake to build their
own plans against Jabba. He heard the rattling of a
grate above. Other footsteps. Malakili cursed the disturbance.

He looked at his chronometer again and was
alarmed to hear Jabba stirring, others talking, the
minions awakening. A visitor had appeared. Not now!

Malakili hissed and paced up and down the dank
corridors. He couldn't have Jabba waking up now.
Perhaps Jabba could take care of the new business
quickly and decide to catch another hour or so of
sleep.

He heard Jabba's booming voice. Something that
might have been an argument. An outcry—and then
from above the trapdoor opened, and two more bodies tumbled into the rancor pit.

Malakili moaned, kneading his fists together. "Why
now?" He looked at his chronometer again. The rescue ship would be coming any moment.

Several of Gonar's replacements pressed forward
next to Malakili to watch the new victims die in the
pit. He couldn't remember any of their names. He
couldn't care about them now. He whispered a message he knew the rancor could not hear. "Just eat
them. Hurry, my pet!"

He saw a young, thin human male—nothing to
worry about there—and one of the stupid Gamorrean
guards. Malakili cringed when he saw the guard still

had his wicked vibro-ax, which could hurt the rancor —but the guard seemed too terrified to remember his weapon.

The piglike brute turned to flee, but the rancor was upon him in a second, grabbing him up and jamming the entire body into its mouth. It chomped down, then slurped the still-twitching legs down into its throat. The rancor turned to the human male and strode forward.

Malakili looked at his chronometer. Lady Valarian's ship would be approaching even now, drifting silently across the sands, creeping to the secret rendezvous. "Come on!" he whispered.

Up above, the spectators cheered and cackled wildly. Jabba's deep-throated laugh echoed into the pit. The watchers seemed to be giving the spectacle more importance than it should have had. Malakili wondered who this victim was.

The young man ran to the other side of the pit, snatching one of the discarded bones on the floor just as the rancor grabbed him in its claws and lifted him up to the jagged jaws.

The human thought fast and jammed the long bone like a support strut into the rancor's mouth, and the monster dropped him as it bit down on the splintery bone, snapping it.

Malakili winced, remembering the shards from the combat arachnids that had caused so much pain to the soft inner lining of the rancor's mouth. "My poor pet," he said.

Malakili calmed himself. *No matter.* Once they escaped, he would have all the time in the worlds to take care of his monster, alone and at peace on their own world.

The young man ran in panic like a spooked Jawa, slamming against the open grille of the access door trying to get out. Malakili batted him back, and the others pushed the young man away.

"Hurry up and get eaten!" he said, glancing yet again at his chronometer. There wasn't much time.

Inside the den the young human ran straight between the rancor's legs, beneath the monster and to the other side.

Malakili slapped his forehead in dismay. The same silly trick the combat arachnids had used, but the rancor had still not figured out how to defend against it.

The rancor turned and lumbered toward the human again, arms outstretched. The human ran into a low chamber where the rancor frequently slept, ducking under the heavy jagged door that could be closed off when others needed to clean the cage.

Malakili felt his heart pounding, and he hissed in a cold breath. Above, the others shouted and cheered even louder than before. Even if the rancor ate this human in the next few seconds, the spectators would not settle down for some time yet. He let another moan escape his throat. Now what was he going to do? Lady Valarian would not wait.

The rancor had the human trapped now, and it hunched low to pass into the sleeping den. The human grabbed up a round ivory boulder—no, a skull— and hurled it at the controls just as the rancor leaned under the jagged door.

The skull triggered the switch, and the massive durasteel door crashed down like a guillotine blade. The jagged end slammed into the rancor's head and spine, hammering the monster down to the floor and smashing open his skull, splitting his hide.

The rancor snorted and whimpered once in stunned pain, as if calling out for Malakili, and then it died.

Malakili stood like a statue. His jaw dropped open

as his ears filled with a roaring white noise of disbelief and utter anguish. "No!" he wailed.

The rancor was dead! The pet he had tended and cared for . . . the creature that had rescued him from the Tusken Raiders . . . who had allowed him to sit on its knobby foot as Malakili ate his lunch.

Other guards opened the cage as angry shouting came from above. They whisked the young struggling human away, but Malakili was too much in shock even to notice.

Moving like a droid, unable to stop himself, Malakili staggered into the cage where he stood in front of the carcass of the dead monster. Most of the other hopefuls, the ones who had wanted to take care of the rancor, melted away, seeing their chances for advancement erased. Only one man, tall and swarthy with dark hair, followed him in.

Malakili watched the ichor ooze across the slimy flagstone floor. The rancor lay still, as if sleeping. Finally, unable to stand it any longer, Malakili let loose his tears like a flashflood on Tatooine. He wailed in grief, ready to faint, not knowing what he was supposed to do now.

The man next to him—Malakili could not remember his name, no matter how hard he tried—put a grimy hand on Malakili's shoulder, patted him and tried to comfort him, but he stumbled away through a blur of tears. All he could see were his own memories of wonderful days with the rancor.

He heard Jabba's angry pronouncement echo through the grille, ordering that the human captive be taken out to the Great Pit of Carkoon and fed to the Sarlacc. Jabba didn't care that the rancor was dead: he was merely disappointed that his anticipated great battle with the krayt dragon could not now take place.

The tears continued to flow down Malakili's chubby

cheeks, tracing clean rivers across his grimy skin. His Adam's apple bobbed up and down, trying to strangle further sobs.

Malakili thought only of how much he hated Jabba, how the crimelord had ruined everything. Even before the grief began to fade, Malakili found ways to replace it, vowing that he would get even with Jabba the Hutt. He would find some way to make the sluglike gangster pay.

Outside in the blistering heat of afternoon, Lady Valarian's rescue ship circled, and waited, and waited, and finally slipped back toward Mos Eisley, empty.

Valarian did not care. She already had the information she wanted.

Taster's Choice:
The Tale of Jabba's Chef

by Barbara Hambly

It started the day Jabba the Hutt acquired his two new droids.

Not that the arrival of new slaves in the isolated desert palace of the Bloated One made a great deal of difference to Porcellus, the crimelord's harassed chef; his only question, when informed of the new additions by Malakili, keeper of the Hutt's rancor, was, "What do they eat?"

"They're droids," said Malakili. He was perched on the end of the long and massive kitchen worktable at the time, picking through two cubic meters of dewback offal and eating a beignet. Minor religions had been built around Porcellus's beignets in Mos Eisley—scarcely the oddest objects of veneration in that port, it should be added. Porcellus had a huge pot of them going on one of his four stoves, and the heat in the long, low-vaulted kitchen was tremendous.

"Good," said Porcellus. It wasn't that he objected to real people coming around his kitchen to cadge snacks. It was just that most of the people in the court of the Tatooine crimelord who *did* come around his kitchen made him extremely nervous.

"Quite polite, too," added Malakili. "High-class social programming."

"That'll be a switch." Porcellus gently tonged the last beignets from the boiling oil at their exact moment of apotheosis, set them on the paper toweling on the counter, dusted them reverently with powdered sugar, and activated the portable electric fence around them. He smiled across at his friend. "Present company excepted."

"Oh, the guards and stuff ain't so bad." Malakili paused as Phlegmin the kitchen boy came in carrying a box of the fragile Belsavian bowvine fruit which had just been delivered. The pimple-faced youth sniffled, wiped his nose on his fingers, and started to take the fruit from their box, looking sullen and offended when Porcellus motioned him sharply to wash his hands. "Well, maybe some of 'em," the rancor keeper conceded. He hopped down from the table, and crossed to where the chef was examining the fruit for subcutaneous bruises with the delicate fingers of an artist. Phlegmin tried in passing to steal a beignet—the electric fence hurled him several feet against the nearest wall. He retreated, sucking his burned hand.

"A word in your ear, friend," Malakili whispered.

Porcellus turned from his work, the familiar sensation of cold panic clutching at his chest. "Eh?"

Back in the days when he had been chef to Yndis Mylore, governor of Bryexx and Moff of the Varvenna Sector and that Imperial nobleman's most prized possession—and how not, when he was a triple Golden Spoon and winner of the Tselgormet Prize for gourmandise five years running?—Porcellus had not been a particularly nervous man. Concerned about the perfection of his art, yes, for what great maestro is not? Worried, from time to time, about the firmness of a meringue served when the Emperor was Governor Mylore's guest, of course, or the precise combination of textures in a sauce to be presented at an ambassadorial banquet . . .

But not prey to chill terror at every unexpected word.

Five years as a slave in the palace of Jabba the Hutt had had its effect.

"Jabba, he had indigestion again last night."

"Indigestion?" Later Porcellus realized his immediate reaction should have been uncontrolled horror; it was actually, at first hearing, only a laugh of utter disbelief. "You mean there's actually a substance he can't digest?"

Malakili lowered his voice still further. "He says he thinks it's *fierfek*. As far as I can make out, that's the Hutt word," he went on softly, "for poison."

Then the uncontrolled horror took over. Porcellus felt himself go white and his hands and feet turned cold despite the oven heat of the kitchen.

The rancor keeper put a big hand on his friend's shoulder. "I like you, Porcellus," he said. "You've been a good friend to me, letting me take a couple scraps for my baby . . ." He jerked a thumb at the mass of steaming meat and meat by-products that occupied a good two-thirds of the table. "I don't want to have to throw you in there with him. So I thought I'd drop you the word before Bib Fortuna gets down here to talk to you about it." Malakili gathered up the corners of the oilcloth upon which the offal was heaped, and lugged it out the door in a trail of dribbled juice.

Porcellus said, "Thanks," though his mouth was too dry to produce actual sound.

"His Excellency is most displeased."

"Entirely without reason, Your Worship. It is wholly the result of a regrettable misunderstanding." Porcellus bent almost double in a deep bow and hoped Bib

Fortuna, Jabba the Hutt's vile Twi'lek majordomo, wouldn't notice the ransacked boxes and canisters which covered every horizontal surface in the kitchen, the result of a frenzied search for anything that might have caused the Bloated One's unprecedented discomfort. Since many of the delicacies which had gone into the Hutt's omelettes, *roulades,* and *étouffées* over the past years were inedible by any lesser species, the search hadn't been an easy one—the chef was still wondering about the goatgrass he'd used the previous evening as a stuffing for the gamwidge, and the small unmarked red canister of unidentifiable paste whose contents had been used to top yesterday's chocolate ladybabies.

The Twi'lek's small eyes narrowed still further; in the kitchen's mephitic light they had the appearance of dirty glass. "You know how solicitous our master is about his health."

Neither of them was going to speak the word "poison," of course.

"Absolutely," groveled Porcellus, reflecting that between Jabba's wholesale consumption of triglycerides, cholesterol, and alcohol—never mind substances less identifiable—and indescribable sexual practices, the Hutt would scarcely *need* poison. Porcellus was still trying to deal with the concept that a Hutt *could* be poisoned. "I scarcely need to assure you that throughout my term of service here I've accepted nothing but the finest, the most healthful, the tastiest ingredients to lay before His Excellency's discriminating palate. I am at a loss to understand this most distressing development."

Arms folded, Fortuna drummed his long nails gently on his own biceps. "Should the situation continue," he said in his soft voice, "explanations for it could be devised."

"Here!" Porcellus whirled, lashed out indignantly with the dishtowel in his hand. "That's the master's!"

Ak-Buz, commander of Jabba's sail barge, backed quickly away from the little electric fence around the beignets, dropping the pair of long-nosed nonconductive machinist's pliers he'd used to poke through the current. A snarl contorted his leathery face—the only expression, as far as Porcellus had ever been able to ascertain, of which Weequays were capable—and he ran out of the kitchen into the hot sunlight of the receiving bay, shoving the stolen beignet into his lipless mouth as he went.

"They seem to think this place is a charity kitchen." Porcellus mopped nervously at the last traces of spilled sugar.

"Shall I suggest to Jabba that the Weequay be punished?" Fortuna's voice was a dangerous purr. "Thrown to the rancor? A little quick, perhaps, though Jabba is fond of the spectacle . . . Lowered into the pit of the brachno-jags, perhaps? They're small in themselves, but a hundred can strip a being's bones in, oh, five or six hours. One alone—if that being is tied up quite firmly—can take four or five days." He smiled evilly. "Would that be a fitting punishment for one who tampers with His Excellency's food?"

"Er . . ." said Porcellus. "I don't think that's necessary."

To his own great distress, his words turned out to be prophetic, as he discovered some hours later when he tripped over the barge captain's dead body in the corridor leading to the lower regions of the servants' quarters . . .

Panic had had its effect. After searching the kitchen for another half hour, dogged by the sullen Phlegmin ("How come you let Ak-Buz take a beignet and not me? There's nuthin' in that box . . . What you lookin' for, anyway, boss?"), Porcellus had discovered, to his horror, that though the time was approaching to begin preparing that night's feast, he hadn't the smallest inspiration about what to prepare. Poached icefish imported from Ediorung on a bed of Ramorean capanata? What if Jabba should choke on a bone? A ragout of Besnian sausage with orange-Madeira sauce? If the spices should disagree with his already irritated digestion, what would his immediate assumption be? *Vegetable broth,* thought Porcellus, *vegetable broth and unspiced rice pudding* . . . He reflected upon the crimelord's probable reaction to such a menu, and the images conjured to mind were not pleasant ones.

In quest of inspiration for the first time in his life, he retreated to his room to consult his cookbooks, take a nap in the relative cool, and relax . . . he had to relax . . .

And there was Ak-Buz's body, sprawled in the corridor halfway to his room, arms outflung and eyes glaring fixedly in the sunken stare of death.

Porcellus knelt beside the corpse. Still warm. Shreds of sugar topping speckled the Weequay's quilted vest.

Maybe after consuming seventy-five kilos of dewback offal the rancor won't be terribly hungry tonight . . . ?

Snuffle, snort, demanded a deep, gluey voice. "What happened here?"

The chef leaped to his feet in a panic of shock and horror, to find himself facing one of Jabba's Gamorrean guards.

Porcellus had always hated the Gamorreans. They were among the worst of the food-cadgers, and he was forever cleaning up drool, dirt, and miscellaneous vermin in their wake. Last week five of them had come to blows in his kitchen over who was going to lick out the bowl from a Chantilly *crème,* with the result that the bowl ended up broken, two rather delicate processors were smashed, and Porcellus was nearly beheaded by an ill-aimed vibro-ax. The Chantilly *crème* had suffered, too.

"Going on?" squeaked Porcellus. "Nothing's going on."

The guard's porcine brow furrowed in a long moment of thought. Then he gestured with his spike-gloved hand at the barge captain's body. "He's dead?"

"He isn't dead," said Porcellus. "He's asleep. He's resting. He said he was tired and he was going back to his quarters to take a nap. He must have . . . he must have fallen asleep right here in the hall."

Ak-Buz's sightless eyes continued to stare at the ceiling.

The guard frowned, turning the information laboriously over in his mind. "Looks dead."

Porcellus could feel the rancor's claws closing around his body. "Have you ever seen a Weequay asleep?"

"Uh . . . No."

"Well, there you are." Porcellus bent down and heaved the body to its feet, draping an arm around his shoulders. For a horrible moment he wondered what he'd do if rigor mortis had begun to set in, but in that heat there was little chance of it. The glaring head with its filthy braids lolled against his cheek. "Now I'm going to get him to his quarters—er—before he wakes up."

The guard nodded. "Want help?"

"Thank you," smiled the chef. "I'm fine."

He concealed Ak-Buz's body in the scrap pile in the machine yard, a heartstoppingly tricky operation because he had to lug it through the dungeons and then out past the barracks where the Weequays lived. The Weequays—silent, deadly, vicious enforcers—were part of Ak-Buz's sail-barge crew, and though they showed little loyalty to anyone, Porcellus had the impression that being found in possession of the body of their commander wouldn't be such a good idea. But they weren't anywhere in sight—*probably in my kitchen stealing the beignets,* thought Porcellus gloomily—and neither was the sail barge's mechanic, Barada. With luck nobody would look under the monumental pile of rusting speeder parts in the yard's corner until decomposition was sufficiently advanced, something which shouldn't take too long in this heat. Ordinarily, on Tatooine, one would have to worry about Jawas raiding the scrap heap for metal, but the pieces of the last Jawa caught doing so were still fairly fresh, nailed to the gate.

Porcellus hastened back to his kitchen, wondering what he was going to do about the banquet tonight and bereft of the smallest crumb of inspiration.

"You call this food?" The Hutt crimelord's huge copper-red eyes swiveled slowly, the pupils contracting slightly with anger as they fixed their gaze upon his unfortunate servant.

Porcellus had never understood Huttese very well, but when Jabba raised one of the exquisite vegetable crepes in a hand surprisingly small and delicate in comparison with the rest of his yellowish, gelid bulk and squeezed it so that the contents plopped thickly to the floor, it was entirely unnecessary for his new translator droid, C-3PO, to explain, "His Excellency is most displeased with the food you have been serving of late."

Porcellus, standing before the Hutt's dais on the ornamental trapdoor that covered the rancor's pit, managed to make a small sound, but that was all. Eight meters below his boot soles, the rancor snuffled softly in the dark.

The horrible eyes narrowed. "You seek maybe to do me ill?"

"Never!" Porcellus dropped to his knees—causing the rancor in the pit below to rear up to its full height and sniff at the grille—and clasped his hands pleadingly. "How can I prove my goodwill?"

Jabba chuckled, a sound like a bantha being gutted —slowly. "We'll let my little one prove," he said, and dragged on the chain he held. From the dais beside him rose the lovely Twi'lek dancer Oola, Jabba's newest pet. Her delicate face showed apprehension, as well it might.

Porcellus had never learned exactly what Jabba did with his "pets"—usually female but always young, lithe, and beautiful—but he knew they seldom lasted long and he'd heard some truly horrible tales from his friend and fellow slave Yarna the Askajian.

At the moment, however, all the Hutt did was scoop up a fingerful of the vegetable-crepe stuffing and hold it out to her, and after a moment, with visible distaste, Oola licked the subtly flavored concoction from his slimy hand.

"Now bring me real food," gurgled the Hutt, turning back to Porcellus. "Fresh—live—*untouched.*"

By the time Porcellus returned to the palace hall with a glass bowl of live Klatooine paddy frogs—in flavored brandy to prevent them from attacking and killing each other, as was the wont of the ill-tempered little creatures—Oola, far from suffering any ill effects from the vegetable crepes, was dancing, swinging her long head-tails in sensual invitation, the chain still around her neck. Her performance, Porcellus thought, should lay aside Jabba's suspicions of *fierfek*— of poisoning—for good.

Ordinarily, Porcellus stayed as far away from Jabba's court as was possible within the confines of the palace, for the vicious and violent rabble of bounty hunters, mercenaries, and intergalactic scum terrified him. But tonight he leaned his shoulders against the arch of a doorway, thin and graying and nervous-looking in his unspeakably stained cook's whites, listening to the jizz-wailers—he'd always been fond of good wailing—and watching the dancing and hoping desperately the beautiful Oola wouldn't drop dead of some unknown cause as Ak-Buz had.

It crossed his mind to wonder what *had* killed the sail barge captain, but in this awful place, who could tell?

Jabba, laughing horribly, hauled on the dancer's chain. Oola shrank back, unable to control the revulsion on her face—it was quite clear that what he intended was not to feed her more vegetable crepes—and for a time the Hutt amused himself, playing her like a fish before triggering the trapdoor and dropping her into the rancor's pit below. She gave one hideous scream and everyone rushed to the grille to see the show; Porcellus shrank back into the archway, shaking like a weed stem in a windstorm. The casualness, the offhanded quality of her murder terrified him . . . The Hutt had killed her with as little reflection as he expended on the next paddy frog he gulped.

Just so, thought Porcellus, pale and almost sick with shock, would he kill his chef, if the slightest rumblings of indigestion brought the word *fierfek* back to his mind.

That was the night the bounty hunter brought in the Wookiee.

It was a mop-up operation, really. The Wookiee—well over two meters of shaggy hair and ill temper—was partner to a Corellian smuggler named Solo whose inanimate body, frozen in carbonite, had been decorating Jabba's wall for months. At one time Porcellus had toyed with the notion of unfreezing the man and bargaining for assistance in an escape, but at the last minute he'd lost his nerve. There was no way of knowing how cooperative he'd be even if Porcellus could keep him hidden long enough for him to shake off the blind weakness of hibernation sickness, and the thought of what Jabba would do to him if he was caught in an escape attempt had brought him into a sweat.

Jabba had advertised bounty on the Wookiee at fifty thousand credits, and was prepared to actually pay half that. After protracted negotiation with the bounty hunter—a ratlike scrap of a creature in a leather breathing mask—which included the hunter's threat to set off the thermal detonator it conveniently had in its pocket, they'd settled on thirty-five. At that point Porcellus retreated to his kitchen, reflecting that he was unsuited for financial dealings of that sort and wondering how he would manage if this particular bounty hunter came to the kitchen demanding beignets or Chantilly *crème*.

The kitchen boy, Phlegmin, was stone dead in the middle of the receiving-room floor.

Darkness seemed to tunnel in around Porcellus's vision—darkness that smelled of rancor. The next moment a huge hand shoved him aside and Ree-Yees, a sleazy Gran swindler and minor member of Jabba's court, barged into the receiving room, three eyes bulging on their short stalks as he stared down at the kitchen boy in disbelief.

"I had nothing to do with it!" shrieked Porcellus. "He never ate a thing in this kitchen! He never so much as touched a dish!"

Ree-Yees, on his knees pawing through the goat-grass in the open packing box beside Phlegmin's body, took no notice.

"Hey," snuffled a basso rumble from the doorway. "He sleeping?"

It was a Gamorrean guard. The same Gamorrean guard, Porcellus realized, who'd found him with Ak-Buz's corpse in the passageway.

His life flashed before his eyes in a kaleidoscope of croquettes and Coruscant sauce supreme. "I didn't do it!"

"You're just in time!" Ree-Yees sprang to his feet. "I just found him—er—just like this—down the hall—near the tunnel to Ephant Mon's quarters! And I brought him here to perform—uh—emergency culinary resus-susperation! Garbage inhalation of the last resort! It's an emergency technique I learned from . . ."

With great presence of mind, Porcellus slipped out of the receiving room and concealed himself in the very darkest corner of the kitchen. From there, a few minutes later, he watched the Gamorrean guard plod dutifully out, carrying the kitchen boy's corpse slung over his shoulder. He was followed in fairly short order by Ree-Yees himself, staggering as though his brain had been set on auto-pickle and reeking of Sullustan gin.

There was very definitely something going on in the palace.

"A plot," rumbled Gartogg, the Gamorrean guard, who returned to the kitchen the next morning, Phlegmin's corpse still slung over his shoulder and much unimproved by the day's rising heat. "Clues." A long pause, while he considered, as if carefully matching the contents of one of his brain cells with the contents of the other. "All tied together." He helped himself to a handful of the packing material which had come around a jar of candied rennet, and snuffled noisily. "Girl. She, um . . ."

"What girl?" demanded Porcellus. "And get that disgusting thing out of here!"

"Mercenary girl. Brought in Wookiee. Last night." Gartogg licked a fragment of plastiform from his lower lip. "Ladyfriend of Solo. The smuggler. Boss caught them." He carefully poked back into its socket the corpse's left eye, which was starting to droop free, and looked inquiringly in the direction of the white-chocolate bread pudding that Porcellus was preparing for tonight's dessert.

"Get that thing out of here!" commanded Porcellus. "I cook in here, this place has to stay clean—clean and *healthful*." He was not anxious to have the Gamorrean start thinking about plots.

But Gartogg was right about the girl. When he was summoned to Jabba's audience chamber at the beginning of the evening's festivities, Porcellus noted the absence of the tarnished brown-black slab of carbonite which for months had decorated the alcove, and the presence of a new "pet" on Jabba's dais.

His heart went out to her in pity. She was very small, slender and fragile-looking in the few scant scraps of gold and silk the crimelord allowed, her heavy, dark-red hair piled thick on her aristocratic head. "I—I'm sorry," he stammered quietly, kneeling on the dais at her side. "If there's anything I can get for you from the kitchen . . ."

It was a hopelessly ineffective offer of aid, and he knew it; but she smiled, and took his hand. "Thank you." She had a voice like smoke and honey; he could see, not fear, but terrible worry in her brown eyes.

Solo, thought Porcellus despairingly. *She's in love with that smuggler Solo*. She was in this position—a prisoner like himself in Jabba's palace—because of that love.

And so, though his own heart hurt with love for her, he made it his business to see that Solo got food from the palace kitchen, not something that was guaranteed in Jabba's dungeons. Many of the prisoners didn't get food at all, for long periods of time. But Porcellus, though his heart was in his throat with terror every time he did it, bribed the guards with beignets and chocolate ladybabies to take meat to the Wookiee, and because he knew hibernation sickness left the body weak and shaky from carbohydrate starvation, smuggled things like stuffed pasties and breaded eggs to the man his beloved loved.

He felt like a fool—the man was going to be executed anyway and he was playing around with a rancor-pit offense himself. But it was all he could do for her, and when, the following night, she took his hand and whispered, "Thank you. Porcellus, thank you," and looked up into his eyes, it was, for one second, worth it all.

Jabba's rumbling, horrible laugh sounded from above them. "You watch out, pretty Leia," the crime-lord said in his slow, almost incomprehensible Huttese. The noise in the hall around them was tremendous, as Jabba's court degenerated into the usual orgy of card games, alcoholism, and testosterone-imbued lying that characterized evenings at the palace: Max Rebo and his band were playing, and Jabba's nasty little pet Salacious Crumb was engaged in a vamped duet with the singer Sy Snootles.

Jabba hefted the golden dish of fricasseed sandmaggot kidneys which was the first of Porcellus's culinary offerings for the evening. After the adventure of the vegetable crepes, Porcellus had gone back to the Bloated One's favorite standbys, but for days now he had produced every one with his heart in his mouth. "I think there's *fierfek* in his cooking. What you think, Chef?"

"No," whispered Porcellus desperately, and checked to see if he was standing on the rancor's trapdoor. He was. "No, it isn't true . . ."

"Here." Leia cast a quick look at the cook's ashen face and stood up, reaching to take the dish from Jabba's hands. "There's no *fierfek* in this, is there, Porcellus?"

"Uh . . ."

"Your Highness," warned the golden protocol droid C-3PO hastily, "I really wouldn't advise . . ."

Jabba generally dispensed with the formality of utensils, but an ornamental border of cracknels surrounded the fetid yellowish glop heaped artistically in the center. Using one of them for a spoon, Leia helped herself to two large mouthfuls.

She turned green and sat down rather quickly.

Jabba roared with obscene laughter. Salacious Crumb, skipping through the crowd around the bandstand, sprang up over the back of the Gamorrean stationed nearest Jabba's dais, an ugly boor named Jubnuk, and, when Jubnuk swatted irritably at him, ran shrieking to his master's side and hurled the rest of the dish of sandmaggot kidneys at the guard. This created enough of a diversion for Porcellus to slip hastily out of the main hall. But throughout the remainder of the night's partying, he returned again and again to the hall to check on Leia, who was looking extremely wan as the night progressed.

Sandmaggot kidneys did not agree with everyone.

And all it would need, thought Porcellus despairingly, would be for *her* to drop dead.

Jubnuk, who had licked all the spattered sandmaggot kidneys off his armor and the surrounding walls, showed no ill effects. Porcellus took what comfort he could from that.

Luke Skywalker, last of the Jedi Knights, entered the palace with the first light of dawn.

The first Porcellus knew of it was when he picked

his way on tiptoe among the sleeping bodies in the audience hall with a cup of vine-coffee and a freshly made jelly doughnut for Leia—also sleeping on the dais at the Hutt's side—and saw Bib Fortuna enter, followed by a medium-sized, slender, and self-effacing young man in black.

"I told you not to admit him," rumbled Jabba, when his majordomo had wakened him to see the young man before him.

Porcellus stepped hastily back, concealing himself behind the bemused and hungover crowd of Jabba's retainers, one of whom—a dark-skinned newcomer in a helmet of gondar tusks—relieved him of the vine-coffee and the doughnut.

"I must be allowed to speak to your master," said Skywalker in his soft voice.

Bib Fortuna turned immediately to the crimelord. "He must be allowed to speak to—"

"You weak-minded fool." Jabba pushed Fortuna aside. "That old Jedi mind trick will not work on me."

Skywalker inclined his head in a respectful bow. "You will bring Captain Solo and the Wookiee to me," he said, and Porcellus felt an immediate urge to run to the dungeon, get the key from Captain Ortogg, and do just that.

"Look out!" piped up C-3PO, who—if Porcellus remembered correctly—had been Skywalker's gift to Jabba. "You're standing on—"

"Your mind powers will not work on me," said Jabba, perhaps deliberately drowning out the droid's warning that Skywalker was, in fact, standing precisely on the rancor's trapdoor.

"Nevertheless," said Skywalker gently, "I am taking Captain Solo. You can either profit by this, or be destroyed."

Jabba smiled evilly and his eyes seemed to grow redder as the pupils narrowed. "I shall enjoy watching you die."

Porcellus had already seen how Skywalker's eyes had met those of the woman Leia when first he had entered. Now she cried "Luke!" as the guards closed in. Skywalker flung out his hand, and somehow the blaster that had been in the holster of a guard four meters away was in it. He had time to fire one shot as they closed around him, Jubnuk the guard reaching to grab. Then the trapdoor beneath his feet fell open, and both Skywalker and Jubnuk plunged into the pit below.

"Luke!" screamed Leia again, dragging fruitlessly against the chains, and the whole court rushed forward—pushing Porcellus along with them—to watch the show in the pit.

It was quick, horrible, the nightmare form of the rancor bursting forth from its den as the bars were raised. Brownish, slimy, hideous beyond belief, it lunged first at the Jedi, who managed to wedge himself in a crack of the rock, then turned and caught Jubnuk as the Gamorrean tried to force apart the barred judas window in the side of the pit. Porcellus was standing among the other Gamorreans as the rancor seized Jubnuk neatly around the waist—Captain Ortogg and his cohorts bellowed with laughter as the monster gulped Jubnuk down in three bites, the noise of their mirth almost drowning his agonized screams. The chef felt faint, feeling those teeth around his own waist, seeing his own arm disappearing like a final fillip of noodle into that round, fanged mouth . . .

Not me, he thought desperately, *not me . . .*

Skywalker saw his chance, and took it. He fled under the rancor's feet, into the smaller den where the beast slept, and from there, as the thing pursued him, hurled a skull at the mechanism which controlled the den's sharpened portcullis of bars. Whether he used some Jedi power to slam the missile home, or whether he simply had the unerring eye of a trained warrior, Porcellus couldn't be sure. But the bars dropped like a guillotine, their pointed ends driving like spears through the rancor's skull.

The beast made a dreadful sound, and fell limp.

In the startled silence of the criminals around him, Porcellus could hear, from the deeps of the pit, Malakili's frantic wail, *"NOOOOO . . . !!!"*

Porcellus was safe.

He straightened up, feeling oddly light-headed. For five years Jabba had threatened to throw him to the rancor . . . and now the rancor was dead. He felt bad for Malakili, hurting with the echoes of that terrible cry, but in the first dizzying flush of relief it was hard to sympathize with his bereft friend. The rancor was dead . . .

Guards were dragging the smuggler Solo, the giant Wookiee behind him, into the audience hall. Solo was still blind from hibernation sickness, but noticeably stronger—Porcellus hoped desperately nobody would ask who'd been feeding him. They were thrust before the dais of the Bloated One.

"His High Exaltedness has decreed you are to be terminated," said the translator droid C-3PO, rather shakily. He looked a little the worse for his few days in Jabba's palace, stained with the Bloated One's slimy green exudations and fragments of sandmaggot kidney. "You are to be taken to the Dune Sea, and cast into the Pit of Carkoon, the abode of the Sarlacc. In his belly you will find new definitions of pain and suffering as you are digested over the course of a thousand years."

"You should have bargained, Jabba," said Skywalker quietly. The guards shoved him, Solo, and the Wookiee toward the door; Leia, on the dais, half started up with anguish in her face, but the Hutt dragged her back by her chain. "That's the last mistake you'll ever make . . ."

Porcellus leaned against the archway in which he stood, knees trembling with reaction and relief. Whatever else happened, the rancor was dead. The threat which had hovered over him for all those years . . .

"And you!" Jabba turned suddenly on his dais, his copper-red eyes seeming to skewer Porcellus where he stood. Drool dripped from his enormous mouth and he pointed one finger. "You also are to die . . ."

"What?" screamed Porcellus.

"You cannot now deny putting *fierfek* into my food. Take him away!" Jabba beckoned to the few guards remaining in the room. "Take him to the deepest dungeon. When my sail barge returns from carrying me to watch the deaths of Skywalker and Solo, then I shall have the leisure to deal with you!"

"But nobody who ate your food died of poison!" wailed Porcellus, as the guards closed in around him. "Jubnuk . . . and Oola . . . You can't—"

"Oh, *fierfek* doesn't mean 'poison.' " C-3PO bustled officiously down from the dais. "It's extremely difficult to poison a Hutt, of course. But all Huttese words derive from food imagery, you see. *Fierfek* simply means a hex, a death curse . . . and you can't deny that Jubnuk, and the unfortunate Oola, both succumbed quite soon after sampling your meals. It's a natural misunderstanding."

And so it was, but Porcellus derived little comfort from the fact as he was dragged away screaming to a cell to await his doom.

That's Entertainment: The Tale of Salacious Crumb

by Esther M. Friesner

Melvosh Bloor had no spectacles to adjust, so he contented himself with polishing the screen of his datapad whenever he felt flustered. Like all good academics, one of his primary reactions to prolonged contact with the real world was to fidget. However, as with all things in his life (so he told himself), it must be fidgeting with a purpose. Melvosh Bloor did nothing without a purpose.

On the face of things, one would imagine that his purpose in infiltrating the lair of the notorious crimelord Jabba the Hutt was a simple one: he wanted to die but lacked the strength of will to kill himself. This, of course, would be dead wrong. Then again, dead wrong might be a pretty good prediction for the fate of Melvosh Bloor.

Oh dear, oh dear, the Kalkal thought as he blundered through the honeycombed underbelly of Jabba's lair. *Where is that fellow? You would think that at the price I paid him—in advance, sight unseen, solely on the recommendation of my colleagues—he would at least manage to be at the rendezvous point on time.*

His cumbersome boots stepped into something thick and sticky on the corridor floor. There was very little light in this part of Jabba's palace but Melvosh Bloor had the excellent vision common to all Kalkals, day or night. Therefore he could not avoid noticing that part of the large and gooey mass he had just stepped in had eyes.

"Mercy," said Melvosh Bloor, placing a trembling hand to his lips as the acidic tide of queasiness surged up his wattled throat. His most recent meal had not been of the finest, to say the least—in fact, it made the refectory fare at dear old Beshka University seem attractive by comparison—so he had no desire to experience it a second time. (Although Kalkals were famous for their ability to eat anything, even university food, there were no guarantees that what they once downed would not make a reappearance if something upset them enough. The goop with eyes was enough to physic Jabba himself.)

"Mercy? *Mercy?*" The dripping darkness exploded with a shrill, harsh voice that mocked Melvosh Bloor's own erudite pronunciation to a tee. Cackling laughter bounced from the maze of pipes overhead and echoed back from the ends of gloomy passageways that led off into the who-knows-where.

Melvosh Bloor gasped, huge yellow eyes rotating wildly in his head as he flattened himself against the nearest wall. "Who's there?" he whispered, tiny flakes of scale falling from his wide, thin lips as he spoke.

Silence answered.

Shaking badly, the academic fumbled for the side-arm his Jawa guide had pressed upon him before they parted ways outside the palace. *Far* outside the palace. Much as he hated the thought of violence and as repulsed as he felt by any of its symbols, Melvosh Bloor thought himself capable of shooting another living being if need be (strictly in the interest of preserving academic freedoms, such as his life). He felt a fleeting spark of gratitude for the Jawa's stubbornness in insisting he take the weapon.

Perhaps the fact that he would be unable to pay the Jawa the remainder of his fee until they were both safely back in Mos Eisley had more than a little to do with the guide's devotion to Melvosh Bloor's personal safety. But that was a low, common thought, unworthy of Beshka University's premier up-and-coming (albeit untenured) professor of Investigative Politico-Sociology. Melvosh Bloor pushed it far from his mind as he continued to scan the shadows.

"Er . . . hello?" he ventured. A glimmer of hope as to the unseen speaker's identity struck him. "Darian Gli, is that you? You're—you're late, you know." He tried not to make it sound like an accusation. Wishful thinking made him certain that the voice he'd just heard coming out of the shadows belonged to his precontracted, pig-in-a-poke guide to Jabba's palace and he didn't want to alienate him. "And—and you were supposed to meet me farther back down this tunnel. Unless I was mistaken in our agreement.

Which I probably was. All my fault. No hard feelings. I apologize.''

Somewhere water was dripping, an eerie sound made even eerier by the fact that Jabba's palace lay in the midst of the Dune Sea, a fierce, unforgiving wasteland where it was cheaper to let blood drip away than water. A faint breeze passed over Melvosh Bloor's face as lightly as a dancing girl's veil. His breath sighed from his wide, flat nostrils as he waited for some response to his words.

A thunderous sound that was half bellow and half shriek shook the wall he clung to. Melvosh Bloor leaped forward, a pathetic cry of startlement involuntarily escaping his lips. Unfortunately for the academic, he landed squarely on the puddle of goo and his booted feet shot straight out from under him. He landed with a nauseating *squosh*. The orphaned eyeballs seemed to regard him with the dumb resentment of an overworked beast of burden.

The same maniacal laughter heard earlier resounded over Melvosh Bloor's head once more. This time, however, a small, rubbery shape detached itself from its hiding place and dropped right into the dazed academic's lap. A wizened face twisted into a mindlessly malevolent grin shoved itself nose to nose with the professor.

Melvosh Bloor was badly shaken by this ugly little apparition, but he had been trapped (and forced to make small talk) with uglier things at faculty teas. "Uh . . . salutations." He raised his right hand in greeting, having forgotten it still clutched the Jawa's parting gift. The creature in his lap gave a yodel of distress and scampered a short distance away. It stood there dancing from foot to taloned foot, chattering angrily.

"I—I'm sorry," Melvosh Bloor stammered, fumbling the weapon away. "I assure you, I have no intentions of shooting you. That would be a fine greeting, heh, heh." He forced a sheepish smile in hopes that the creature had a sense of humor. "Heh?"

"A *fine* greeting!" There was not a trace of humor in the creature's reply, merely resentment. He folded his flabby arms across his chest and glowered at the unhappy academic.

"Oh dear, I *do* apologize most sincerely. You must think I'm an awfully big muckhead." Melvosh Bloor got to his feet unsteadily, then took a dainty step away from the remains of who-or-whatever's final rest he had so messily disturbed.

"An awful . . . *biiiiig* . . . muckhead," the creature echoed, each word ripe with disdain. His grasp on Melvosh Bloor's highly refined accent seemed to grow firmer with each word. In fact, his posture now appeared to mimic Melvosh Bloor's own slightly stooped and timorous stance. If the academic did not know better, he would almost think this creature was making fun of him. That had *not* been in the contract.

Melvosh Bloor holstered his sidearm and, in the name of accomplishing his mission, decided to overlook the insult. "There," he said. "That's better. Now we may proceed."

"Proceed?" The creature shook his head rapidly in the negative, making his tasseled ears bob and shake wildly.

"Eh?" Melvosh Bloor's momentary brush with relief at having encountered his promised in-palace guide winked away like a candleflame in a sandstorm. "Do you mean it's too dangerous to go on? Or—or has there been a change in the situation since last we communicated?" He lowered his voice and in a hoarse, terrified whisper begged, "Don't tell me that Professor P'tan has actually turned up *alive*?"

"P'tan! P'tan! Hahahahaha!" The little creature convulsed with insane merriment, rolling around on the floor as Melvosh Bloor watched, aghast.

"Oh my," he murmured. "Professor P'tan is alive after all. Oh dear, dear me, this ruins *everything*."

The creature stopped its mad tumblings and pricked up one ear. "Everything?" it inquired.

Melvosh Bloor heaved a tremendous sigh. "Is there somewhere we can talk? Somewhere safe? Somewhere"—another sigh—"I can sit down?"

For an instant, the unthinkable happened: the creature's face-splitting grin got even wider than ear to ear, physical possibility or not. Then it leaped forward and seized Melvosh Bloor by the hand, yanking and tugging violently (and painfully) as it urged him to follow it down one of the narrower passageways. Stumbling from weariness and bewilderment, the Kalkal allowed himself to be led away into the maze of corridors.

At length they stopped before a dully gleaming metal door. "In there?" the academic asked doubtfully. "Is it—? Are you sure we shall be secure in there?"

"In there." His guide spoke decisively and gave him a hard shove. "*In* there!"

Still possessed by an uncertain, creepy feeling (hadn't that charming-for-a-Whiphid Lady Valarian assured him that his in-palace contact, Darian Gli, was a Markul? This creature did not look anything like a Markul. But Melvosh Bloor was an Investigative Politico-Sociologist, not an Eidetic Xenologist, so he figured he *could* be wrong), the academic did as he was told. He laid hands on the massive door and was mildly surprised when it swung back easily on its hinges.

"How . . . primitive," he remarked as he peered into the darkened chamber beyond. The spill from the dim illuminations in the corridor was enough for him to see by. He hesitated on the threshold until his guide gave him another of those forceful shoves, making the Kalkal trip over his own boots and fall on his face. Chittering and squealing with glee, the little creature scampered over Melvosh Bloor's prone body. There was a scrabbling sound and a faint amber light flared on at the far end of the room.

Melvosh Bloor picked himself up cautiously. "Shall I— Shall I close the door?"

"Close the door! Close the door!" his guide commanded imperiously. He was seated on a block of rough-hewn sandstone about the height of a table. The amber light came from a small, crystal-shielded niche in the wall nearby. The only other object to break the cubic monotony of the room was a second slab of rock approximately the dimensions of Melvosh Bloor's bed back in the university cloister.

Melvosh Bloor hurried to comply, then took a seat on the sandstone slab. He covered his face with his hands and let the full weight of misery bow his shoulders even more. "I suppose I'm to blame for not having done sufficient research before undertaking this mission," he said. "As, no doubt, Professor P'tan will be the first to tell me once we return to the university. Insufferable old gorm-worm. Oh, I can just hear him now, spouting off the same way he always does when he speaks to the junior faculty." Melvosh Bloor struck a stiff pose and, in a voice blubbery with pomposity, intoned, " 'Melvosh Bloor, do you call that *teaching*? You merely drum facts into your poor pupils' rocky heads and give them passing grades if they spew the same swill right back in your lap! Small wonder, when it's the same swill *you* swallowed whole from your professors.' " The Kalkal snorted. "*Then* he has to go brag about how *he* doesn't rely on secondhand knowledge when he teaches; *he* goes out and does research in the field. If I hear him say 'Publish or perish' one more time, I shall—"

"Research in the field?" the creature broke in,

cocking its head. Then it made a rude noise with one or more parts of its rubbery body.

"My sentiments exactly," Melvosh Bloor agreed. "Oh, I do wish we had more honest folk like you at the university. Have you ever had any academic experience, Darian Gli?"

The creature repeated the rude noise, louder this time, and with a few extra flourishes.

"Ah," said Melvosh Bloor dryly. "I see you have."

"Professor P'tan?" the creature prompted.

Melvosh Bloor was not used to enjoying the company of such a good listener. "You wish me to . . . go on?" he inquired timidly.

"Go on, go *on*!" the creature responded with an expansive gesture. Melvosh Bloor found himself liking this quaint being more by the minute.

"My good fellow, your, ah, rather substantive evaluation of Professor P'tan's character leads me to believe you have encountered him, even though he swore he'd have nothing to do with you. Which—correct me if I'm wrong—strikes me as stupid."

"Stupid."

"Ah! Then we're in agreement. When I was first plotting—I mean *considering* this expedition, my fellow academics Ra Yasht and Skarten told me I couldn't go wrong with you by my side. Perhaps you remember them? You helped them research that *fascinating* monograph on *Torture Observed: An Interview with Jabba's Cook.*"

The creature made a retching sound, though whether this was a literary or culinary critique remained unspecified.

"You're certainly entitled to your own opinion, but that monograph was the making of their reputations at the university. *Instant* tenure. Professor P'tan was infuriated—they hadn't suffered enough yet, by his standards—but the board overruled him. Right then I sent in my own request for leave to do a project so challenging, so sweeping in its scope, that even were Professor P'tan to bully the board into siding with him, the sheer *audacity* of my work would compel them to renege and end by favoring me. I would delve into one of the greatest and least-known sociopolitical mysteries of the galaxy. I would lift the veil between polite society and the darkest, slimiest, most hideously profitable phenomenon of our time. I would interview . . . *Jabba the Hutt!*" Melvosh Bloor's eyes shone as he recalled the grandeur of his scheme.

"Interview the Hutt?" Thick chuckles, like laughter emerging from a pudding, bubbled up from Melvosh Bloor's guide.

"Uh . . . quite. Sit down nicely with him, like civilized beings, and—"

"Nicely? *Nicely!* With *him?*"

In the face of such obviously open ridicule, the academic went on the defensive. "I fail to see the humor," he said stiffly. "I realize that the—the Bloated One as he is so colorfully called, has a certain reputation, but still—" Melvosh Bloor pursed his lips as well as any Kalkal could manage. "When you were originally contacted about this, you said you could arrange it. You represented yourself as one very close to Jabba."

"Close to Jabba?" The creature's chuckles burst into full-fledged cackles once more, but he bobbed his head.

"Then you can take me to him? Not merely as far as his, ah, majordomo or secretary or whoever it is weeds out the riffraff, but all the way to Jabba himself?"

"Take? *Can* take, ha!" Now the creature's head was nodding so exuberantly his ear-tassels looked ready to fly off any moment. "*All* the way!" He grabbed his long, flexible feet and rolled back and forth on his flabby bottom. "To Jabba, to Jabba, to Jabba!"

"The way Professor P'tan's guide took him?"
Melvosh Bloor replied coldly. In this small chamber it
was possible to believe oneself safe, possible to forget
for a time that one was burrowed deep into the
stronghold of the galaxy's most ruthless crimelord. In
such an environment of self-deceit, the academic re-
verted to his classroom manner, a style that combined
frigid disdain for underlings, shameless toadying to su-
periors, and backstabbing ad-lib, as the opportunity
presented itself.

"*He* got wind of my plans, P'tan did," Melvosh
Bloor went on. "He came barging in while I was peti-
tioning the board for leave and financing. He said that
it was ludicrous to entrust a study of such magnitude
to a junior faculty member—never mind that it was my
idea! He claimed I'd get the data all bollixed, or be
taken in by the Hutt's, ah, propensities for elasticizing
the facts."

"Lies, lies, lies," the repulsive little creature opined.
"Like a Gran!"

"Well, I suppose I agree with you there," Melvosh
Bloor allowed, giving his guide a condescending
smile. "But I won't tell Jabba you said that about him
if you won't tell him I agreed with you."

"Ohhh, *I* won't tell Jabba. Hahahahaha."

"Er, good." Really, the creature's unseemly attacks
of hilarity were becoming most distressing to the academic's timid nature. "Jabba's ethics aside, Professor
P'tan went on to insist that *he* undertake *my* proposed
study. Which he did. Perhaps the board felt that one
miserable thief was best qualified to interview another."

"Miserable thief? Jabba the Hutt? Jabba, miserable
thief, lies like a Gran?" The guide's tasseled ears
pricked up.

"Do excuse my language. Heat of the moment. Al-

though, um, I believe that last bit—lies like a Gran—
you said that . . . didn't you?"

"Didn't." The lipless mouth snapped shut.

"But you did! I admit, I said Jabba lies, but you were
the one who—" A glance at that hard little face made
Melvosh Bloor realize he was engaged in a losing battle over a minor point. He sighed wearily. "Very well,
have it your way, if you insist: *I* said Jabba lies like a
Gran. Now may I continue?"

A taloned paw executed a parody of a fine lady's
gesture when dismissing an unwanted servant.

"So P'tan came here." The Kalkal's wide mouth was
exceptionally well suited to a grim expression. "And
was never heard from again. We all hoped—*assumed*
he was dead, but the board likes to be sure. That way
they have a solid reason for cutting off his wife's benefits. That is why they sent me, to determine conclu-
sively whether Professor P'tan still lived. Ridiculous, of
course; he had to be dead. I resolved to turn this trip
into the expedition it should have been in the first
place—*my* expedition to interview Jabba the Hutt.
Now you tell me Professor P'tan is still alive." The
academic's teeth ground together.

"Still alive." The creature leered. "Sarlacc eat one
meal looooong time, hahahahaha!"

"The Sarlacc!" Melvosh Bloor was horrorstruck.
While he was no expert on life beyond the university
walls, he had heard enough shivery tales of the Sarlacc
and its protracted digestive habits while he was awaiting his Jawa guide in Mos Eisley to more than com-
pensate for that lacuna in his education. "You mean
Professor P'tan fell into the—the—?"

"Splat," his guide provided smugly. "Splat, ow,
shrieeeeeek!" he added as an afterthought.

"Not so loud, not so loud!" Melvosh Bloor hissed,
making desperate hushing motions with his hands.

"Huh! Coward. Think I stupid?" The creature put

on an air of the highest dudgeon. "Like *fool* guide *fool* P'tan hire? Fools for Sarlacc pit! I *offer* be his guide. He listen? Nooooooo. He *lunch*! Dinner. Breakfast. More lunch. Snack. Sup—"

The academic was taken aback by this diatribe. "Mercy on us, P'tan's guide must have been a fool of the first water. Whom did he hire? How stupid was he?"

For an answer, the creature flew into gales of wheezy joy. "How stupid was he? *How stupid was he?* Fool P'tan went hire"—snorts and guffaws—"went hire"—gasps for air and fresh howls of mirth—"went hire *Salacious Crumb*!" Having communicated this intelligence, the whole effort proved to be too much for the small creature and he laughed so hard he fell off his perch onto his head. He then said a nasty word so arcane that Melvosh Bloor made haste to enter it in his datapad for later linguistic study before asking:

"Who—who is Salacious Crumb? I'm afraid I don't know—"

"Uh-*huh*." The creature grunted emphatically, clambering back onto his sandstone block.

"But . . . what's so foolish about hiring this Salacious Crumb? Has he no experience with the layout of the palace?"

"Experience? Hee! Knows palace like back of my—his right paw. Ha!"

"In that case . . . not a good contact for approaching Jabba? He is one of the Hutt's enemies, perhaps?"

"Hutt's *enemy*?" A groan of melodramatic proportions shook the small creature as it covered its face with its paws. "No one closer to Bloated One! *No one!* All day, every day, Hutt say 'Crumb, Salacious Crumb,' he say, 'Salacious Crumb, make me laugh now or I eat you!'"

"Er, I see," said Melvosh Bloor, who didn't. "I'm afraid I don't quite get the joke, but—"

"Better you don't than Jabba don't. Every day, every day, fresh jokes. All time, fresh, fresh, fresh! *Try* tell Bloated One same joke twice!" The creature's face doubled in on itself in a frightful grimace.

"Are you saying that this Salacious Crumb deliberately led Professor P'tan to fall into the Sarlacc pit as a —a joke?"

The creature turned a totally innocent gaze to the academic. " 'Smatter? You don't get it?"

Melvosh Bloor shook his head.

The creature sighed. "Bloated One too don't. Seen it. He say, 'Next time, louder and funnier.' "

Melvosh Bloor's yellow eyes narrowed suspiciously. "You seem to know an awful lot about the doings of Salacious Crumb."

"So?" The creature sprang to its feet, its pelt standing out in spikes that made it even more unattractive to the eye. "You know lot about Jabba. This makes you Hutt?"

Melvosh Bloor shuddered. "I hope not."

The creature snorted. "Come."

For once it was the academic who became the echo. "Come? Come where? You don't mean come with you to meet—to meet—Jabba the Hutt?"

"Jabba . . . the . . . Hutt!" The creature pronounced the crimelord's name in a low, rolling, impressive voice reminiscent of Lord Vader himself.

"So—so quickly? So easily?" Melvosh Bloor didn't know whether to tremble with delight or trepidation, so he settled for a generalized case of the shakes. "You can take me to him now?"

"*Right* now. Timing, timing, *timing*! Time is ripe!" It made a great show of sniffing its own armpits, then cheerfully added, "Me too!" It loped across the floor on all fours and flung open the cell door. "Last one out, Sarlacc food."

Such an invitation coming hard on the heels of Professor P'tan's reported fate was impossible to ignore. Melvosh Bloor fairly sprinted out of the cell in pursuit of his guide. Once back in the corridor, the creature climbed the academic's body as if it were a sail barge mast and perched on his shoulder. "You listen," it hissed in his ear. "*I* do talk, get it? Else—" It drew one claw across its own scrawny throat and uttered: *"Sskkkr-rrhtt!"*

"You mean you'll conduct the interview? But my questions—" Melvosh Bloor gestured helplessly with his datapad.

His guide grabbed it from his hands and chewed on one corner experimentally. "Naaaah. You shut up until throne room. *Then* you talk." He chortled. "Oh boy."

Melvosh Bloor snatched back his datapad and secured it from the creature's covetous fingers. "That is agreeable," he said. "Let's go."

The sights and sounds that greeted the Kalkal in the palace vaults would have been fodder for a score of monographs on debauchery, suffering, and substandard hygiene, had he been minded to turn back from his original goal. From its piggyback perch, his guide greeted every other being they passed—Twi'lek, Gamorrean, Quarren, and the rest—with an easy camaraderie that was . . . Well, in truth, it was downright rude. Insults and jibes flew from the ugly little creature's mouth with astonishing fluency. Melvosh Bloor's fingers almost fell off from the rapidity with which he had to enter the many terms with which the other inhabitants of Jabba's palace showered his guide. (All of them filed under "U" for "Unbelievably Foul.")

At last they came to a curtained portal. A tusked Gamorrean raised his vibro-ax in challenge until Melvosh Bloor's guide poked his head up over the Kalkal's shoulder and loosed an ear-splitting cackle.

The Gamorrean snorted in reply and waved them through.

As Melvosh Bloor stepped into Jabba the Hutt's throne room he felt an overwhelming sense of awe that was almost as heart-shaking as the dread that had possessed him when he went in to take his doctoral oral examination. Jabba the Hutt in person was indescribably more imposing than the mountains of research the academic had accumulated to prepare himself for this moment. He felt the weight of his guide drop from his back and saw the creature scamper across the vast chamber to the Hutt's very throne. Such boldness should by rights result in immediate consumption (so the Kalkal's research led him to believe) but was not. Instead, the crimelord actually permitted the creature to scale his monstrous body and whisper something for Jabba's ears alone. The academic's heart leaped at this irrefutable evidence of his guide's favored status with the Bloated One. He could almost taste his tenure now.

"Er . . . Exalted One?" The academic faltered as he approached the throne. Jabba regarded him impassively, which he took as a good sign. He dared to move closer yet. "I am Melvosh Bloor of Beshka University and I—"

"University?" the Hutt thundered.

"Y-yes. I have come here to—to honor and immortalize you by publishing an in-depth study of the thoughts and motivations that guide you in the establishment and maintenance of your crimin—extrasocial empire."

"Mmm." The sound of rumination rumbled through the Hutt's enormous body. "In other words *you* expect *me* to tell you all my secrets freely, so that you can then put them on display where any of my rivals may study them?" He leaned forward, his mouth uncomfortably close to Melvosh Bloor's head. The academic tried to back away, but something sharp was there, in the small of his back, to make retreat a suicidal alternative. He thought he detected the grunting of a Gamorrean guard.

Jabba's body shook. His mouth fell open. Melvosh Bloor froze, positive that his life was about to end in one gulp. And then, the unthinkable: booming mirth engulfed the throne room. Jabba was laughing, a sound duly taken up by the Hutt's lackeys and retainers. At length the shaking and the laughter stopped. Jabba drew a deep breath. "*Me* tell *that* my secrets and I'm to consider it an honor? Now *that's* funny," he said.

"What I say, Master?" Melvosh Bloor saw his guide come dancing in between him and the Hutt's looming bulk. "This guy a riot!"

"A . . . riot?" the Kalkal echoed, stunned.

"Indeed. I am surprised," Jabba admitted. "Usually academics are too dry to be funny, or even digestible. I know: I never forget a taste."

Melvosh Bloor's skin went cold. "Taste?" he peeped. "You mean you—you—? Professor P'tan—?"

"*That's* the name." If Jabba had possessed the ability to snap his fingers at a memory recaptured, he would have done so. "You are the second academic to disturb my court, thanks to the insolence of my miserable servant, Salacious Crumb." One of the Hutt's truncated arms gestured at the madly prancing creature. "At least *you* were worth it."

All that Melvosh Bloor could say was, "Sa-Sa-Sa-Salacious Crumb?" as he goggled in shock at his erstwhile trusted and beloved guide. "But I thought—I was sure— *You said you were Darian Gli!*"

"*You* said," the lizard-monkey gloated.

"Darian Gli?" Jabba was momentarily at a loss. "Ah yes, the Markul who brought in those two pests who upset my cook." He smacked his lips nostalgically. "Delicious."

"*You* said, *you* said, not me!" Salacious Crumb taunted him. The Kowakian lizard-monkey was in his glory. "Hoooo! *Stupid?*" He waved at the shivering academic so that none of Jabba's courtiers could mistake the insult's target.

None did. In fact, someone from the back of the crowd shouted out, "How stupid *is* he?"

"How stupid? *How stupid?*" Malice beamed from the Kowakian's beady eyes. "He say Jabba *lies like a Gran!*"

Jabba's roar of outrage swallowed the Kalkal's weakly uttered protests of innocence even if Jabba did not swallow the Kalkal . . . yet. While Melvosh Bloor sputtered "But I—but he—but we—" the Hutt bellowed for his Gamorrean guards. Somewhere in Jabba's outpouring of indignation, Melvosh Bloor distinctly heard the word "Sarlacc."

Desperation can work astounding transformations. Stung to the quick at being played for a fool by someone without a doctorate, insulted past bearing, trapped, bereft of hope, the normally placid academic exploded. Salacious Crumb uttered a squawk as one of Melvosh Bloor's hands shot out to seize his neck while the other drew the borrowed sidearm and jammed the barrel halfway up the Kowakian's nose.

"He came into my presence *armed?*" Jabba boomed as his bodyguards hastened to throw themselves into a living wall between their master and danger.

"Soddy, Baster," Salacious Crumb replied as best he could. "I thod you eed hib zoon as he—"

"Blast you, Salacious Crumb, that's a Klatooine handblaster he's got there! You know they give me gas!"

"I mean you no harm," Melvosh Bloor gritted at the Hutt. "I just want to blow the head off this loathsome little cretin, then you can eat me. At least I'll die happy." To his captive he snarled, "Cheat *me* out of tenure, will you?"

"Hey hey hey! You wad denure? Baster, Baster, gib hib wad he want, adzer questions, led hib ged denure, led Zalacious Crub keeb head—"

"He said I lie like a Gran," Jabba replied.

"Uh . . . thad wuz be," Salacious Crumb confessed.

"You!"

"Wuz goblibent, *goblibent*! Gan't dake a choke?"

Jabba settled deeper into his own fat to consider this. "A compliment?" he mused. "From a Kowakian . . . mmmperhaps." He reared back on his throne and gave a string of commands.

Melvosh Bloor could hardly believe the complete about-face in his fortunes. Whereas moments earlier he had been on the brink of extinction, ready to take the duplicitous Salacious Crumb with him into oblivion, he now found himself comfortably seated before Jabba's throne, on a heap of cushions which Salacious Crumb himself took special pains to arrange just so. The Hutt proved to be a surprisingly forthcoming interviewee. Before long, Melvosh Bloor's datapad memory was stretched to the limit, which was just as well: he had run out of questions.

"I can't thank you enough, sir," he said, hugging the precious datapad to his bosom as he stood up in the midst of the cushions. "I must say, your reputation does not do you justice. Your kindness, your tolerance, your indulgence—" He gave Jabba his most ingratiating smile—one which, in the past, had *almost* fooled the late Professor P'tan, and that was saying something. "If there is ever anything I can do for you—"

"There is," Jabba replied. His eyes closed to slits. "Make me laugh."

Taken aback, the academic could only reply, "Uhhhh . . . what?"

"You heard me. I weary of Salacious Crumb's antics. This is the second time he has attempted to use academics to amuse me. I don't like to hear the same joke twice. Make me laugh—"

"So he said. Um, well, sir, you see, humor does not generally fall within my area of study—"

"—or I will devour you where you stand."

"—however, I *did* take a course on the analysis of comedy and I would be happy to send you my notes on the subj—"

"Make . . . me . . . laugh."

Melvosh Bloor sucked in his lower lip—no mean feat—and tried to maintain his composure. Make the Hutt laugh? He cast his eyes about the throne room, desperately seeking some clue, some inspiration that would save his skin. His roving glance lit upon the repugnant figure of Salacious Crumb. The Kowakian lizard-monkey grinned and made obnoxious faces at him. *How dare he!* Melvosh Bloor thought, the color rising to his cheeks. *I should have blown his head off when I had the chance. If that obscene little pimple can make the Hutt laugh, then surely I, with my university education, my knowledge, my vastly superior breeding, ought to be able to do the same.*

And then it came to him, a joke he had heard from Professor P'tan himself at a faculty meeting. Melvosh Bloor recalled that all the junior faculty had laughed loud and long, so it must be a good one.

The academic cleared his throat, smiled amiably, and began: "Stop me if you've heard this one before. How many Sarlaccs does it take to do in a Jedi?"

Jabba stared at him. Too late, Melvosh Bloor remembered that junior faculty will laugh at any joke a senior professor tells.

"I've heard it," said Jabba. He twitched his tail over

a control device he alone commanded and the floor beneath Melvosh Bloor's feet vanished. The academic plunged into the pit beneath, cushions and all. The datapad went flying from his upflung hands to land with a clatter at Salacious Crumb's feet. There was a horrendous, bone-chilling cacophony as Jabba's favorite pet, the rancor, made the acquaintance of its newest playmate. "And I've heard *that* one before too," the Hutt concluded.

He turned a stern look on his court jester. "Well, Salacious Crumb," Jabba remarked, "that was louder, but I don't think it was funnier."

"Eh! Academics." The Kowakian shrugged. "Publish or perish, publish or perish," he parroted. He stressed each word with a whack of Melvosh Bloor's datapad against the floor.

"Publish or . . . ?" A slow, skin-prickling sound began to work its way out of the Hutt's bulk until it broke from the Bloated One's maw in a geyser of approving laughter. "Now *that's* funnier!" Jabba decreed.

Salacious Crumb screwed up his face into a look of all-encompassing contempt for his master's idea of a punch line. He tossed the datapad into the rancor pit. The rancor, who had no need to fidget and absolutely no sense of humor, tossed it back.

But of course the rancor already had tenure.

A Time to Mourn, a Time to Dance: Oola's Tale

by Kathy Tyers

Oola's back throbbed from the roots of her lekku to the sandaled soles of her feet. She perched on the edge of Jabba's dais, just as far from the Bloated One as her chain would allow. Foul smoke curled from his hookah. It hung acridly in the air, stinging her throat.

She shook her head, and the chain rattled. She'd tested every link of it, hoping it had a weak spot. It didn't. For two days, two endless rounds of Tatooine's twin burning suns, she hadn't seen daylight. And she guessed she had only thwarted the hideous Hutt's slobbering advances because he enjoyed punishing her as much as he anticipated her eventual submission.

They'd been careful, the Gamorreans who beat her this morning. She'd refused to dance closer to Jabba. Oola hunched down and tried to forget. Jabba's flag-eared lizard-monkey had perched on her heel and cackled as the Gamorreans stretched her out and scientifically pummeled her. She'd hoped for bruises. They might make her repulsive to Jabba.

Her sponsor and fellow Twi'lek, Bib Fortuna, had crouched close and wrinkled his knobby brow. He communicated with twitches and whisks of his thick, masculine lekku. "Learn quickly! You cost me a fortune. Two fortunes. You will please him—even if his only enjoyment is watching you die."

Oola had only two hopes left: to escape from this palace of death or, barring that, to die cleanly and well, and escape that way. Fortuna was the only person inside who spoke her language. The thought made her unbearably lonely. Master Fortuna sat at an alcove table, draping his lekku over the shoulders of Melina Carniss—a human dancer, dark-haired and almost pretty.

Jabba's tail twitched. Oola wrapped her arms around her ankles. She'd learned only a few words of Huttese ("no," "please no," and "emphatically no"), but she was getting very good at reading the Hutt's body language. Some thought had just pleased him.

An ancient free-verse song sprang to her mind: "Only a criminal prefers survival to honor. Love life too much, and you'll lose the best reason for living." She'd learned that song as a child. Life was dangerous. Oola desired life like water and she meant to drink death like wine, deeply and quickly.

But not too soon.

Then she heard what had already excited Jabba: struggling and shouting noises drifted down the entry stair. She could barely hear them through her headpiece. She'd seen Master Fortuna display the studded leather band to Jabba, speaking Huttese and stroking one knobby protrusion with a sharpened claw. Then he buckled it under her chin, the finishing touch on her costume.

Metal knobs on the headpiece protruded through leather into her delicate ears, blocking all but the loudest noises—such as Max Rebo's contemptible singer Sy Snootles, and Jabba's abhorrent invitations.

She raised her head to stare toward the entry. All around the throne, in dark recesses and corners of Jabba's sand-strewn floor, courtiers roused from their daily business. Bib Fortuna turned toward mid-floor, then rose and glided forward.

Once she'd admired him. Now she despised his obsequious shuffling and the touch of his claw-fingered hands.

Two tusked Gamorrean guards dragged in a struggling creature. Although half the size of either guard, the prisoner jumped left and right, desperately kicking the thick hide of their knees. Whenever a kick landed, the Gamorrean whuffled. She guessed that was their laughter.

Jabba yanked Oola's chain. Choked, she fell back against gooey flesh. A warty, vestigial hand grasped her sensitive left lek from behind and stroked it.

Jabba rumbled at his luckless new captive. One Gamorrean seized its roughly woven brown robe by the collar and yanked it off, revealing a scrawny creature with a shrunken face and glowing yellow eyes. He babbled at Jabba in a quick, high voice. Jabba belched something that sounded like a command. From behind the hideous guards scuttled a squatty crustacean with four green-shelled legs. Several courtiers recoiled from it; others edged forward. Even Master Fortuna kept a respectful distance.

The crustacean brandished a forefoot. Two pairs of pincers snapped open. A straight, slim talon protruded between each pair of claws. One talon glistened wetly. The prisoner shrank down and screamed.

Jabba's rumbling laugh vibrated his belly. Oola trembled. She hadn't slept in two nights; if this went on much longer, she'd be too tired to escape if she got the chance. Jabba's exclusively chained dancing girls must live short, miserable lives. The ancient song haunted her: "lose your best reason for living . . ."

As the captive cowered, the crustacean's twin claw seized his upper arm. Pincers clamped. The captive shrieked again, a long, thin screech that arched Oola's neck. She spun around, pushed her face into fetid hide, and then scrambled up Jabba's hideous midsection. Momentarily she forgot the rotten flesh under her bare arms and legs. Jabba chuckled but loosened her chain, possibly the better to concentrate on his victim's last agony.

Oola slithered down Jabba's other side, cautiously testing the slack he was giving her. She managed to slide off the back of his dais before snapping her neck tether tight. Jabba didn't seem to mind having its links dragged over him. He'd find her when he wanted lighter entertainment.

She slid her hated headpiece's strap up her chin and flung it off. Then she tugged her skimpy net costume, straightening flimsy fabric to cover her body as well as it could. Narrow leather strips belted it at her waist, hips, knees, and ankles.

She'd hoped for dancing veils.

Her eyes adjusted slowly. To her surprise, two other

creatures shared her refuge. Her fellow dancer—
Yarna, a heavy-bodied Askajian with room at her
breasts for a large litter of children—had spoken
"comforting" words after this morning's long beating:
"Do what you have to. Anything that works. As long as
you're alive, there's hope." Oola frowned. Death was
the ultimate enemy, but beyond it lay bright, clean
eternity and the Great Dance.

The humanoid-looking droid cowered back here
too. Almost as tall as Fortuna, he gleamed gold where
Jabba's slime hadn't fouled him. She'd seen him earlier when he arrived with his squat, silvery partner,
and she hadn't forgotten the towering human image
they projected into foul, murky air . . .

Yarna lounged, stretched out as if for a peaceful
nap after breakfast. The droid pressed metal-jointed
hands over his invisible ears. Oola hunkered closer to
him. She racked her memory for words that might
comfort him, but she didn't know enough Huttese to
make a start. She might try Basic, although she didn't
speak it well.

His metal head turned. He straightened—avoiding
her, she thought at first—and then made a stiff but
courtly bow. "Miss Oola," he said.

He spoke Twi'leki. The shock of familiarity hit her
again, as when his partner had projected that image.

"I am See-Threepio, human-cyborg relations," he
announced, managing Twi'leki as well as she'd ever
heard a creature without lekku speak it. "I am fluent
in over six million forms of communication. I apologize for my disreputable condition," he added, and
swiped one metal hand at the green ooze on his body.
"If I truly am doomed, I would prefer to face the
scrap pile in a more pristine condition."

"Don't be cowardly," she whispered, but she
couldn't put any strength into her voice.

"He threatened to flush my memory. That would be even worse," the droid whined.

"Nothing is final," Oola murmured, trying to echo things she'd thought she believed in, before fear nibbled holes in her faith. "Not even death. It only frees your spirit from the confines of gravity, to dance—"

"You don't understand." Threepio lowered himself with a metallic squeak onto the chamber's sandy floor. "Even a partial memory wipe would be disastrous for a droid of my programming. I might have to start from basic imitative body movements. I'm not even certain I would retain my primary communications function."

Whatever that means, she signed with her lekku. No non-Twi'lek could read lek gestures.

Surprising her again, he spread his metal hands. "It would mean doom," he explained. Then he spoke again, almost shyly. "Might I offer condolences for your unhappy position, Miss Oola?"

Those were the first genteel words she'd heard in two days. Regretting her bravado back at the town, when she could have escaped Master Fortuna, and then her obvious lack of courage in this place, she curled up into a tight little ball and cradled both lekku between her knees. "Thank you, See Pio," she murmured. "Do you have any idea what's happening?" She indicated the other side of Jabba's throne with a quick jerk of her head.

"Threepio," he corrected, but he tried to be gallant. "As I understand, His High Exaltedness is punishing a Jawa. Someone he caught plotting against him, I suppose. Everyone here hopes to kill everyone else, so far as I can ascertain. I—oh!"

Another shriek cut him off. His head turned.

Oola nudged his hard, cool side with a bare elbow. "Tell me about that . . . picture that the other droid projected this morning," she said urgently. She needed to know *now*. She'd learned not to hope for second chances.

"What?" Threepio swiveled his head toward her.

"The . . . human." Humans looked almost Twi'leki, but pitiably maimed . . . just as Jabba looked horribly mutated, one lek bloated to obscene proportions. "Who was it?"

Threepio's tone brightened. "Oh! That is my—" He halted before saying "owner," or "master"—he belonged to Jabba now—but his speech had clearly started to imply ownership.

She touched her collar in unexpected empathy. Ignoring his faltering, she said, "I've seen him."

He drew up with a grandiose sweep of both arms. "I am afraid that's impossible."

"Is his name Luke?" Oola asked.

Threepio's eyes glimmered in the dark, smoky air. "My goodness. Yes. Yes, it is. Where was he?"

Mournfully, Oola explained.

Oola relaxed on her deceleration chair, relieved that her first spaceflight had ended smoothly. Jerris Rudd, Bib Fortuna's employee and their pilot-escort on the short trip from Ryloth to Tatooine, had warned her that unexpected sandstorms or hostiles might agitate their landing. Oola flexed her legs, eager to spring from this cramped cabin. At her twilit home on Ryloth, deep in underground warrens where eight hundred people acknowledged her father as clan chief, she'd been known as an exquisite dancer. The height of her kicks and the sensuous swing of her lekku had won dozens of admirers.

Four months ago, Bib Fortuna had coaxed her aboveground. He'd abducted her, instead of paying her father as custom dictated. He'd enslaved her—and another Twi'lek girl, even younger and more petite—at a complex on Ryloth where he'd once conducted a lucrative smuggling business. He'd bought them the most expensive training on six worlds: four months with Ryloth's most elegant, experienced court dancers.

The older dancers disdained her clan's quaint, primitive ways. To Oola's way of thinking, her clan preserved faith and dignity that the rest of the world had lost in its rush to accommodate slavers and smugglers. Expediency was a deadly god to serve.

Still, Oola rose to her training. She couldn't escape, and she did love to dance. The twin temptations of power and fame set hooks in her soul. Fortuna's performers selected the girls' dancing personae: Sienn would appear slightly younger, naïve, and guileless; Oola would seem knowing, worldly-wise, and callous. Sienn sat stoically as Fortuna's grim groomers tattooed delicate floral chains up and down her nerve-laden lekku. Oola held Sienn's hand and wiped her silent tears of pain.

Sienn was too young and vulnerable for work that made her beauty a commodity. Twi'leks called her kind a "morsel"—one gulp and a client could eat her. Their aging head trainer, who still boasted some beauty, tried hardening Sienn. "Don't play with that kind of appetite," she'd warned. "Make them drool, but don't let them bite."

Oola sleeked her lekku and shimmied her shoulders infinitesimally. She and Sienn had been trained by the best. Groomed for the best.

Sienn sat in another deceleration chair, wearing a simple hooded coverall—like Oola's, but pale yellow instead of dark blue—and stroked her freshly tattooed lekku. "Do they still hurt?" Oola murmured.

"They're fine," insisted Sienn. "They—"

The cabin door slid aside. Jerris Rudd stepped through, one point seven meters of scum. Rudd was the first human she'd met. Perhaps all humans dressed in baggy, torn clothing. Perhaps they all smelled this foul, with matted fur covering their heads (the worst of Rudd's stench came from that fur). If so, humans were scum. In keeping with her worldly-wise role, Rudd had given her a tiny dagger. "Help Sienn," he'd taunted, "if you can." She'd bristled, but she'd made sure the dagger was sharp, then tucked it into her belt.

"Nice fly, girls?" Rudd rubbed his stained hands. "Pretty good landing, I think. No *boom*." He clapped his hands at Sienn's face.

Sienn shrank into her chair. Evidently Rudd had tried to evaluate Sienn's training during their hyperspace hop.

Oola could speak only a few hundred words of Basic, but her ear knew the way pidgin limped. It offended her. She could guess-translate most words in context. "It was a good landing," she said firmly.

"Time to unbuckle"—he pantomimed releasing their harnesses—"and hit dirt. You'll love Tatooine."

Sienn touched a control on her seat. Her flight harness withdrew into its side. "What's it like?" she asked.

"A little like Ryloth. You'll see. Come on."

They'd barely climbed down into the docking bay's heat—and the sandy back lot was like Ryloth's hot, perpetually uninhabitable bright side—when a metallic voice announced, "Hold it right there. Nobody moves."

That voice had no music left in it. It grated in her ears like metal on slate. Oola did as it ordered.

The voice came from a human wearing white metal. Oola stared. She'd seen tri-D images of Imperial stormtroopers. Three of them stood between the battered fore pod of Rudd's small transport and the only gate in the docking bay's sandstone walls. One whiteskin marched up to Rudd. "Let's see some identification."

Oola had no trouble translating *that* word. Moving slowly and keeping his eye on the stormtroopers' blast rifles, Rudd dug into his sweat-stained shoulder pouch. A stormtrooper grabbed it. Sienn stood still, trembling.

Eventually the whiteskin returned Rudd's pouch. His partners lowered their weapons. "This is a very common class of ship," he explained. "Just what we'd expect someone to use if they were trying to sneak past surveillance."

"I," said Rudd, "am a respectable escort. I—"

"Can it," said the head stormtrooper. "We know your boss. Jabba's in for a surprise. Real soon." The whiteskin beside him laughed.

The third stormtrooper kept his weapon up. "I say we search their ship," he drawled.

"Not necessary," Rudd insisted. "I'm clean. I've got an appointment in just a few minutes."

Evidently that was the wrong thing to tell a stormtrooper. Oola, Sienn, and Rudd spent the next hour under Imperial guard, crouched in marginal shade while two stormtroopers examined every square *glekk* of the shuttle. They emerged with officious shrugs. "Move along," said the head whiteskin. "No charges this time."

"Thanks so much," Rudd growled, but he said it softly. Whatever "charges" were, they scared him. "Come on, girls." Oola walked a little faster and so avoided letting his swat land. Out of the corner of her eye, she saw that Sienn wasn't as quick.

"What are they looking for?" Oola asked as they hustled up a narrow alley.

"Not what. Who. From the way they searched us, they're looking for a person."

"Who?"

"Don't know. Don't care. Don't ask. I'm off schedule now," he grumbled, forgetting to condescend and speak pidgin. He bundled them into a wheelless craft with three aft-mounted engines. Oola claimed the back seat. "Fortuna's going to be busy for more than an hour. We'll have to—" His testy words faded under engine noise.

Oola stared over the side of the craft as Rudd steered across the ugly little town. It was all aboveground, not sensibly nestled in solid rock. Already she felt homesick. Debris lay heaped alongside square buildings the same ugly orange as Tatooine's sand. Rudd steered around several turns, until Oola would've gotten lost except for her unfailing sense of the suns. If you couldn't orient yourself on Ryloth, you could die before your time. "Just a little farther." Rudd stroked Sienn's leg as she sat in the front seat beside him. "And we'll—whoops." He'd been decelerating. Abruptly he sped up again and raced around a corner.

"What was that?" Oola asked. She craned her neck to look back. Nothing interesting showed.

"Visitors outside Jabba's town house. Not the kind I want to show you girls to. Let me think." Moments later, he braked the craft beside a sizable pile of debris. Metal spars and hull plates lay tangled with shredded cloth shrouds: evidently two airships had collided over Mos Eisley, crashed, and been preserved in Tatooine's dryness . . . except for their removable parts. Those were long scavenged, judging by the sand that drifted through holes in what remained. "Out," said Rudd. "Out."

"Here?" Sienn's lekku wriggled in confusion. It was a natural gesture their teachers had taught her to emphasize, just as Oola had learned to swing her lekku in free, wild arcs.

"Yep." Rudd gave Sienn a shove that sent her over the side. Oola vaulted down with a long, lazy flip.

Rudd followed. He poked at a long metal engine shield, slid a spar aside, and finally lifted a large sheet of yellowish cloth. It might have once served as a sail, attached to a long straight boom and ripped into weathered yellow strips at one end. "Climb under this. Wait till I get back. Don't make a sound. Mos Eisley is full of predators." He mimed a toothy growl and pretended to claw her. "Predators eat nice little girls. Put your hoods up."

Sienn had already rolled into the sail's stuffy shade. "Get in here, Oola," she whispered. "Hurry. Someone might see you."

Oola crawled close, curling her lekku close to her neck inside the hood. She couldn't let sand scratch their sleek skin. That would hurt . . . and it would decrease her value to Bib's famous employer.

It was finally sinking in: they were on the same world as the fabulous Jabba the Hutt. Master Bib Fortuna had spun mouth-watering tales of Jabba's wealth and splendor—his legendary palace, his exquisite taste in food, females, and other luxuries. Oola imagined soft cushions and costumes that fluttered in every breeze, composed solely of artfully draped dancing veils. Her handsome new master would be suave, powerful, and very deeply impressed with her . . . a station worth the insignificant price of the freedom she'd flung aside.

But she lay hiding in a pile of garbage. Sienn sniffled behind her.

Several minutes later, Oola blinked a runnel of sweat out of one eye. She'd changed her mind about Tatooine: it was hotter than Ryloth. Her vision blurred in heat that shimmered the air. An ill-defined shadow seemed to detach from the nearest building and flow toward the rubbish heap.

That was ridiculous. Even at midday, shadows didn't—

Sienn grabbed Oola's leg. "Oola," she whispered. "What's that?"

Oola blinked. It wasn't an hallucination, but a black-robed . . . person. *Mos Eisley is full of predators.* Even Rudd traveled cautiously here. Oola toed Sienn's shoulder. "Get deeper!" Once Sienn started to move, Oola wriggled backward. Hot, scratchy sand ground through her coverall against her knees, elbows, and belly, but she managed another meter deeper under cover.

The far edge of the sail lifted. he dark creature crouched on its heels, extending a hand as if to raise something . . . but his hand did not touch cloth or spar. A black cloak, hooded like theirs, draped his face.

Sienn whimpered. Oola scrabbled at her belt with sandy fingers, fumbling for her decorative little dagger. "Keep away," she hissed and signed in Twi'leki.

The shrouded creature leaned onto one hand. Deep under his hood, Oola caught a glimpse of chin and a glint of blue. Twi'leks never had blue eyes.

"Keep away," she repeated. The words didn't sound as menacing in Basic.

The creature shed his cloak and edged forward. Human like Rudd, he had clean, tow-colored fur. Unlike Rudd's kitchen-rag garb, his black undercloak clothing looked intact (although well worn) and tucked down. If this was a predator, her impression of Rudd had been right: Rudd was scum, even among his own people. Bib Fortuna's organization dropped in her estimation. So did her decision to cooperate.

The human's unnatural blue eyes glanced from Oola to Sienn, back to Oola. "I feel your fear," he said softly. "Come with me. I've got a—" He used several more words that she didn't understand, but he finished with two that she did: "safe place."

Oola laughed shortly. "No safe place on this world," she guessed aloud. It alarmed her that this human's way of speaking, whether or not she understood his words, dispelled her logical fear of him.

Sienn shook like one of Master Fortuna's collar ornaments. Oola raised up on her elbows and knees, lizard-style, and brandished Rudd's little dagger like a claw. "Who are you?" she demanded. "What do you want?"

"I mean you no harm." He didn't flinch from her blade. "My name is Luke."

She rolled the word down her tongue. "Luke. Go away, Luke."

"I was born on this world." Every word tried to soothe her. "I've returned on important . . ." He used another word she didn't know and couldn't guess at. Maybe it was the name of his spaceship.

"Then go do what you came back for," she said. "Leave us alone."

He leaned down onto both hands and crawled closer. Something dangling from his belt caught her attention. It didn't look like a blaster, and it certainly wasn't a knife. But she'd never seen a money pouch shaped like that. If it was a weapon, he wasn't reaching for it. He must not think her quick enough—or determined enough—to use her knife. She wriggled her knees up under her hips and dug her toes into the sand. This lizard could spring.

"What's *your* name?" he asked. He was almost close enough to touch.

"Nothing, daughter of nobody." She didn't want to hurt him, just chase him away. She picked her target —his left arm was extended. She could jab his elbow. Just enough to—

His right hand flicked, a beckoning gesture. Her

arms collapsed. She dropped chin first onto the sand and lost her grip on her knife.

He crooked one finger. The dagger spun across the ground into his grasp. "Sorry," he said. "But I won't hurt you. You mustn't hurt me. Are you slaves?"

What was this Luke creature? His face looked placid, even kind . . . but she couldn't trust that power in his voice and his right hand, and she didn't want to be kidnapped twice. She backed off again. Her left foot struck something. "Ouch!" squeaked Sienn.

"Come with me," Luke whispered. "I'll hide you. If anyone sees me, I have to . . . hide." Now he was underestimating her grasp of Basic. "Or . . . I have to get rid of them."

Oola scooted deeper and scooped up a handful of sand.

"I don't mean you." His smile seemed genuine, though she was no judge of humans. "I'll get you to the Rebel Alliance. They don't buy or sell anyone."

According to Master Fortuna's people, the Rebel Alliance was even more dangerous than the Empire. She held her ground.

The human—Luke—turned to address Sienn. "Come with me?" he cajoled.

Oola twisted around to warn her partner against it. Sienn widened her eyes and smiled. She raised up on hands and knees and crawled forward.

"That's it," the stranger encouraged her.

"Sienn!" Oola hissed. Sienn scrambled past her.

Luke touched Sienn's shoulder, resting one hand on silky yellow fabric. "Hurry," he urged. Backing out of the sweltering shelter, he eyed Oola again. She fancied that he pitied her. "Won't you let me help you? You won't get a second . . . chance. Do you know 'chance'?"

Even as Oola felt the tug of his influence, her pride and jealousy flared. "We've been chosen to dance in

Jabba's palace," she insisted, "the grandest on Tatooine. We're a pair. We go to Jabba together."

"It's the grandest on Tatooine, all right," Luke admitted. He draped his cloak over Sienn. "But I have" —again the "bizz-ness" word she couldn't translate— "there. It won't be pleasant. Jabba's palace isn't what you think."

Abruptly Oola remembered stormtroopers at the spaceport, searching incoming ships . . . for someone. She stared at the crouched figure in his rough but dignified black. Built like a dancer, he moved with controlled energy. And he still held her knife. She hadn't seen much of the galaxy, but she knew how to piece clues together. She made a swift guess. "Are *you* the one the Empire is looking for? At the spaceport?"

Luke shrugged. He glanced over his shoulder. "Probably. We have to hurry. Come on. I'll set you free."

Free? On this planet? What kind of life would that be?

She'd tried to reconcile herself to slavery. But freedom was better than servitude, even in the finest palace.

Then again . . . Oola envisioned herself lying on soft tufted cushions, savoring the finest raw fungi, summoning energy for another glorious dance. She thought of the thunderous praises she'd win. She hesitated.

Jabba was the wealthiest gangster in a hundred worlds.

"Please come," Luke whispered. "Jabba will k—"

"Hey!" shouted a familiar voice. "Get away from those girls!"

Oola peered out from under the sail toward the street. Rudd had reappeared around the corner of one blocky building. Bib Fortuna hung back, looking as darkly elegant as ever with his high bony crest and thick lekku. Protruding from his cloak, half-gloves and studded wristbands set off his long, clawed fingers. She'd found his hands fascinating, that fateful night back at home.

He was temptation.

He was evil, she realized with a shock that almost leveled her. *Evil.*

Rudd held his blaster at the ready. "All right, you. You're asking for it. That's Jabba's property."

"I don't care much for Jabba." Luke thrust Sienn behind him. Slightly shielded, she plunged toward better cover. A crushed nose cone jutted out of the debris pile. Sienn dove behind it. Luke pressed into the nearest alcove and shoved at what looked like a door. It didn't open.

Oola cringed.

"Hah!" Rudd fired. His shot splattered into sand just behind Luke's left leg. The sand melted into a glassy puddle. "I'm not killing you yet," he jeered. "First, you're going to learn not to tinker with Jabba's belongings."

Luke flattened against the building. His face looked deadly calm. Fortuna had warned her: please Jabba, and she'd reap the finest rewards. Cross him, and expect worse than her worst imaginings.

Jabba must be evil too. She had to stop this. Somehow. What could she do?

Finally Luke seized the strange object at his belt and unhooked it, then held it out two-handed. To Oola's astonishment, a glowing green shaft appeared at one end. Luke stepped out of the doorway toward Rudd. The step dropped him into a deep dueling stance, and he wielded the glimmering weapon with long, strong sweeps of his arms and shoulders. The weapon's weird metallic hum changed pitch as he swung it. Blaster bolts deflected in all directions. Not one touched him.

Oola gaped. He wasn't just built like a dancer. He moved like one.

His head turned. "Go!" he shouted at Sienn. "Run!" That was for Oola.

Oola hesitated. Rudd had seen Luke. As Oola understood, Luke had to kill him now. He was hiding from the Empire.

What about Master Fortuna?

"Stop that!" Rudd crouched. He steadied one elbow on his knee and fired off a continuous volley. Luke stepped closer and continued to parry. Rudd didn't seem to realize his own danger.

Oola cast a glance around for her tall master.

At the edge of the debris, Fortuna slunk toward Sienn. He brandished a blaster of his own. He probably meant to stun Sienn, then kill Luke . . . if Rudd didn't get him. He rounded the nose cone and aimed his blaster. Sienn shrank against jumbled debris, trapped like a child with no place to run or hide. Oola had one moment of choice.

"Sienn!" Oola shrieked. "Go! Run!" She dashed at Fortuna, seized the flapping edge of his black robes, and twined her lekku around his shoulders in mock passion. Rolls of fat shook at the base of his neck. The blaster fell from his elegant hand. He bent backward to grope for it. "Get off," he seethed. "Get off me, you little fool."

Oola's sudden panic made Mos Eisley seem chilly. If Luke meant to kill Fortuna, she'd just jumped into his line of fire. She tried to pull free. Her lekku tangled with Fortuna's.

Bib caught her wrist in a grip that drove his nails into her flesh. Gasping, Oola collapsed. Her lekku fell flaccid. Fortuna pulled free of them.

Oola let him drag her to her feet. She hadn't been shot. Neither had Fortuna, but Rudd lay facedown and twitching. Sienn was dashing up the street. Both of her lekku swung down the back of Luke's too-long cloak. She had almost reached the street corner beyond that debris heap. Luke followed her, carrying his weird weapon . . . but the glimmering shaft had vanished. As Sienn dashed out of sight, Luke slowed. He glanced over his shoulder, caught Oola's stare, and hesitated.

Sienn wouldn't survive two minutes alone in these streets. "Go!" Oola shrieked.

Luke raised both eyebrows in a pained expression, as if she had finally jabbed him. He spun away, and then he too was gone.

"So you want Jabba to yourself." Bib pulled her so close to his leather chest protector that she could smell rancid breath venting between his long, pointed teeth. He dug his blaster muzzle into her stomach. "All of the goodies for Oola. No rivals."

"No rivals," she sneered back, full of adrenaline and bravado. It was either that or recoil. She mustn't show fear.

Fortuna flung her away. Oola caught her balance with a languid handspring, turned back to Bib, and waited.

"My speeder is parked around the corner," he growled. His orange-pink eyes glowered. "This way."

Oola sighed away the memory. She'd lost daylight and hope, and she'd never wielded power. But no one could steal her honor. She would never again lose her best reason for living.

"Fortuna hates me now," she murmured. She fingered the hideous leather headdress. "Here are my soft cushions." Mocking her own words, she ran a finger over the stony lip of Jabba's bed. Her dainties? Scraps Jabba tossed when she groveled . . . or food he suspected of harboring poison.

Threepio finished translating her tale for Yarna, then they both shook their heads. Beyond Jabba's throne, a scream faded into the floor. Oola shuddered. She'd seen Jabba feed his stinking, hideous underground monster. The rancor usually devoured its prey whole. By the standards of this place, it looked like a quick death. She'd rather be next on the menu than watch it again, and that was likely enough. She'd choose it over Jabba's ardent embrace. How ironic that Sienn, the obvious morsel, had escaped . . . but Oola was glad that she had, and proud to have helped.

"At least you can dance," Yarna pointed out. "Be thankful Jabba doesn't have your cubs in his clutches."

Oola raised her head. "I can dance," she agreed. "If I could have one wish . . ."

"What?" Yarna encouraged, straightening her own headdress.

"I would dance the perfect dance. Once. It wouldn't matter who watched. I would know it was perfect."

Threepio's head swiveled jauntily over his metal shoulders. "But Miss Oola, Master Luke is close by."

"You do know him?"

"Oh yes. I—"

"I wasn't heat-crazy? He can do all those things?"

"Oh yes. I too was a gift to Jabba." His singsong voice sounded giddy. "Master Luke is a Jedi Knight, a very important person in the Rebel Alliance. He's very good at rescuing people. You should have—"

"Don't," she groaned. What had Luke tried to warn her? That Jabba would . . . k-something. Kill her? Surely he couldn't predict the future.

Threepio touched her shoulder. "He's coming here to rescue me. I'll see that he rescues you ladies, too. Leave that to me."

Oola eyed the droid critically. "He used so many

hard words in that message—the one your friend . . . *projected*," she finished in Twi'leki.

"Oh, that. Perhaps you should play along with His High Exaltedness just a little longer?" Threepio imitated a human shrug.

Yarna nudged her, her face compassionate. "Listen to Metal Man, Oola. If I can survive this, you can."

"Not for long. Not with my—" The court rang with raucous laughter. At any moment, she'd feel the tug at her slave collar. "Threepio, help us escape. You must."

Threepio touched her stout chain and then the greasy round bolt on his chest. "Creating a plan," he dithered in Twi'leki, "is beyond my capacity. Artoo has a vibro-cutter among his appendages, but he has been assigned to the garages."

Oola forced down her glimmer of temporary hope. She mustn't forget bright eternity, nor the Great Dance. Not in here. Not for a moment. "That's the difference between us," she muttered. "For all of your six million forms of communication, you're faithless."

"I beg your pardon." Threepio brushed his midsection again. "I have every faith in Master Luke. He will rescue me." Since hearing her story, he'd called Luke "Master" twice—a term he'd hesitated to use before. Evidently her story had done *him* some good, anyway.

And if "Master Luke" was coming, she might get a second chance after all. She eyed her fellow dancer. "Perhaps I can survive this," she agreed. And perhaps Sienn was already safe somewhere. "I'll do my b—"

Her collar tugged up and backward. Half strangled, Oola yanked her headpiece back on, flailing for balance as Jabba hauled her over his side. She dug her fingers and toes into fetid flesh. Jabba purred as if tickled by her struggling. His jizz-wailers swung into a new dance tune.

Furious, Oola leaped off her grotesque master's

dais. She vaulted into the middle of the floor, defiantly landing on the rancor pit's grate. Jabba's trapdoor had closed again. Maybe he hadn't even opened it.

Maybe.

Yarna joined the dance, as did Melina Carniss with her long dark fur. Oola kept at the far end of her chain. In one dark alcove she seemed to see blue eyes watching from under a roughly woven black hood. She would dance for him this time. For a second chance. She kicked head-high and higher, powerfully swinging her fleshy lekku. Her grace was her glory. The physical rapture of dancing swept through her and owned her, freely and naturally. Every step and each gesture marked out a melody. She'd found perfect sensual poise. At last.

Evidently Jabba thought so, too. He tugged her chain.

More angry than frightened at first, she grasped it with both hands and yanked back. She didn't care if the Gamorreans beat her again—she would not dance closer. She only knew a few words of Huttese. She shouted them. "Na chuba negatorie!"

Jabba tugged again, drooling.

Oola braced her feet at the trapdoor's edge. Though terror robbed her of poise, she would not yield. "Na! Na! Natoota . . ."

Let Us Prey:
The Whiphid's Tale

by Marina Fitch and
Mark Budz

Feeding time again. The crunch and snap of bones resonated through the walls of the Whiphid J'Quille's room as Jabba's "pet" rancor snacked on its latest morsel.

J'Quille paced his stark room. Huntlust vibrated through his tall, golden-furred frame, wrinkled his broad snout. His tusks tingled even though it had been several hours since Jabba dropped the Twi'lek dancer into the rancor's pit. The screams had ceased long ago, but J'Quille couldn't stop salivating. The savory aroma of fresh blood warmed the pit of his stomach.

The warmth wouldn't last long. J'Quille snarled low in his throat. Next time it might be J'Quille the rancor feasted on. Jabba grew bored so easily. What if the novelty of employing a former lover of the Whiphid crimelord Lady Valarian to ferret out conspiracies wore thin?

No doubt the kind of reminder Jabba intended when he gave J'Quille quarters this close to the pit. If Jabba suspected J'Quille still worked for her . . .

Owner of the Lucky Despot, Lady Valarian was Jabba's most powerful rival. Not only was her nightclub the most successful in Mos Eisley—on the entire planet of Tatooine—she siphoned business from Jabba as easily as she sipped Sullustan gin.

As easily as the rancor would sip the marrow from J'Quille's bones if he was discovered.

J'Quille snorted. All he had to do was keep his tusks clean for a few more days. Then the rancor and his devoted keeper, Malakili, would be gone, free of Jabba. J'Quille had helped arrange their escape with Lady Valarian. One of the few good things he'd been able to do behind Jabba's back.

That, and bribing the kitchen boy, Phlegmin, to lace Jabba's snack tank of freckled toads with slow-acting poison. A little too slow by the look of things.

Another bone snapped.

J'Quille's claws tensed. He smoothed the fur bristling around his neck, raised by the scent of the Twi'lek's blood and the huntlust surging through him. But was he hunter or prey? Or both?

He stopped pacing and glanced at the room, barren except for his sleeping pallet. Built by the B'omarr monks, the room's stark ascetic reminded him of the rock-and-bone shelters of his homeworld, Toola. Two ceremonial trophies hung on opposite walls: a necklace of Mastmot teeth, dipped in poison; and the skull of a young bantha he had brought down one night with his bare claws. He was a hunter, not some weak Ice Puppy that sat back and waited for death to come.

He jerked open the door and slipped into the hallway. A pain-filled moan issued from one of the rank cells. A Gamorrean guard grunted as he pushed past J'Quille, bleary with sleep or too much Sullustan gin.

J'Quille stroked the spiky hairs along his lower lip. Lady Valarian liked gin. If only he were back at the Lucky Despot! Two days ago, when it looked like everything was going according to plan, it had seemed a possibility. His "falling out" with Lady Valarian would end and they could finally stop pretending.

That was before the note. Someone knew he was bribing Phlegmin. He had already paid a hefty ten thousand credits to keep the blackmailer silent. But it was only a matter of time before Jabba found out.

How much time? That was the question.

The crunch and snap of bones stopped. Blast. Sweat beaded J'Quille's forehead and long, broad snout. When was the last time he'd been cool? He wiped his face with the back of his paw. Strands of fur clung to the sweat. He grimaced. Shedding again. Tatooine's dry, sweltering heat sucked the energy out of him. What he wouldn't give for a couple of minutes in one of the Lucky Despot's ice saunas.

Something scuttled past him—one of those spider-like droids enlightened B'omarr monks used to ferry around their pickled brains. The glass jar winked in the dim light, then droid and brain disappeared around the corner.

J'Quille snarled in disgust and hurried on, stopping outside the rancor's pit. The inner gate stood slightly open, as he'd known it would. Malakili was cleaning the outer cage.

The scent of blood was stronger here. J'Quille closed his eyes and breathed deeply. The intoxicating scent soothed his taut nerves, taking the edge off his repressed frustration. If he could just track down the blackmailer and kill him . . .

A foot scraped on the stone floor near him. His eyes snapped open. One hand jerked up, claws extended, while the other reached for his vibroblade.

"Hey, it's just me," Malakili said softly, stepping out of the cage's shadows. Sweat glazed his bare chest and heavy arms. He patted J'Quille's shoulder with a black-gloved hand. "Easy. You're stiffer than an Imperial stormtrooper."

"Been a bad night," J'Quille said, letting go of his vibroblade.

"Tell me about it," Malakili said, adjusting his black headband. His eyes narrowed in his thick, doughy face. "Something's in the air. Even my friend here is jumpier than usual."

"This place is a tomb," J'Quille said. "Even the living are dead inside these walls. Might as well stuff our brains in jars."

"Yeah, but the monk's brains aren't dead." Malakili leaned closer to him. "Listen, I heard something I think you should know."

J'Quille tensed. "What?"

"This afternoon Bib Fortuna tried to get Jabba to throw you into the pit. Thinks it would be an interesting contest."

J'Quille peered at Malakili. "What did Jabba say?"

"I tried to talk him out of it. You'd inflict too much damage before my friend killed you. But Jabba wasn't convinced. He said he'd give it some thought."

"So I have a little time," J'Quille said.

Malakili nodded. "A little. With luck, we'll both be out of here soon."

"Alive, I hope," J'Quille said, curling the corners of his lips back around his tusks in a smile.

Malakili smiled. "I'll let you know if I hear more."

"Thanks," J'Quille said.

Gnashing his tusks, J'Quille hurried back to his room. Things were moving much too fast, forcing his hand. Jabba's increasing coolness, the blackmailer . . . and now Bib Fortuna's plotting. Time to get Phlegmin to increase the dosage of slow poison. The sooner Jabba was reduced to a vat of gibbering slug jelly, the sooner J'Quille could return to Lady Valarian. He'd wanted to increase the dosage earlier, but he'd been afraid someone would notice a sudden change in Jabba.

Now he could no longer afford the luxury of caution.

J'Quille slipped into his room and went to the string of Mastmot teeth hanging on the wall. Lifting the necklace from its peg, he slipped it over his head. Luckily most people, including Jabba, considered him a mindless brute with a taste for crude jewelry. No one suspected the teeth had been dipped in poison.

J'Quille started at a low mechanical warble outside his door. His nostrils flared, crinkling at the acrid stench of oil and metal.

A droid.

The claws of J'Quille's right hand curled involuntarily around the grip of his vibroblade, then slowly relaxed. An assassin droid wouldn't announce its presence.

The warble repeated. J'Quille yanked open the door.

The maintenance droid, a blue U2C1 housekeeping model, chirped and took a step back. Both of its flex-tube arms quivered. With a whine, it sucked in air through the stiff brush at the end of its left arm and the upholstery attachment on its right.

"I hope I'm not disturbing you," it said tinnily. "I've been instructed to clean this room."

J'Quille stepped aside, allowing the droid to enter. Another calculated nuisance on the part of Jabba or one of his servants—most likely Salacious Crumb. That drool-lapping Kowakian lizard-monkey probably scavenged the droid's waste tank for between-meal snacks. J'Quille sneered. He'd love to program the cleaning droid to suck up that cackling little rubbish heap.

"Please close the door," the droid said. "This won't take long."

J'Quille grumbled.

The droid's right arm snaked out to sweep the floor. The loud whine grated on J'Quille's nerves. He reached for the doorknob.

"I have a message," the droid said.

J'Quille hesitated. "A message?"

"From a friend." The droid paused, but left its vacuum running. " 'I know who's blackmailing you. Meet me on the citadel roof at sunrise and I'll give you his name.' "

The rampart on top of the guest quarters. J'Quille had gone up there more than once to escape the press of the walls and drink in the cool night air.

"I have been instructed to wait for your response," the droid said.

J'Quille's hackles rose. A clever ruse by Jabba to lure him out? If the message had been sent by a friend, why the secrecy? Why not just give him the name of the blackmailer?

Obviously the person wanted something more from him . . . but what?

Money? Or to enlist him in another plot to kill Jabba? There were certainly enough of those. J'Quille had only leaked a fraction of them to Jabba. Only the least promising.

"How will I recognize him?" J'Quille asked.

"You won't," the droid said. "You'll recognize what he's wearing."

J'Quille exhaled sharply, tired of playing these games. If it turned out to be a setup, he could always claim that he was just doing his job, following up on a suspect. For Jabba.

J'Quille wet his lips. Yes, that was the way to handle it. A thrill ran through him, not unlike the one he got while tracking an Ice Puppy or a Sea Hog back on Toola.

"I'll be there," J'Quille said.

He ducked into the hall and up the stairs to Jabba's main audience chamber. Jabba and his minions dozed on the crimelord's dais. The band played on, melodic jizz and dense smoke cavorting in a sinuous dance of sound and smell. Frozen in carbonite, Han Solo stared at him from the display alcove.

J'Quille eased past the bandstand, skirting the trapdoor to the rancor's pit. He caught a glimpse of Malakili through the grating, still cleaning the pit while the rancor gnawed contentedly on a wet bone.

The rancor belched. The band missed a beat but picked up quickly, as if trying to drown out the disturbance.

Jabba opened one eye, then closed it again, clearly unconcerned. His tail twitched, a sure sign that he was wide awake. Even the new gold droid beside him stood alert, ready to translate the orders of its master. Bib Fortuna slept on the floor, next to Salacious Crumb, who was snoring loudly. Not even sleep could silence the little garbage disposal.

J'Quille descended the steps to the kitchen. Someone watched from a darkened recess—one of the B'omarr monks that still lurked in the palace. The monk's broad, round face was moon-pale, his twisted nose casting a craterish shadow along one cheek.

J'Quille scowled and picked up his pace.

He slowed near the kitchen door. The scent of bruised goatgrass wafted from the darkened room. He crept closer. Dim light spread from one of the inner rooms.

He pricked up his ears.

Two voices rose in argument: Ree-Yees's perpetual slur and the guttural grunts of a Gamorrean guard. Hiding behind the door frame, J'Quille peered into the room.

Goatgrass littered the kitchen like feathers from a fresh kill. Even more unsteady than usual, Ree-Yees teetered over a body sprawled beside a broken crate. Ree-Yees's three eye stalks trembled as they tried to focus on the Gamorrean. The guard glowered at Ree-Yees, then waddled forward and bent to look at the corpse.

Ree-Yees shifted slightly, giving J'Quille a clear view.

Phlegmin, the kitchen boy.

J'Quille's foot claws curled reflexively, digging into the stone floor. His heart hammered in his ears, blotting out the guard's piglike grunts and Ree-Yees's drunken bleats. What had that goat-faced, three-eyed bar rag done? Clenching and unclenching his claws, J'Quille quelled the urge to stomp forward and rip out the thieving Gran's throat.

J'Quille growled under his breath and drew back. Better to wait. He could hunt the murdering drunk later. There wasn't anything he could do now—not without arousing the guard's suspicion. He swallowed, backing away from the kitchen.

He retreated the way he came. Hurrying past the darkened recess, he stopped. The B'omarr monk was gone.

J'Quille's mind raced. Maybe Ree-Yees hadn't murdered the kitchen boy after all. Maybe it was the monk. Phlegmin might have sent the droid to J'Quille after discovering the monk's blackmail plot. The monk found out and killed Phlegmin . . .

But why would a B'omarr monk blackmail J'Quille? He suspected the monks wanted Jabba out of their citadel as much as anyone, more. But if Jabba found a discontented B'omarr to work as a spy for him . . . hardly surprising. In fact, it would be more surprising if he hadn't.

But why not simply turn J'Quille over to Jabba?

J'Quille let out a breath and hurried up the stairs to the audience chamber. Lady Valarian would know what to do. The last time he'd contacted her, she'd told him not to call until Jabba was a chortling, mindless slug.

But without Phlegmin that might take a while. Besides, she needed to know what was going on.

The band was packing it in when J'Quille eased past them. The rancor snored in its pit, and even Jabba's tail had slowed its pensive rhythm. J'Quille curled his claws to keep from touching the necklace of Mastmot teeth. He averted his eyes from the tank of live toads.

Climbing the stairs to the guest rooms, J'Quille passed the masked bounty hunter who had brought in the Wookiee and threatened to blow up the palace with a thermal detonator earlier that evening. J'Quille smiled. A fine, subtle display of huntlust. Truly admirable.

The bounty hunter nodded once, then continued down the stairs. No doubt on his way down to the dungeon to taunt the Wookiee. J'Quille's nostrils twitched. Something about the bounty hunter smelled odd, out of place. There was no time to wonder about it now. J'Quille raced up the stairs.

He panted, his lungs aching with the still, hot air. Doors lined both sides of the curved guest wing, most open to reveal empty rooms. In the past they had served as individual sleeping and meditation chambers for the monks, but now the moldy breath of neglect filled the hallway. Jabba had few guests at any given time. Even two or three tended to nuture his pampered paranoia.

Glancing over his shoulder, J'Quille crept to an empty room near the stairwell leading up to the roof. He shut the door softly behind him.

J'Quille went to the window slit in the far wall. Peering out at the night sky, he flared his nostrils, sucking in the soothing breeze. The cool air smelled faintly of dust. A whiff of goatgrass clung to the breeze, no doubt rising from the kitchen. A delicious shiver traveled through him. Blood stained the wind tonight too.

He turned from the window and pried the cap from the pommel of his vibroblade. Sliding a holo-projection tube hidden in his vibroblade, he set it on the thick windowsill, making sure the tiny lens in the side faced him.

He pushed the transmit button and waited for Lady Valarian to respond. It shouldn't take long. She didn't go to bed until dawn, when the Lucky Despot closed for a short time to get ready for the next day's customers.

A light flashed on the cylinder. Half a second later the lens projected a hologram of the entry hatch and bulkhead where Lady Valarian conducted business. Part of the Lucky Despot's charm was that it had once been a cargo hauler. Lady Valarian had used the spaceship's decor to create an atmosphere comfortable to spacers and exotic enough to lure planetbound clientele. A low, wistful growl rumbled in J'Quille's throat.

And into the middle of the holo stepped Lady Valarian, dazzling as always. Her curled mane, tinted a burnished red, spilled down the sides of her face. She had painted her tusks blue and wore a gold ring on the left one. Earrings glittered on her ears.

A wave of longing sped through J'Quille. His nostrils tingled with the remembered allure of her pheromone perfume, the softness of her fur against the flat of his nose, the way she snuffled in her sleep . . .

"J'Quille," she said, waving one claw-polished hand. The blare of music and sabacc players from the Star Chamber Cafe tinkled in the background. "How wonderful to see you! Oh, my little Mastmot, how thin you are! You've been shedding again. Well, now that you've completed that little task you promised to do for me—"

"Not yet, my little ice tiger," he said. He clucked his tongue. "There's a problem. I need to talk to you."

Lady Valarian's eyes narrowed. "What kind of problem, dearest?"

The massive hand of a Whiphid male reached from the edge of the hologram and offered her a Sullustan gin ice blaster. J'Quille's throat tightened. A male, in Lady Valarian's chambers . . .

"J'Quille?" Lady Valarian said. "Darling?"

J'Quille cleared his throat. Probably just a servant. "I'm being blackmailed," he said. "Someone knows the kitchen boy was poisoning the toads. He was killed minutes ago."

Lady Valarian removed the siptube from her lips. "What are you trying to tell me, dearest? Does Jabba know you're trying to poison him?"

"Not yet," J'Quille said, wishing he could be that certain.

Lady Valarian sighed. "Then why are you calling, darling? Please get to the point. I have other business to attend to."

J'Quille's nose flaps flared.

Lady Valarian's eyes teared under her worried brow.

"And this is much too dangerous. If someone caught you, my precious . . ."

J'Quille leaned toward the holo. "I need help. I need to find out who killed the scullion. Do you have any idea who killed him or who might be blackmailing me?"

"There's a B'omarr monk—"

A deep laugh rumbled through the palace walls below, drowning the words.

Jabba.

J'Quille stiffened. The fur on his spine prickled with a rush of fear.

Lady Valarian's eyes widened. "J'Quille—"

"I won't fail," J'Quille said, reaching for the projection tube as another laugh reverberated through the walls. He severed the uplink and slammed the tube into the grip of his vibroblade.

Muscles taut, J'Quille held his vibroblade ready in front of him. He listened for even the slightest sound . . . the scraping of feet on stone or the rattle of weapons.

Silence.

Were the guards waiting for him in the hall? Better to face death head-on. He opened the door, expecting a blaster shot or the slash of a vibro-ax.

Nothing.

The corridor was empty. J'Quille dashed toward the far stairs. Distant voices, human voices, drifted from Jabba's audience chamber, punctuated by the unmistakable cackle of Salacious Crumb.

J'Quille took the steps two at a time. Just before he reached the bottom step something caught his eye. He drew back.

The carbonite slab.

Empty.

J'Quille's tail twitched. The human pleading with Jabba must be Han Solo. But that was impossible. A person stood a better chance stepping out of the heart of a Toolan iceberg than breaking free of carbonite's freezing grip—

Another round of laughter filled the audience chamber. A cacophony of voices joined Jabba's bass chuckle. Hugging the wall, J'Quille peeked into the room.

The bounty hunter, a human female, stood helmetless beside Solo facing Jabba. J'Quille hissed in surprise. A human! That's what the smell had been!

Solo's head bobbed and wobbled, his eyes unfocused and not quite fixed on Jabba. "I'll pay triple," he said as the Gamorrean guards dragged him off. "You're throwing away a fortune here. Don't be a fool!"

Jabba smiled, then turned to leer at the human female with the same cruel lechery he had gazed on the Twi'lek dancer. His slimy lips gleamed with spittle.

J'Quille slid back into the shadows and quietly sheathed his vibroblade. It wouldn't look good if a guard stumbled across him lurking in the stairwell with his weapon drawn. He took a deep breath and let it out slowly.

The Crumb's hysterical screech covered J'Quille's retreat up the stairs. There was still time. As much time as Jabba remained preoccupied with the human female.

J'Quille trotted down the corridor to the guest room. That would be safer than his own quarters if Jabba suspected him. He closed the door and sat on the floor facing the window slit, his vibroblade lying across his legs. Framed by the slit, the night sky had faded from black to deep blue. It would be dawn soon.

He stared at the stone wall opposite him. Jabba had to know. Why else would Phlegmin be dead? The blackmailer, the monk Lady Valarian warned him about, had told Jabba about the poisoned toads then killed the kitchen boy to prove his loyalty. J'Quille grimaced. Jabba was always demanding proof of loyalty. J'Quille had been forced to hunt and "kill" his own servant in a display of fidelity. Fortunately that great sack of nearsighted slug gel couldn't tell a Whiphid tusk from a greater Mastmot tooth.

Footsteps tramped heavily down the hall. J'Quille leaped to his feet, drawing his vibroblade. The thick, swinish grunts of several Gamorrean guards echoed in the corridor. Holding his breath, J'Quille stepped behind the door.

The guards lumbered past.

J'Quille listened till their footsteps faded, then sank down onto the floor again. He slid the vibroblade in its sheath. Lady Valarian had given him the weapon.

Lady Valarian. For whom he risked his tusks daily.

And who had a strange male in her chamber. Just a servant? Or a rival? J'Quille's mane bristled. Perhaps this blackmailer had more to do with Lady Valarian and less to do with Jabba.

Perhaps Lady Valarian had tired of waiting for him to act and decided to rid herself of the potential embarrassment of an inept spy in Jabba's palace. She had always despised foolish, weak males. Look at D'Wopp, her first husband. The fool had been too stupid to turn down a bounty offer by Jabba during their wedding reception. Lady Valarian had shipped him back to Toola in a box.

J'Quille was no fool and he was not weak. The slow poison had been Lady Valarian's idea. "Let's not be too obvious, my sweet," she'd crooned.

J'Quille stared at the vibroblade. Beautifully crafted, the finest weapon credits could buy. Was he jumping to conclusions? Still, she knew about the monk . . .

Slamming and banging echoed from the direction of the hangar. J'Quille listened at the door, then stalked to the window slit. In the gray light people were scurrying about, preparing Jabba's Ubrickkian sail barge. Evidently Jabba was planning a trip to the Great Pit of Carkoon sometime in the near future, probably to feed Han Solo and the Wookiee to the Sarlacc.

Was J'Quille on the menu, too?

He shivered, then peered across the sands at the welt of brightness along the horizon. One of Tatooine's two suns was rising. The light spread slowly like water, dousing the glitter of stars. He had better head up to the roof to meet the informant. J'Quille unsheathed his vibroblade and opened the door.

Someone shuffled down the hall. J'Quille waited in the doorway and listened to the dry whisper of clothes. Instead of diminishing toward the stairs to the main audience chamber, the steady shuffle grew louder.

A shadow materialized around the curve in the hall. It passed an open door. A pale, round face with a twisted nose peered warily into every shadow.

The same monk who had hidden in the recess outside the kitchen.

J'Quille eased into the room and waited for the monk to pass. The man's loose robes swayed with each step. Light from the partially open door illuminated the side of his face. His head and face were devoid of all hair.

Anger surged through J'Quille. He narrowed his eyes, deepening the shadows in the hall. His pulse throbbed in his claws as his chest tightened around the beating of his heart.

J'Quille stepped into the hallway. The monk paused and turned, his hands hidden in the folds of his robe, a robe ample enough to conceal a blaster or a vibroblade.

"There you are," the monk said. His gaze flitted to

the vibroblade. "Let's go to the roof, friend, where we can speak freely."

The vibroblade trembled in J'Quille's hand. He tightened his grip. "What do you want from me?"

The monk glanced nervously down the hall. "This is not a good place to talk. It's too easy to be overheard. Trust me."

"You were there when the kitchen boy was killed," J'Quille said, unmoving. "I saw you."

"There was nothing I could do," the monk said. His hands shifted under his robes.

Before the monk could free his hands, J'Quille slashed upward with his vibroblade. The blade sliced through the robes and the man's chest. The monk stared at J'Quille, a look of surprise on his face, then toppled forward onto the floor.

The pressure in J'Quille's chest eased. At last he could breathe again. He took a deep breath, filling his lungs with the ripe, giddy scent of fresh blood.

Sheathing his vibroblade, he knelt down and rolled the body over. The monk gurgled. "Phlegmin . . . black . . . mailer," he rasped, then shuddered and died.

Phlegmin? J'Quille frowned and leaned closer.

Something winked in the dim light.

An earring. J'Quille turned the monk's head to get a better look at the chartreuse gemstone set in a single gold ring. His blood went cold. "You'll recognize what he's wearing," the cleaning droid had said.

The earring was Lady Valarian's.

J'Quille had given her the pair the day after their first night together. She'd growled with delight and clipped the earrings on immediately.

J'Quille unclipped the jewel from the monk's earlobe.

The monk had been working for Lady Valarian.

J'Quille flexed his claws around the earring. What was he going to tell her?

A grunt filtered down the corridor. J'Quille grabbed the monk's robes and dragged the body toward the nearest guest room. The monk's hands fell free of the robes.

His right hand clutched a thermal detonator.

The one the bounty hunter had used to threaten Jabba?

J'Quille snatched it from the stiffening hand. Whatever he had done, here was a chance to redeem himself.

Heavy footsteps accompanied another grunt. J'Quille glanced over his shoulder. No one yet, but the person was definitely headed his way. He looked around wildly. Where could he hide the detonator? His belt pouch seemed too small—

J'Quille crammed the detonator into the pouch anyway, praying he wouldn't trigger it. The pouch bulged, refusing to close. J'Quille smoothed his fur over the pouch's gap, his shoulders rising as the approaching stranger called out.

Or rather, *squealed* out. J'Quille turned slowly, forcing himself not to smirk, and looked up into the face of a squat Gamorrean guard.

Stupidity on the hoof.

The guard carried Phlegmin's dead body over one shoulder. This must be the same Gamorrean who had been talking to Ree-Yees in the kitchen.

The guard trudged up to him, wheezing and snorting. He uttered a few more incomprehensible grunts, then looked at J'Quille expectantly.

J'Quille's mind raced frantically. Just how stupid were these guards? If this brute could believe Ree-Yees, he'd believe anything.

The Gamorrean grunted impatiently. One of the squeals sounded like "dead."

J'Quille stood. "He's not dead, he's, uh, meditating. Gone into a deep trance. Pondering the imponderables."

The guard bent over the monk. He wrinkled his nose at the blood and snuffled a short, bewildered snort.

J'Quille wet his lips. "The blood? He wanted to see if he'd reached the final stage of enlightenment. He decided to do a little testing on his own to see if he was ready before asking his friends to put his brain in a jar."

The guard's eyes narrowed. He grunted and pointed first at the monk's head, then at his chest.

J'Quille shrugged. "That's where their brains are. In their chests. It makes it easier to remove them."

The guard's brow puckered. He snuffled, then grunted something that sounded like, "Can't meditate here," then bent down and hefted the body of the monk onto his other shoulder.

J'Quille watched the Gamorrean shamble off, then heaved a sigh of relief. He touched the thermal detonator.

Slipping into the nearest guest room, he walked over to the window. He held up the earring and admired the sunlight shining through the clear stone, then set it on the windowsill. He opened his pouch.

J'Quille cradled the thermal detonator in his claws. He knew just what to do with it. He'd been given a second chance to get rid of Jabba—this time he wouldn't blow it.

Sleight of Hand:
The Tale of Mara Jade

by Timothy Zahn

The dance ended, and the music was silenced. She stood as she had finished: on single tiptoe, her opposite arm upstretched, reaching with silent eloquence for the stars or the Empire or perhaps merely the approval of her master. For a pair of heartbeats she held the pose. Then, with a dramatic flourish, she collapsed again to the floor, arms sweeping around and onto the floor in front of her like the wings of a downed bird, legs shifting to curl half around her, one in front and one behind, torso bent forward over her arms. Grace and beauty and style, transformed in an instant to unworthiness and submission and humility. The precise combination, or so she'd been told, that Jabba the Hutt liked in his dancers.

As did, presumably, the fat, scar-headed man sprawled on the couch in front of her. But the seconds dragged on and he just sat there, not speaking, watching her. She held her pose, breathing quickly and shallowly into cramped lungs and wondering if she should go ahead and get up without waiting for permission. But the fat man had already demonstrated his enjoyment of giving orders, particularly to helpless underlings. If she wanted to become one of those underlings, it would be best to allow him that extra little bit of egotism.

So she waited for his orders, and after a few seconds more he was ready to give them. "Rise," he said, his tone as indulgent as the rest of him. "Come here."

She did so. Up close he was even more repulsive, his vaguely greasy aroma approaching suffocation level. But Jabba himself, she knew, would be worse. Maybe this was part of the test.

"You dance very well, Arica," he said, looking her up and down. "Very well, indeed. Tell me, what else do you do well?"

"Whatever my master Jabba the Hutt would require of me," she said.

He smiled, his small eyes almost disappearing into folds of flesh. "Very good," he said. "Not what I would require, but what Jabba your master would require. A wise answer; but perhaps not wise enough. Tell me, would it surprise you to know that I once *was* Jabba the Hutt?"

She blinked, giving him her best stupid-helpless-lost look. "You were—? I don't understand."

"I was Jabba the Hutt," he repeated smugly. "Not really, of course, but for a time many on Tatooine thought so. I was the one, you see, whom Jabba always sent outside the palace to meet with people. Kept his anonymity that way. A good smuggler always keeps a few secrets." His smug smile vanished. "You see now who exactly you're dealing with here."

"Yes, I see," she said. She did, too. He was the expendable one, the man Jabba had sent out to take whatever blaster shots his many enemies might care to fire in his direction. The stupid one, moreover, too dazzled by the pseudoglamour and pseudopower of the role to realize he was little more than assassin bait.

But for all that, a man Jabba must have trusted at least enough to finalize his deals and not flop the charade in the process. And who thus had probably earned whatever microscopic gratitude the Hutt was capable of.

Someone not to be crossed. At least, not openly.

"Good," the fat man said softly. "Well, then. You're hired. You'll start on the midnight shift—you never know when Jabba might want some entertainment." He looked at the door and snapped his fingers. One of the Gamorrean guards detached himself from the door and lumbered over. "The guard will show you the way. I'll see you later, Arica."

"I will be honored," she said, bowing humbly as she backed away. Groveling before him.

But that was all right. Let the petty man revel in his petty power over her. Trusted underling of one of the most powerful crimelords in the Empire, he was still nothing. She could crush him with a word; could bring down Jabba's entire organization on a whim; could burn this backwater planet to a core of glazed sand with a single order. And if none of that happened, it was merely because she had more important matters to attend to.

For she was Mara Jade, the Emperor's Hand. Here to await the arrival of Luke Skywalker. And to kill him.

The Emperor's face seemed to hover in the air in front of Mara, his yellow eyes glittering with satisfaction. *So you are inside,* his thoughts said. *Skywalker has not yet appeared?*

Not yet, she thought back at him. *But Solo is still here. When Skywalker comes, I'll be ready.*

The eyes glittered again, and Mara felt the warmth of his approval fill her mind. *Excellent,* his thoughts said. *Such a threat must be eliminated.*

Mara permitted herself a small smile. *He will be,* she assured her master. *Jabba may even get to him first.*

Abruptly, the warmth withdrew, leaving an icy chill behind. *Do not underestimate this opponent,* the Emperor warned, his thoughts dark. *Remember Bespin.*

Mara grimaced. Yes. Cloud City on Bespin, and the duel between Skywalker and Darth Vader. Skywalker had acquitted himself well in that battle—far better than either Vader or the Emperor had expected him to.

And in the midst of that battle, Vader had proposed that the two of them form an alliance against the Emperor.

Vader had later denied it, of course, claiming that the offer had merely been part of his lure to confuse Skywalker and entrap him to the dark side. But the Emperor knew Vader's thoughts and feelings, and he knew that was not the entire truth.

Which was why Mara was here, and why she had come alone. She was the Emperor's Hand, with powers in the Force that had been trained, nurtured, and strengthened by the Emperor himself . . . and one of those powers was the ability to cloak her feelings from even so powerful a Dark Jedi as Lord Darth Vader. He might wonder afterward if the Emperor had had a role in Skywalker's death, but he would never know for certain. And with Skywalker gone, the matter would be over. Vader would never defy the Emperor alone.

I remember Bespin, Mara promised. *Skywalker will die here.*

The Emperor smiled . . . and then another face was there, superimposed on Mara's vision. A young woman with dark hair, wearing a dark red jumpsuit. "Are you Arica?"

Mara blinked and the Emperor's face vanished, only the lingering sense of his distant presence remaining. "Yes," she said. "Sorry, I was just thinking."

The other woman gave her a knowing smile. "Sure

you were." She waved a hand around her. "I'll bet your first week's pay that you were thinking you'd made a big mistake coming here."

Mara looked around. The Dancers' Pit, they called the prep room, and it was fully deserving of the name. "Oh, I don't know," she said diplomatically. "I've been in worse places."

"Better than the rancor pit, anyway." The other shrugged. "Don't worry, the money's a lot better than the facilities."

"I hope so," Mara said, wondering what a rancor pit was. "The implied fringe benefits weren't all that enticing."

The woman laughed. "Ah, yes—the Fat Man. He gave you his Important Person routine, did he?"

"Something like that."

"Well, don't worry, he's mostly harmless. I'll tell you later what buttons to push to keep him off you. I'm Melina Carniss, by the way. Former dancer, current dance designer, sort of general runaround person. Come on—let's go to the throne room and I'll present you to His Exaltedness."

They headed down one of the dark tunnels that seemed to make up the bulk of this place. Mara crinkled her nose at the odors, wishing the quick briefing she'd had on Jabba and his palace had been more comprehensive. Perhaps she should consider wangling herself a trip over to Bestine, see if she could get some up-to-date information on Jabba and his entourage from Governor Aryon's office.

Still, that might prove dangerous in the long run. To access Imperial data files, she would have to identify herself as a high Imperial agent . . . and truly capable governors were not assigned to dustballs like Tatooine. Governor Aryon could be too lazy or incompetent to keep Jabba's spies off her paylist, or could be on Jabba's paylist herself. Worse, even the slightest exposure here could eventually find its way back to Lord Vader.

Besides, this was just a simple assassination: quick in, quick kill, quick out. No, she would handle this one on her own.

"There's the throne room," Melina said, pointing ahead toward an archway that opened into a well-furnished chamber. "Oh, and look—we seem to have a show going."

Mara caught her breath. The show was Luke Skywalker.

Or rather, a holo of him. A prerecorded message, projected by a squat R2-D2 astromech droid with a C-3PO protocol droid hovering nervously beside him. Skywalker's droids, all right. The ones who'd played key roles in the destruction of the Emperor's prized Death Star.

"—I present to you a gift: these two droids."

The protocol droid squawked. "I wonder who that is," Melina murmured.

"I don't know," Mara said, frowning at the image. She'd read all that the Emperor had on Skywalker: his background, his upbringing right here on Tatooine, his brief training under Obi-Wan Kenobi, the immense trouble he'd been so far to the Empire. But this was not the tentative, callow kid she'd seen in those records. The Luke Skywalker she was seeing and hearing now was poised, self-assured, confident of his power.

And with a lightsaber prominently displayed at his belt too. A replacement, probably constructed himself, for the one he'd lost at Bespin.

The Emperor had been right. Skywalker was indeed more dangerous than Mara had given him credit for.

The message finished, and the droids were hustled away, the 3PO wailing the whole way. "Okay," Melina said, taking Mara's arm. "Chin up, Arica. Let's go meet the Hutt."

By the time the protocol droid was brought back, the throne room had become crowded, thick with humans and aliens and smoke and noise. In the background a third-rate band was playing; in the center, in front of Jabba's throne, a young Twi'lek woman was dancing.

Her name was Oola, and she was pretty good.

Standing by the archway leading back to the Dancers' Pit, staying to the background, Mara kept half an eye on Oola's performance as she studied the room and its occupants. A decidedly motley crowd, no doubt about it, ranging from obviously hungry nobodies trying to impress Jabba with their toughness right up to some of the nastiest names on the Imperial locate-and-detain list. If Skywalker got this far, he was going to have his hands full.

She stiffened. In the back of her mind, her danger sense had just gone off.

Deliberately, she took a slow breath, calming her mind and preparing her body for action. Her eyes and mind swept back across the room, seeking the source of the danger—

Just in time to see Jabba hit a button on his throne, opening a section of the floor directly beneath Oola.

The dancer's scream was piercing, fading off into the distance. Jabba's throne slid forward over the trapdoor toward a large grating that had opened up in the floor, a grating the rest of the company was already scrambling to get a place at. Mara spotted Melina Carniss crouching at one edge, peering eagerly at whatever was happening down there. There was another, more distant scream—

And then, suddenly, the show was forgotten. From the archway on the far side of the throne room came the sound of blaster fire. There was a brief commotion; and then, pushing haughtily past the guards, an armed and armored figure appeared, leading a Wookiee in chains.

Not just any Wookiee. Chewbacca, companion and co-pilot to Han Solo.

"Boushh," someone beside her muttered. "Well, so much for the bounty on Chewbacca."

Mara smiled tightly. So simple, so classic, so unimaginative. The best way to infiltrate an enemy's stronghold, they always thought, was to come in disguise, bringing something or someone the enemy wanted.

But this time it wasn't going to work. Frowning slightly with concentration, trying to ignore the noisy clutter of all the other minds in the room, she drew on the Emperor's power within her and focused on the figure in the armored suit. She touched the mind . . .

And blinked in surprise. It wasn't Skywalker at all. It was a woman.

A woman?

There was some byplay: Jabba offering too low a price, the figure arguing the point with a thermal detonator. Mara waited until it was over and the Wookiee had been dragged away. Then, she made her way through the reinvigorated party atmosphere to where the bounty hunter Boba Fett stood silent guard. "Excuse me, sir," she said timidly, reaching a hand almost to his shoulder and then stopping, as if she'd been planning to tap him there and had suddenly thought better of it. "My name's Arica—I just came in today. That thing with the bounty hunter—that was pretty scary. Does that sort of thing happen often?"

For a long moment he just stared at her, and for that same long moment Mara thought the game was up. Boba Fett had done a fair amount of quiet work for the Empire over the years, and it was entirely possible that he had spotted her at some point in the Emperor's entourage. She reached out with the Force, trying to touch his mind. But his control was excellent, and nothing she could read gave her any clues.

"Nice to meet you, Arica," he said at last, in that flat voice that so terrified his victims and impressed his employers. "Don't worry about Boushh—he might have looked crazy right then, but he's not. And don't worry about anyone else. Jabba knows who can be trusted. No one else gets in." He tapped the blaster rifle at his side. "And I stay around here a lot between jobs."

"I'm glad," Mara breathed. "Thank you—I feel much better."

"My pleasure."

She smiled at him and moved away. So Boushh was indeed a man. Or at least, the real Boushh was.

So who was this woman? One of Skywalker's allies? Or someone from the Fringe trying to make a name for herself, and the Wookiee had just gotten careless?

It almost didn't matter. Mara was here to get Skywalker, and Skywalker alone. Anyone else was just clutter; and Jabba's people ought to be capable of handling clutter. A quiet word about this Boushh impostor in the Hutt's ear should do the trick.

Eventually, when he ran out of allies and droids, Skywalker would have to come himself.

He came a day later in the morning, at the break of dawn, as Jabba and his entourage were still snoring away the aftereffects of their late-night celebration over the unmasking and capture of Princess Leia Organa.

Mara's danger sense gave her advance warning. To her surprise, it was all the warning anyone got. Without a whisper of noise or trouble from the supposedly alert guards outside, Skywalker was suddenly there in the throne room, Jabba's Twi'lek majordomo docilely leading him in.

Skywalker's holo had prepared Mara for an achievement of this caliber. Even so, she was impressed.

Some of the guards were beginning to move into positions around Skywalker as the Twi'lek stepped to his master's side and murmured in his ear. Jabba came awake with a jerk, his huge bleary eyes blinking as he took stock of the situation. He looked at the Twi'lek and at Skywalker.

And then he laughed.

The deep rumbling echoed through the throne room, rousing the rest of the company into a sleep-fogged scramble for consciousness and their feet. A few blasters appeared, but most weapons stayed in their holsters as brain-fuzzed courtiers tried to figure out whether this silent figure in hooded cloak was a friend or some unlikely foe.

It was the moment Mara had been waiting for: quiet confusion, no one quite sure what was happening, no one quite sure where anyone else was. The moment to strike. Danger sense still tingling, she took a silent step to her right, to where one of Jabba's younger human guards was gripping his force pike and trying mightily to make sense of the situation. His blaster rested ignored in its holster. Reaching smoothly around behind him, Mara got a grip on it—

And froze as a hard object jabbed firmly into the small of her back.

She'd been wrong. That tingle of danger hadn't been coming from Skywalker.

"Nice and easy," Melina Carniss murmured in her ear. "Let's just ease our way back down the tunnel. Unless you'd rather die right here."

Silently, furious with herself, Mara let Melina guide her backward out of the throne room. A quiet security guard. One of many, probably, forming an extra barrier between Jabba and his enemies. She should have known such a layer would exist in a place like this, and been watching for it. Concentrating exclusively on Skywalker and his friends instead, she'd been sloppy.

From the throne came a sudden commotion, and a single blaster shot. Mara craned her neck, but they were too far away for her to see what was happening. "Curious, huh?" Melina commented. "Was he one of yours? Turn here—very carefully."

Mara did as ordered, studying Melina out of the corner of her eye as she turned and stared down the indicated tunnel. Melina had the blaster; but she, Mara, had the training, with the Emperor's strength and will to drive it. If she reached out through the Force right now and snatched the blaster away . . .

She glanced down at Melina's hand. No. Not from a grip that tight. Not without the other getting at least one shot off first.

Mind tricks, then? There were several ways to soothe or confuse or just plain incapacitate an enemy by jabbing with the Force directly into the victim's mind. But all the techniques required at least a little time to take effect, and in Melina's alert state of mind there was a good chance she'd again get off that one shot.

"You're being awfully quiet," Melina commented as they walked.

"That's because I don't have any idea what's going on," Mara told her. "I haven't done anything."

"Sure you haven't," Melina said grimly. "You haven't infiltrated here under false pretenses. Or lied about who and what you are. Or conspired with the Lady Valarian to assassinate Jabba." She jabbed the blaster muzzle again into Mara's back. "Have you?"

Mara blinked. An assassination plot? Here? And without her even noticing? That wasn't just sloppy, that was embarrassing. "I don't know what you're talking about," she protested, trying one last time. "I have nothing against Jabba. Really."

"Sure you haven't. You just wanted that guard's blaster as a souvenir." Melina jabbed again. "In here."

It was another tunnel, this one slanting sharply downward before leveling out and bending away out of sight. Loitering just inside the tunnel entrance were a pair of Gamorrean guards, leaning casually on their force pikes and grunting quietly to each other. "What in blazes are you two doing here?" Melina snarled at them. "Straighten up. Now."

Slowly, obviously bewildered as to why a lowly dance designer should be giving them orders, they pulled themselves a little more upright. "That's better," Melina growled. "But just marginally. Who do you think you are anyway, the Imperial Royal Guard? Get off your rears and take this woman down to the dungeons for me."

She gave Mara a shove toward them. "Get going. Be a good girl and maybe I'll ask Jabba to let you die quickly."

"I appreciate it," Mara said, looking back over her shoulder. She still couldn't safely snatch the blaster from Melina's grip. But what she *could* do . . .

Reaching out with the Force, she gave the muzzle a sharp twist to the right. There was a flash as Melina reflexively fired, the blast sounding twice as loud as usual in the confines of the tunnel.

It was followed by a grunt of pain and rage from the Gamorrean Melina had just shot. The other Gamorrean grunted, too, and the two of them lowered their force pikes and lumbered toward this human who had unreasonably attacked them.

Melina's expression at what she'd just done was priceless, but Mara didn't have time to enjoy it. With her captor's attention distracted, now was the time to act. Ducking between the Gamorreans, she sprinted down the tunnel.

"Stop her!" Melina shouted. But the guards paid no attention. A pair of quick shots lit up the tunnel, scattering rock chips and spurts of dust.

And then it was just the grunts of the slug-brained Gamorreans and Melina's angry and increasingly frantic shouts. Mara kept running, hoping she could get out of the line of fire before they got things straightened out up there. Near the bottom of the tunnel came her first opportunity: a curved and highly odoriferous cross tunnel that branched off to the left. Throwing a last glance back at the noisy confrontation, she ducked down it.

It was short—no more than twenty meters—and was almost a dead end. Almost. At the end was a rock wall with a half-meter-square ventilation grating cut into it, a grating that was literally shaking with the growls of something behind it. Cautiously, she stepped up to it and looked in.

The roaring was coming from probably the largest and ugliest biped creature she'd ever seen. A creature which, judging from the number of bones lying around the stinking filth of the pit, was both carnivorous and ravenous.

And which at the moment seemed intent on making a snack out of Luke Skywalker.

Pressing her face against the grating, the stench forgotten, Mara watched as Skywalker scrambled out from beneath a small ledge and dashed between the creature's legs toward a tunnel-shaped area of the pit she couldn't see into from her angle. This was perfect. The creature would make short work of Skywalker, in front of the dozens of witnesses she could hear cheering it on, and without a single link Vader could backtrack to either her or the Emperor. And if for some reason the creature needed help, well, she was right here to give it.

The creature had turned around now and was thudding its way in pursuit. Skywalker himself was out of sight, but from the noise coming from that direction she could tell that Jabba's people were blocking his escape. It should be over quickly.

And then, without warning, something small came flying through the air right at the edge of her vision, slamming into a control panel set into the stone wall. There was a flash of sparks—the creak of released machinery—

And a heavy, serrated-bottom door dropped out of the ceiling, catching the creature across the back of its massive neck and driving it to the floor. It growled one last whimper and lay still.

Mara stared at the hulk, not believing it. Skywalker had killed it. Alone, unarmed, he'd actually killed it.

And judging from the tone of the Huttese words rumbling down through the stunned silence from above, Jabba wasn't at all happy about it.

Mara took a deep breath of the fetid air. All right. Fine. So the creature hadn't killed Skywalker; but now Jabba would. Probably viciously too, if even half the stories about the Hutt were true. Served Skywalker right. He had to have been grossly stupid and grossly overconfident both to have come here alone and unarmed this way—

The stinking air seemed to freeze in her throat, two mental images abruptly superimposing themselves on the scene in front of her. Skywalker running away from the creature; Skywalker delivering his holo message to Jabba.

His new lightsaber. He hadn't brought it with him. Or rather, he hadn't brought it himself.

The Wookiee didn't have it—he would have nowhere to hide it. The protocol droid didn't have it. Leia Organa certainly didn't have it.

The astromech droid.

She cursed under her breath. No, it wasn't Skywalker who was being overconfident. It was Jabba. And suddenly this whole thing was up to her again. Stepping back from the grating, she looked for some kind of opening mechanism—

Her danger sense triggered a split second before she heard the shuffling behind her on the tunnel floor. She spun around, dropping into combat stance.

The Gamorrean guards she'd left at the top of the tunnel had caught up with her. And they'd brought a half-dozen friends with them. Two by two, blocking her exit with their bulk, they started toward her.

Mara didn't have time for this, and she wasn't in the mood for it anyway. Reaching out with the Force, she jabbed hard at the minds of the first two guards. They stopped short, quivered for a moment on their thick legs, their long force pikes dropping with a clatter from limp hands. Then, to the obvious consternation of those behind them, they collapsed.

Mara had one of the force pikes in her hands before they hit the floor. Swinging it expertly around in the confines of the tunnel, she feinted past the weapons of the second row of guards and slashed the deadly power tip across their faces. They staggered, clutching their wounds, and fell back against the third row. Jumping up on the backs of the first downed Gamorreans, Mara again jabbed past the momentary tangle to cut into the next row.

A brief minute later, it was over.

Breathing heavily, she turned back to the grating. The force pike's vibroblade made a fair racket as it cut through the metal, but there was probably enough of a ruckus coming down from Jabba's throne room to cover it. Pitching the force pike through the opening, she squirmed her way into the pit.

The place was even more disgusting than it had looked from the outside. The door that had killed the creature was blocking any exit in that direction, but there was a small round hatchway partway up the opposite wall. The force pike made quick work of the hatchway, revealing a steep but climbable slide behind it. Probably the end of the route that started at Jabba's trapdoor. Grabbing a nearby bone that was slightly longer than the slide's width, she wedged it into the opening and pulled herself inside. Alternating her bracing between the bone and her own leg, she started up.

She came out a couple of meters short, the section directly beneath the trapdoor turning out to be a wide, straight drop that funneled the victim into the slide. Wedging the bone against the slide opening, she eased her way up to a precarious standing position. A small connection box was set into the wall; a careful prodding of the right connector, and the two sections of the trapdoor dropped open above her.

No one fell through or peered down at her. In fact, what conversation she could hear sounded distant. Grimacing to herself, hoping she wasn't too late, she got a grip on the edge of one of the trapdoors and started climbing.

The throne room was empty as she pulled herself over the edge, but the rapidly fading noise showed her which way they'd all gone. Following the sounds, watching for guards who may have been alerted about her, she headed in pursuit. Skywalker was out there somewhere; with luck—and the Force—maybe she could still catch up with him.

• • •

Beyond the milling crowd in the vast vehicle hangar was a large sail barge, busily taking on passengers. To one side a pair of skiffs were similarly being loaded. Guards were everywhere: human, Gamorrean, a half-dozen other species; on the skiffs, on the sail barge, roughly controlling the crowd as they weeded out those apparently not invited to go along. Wherever Skywalker was in all that—assuming he was there at all —Mara couldn't spot him.

But she could see Jabba. He was on his float, surrounded by guards and lackeys, being maneuvered toward the sail barge's lift. Pushing through the crowd, she hurried toward him.

The guards were watching as she approached, but she couldn't read anything but normal caution in their faces and stances. Apparently, word of her alleged involvement with this Lady Valarian hadn't gotten to them yet. "Your Exaltedness?" she called, stopping just short of the warning ring of weapons. "Your Exaltedness? Please?"

Jabba turned his head toward her. "I'm Arica, Your Exaltedness," she called. "One of your dancers. Could I please come along with you?"

The Hutt rumbled something and gestured to one of the guards, who in turn prodded the C-3PO protocol droid. "Oh—ah—the great Jabba the Hutt says no," the droid translated distractedly, not even looking at Mara. She followed his gaze to one of the skiffs—

Just in time to catch a fleeting glimpse of Skywalker, standing proud and straight, as the skiff took off through the hangar door.

And he was getting away. "Please, Your Exaltedness?" Mara begged, putting all the strength of her most powerful Force mind-control technique behind the words.

She might as well have spat at a stone wall. The Hutt

chuckled, his eyes swiveling to face her, and spoke again. "The great Jabba the Hutt says you are to leave him now," the protocol droid said, still gazing forlornly after the departing skiff. "He says a landspeeder will be placed at your disposal, and that you are not to be seen here again."

For a moment Mara locked eyes with the Hutt, trying futilely to read that impenetrable alien mind. Did he have some idea of who she was, perhaps even of why she was here? Or did he merely suspect, as Melina had, that she was part of a conspiracy and was hoping she would lead him to his enemies?

It didn't really matter. She couldn't catch Skywalker's skiff with a landspeeder, and she couldn't fight all of them. One way or the other, it was time to go. "I thank Your Exaltedness for his kindness," she said, matching ambiguity with ambiguity. "May you live forever."

So you have failed, the Emperor's thoughts said, the chill of his anger sending a shiver through Mara despite the blazing heat of Tatooine's twin suns. *I am disappointed, Mara Jade. Disappointed, indeed.*

I know, Mara answered, the bitter taste of defeat mixing with the grit of sand in her mouth as the landspeeder skimmed across the desert. *But perhaps Jabba can deal with him.*

His anger had made her shiver. His contempt now made her ache. *Do you seriously believe that?*

She sighed. *No.*

For a moment he was silent, and Mara could sense him reaching deeply into the Force. Searching into the future . . . *Skywalker is of no immediate importance,* he said at last. *Continue on to Svivren. We will discuss this when you return.*

The image and sense faded, and he was gone.

With a sigh, Mara returned her full attention to the desert landscape before her. So she had failed. Her first true failure since the Emperor had designated her his Hand. It hurt. Terribly.

But it was all right. She would make it all right. Skywalker might escape now, but he couldn't avoid her forever. Eventually, somewhere, she'd catch up with him.

And then he would die.

And Then There Were Some:
The Gamorrean Guard's Tale

by William F. Wu

Gartogg the Gamorrean guard was waddling through the dimly lit corridor of Jabba the Hutt's palace toward the servants' quarters on his assigned patrol when he heard a disturbance behind him. The main entry slammed shut and chains rattled; he paused, snorting thoughtfully. At the sound of a Wookiee roaring in protest, Gartogg hurried back toward the main entry, anxious to prove his worth to

Ortugg, leader of the nine porcine Gamorreans working here for Jabba.

"Ortugg," he gurgled. "Wait."

The Wookiee roared again as a bounty hunter pulled his prisoner by his chains down the steps to the main audience chamber. Gartogg lumbered after them, hoping to get in a good shove or two, but he was too late—as usual. Ortugg and Rogua, the other Gamorrean posted at the main entry with the chief, followed the bounty hunter and the Wookiee.

"Prisoner?" Gartogg came up behind Ortugg.

"Shut up," said Ortugg.

"Yeah, shut up." Rogua shouldered Gartogg back out of the way.

Gartogg said nothing as he stumbled backward. Ortugg always treated him this way, but Gartogg knew he deserved it. He had never really earned his chief's respect. Members of other species here always joked and complained about how stupid the Gamorreans were, but Gartogg didn't believe that; to him, Ortugg, Rogua, and their other fellow guards seemed as intelligent as the rest of Jabba's followers.

Jabba dickered with the bounty hunter as the crowd watched carefully.

"Boba Fett?" Gartogg asked, trying to shove between Ortugg and Rogua again.

"Of course not," Ortugg muttered impatiently. "Boba Fett's over there." He pointed through the crowd with a thick green arm. "This bounty hunter's called Boushh."

"And the others call *us* stupid." Rogua shook his head.

Jabba spoke to the visiting bounty hunter.

"He agrees!" one of the new droids interpreting for Jabba announced from Jabba's dais.

Jabba signaled for the Gamorrean guards to haul the Wookiee down to the dungeon.

Ortugg and Rogua stepped forward to take the Wookiee's chains.

"Me, too." Gartogg lumbered after them.

Ortugg put a big green hand on his chest. "No. Go back to your patrol."

"Sail barge," Gartogg grunted frantically.

"What?"

"Sail barge?"

"Speak plainly, you idiot. What about it?"

"Want to go. Next time."

"The rest of us Gamorreans speak in complete sentences!" Rogua whacked Gartogg on the side of his head with his open hand. "Why can't you?"

Gartogg blinked dizzily from the blow, snuffling. "Huh?"

"You want to be assigned to the sail barge next time Jabba takes it out?" Ortugg demanded.

Gartogg snorted in the affirmative.

Rogua snorted contemptuously.

"You must earn that kind of assignment," said Ortugg. "You never have."

"Audience chamber?" Gartogg asked hopefully.

"No! Return to your patrol!"

Stung, Gartogg watched in disappointment as Ortugg and Rogua grabbed the Wookiee's chains and dragged him away to the dungeon. As the band struck up their music, and the crowd in the audience chamber resumed their party, Gartogg plodded away. He never had any fun.

As he wandered the dark, empty corridors alone as usual, he snuffled and muttered to himself. Ortugg always ordered him to sentry duty at places where nothing ever happened. When off duty, Gartogg wandered Jabba's palace in the hope of finding something important to do. Even his fellow Gamorrean guards didn't want his company. Every time they had a special assignment, like protecting Jabba the Hutt on an excursion in his sail barge, they left Gartogg behind.

Footsteps up ahead told him someone was coming this way. Eagerly hoping for company, he looked up and saw two familiar humans, a pale, slender, brown-haired woman and a stocky man with black hair and slanted eyes. Gartogg had heard they were a couple of thieves hiding out with Jabba.

"Good evening," he snorted enthusiastically.

Both humans flinched in surprise and stared at him.

"What did he say?" Quivering, the woman whispered without taking her eyes off Gartogg. "Ah Kwan, did you understand him?"

"Sorry, Quella," said Ah Kwan. "I can't tell what language that was."

"Good evening," Gartogg snorted, more loudly.

Both humans drew back.

"What do you want?" Ah Kwan rested one hand on the handle of a long knife at his belt. "What did you say?"

"Good evening!" Gartogg roared in frustration, raising his clawed fists.

The man and woman whirled and ran up the hall; in a moment, they vanished around a corner.

Gartogg sighed. No one liked him. Alone, he trudged up the corridor. It was always the same.

Earlier that day, as Gartogg had plodded alone through the shadowed, empty corridors of the palace, he kept the peace by his very presence. After all, nearly everyone he met, even the other Gamorrean guards, hurried away when they saw him coming.

Gartogg heard a couple of loud footsteps, as though someone had tripped, echoing in the corridor leading down to the servants' quarters. He hurried to investigate, still longing for some special accomplishment he could show his fellows, a contribution that Ortugg would respect. Maybe then Ortugg would let him go the next time Jabba journeyed out on the sail barge.

As fast as his thick, muscular legs could move, Gartogg thumped down the corridor and turned a corner, hefting his ax optimistically. He saw Porcellus, the human chef, kneeling over someone on the floor. The chef was a very thin, jittery man with receding, dark blond hair; as usual, he wore his white chef's uniform, perpetually smeared with all sorts of ingredients with interesting aromas.

Gartogg liked Porcellus. The chef always had plenty of food lying around the kitchen. All the Gamorrean guards went snorting and snuffling around there for snacks. Last week, Gartogg had found four of his fellow Gamorreans fighting in the kitchen over who could lick out the bowl from a dessert. Delighted to join in the fun, Gartogg had almost chopped off Porcellus's head with his ax by accident, but the chef didn't seem to hold it against him. He was a good fellow.

Now Porcellus knelt over Ak-Buz, the commander of Jabba's sail barge. Ak-Buz, a Weequay, lay motionless, sprawled on his back with his arms outstretched and his eyes staring vacantly.

This was Gartogg's chance to think out the situation on his own. He studied the scene. In his opinion, Ak-Buz did not look well.

"Hey!" Gartogg snorted. "What's happened here?"

Porcellus leaped to his feet, quivering. "What?"

Gartogg walked up to Ak-Buz and frowned down at him. "He's dead?"

"He isn't dead," Porcellus said quickly, his face shiny with sweat. "He's asleep. He's resting. He said he was tired and he was going back to take a nap. He must have . . . he must have fallen asleep right here in the hall."

Gartogg studied Ak-Buz's unmoving face. Those staring eyes did not move. Gartogg snuffled thoughtfully. "Looks dead."

"Have you ever seen a Weequay sleep?"

"Uh . . . no."

"Well, there you are." Porcellus crouched and lifted Ak-Buz, tugging one of the commander's arms around his shoulders. "Now I'm going to get him to his quarters—er—before he wakes up."

Gartogg nodded. That would be good; Weequays shouldn't sleep in the hallway. Someone could trip over him. "Want help?"

"Thank you," the chef said, smiling. "I'm fine."

Gartogg sighed. For a moment, he thought he had found something important, like a corpse, but he was mistaken. Now he had been left alone again, with nothing much to do.

Snorting in disappointment, he had plodded back upstairs.

Late that evening, Gartogg was wearily climbing the stairs up to the guest quarters when he heard a single set of footsteps behind him. Hoping something horrible might happen so he could catch the guilty party, he stepped around a corner and waited in the shadows. A moment later, a silhouette thrown against the far wall sauntered near.

The lanky figure stood tall, lean, and broad-nosed; he wore a jacket with a high-necked collar. Even Gartogg held his breath, trying not to snuffle unnecessarily. Dannik Jerriko, an assassin, was the only one in the palace he feared except for Jabba himself. Gartogg had never seen this killer in action, but he had heard all the rumors about how Jerriko conducted his business: he was a snot vampire.

When the assassin had passed, Gartogg covered his

upturned snout protectively with one hand and hurried in the other direction.

As Gartogg plodded along the corridors on his usual patrol, he worked his way through the back hallways and neared the main entry. He heard shouts from the direction of the kitchen and hesitated, wondering if he should go and look. Then he remembered that he liked going to the kitchen. He could always find a snack.

At first, Gartogg saw no one in the kitchen. He walked inside, pausing to pick up a handful of plastifoam to munch on. Then he saw someone in the receiving room.

Still crunching plastifoam, he moved forward. He stopped when he saw Ree-Yees, the three-eyed, goat-faced crook, kneeling by a shattered box. Porcellus stood to one side, over Phlegmin, the kitchen boy. Unlike Ak-Buz, Phlegmin lay in a tangle of arms and legs with his eyes closed.

"He sleeping?" Gartogg asked from the doorway.

"I didn't do it!" Porcellus screamed.

Ree-Yees started in surprise, almost knocking himself over. His three eyes froze on Gartogg. Silvery-green goatgrass, smelling sweet, had been scattered on the floor from the broken box.

"Kitchen boy sleeping, huh?" Gartogg asked again.

"Uh . . ."

Gartogg blinked, waiting, and grunted encouragingly.

Suddenly Ree-Yees scrambled to his feet, knocking Porcellus aside, and spoke breathlessly. "You're just in time! I found him—just like this—down the hall—near the tunnel to Ephant Mon's quarters!" His three eyes narrowed. "I brought him here to—to—to perform resus—suspiration!"

"Huh?"

"You know—emergency culinary resuspiration! The smell of food so—so—so ripe it can bring the dead back to life! An ancient art, one I learned from my great-uncle, Swee-beeps. We call it—er—garbage-sniffing of the last resort. But alas, I was too late." His eyestalks drooped and he sighed.

Gartogg shuffled forward, bent his knees, and leaned forward slightly. He wondered if the emergency culinary resuspiration would work belatedly, and still wake up the kitchen boy. When he sniffed, though, he didn't smell any garbage. Maybe it was too late.

"So you see?" Ree-Yees said anxiously. "Someone must take over now. Someone with authority. To investigate, put together clues, solve this crime. Jabba will be impressed—and grateful."

"Kitchen boy murdered!" Suddenly understanding the problem, Gartogg bent down to grab one of Phlegmin's ankles. He straightened and dangled the body up where he could see it clearly. Blood covered Phlegmin's face.

Ree-Yees stared at Gartogg, not speaking.

Gartogg nodded and flung the body over his left shoulder. Turning, he snorted thoughtfully and plodded back out through the kitchen, grabbing another handful of plastifoam with his other hand.

"Don't forget!" Ree-Yees called out. "I found him near Ephant Mon's quarters!"

Gartogg walked down the corridor away from the kitchen with unaccustomed cheer. If he could find out who killed this kitchen boy, Ortugg would at last be impressed. Gartogg might be assigned to the sail barge's next outing after all.

• • •

As Gartogg plodded endlessly through the dank, shadowed halls of the palace, wondering how he could solve the mystery, the weight of the kitchen boy began to tire even him. He shifted the body to his other shoulder, which helped for a while. On this third pass by the guest quarters, he finally remembered an important clue: Ree-Yees had found the corpse near Ephant Mon's quarters. Thinking that perhaps he could ask Ephant Mon about the crime, he knocked on the door. When no one answered, Gartogg sighed and trudged on down the corridor.

Wearily, Gartogg snuffled in resignation. It probably wouldn't matter. Ephant Mon didn't like him either.

For days it seemed (and maybe it was), Gartogg had patrolled most of the palace several times over without finding anyone to question. A few people had seen him from a distance, but they all covered their noses, if they had one, and ran off. Gartogg felt that behavior was inconsiderate.

On his fourth pass through the rancor tunnels, he heard the rancor shifting and rustling in the sand behind its grate.

"Come on," Gartogg said to the lifeless face of the kitchen boy dangling over his shoulder. "Visit rancor."

In response, the kitchen boy dripped some sort of cloudy fluid on the floor of the tunnel.

When Gartogg reached the area by the rancor grate, he found Malakili, the pudgy rancor keeper, struggling to carry a limp human to the grate.

"What this?" Gartogg asked.

"Huh?" Malakili jumped in surprise, dropping his burden with a thump. "Uh, I'm feeding the rancor, what does it look like I'm doing?"

"Oh." Gartogg snorted in disappointment. "Need help?"

"No, no, I'm doing just fine."

Gartogg kept the kitchen boy balanced on his shoulder as Malakili opened the grate for the waiting rancor and heaved the other body inside.

"You want to unload him too?" Malakili nodded toward the kitchen boy, grimacing.

"No! Evidence of crime."

"Well, he's decomposing pretty fast. You sure?"

"No!" Gartogg turned and hurried away.

Gartogg trudged to the kitchen, still carrying the corpse of Phlegmin over one shoulder, the head and arms dangling forward. The dead kitchen boy had a much stronger odor than before, and tended to drip fluids on the floor occasionally. Gartogg snuffled politely.

Porcellus looked up from his daily work.

"A plot," Gartogg rumbled. "Clues. All tied together." He reached out with his free hand to grab some pieces of plastifoam. Munching on them casually, he added, "Girl. She, um . . ."

"What girl?" Porcellus demanded. "And get that disgusting thing out of here!"

"Mercenary girl. Brought in Wookiee. Last night." Gartogg licked a bit of loose plastifoam from around his mouth and snuffled contentedly. "Lady friend of Solo. The smuggler. Boss caught them."

Gartogg saw that one of the corpse's eyeballs had started to ooze out of his head. That was bad; he might need this evidence of the crime. Snorting in annoyance, Gartogg poked the eye back in with a thick, stubby forefinger.

"Get that thing out of here!" Porcellus shouted. "I cook in here; this place has to stay clean—clean and *healthful*!"

Hurt, Gartogg turned to go, keeping the corpse balanced over his shoulder. After all, the chef was boss here. As he plodded out, he snatched up some more plastifoam and stuffed it into his mouth, though some of it spilled behind him on the floor.

Gartogg wandered the corridors of the palace all day, ignoring sleep, but he discovered nothing. On the night shift again, he waddled through the shadowed halls all night with the kitchen boy still on his shoulder. By the end of his shift, he was exhausted, but had found nothing.

Finally, as dawn approached, he trudged back to the guards' quarters in weary disappointment.

"Gartogg!" Ortugg jumped forward to block the entrance. "What are you doing with that . . . thing?"

"Evidence," Gartogg snorted defensively.

"It's rotting," Rogua shouted, appearing behind Ortugg. "You can't bring that in here!"

"Can't?"

"What did you do with it last night?" Rogua demanded.

"Night duty," said Gartogg. "Kept it."

Some of the other Gamorrean guards in the quarters snorted and snuffled derisively.

"Get rid of it," Ortugg ordered. "Feed it to the rancor or something."

"Evidence," said Gartogg, eyeing the oozing, discolored face of the kitchen boy. "Murder."

"Forget about coming in here," said Ortugg. "We're ready to go on the sail barge. Rogua, select the guards who will go."

"Yes, sir."

"Sail barge?" Gartogg's eyes widened as he snuffled excitedly. "Now?"

"No—for the next time Jabba goes out to the Great Pit of Carkoon to feed some prisoners to the Sarlacc."

"Take me!" Gartogg bounced up and down excitedly, jiggling the body of the kitchen boy. One of his fingers fell off and hit the floor. Several bugs crawled out of his mouth; many more buzzed away from the corpse, disturbed by the motion.

Ortugg snorted in disgust. "You're looking for the boy's killer?"

"Yes!"

Ortugg snuffled, chuckling, and caught Rogua's eye. "You figure it out by the next time we leave, you can come. Now get out! And don't bring that thing back here!"

"And try speaking in complete sentences!" Rogua yelled.

Snuffled and snorted laughter followed Gartogg as he turned and trudged away from the quarters.

Now, however, Gartogg no longer felt as tired as before. He was too excited. This could be his chance.

"Maybe sail barge," he said optimistically to the kitchen boy.

Some sort of maggot crawled into the kitchen boy's ear. A blackened tongue hung from the slack mouth. Other bugs wandered all over the corpse's face.

"Go see sail barge," said Gartogg. "Want to?"

The corpse still dripped fluids of various colors and viscosities and the bugs ate more and more of the remaining tissue. Still, the body had become only a little lighter than before. Gartogg plodded toward the docking area behind Jabba's throne room where the sail barge waited, just to gaze at it for a moment.

On the way, Gartogg saw a B'omarr monk wearing an earring moving along a darkened hall up ahead.

"Monk," Gartogg snuffled softly to the kitchen boy. "Ask monk for clues. Okay?"

The monk slipped away around a corner. Gartogg hurried after him, but did not call out. He was afraid of waking people up.

For a moment, Gartogg lost track of the monk. Then he heard a couple of voices around another corner and hurried toward them. Before he saw anyone, a thump reached him.

When he came around the corner, he found J'Quille, a Whiphid, kneeling over the monk, who lay on his back covered by the bloody folds of his robe. The Whiphid wore a vibroblade in his scabbard and clutched something in his hand. Startled, Gartogg wheezed and snorted in surprise, then grunted uncomfortably.

J'Quille said nothing.

Gartogg adjusted the kitchen boy over his shoulder and moved forward cautiously.

The monk didn't move.

"Is he sleeping?" Gartogg asked. That was a complete sentence. He wished Rogua had heard him.

J'Quille stood up. "He's not dead; he's, uh, meditating. Gone into a deep trance. Pondering the imponderables."

Gartogg wrinkled his snout and snorted thoughtfully, studying the monk.

"The blood? He wanted to see if he'd reached the final stage of enlightenment. He decided to do a little testing on his own to see if he was ready before he asked his friends to surgically remove his brain."

Gartogg grimaced. Grunting in puzzlement, he pointed at the monk's head and then to the blood on his chest. "Uh—"

The Whiphid shrugged. "That's where their brains are. In their chests. It makes it easier to remove them."

Snuffling nervously, Gartogg frowned. If the monk's brain was in his chest, what did he need a head for? In any case, the monk shouldn't meditate in the hall any more than that Weequay should sleep in one; someone might trip over him.

J'Quille watched Gartogg carefully, silent now.

"Can't meditate here." He bent down and worked

the body of the monk over his free shoulder. Then he straightened. Maybe this mysterious monk, meditating with the brain in his bloody chest, was part of a conspiracy regarding the kitchen boy.

The Whiphid stepped aside and waited without speaking.

Gartogg, hoping he was about to find the answer to these murders, plodded away under the weight of the two bodies, one meditating and one rotting . . .

As Gartogg continued his endless trudging up the hall, he watched the floor carefully for more meditating monks. If he tripped over one, he would drop the two guys he was carrying and might fall on the new one. However, he found no one all day.

"We better stop," said a woman's voice from around another corner. "I heard something—heavy footsteps coming this way."

"Maybe we should see what it is," said a man.

"Forget it," said the woman. "Not in this place. Just leave it alone."

"All right, come on."

Gartogg heard their footsteps going away from him and he hurried, even under the weight of the two bodies he carried. The fresh one, the monk, weighed more than the older one. He thumped heavily down the hall.

When he turned the next corner, he saw Quella and Ah Kwan walking quickly away from him.

"Good evening," he snuffled cautiously.

Both humans whirled to face him; Ah Kwan grabbed the handle of his knife again.

"Yeah?" Ah Kwan's eyes shifted from Gartogg to each of his burdens and back. "What do you want?"

Gartogg spoke as slowly and carefully as he could, with a minimum of snuffling. "See anybody?"

"Anybody like who?" Ah Kwan demanded.

"Is that the same guard?" Quella asked. "The one who chased us? Is that him?"

"You got me," said Ah Kwan. "All the Gamorreans look alike to me."

"Killer," Gartogg said clearly. "Looking for killer."

"He wants to know if we saw a killer," said Quella.

"How recently?" Ah Kwan grimaced at the kitchen boy. "He's been dead for some time."

"This not dead," said Gartogg, jiggling the limp monk slightly. "Just meditating."

"You think the same person killed them both?" Quella asked.

"Meditating," said Gartogg, still struggling to speak plainly. "This one." He wiggled the monk again.

"You think he's right?" Ah Kwan asked quietly.

"Aw, who knows around this place?" Quella clutched Ah Kwan's arm. "People get killed here all the time. Let's go, all right?"

"Yeah."

"See killer?" Gartogg snuffled uncertainly.

"No, we didn't see anybody." Ah Kwan shrugged. "It's been a long night. We were down in the audience chamber. That Jedi Knight got thrown to the rancor, but he survived."

"Jedi came here?" Gartogg had missed something else good.

"Yeah, and he killed the rancor."

Gartogg grunted in shock. "Killed rancor?"

"It was a great fight," said Quella.

"Not so loud," Ah Kwan whispered. "Someone might think we like that Jedi."

"Jedi killed rancor?" Gartogg repeated.

"Yeah, but Jabba's taking him with the smuggler and the Wookiee to the Great Pit of Carkoon."

Gartogg snuffled thoughtfully.

The two humans nodded politely and walked away arm in arm.

Gartogg studied the rotting kitchen boy, then turned to the monk's immobile face. "That it? Eh? Mm!"

Grunting and snuffling sternly, he shifted his burdens slightly and headed for the sail-barge docking area. It would be a good place to sit down with his two companions. The mystery would require more thought and he didn't have much time.

Thumping footsteps woke Gartogg in the docking area. He had dozed off for a few minutes, sitting on the floor with his back against the wall between the other two; they too sat propped on each side of him. As Ortugg stopped in front of him, Gartogg struggled to his feet.

"Gartogg!" Ortugg glowered at him. "What are you doing here?"

"Solved mystery!" Gartogg gurgled sleepily.

"Yeah? Well, make it quick. I sent Rogua and the other guards down to the dungeon to drag the prisoners up here." Ortugg pointed to the motionless monk. "You got another one? So who killed them?"

"Not killed—meditating."

"Speak in complete sentences, you idiot!"

"Conspiracy!" Gartogg drew himself up proudly.

"Eh?" Ortugg cocked his porcine head, eyeing Gartogg with more regard than usual. "*You* uncovered a conspiracy?"

"Aha!" Gartogg shouted. "You wanted to kill Ak-Buz the Weequay sail-barge captain, because he might have invited me on board himself!"

"What?" Ortugg blinked blankly.

"But you didn't kill him. Instead, Porcellus the cook put him to sleep with special sleeping recipes in the plastifoam appetizer!"

"Plastifoam? That's packing material, not an appetizer. Why—"

"Not finished!" Gartogg declared, holding his head high. He nodded toward Phlegmin. "Kitchen boy was friend of Ephant Mon!"

"Yeah, so?"

"I know because he was found near Ephant Mon's quarters!"

"But what about it?"

"Ree-Yees said so!"

"What does that have to do with *anything*?" Ortugg demanded.

"Conspiracy!"

"Go on, get to the point!" Ortugg glared angrily.

"So, Malakili the rancor keeper needs no extra rancor food!"

"Gartogg, you bag of rancor droppings! What is your *point*?"

"Point?"

"Who killed these people you're carrying?"

"This one meditating, not dead." Gartogg jiggled the monk again. "Testing himself, before friends remove his brain from his chest."

"What?" Ortugg screamed in frustration.

"What, what? What's wrong?" Gartogg searched Ortugg's face in puzzlement.

"Who's behind this conspiracy?"

"Oh—process of elimination. All dead killed by snot vampire!" Gartogg smiled triumphantly.

"Who?"

"Snot vampire!" Gartogg shouted.

Ortugg's voice dropped to a cautious whisper. "Dannik Jerriko?"

"Aha!" Gartogg yelled again. "Um, go sail barge now?"

Ortugg glared in mystified silence at Gartogg.

"Go sail barge?" Gartogg repeated hopefully.

"And why do you think Dannik Jerriko killed this kitchen boy?"

"No evidence!"

"There is no evidence?"

"And snot vampire never leaves evidence—so he must be guilty!"

Ortugg's shoulders sagged. "Gartogg, get out of here before I cut your head off for the sand inside it!"

"Snot vampire not guilty?" Gartogg whimpered.

"No! And when I come back—you'll be ground up and sent to Porcellus to cook for Jabba's dinner!" Ortugg shoved him out of the way and stomped angrily to the sail barge, leaving Gartogg alone with his companions.

"No sail barge?" Gartogg snuffled sadly. "Ground pork?"

From the dungeon, the roar of the Wookiee and the rattling of chains reached him distantly. The other guards would drag the prisoners onto the sail barge and go out for a trip. As usual, Gartogg would be left behind.

On the other hand, he was no longer alone. Now he had friends, even if they weren't exactly talkative. He squatted down facing the two seated figures.

Gartogg looked from the kitchen boy to the monk and back, making sure he spoke in a complete sentence. "What do you guys want to do now?"

Old Friends:
Ephant Mon's Tale

by Kenneth C. Flint

I saw Skywalker the first time right after he came into Jabba's palace.

He was just a black figure then, wrapped in a big cloak, face hidden by a cowl. Still, there was something about him that raised the hackles on me.

That old merc instinct made me duck into the cover of a pile of crates—not so easy for a guy over two meters tall—to scan the stranger like a scared range dog.

At the moment he was being confronted by Jabba's head boy Bib Fortuna while a couple of drooling Gamorrean guards stood by.

I stared at him real hard. There was something about him that made a funny ripple run through me. All kinds of things were stirring, and I couldn't peg 'em down. Fear? Naw, not for me. But confusion and wonder? Yeah, them for sure.

Anyway, the little discussion between him and Fortuna lasted only a few seconds. Then Jabba's major-domo turned and led him right on in like he'd bought the place. They headed along the corridor toward Jabba's throne room, the guards falling in behind.

I ducked back further behind the crates, some impulse still wanting to keep me well hidden. It worked, but only for Fortuna and the trailing guards. None of them noticed me as they went past. But that one in black, he turned his head as he walked by to flash me a straight look.

When his gaze met mine, I felt some kind of . . . of . . . Well . . . a power hit me like a gaffi-stick butt right between the eyes. I felt an explosion of white energy shoot through me, lighting my insides right to the very core.

It riled up things way deep down in my skull. They rose from the black depths like a ripe corpse from a swamp. There was some ugly stuff there, memories of some things better left submerged. But one bright vision gleamed amongst the slime: the green-gold recollection of a land of trees and sun.

And that gave me a pang for something lost I suddenly knew I'd loved.

I shook my head to clear it of the crazy feeling and blinked a few times. When I looked again, they'd all disappeared around the corridor's bend.

It was too many late nights carousing with Jabba, I

told myself. Nothing more. And, even though I had a nagging urge to go after them and see if there was more, I shoved it away. I had an appointment, and I was already late. I took off for the garage at my best trot.

I found Barada there, as usual, head buried in the engine compartment of one of his pet vehicles, as usual. He always seemed to be working on one craft or another of Jabba's big repulsorpool. I think it helped him forget what a trap his life was.

The poor Klatooinan was indentured to the Hutt forever, I guessed. He was too valuable to Jabba. The Bloated One was never letting this poor sucker buy his way out. But the guy was still dead loyal to his boss, and dead honest, too. And he was one of the few there I really liked.

"How's it going, chief?" I saluted, slapping him on the back. "Got a machine for me?"

He waved around without pulling his head from the craft's guts. "Take any skiff you want."

There were a number of the little utility vehicles parked around us. But they weren't good enough.

"I need something faster. I'm in a hurry, pal."

He pulled his head out this time and turned toward me. His face was set in a scowl, but it was always that way. The personality behind it was very earnest and mostly good-natured.

"For you, Mon, okay. Take that XP-38A there." He pointed out a low, sleek-bodied landspeeder. "It's as hot as I have. But, watch it! Steering's real loose."

Its steering was as advertised, but so was its speed. I'd made up my lost time when I sailed into Mos Eisley spaceport and pulled up in front of the Lucky Despot hotel.

I climbed out and looked around, taking in the place. Sure, the sprawling spaceport was pretty much a dump for the refuse of the galaxy, but I still liked getting in there once in a while. I'd come from a planet of all open space and light. The closed-in feel of Jabba's pile got to me pretty fast. I took any chance to stretch my legs, such as they were.

I walked toward the hotel. The old place wasn't really a building. It had been converted from a beat-up cargo hauler by some investors with more credits than brains. It had never been successful and was open now only as a front for Lady Valarian's operations.

Now that Whiphid dame was one gutsy customer, trying at big odds to carve out a piece of Jabba's pie right under his . . . uh . . . chins. It seemed to me she might just do it too.

I went up the steep outside ramp to the top level where the hotel lounge and casino were. Those too-pretty, too-smooth humanoid twins Sturn and Anton were at the front desk and waved gaily at me as I passed through the lobby. They made my skin crawl—and that's a lot of skin.

Beyond them, on the left, was the hotel's lounge. I turned in there, hoping for a quick drink before my meet.

It had a shabby look, like the whole place did. The rich fittings and fancy furniture had long since worn to third-hand junk, and the lady hadn't spent one thin credit on restoring things.

There were a few score assorted beings drinking there. I gave them a casual glanceover as I headed for the bar. The only one of note was that weasel-faced Prefect Talmont, the Empire's local stooge. Ineffectual by breeding. Slimy by birth. Untrustworthy by nature. He sat drinking at a table with some of his officers, taking a rare moment for a laugh.

But he sucked that up sharp to stare at me when I came in.

I made the bar next to a pair of humanoid-type

boys. They were big, beefy, and riding pretty low on the forehead. Manual workers, I guessed, but not from Tatooine. A little too clean for that. And no local smell.

The bulb-headed Bith tending bar approached.

"Good seeing you, Mon," he greeted. "Here to see the lady?"

I nodded. "Let her know I'm here, will ya? But first, give me an ale. Usual brand."

"Better put it in a bucket, barkeep, for a mouth like that," said one of the humanoids, and they both guffawed.

"Yeah," said the other. And to me, "Hey, face-guy, how d'ya even get a drink to your mouth with those arms?"

I ignored them both. Waiting for my drink, I gazed across the bar's top at my reflection in the dirty mirror behind. I suppose that to these oddly built humanoid types I did seem mostly a long face set on two stubby trunks of legs. And maybe my thick arms didn't seem capable of reaching to my mouth. But for a Chevin I'm considered a decent specimen. Or, I was. Admittedly I've put a few more wrinkles on the old snout. But it's seen a lot of hard wear over the years, being shoved into places it likely shouldn't have been.

Besides, beauty's relative in the galaxy, and most seasoned travelers respect that. These two jokers must have been greener than a moisture boy as well as bad-mannered.

"Hey, ugly," one of the two persisted, giving me a shove, "we're talkin' to you."

This time I turned around to him. "You bantha fodder looking for trouble?"

"You're sure not gonna give it to us, face," he sneered.

"You're asking to buy the Depp, boy," the barkeep warned him. "That's Ephant Mon. He—"

The other broke in. "He's a big talking head with too much face! Watch me carve him a bigger nose!"

I saw the broad knife flash into his hand. I jerked forward, slamming my forehead down on the top of his skull.

A Chevin's topknot is like iron. A humanoid's skull isn't. It cracked like an egg and he went down hard.

The other idiot still charged in, dragging a blaster out from under his coat. My vibroblade was faster. I had it out and into his chest before his gun cleared holster. He'd made the final jump before he hit the booze-stained floor.

The officers with Talmont stood as one, hands going to their guns. But the Prefect waved them down. He got up and strode casually over to me, looking at the bodies sprawled together on the floor.

"Well, well, my dear Ephant Mon, you've freed two more tormented souls, I see."

"Speaking of seeing, I'm surprised you recognized me," I told him, slipping my blade away.

"Can't mistake your style," he said, peering squintily at me. He was pretty shortsighted.

"No complaints?"

"For ridding me of some riffraff?" he said lightly. "Certainly not. We've no place for them." He eyed me more curiously. "But what about you? Come here on some business?"

"Just a drink."

"Really? Surprised your boss Jabba let you off the leash."

"No one tells me when to go or when to come. Including Jabba!" I said sharply. "I'm a free agent."

"So I've heard." He sounded skeptical. "Nobody understands why."

"Too bad," I said bluntly.

"Most intriguing," he mused on. "Someone like

that would be in a position to take great advantage of the Hutt."

"I don't take advantage of my loyalties, Talmont."

He colored at that shot, but before he could answer the barkeep approached.

"Ephant, Valarian says to go on back," he announced. He gestured to the dead bodies. "I'll take care of things here."

"Thanks." I turned to go.

"Seeing Valarian, eh?" Talmont called after me. "Did you mean what you said about loyalties? She is Jabba's rival."

"If you're so interested in intrigues," I tossed back to him, "why don't you talk to Tessek?"

I didn't even have to look around to know I'd scored with that one. I could hear his surprised gasp.

A short corridor from the bar led into the casino. Of course, it was only that in name now. Jabba had blocked all the Lady's attempts at getting a gambling license, so these days it wasn't much but a dining room, deserted at that hour.

Once it had been a classy place with a holographic star display on the ceiling and exotic fish in porthole aquariums on the outside walls. But the display was shut down and most of the tanks were lifeless now, and the empty tables with their threadbare tablecloths looked pretty forlorn in the half-light.

I went through the door in one wall and into a little office. Venutton, Valarian's scrawny and strung-tight human assistant, ushered me right on through into her office.

It was a stark place. No useless decoration for that Lady. The boss herself sat behind a big desk in the room's center.

Lady Valarian was a pretty young Whiphid—hell, a pretty young anything!—to be running so big an operation. But when you saw her, you weren't surprised.

Her presence was considerable. Her massive bulk filled up the chair, dominating the room. Her tusked face and glaring gaze were fierce.

Yeah, she had a pretty big face, maybe a little like mine. Maybe it's why she'd taken kind of a shine to me. But her big interest was in my connections.

"Well, Lady V," I greeted. "How's it going?"

"Lousy, as usual," she said in a deep growl of a voice. "Look, let's neither of us waste time in pleasantries. Have you thought any more?"

"There wasn't a need to," I said flatly. "You know what I think."

"I can't believe you can stay loyal to that rotting pile of fodder after what I've offered you!"

"Sorry. That's how it is."

"I'll tell you how it is!" she snarled, rising. She moved out toward me, body taut with anger. "The Hutt blocks me at every move. He wrecks my operation with sabotage, sics the law hounds on me, steals my business, sucks me dry with payoffs." She came up almost toe to toe with me, meeting my eye threateningly. Since she's as tall as me and a lot bigger built, she made a pretty good threat. "So here I've got a chance at getting someone on my side, and he turns me down. I don't like that, Mon!"

I stood my ground and answered coolly: "I was hoping not to fight you, Valarian. I thought we were friends."

Seeing I couldn't be intimidated, she sighed and stepped back, dropping the tough act.

"Okay, you're right," she said resignedly. "I won't try muscling you. But look," she tried more reasonably, "he will fall soon. You can't deny that. If not from my pushing, then from someone else's."

"Don't you think I know?" I told her. "I've already got an idea Tessek's up to something, with Ree-Yees and a few others helping, too. And I'm pretty sure

Talmont's been cut in on the deal. I try to warn Jabba of plots when I find 'em, but I can't find them all."

"Then why not leave him?" she cajoled, putting a hand on my shoulder. "We could have a beautiful deal together, you and I. We're alike, aren't we? Both fighting our way up from nothing."

"Maybe for you it was nothing," I answered. "For me it was different." Somehow her words had pulled up a memory again and I was seeing the sunlit, wide grasslands of a planet far away. "It was something all right. I had something. Simple maybe, but clean, open, and honest. Funny, but I haven't thought about it for a lot of years. But, twice today—"

"What?" she asked, dropping her hand and stepping back to eye me questioningly.

Realizing I'd slipped off into a weird reverie, I jerked myself back. "Oh . . . nothing," I said sharply. "But look, please just believe me, Valarian. There's a knot tying me to Jabba that no money or promises are gonna cut."

She looked hard into my eyes and nodded acceptance. "Okay." She smiled. "I should call you my enemy, but I can't. No hard feelings."

I smiled, too. "None. Well, I'd better get back now. Been gone an hour already." I turned to the door.

"Just remember," she called to me as I went out, "if you do survive the fall, you can still come work for me."

When I went back through the lobby, the dead-meat squad was coming in to scrape up the stiffs. Talmont was there, and his squinty gaze followed me out. He was worried now.

Both suns were high in the sky when I got back to the palace. I came into the throne room to find the place in an uproar. Seemed I'd missed quite a party!

I'd already gotten part of the story from Barada in the garage. All about how that guy in black had been

in cahoots with that other bunch out to rescue Han
Solo. How he'd claimed to be a Jedi named Skywalker
and had threatened the Hutt with being destroyed.
How he'd killed Malakili's pet rancor in the pit. And
how he was now cooling his heels in the dungeon
along with Solo and that Wookiee we'd caught before.
Soon they would all climb aboard the sail barge and
head out for the Great Pit of Carkoon.

I moved through a bustling throng headed for
Jabba's throne. He was blithely pulling away at his
hookah, giving proprietary tugs at the chain of that
captured woman who'd replaced poor Oola. But I was
hijacked halfway there by Tessek, one of Jabba's least
trustworthy lieutenants.

The Quarren was nervous. Every appendage on his
head was twitching. He pulled me aside and talked in
low, quick tones: "Have you heard what happened?"

"I heard all about it."

"All?" he said. "But I'll wager you do not know
this!" His voice dropped lower, taking on a confiden-
tial tone. "I checked on this Skywalker. I believe he
truly is a Jedi Knight."

Though intrigued by this, I didn't show it. "So
what?"

"There is more. I used my contacts to check the
Imperial wanted lists. All our prisoners are on it, even
the two droids! And they are considered most dangerous."

"Dangerous to the Empire."

"I think to us, too. These people destroyed the
Death Star! This Skywalker fought Darth Vader and
survived! Why would they come here and so easily be
caught—unless it is on purpose."

"What purpose?"

"To destroy Jabba. I believe . . . Wait!"

He had spotted that wretched little vermin Salacious Crumb creeping close around, and he took a

kick at the being. Crumb gave a high-pitched cackle and scampered away.

"Filthy scum," Tessek said with disgust. "I am certain it spies on me! Anyway, I believe there is an Alliance plot afoot. Their forces no doubt wait now to destroy us when we are most vulnerable."

"You really think they set this all up just to get the Hutt?" I asked. It seemed hard to believe.

"I do. And I want you to warn Jabba of it. He will listen to you. You are his most trusted ally. Maybe his only friend. You must tell him."

Noting that Crumb was still watching us keenly from the safety of an overhead fixture, Tessek broke off here and wheeled away. He left me staring after him in deep thought.

His story was pretty farfetched, and I was sure he was up to a few tricks himself. Still, there was something about that black-dressed man I'd seen. Something powerful. I decided I had to see this Skywalker myself, close up. Before I'd talk to Jabba, I'd talk to our "Jedi Knight."

In the lower corridor to the dungeon, I ran into Ree-Yees, quarter-rate scam artist, sometime killer, and all-around plug-ugly. The three-eyed Gran was stinking drunk, as usual, and it didn't make him any friendlier. I wondered what he was doing creeping around down there at this hour, and he sure didn't seem glad to see me.

"Whadarya doin' down 'ere?" he demanded, sticking his drooling goat-face up near mine.

I shoved him and he staggered away a few steps. "Going to see the prisoners," I told him, moving past. "I'm doing it for your pal Tessek too."

He went after me, grabbing my arm to jerk me around.

"Whadyamean, my 'pal'?" He slurred his words. "Whadaya know about us?"

"Why?" I fired back. "What should I know?"

"Don' gimme that!" he cried in drunken rage. "You know! I'll make you talk, you—"

He started to pull a blaster. My hand shot up open-palmed into his chest and I shoved him back against the wall hard. In his condition he could only struggle helplessly, my big hand pinning him tight.

"Now you'll do the talking," I said in my hardest voice. "I'm tired of this sneaking around. What's Tessek up to?"

"Go . . . to . . ." he gasped out through constricted lungs.

I leaned harder. "Tell me or get squashed right now!"

His chest cage creaked with the pressure. He gasped, his three eyes starting to bug out.

"Okay! Okay!" he said in panic. "Tessek's got a . . . plan! Deal with the . . . Empire! Gonna . . . raid!"

His breath gave out and he sagged forward. I pulled my hand back and let him slip unconscious to the floor.

So, there was a plot! And the Empire was in on it. Well, Jabba would have to be warned about that. But first, I had to satisfy my itch to see this supposed Jedi.

I reached the dungeon, signaled the guard there to move away, and slid open the barred window in the cell door. Beyond I could see the three prisoners huddled together in a far corner. The captured Wookiee was cradling the still recovering form of Han Solo while a blond human dressed in black stood by.

But the one in black turned right away and came over to the door, peering out through the little opening at me.

"You're the one called Skywalker," I said.

He nodded. "And you . . . you are a friend of

Jabba's," he said in a voice as calm as if he were on vacation here.

"The name's Ephant Mon. I'm one of his . . . associates."

He shook his head. "You are much more. I can feel it in you. You are his true friend, and he is yours."

"Not a bad mind-reading trick," I said, impressed. "Maybe you really are a Jedi."

He ignored that. "You can talk to him," he went on more earnestly. "He listens to you. He'll believe."

"Believe what?"

"That he's in danger. Listen, you can still save him. If you are his friend, convince him to release us. We mean him no harm. But if he persists in trying to harm us, I'll have no other choice."

"So you are going to destroy him," I said. "With what help?"

"No help," he assured me. "Not beyond us."

Though that sounded impossible, I found myself believing. I couldn't help it. That he could do exactly what he said was in the cool sound of his voice and the sure look in his eyes. Still, it didn't mean I could just buy in.

"Maybe you've got the power to do that, maybe not," I hedged. "It doesn't matter. Even I can't make Jabba let you go if he doesn't want to. It's impossible. I—"

One of his hands shot out through the opening so fast I couldn't react. It took a grip on my shoulder and hung on while his eyes fixed hard on mine. I couldn't break away. I was suddenly paralyzed by that probing gaze. If he'd wanted to kill me, he could have.

But that wasn't what he wanted.

I felt like some energy current was surging into me from him, crackling through my whole body. A thousand time-dimmed memories were lit up all at once. Images of my past life flashed by like I was a drowning man. I saw my own childhood with my parents' clan. I saw myself growing up on my home planet's vast plains. I relived the beauties of a time when I had once reveled in open skies and bright sunsets, freedom and space, family and comrades and a simple code of honor. I saw it all—all it had been, all I had left behind. It glowed before me like a paradise.

He pulled his hand back, broke eye contact, and the images faded. I stared. I blinked, seeing the reality of dark, wet corridor and prison bars. The ugliness of the dungeon of Jabba's lair closed me in.

"You're not evil," he told me. "Not like Jabba. I feel the good in you. You've just come so far from it, and you've lost your way back. Find it now. Help us. Save Jabba."

"I . . . I could try," I said. "I will try. But I still don't think he'll listen."

"I understand," Skywalker said softly. "But I don't want to destroy you with the rest. There's still a chance for you if you want to take it. If you can't free us, then don't stay with him. Escape yourself. Find your true life again. And may the Force be with you, friend."

With that he turned away and rejoined his comrades.

I went away from him shaken to my core. I'd never before questioned the way my life had gone. I'd just charged blindly ahead. My encounter with this Jedi had opened my eyes. I didn't like what I was seeing.

As I made my way back out of the dungeon, I noticed that Ree-Yees was gone. But I didn't care about him or Tessek or any of that now. I needed someone to talk to.

I went straight to the big docking area right behind the throne room. It was where Jabba's sail barge was kept, convenient for boarding by the Bloated One. I knew I would find Barada there, checking the barge's engine for the imminent departure to the Great Pit of Carkoon.

He quit work right away when I came in. The look on my face must have told him something big was wrong.

"What's the matter?" he asked me.

"It's hard to explain it," I told him truthfully, plopping down on a crate. "Things have happened."

He sat down beside me. "Things?"

"I saw the Jedi. Barada, I know Jabba's wrong. He's done a lot of things, and most of them weren't good. But this is different. I've gotta stop him this time."

"Stop him?" He shook his head. "I don't think even you can do that. He's pretty set on getting that whole bunch who came after Solo. They tried making a fool of him."

"I know. But if I don't stop him, I think he might be the one who gets hurt."

"What?" he said in disbelief. "And by what army?"

"Tessek's bet was that the Alliance was going to take a hand. He wanted me to pass that on to Jabba, probably to shift attention from his own plot. But the joke's on him. There's no Alliance reinforcements, but the danger to Jabba's bigger than anything Tessek could imagine."

"Just from that kid and his friends? It can't be."

"It can," I said stubbornly. "And I'm going to tell Jabba so."

"He won't like it," Barada warned. "You know how he gets. If he thinks you're crossing him, he might just drop you in that pit too."

"Okay. Okay," I said. "I could just let it go and save myself. But I owe him."

"Enough to risk your life?"

"Why not? He risked his life for me once."

"Did he?" Barada asked with interest. "How?"

I'd always kept this to myself before, but there didn't seem any reason not to spill it now.

"Well, he and I were partners in a little gunrunning scheme way back, right after I quit mercenary work. We were going to liberate a cache of Imperial weapons and sell them to the highest bidder. It was on a moon of Glakka, nothing but a rough chunk of ice."

"We were pulling out the weapons when an Imperial goon squad arrived. We'd been ratted out by one of Jabba's boys.

"The rest of our gang either ran for it or bought it real quick. But he and I put up a better fight. He was thinner then, quick and tough and strong. Never seen a better fighter, except maybe me.

"So we made a stand there, fighting back to back against them all. They came in close enough to smell 'em. I had to blast some right off his back. In the end only we were left, shot up bad, but alive. It was the weather that tried to finish us off.

"When night came, it dropped to sub-subfreezing. I was worse off than him and not so well insulated, so he saved me, wrapping his own body around me. Not too pleasant a night, but better than turning icicle.

"By dawn, he was nearly frozen himself. We only made it off that cube 'cause some of our bunch who had escaped before came back looking for us."

"I'll be blasted," Barada said in awe. "I always wondered why you stayed hanging around here when you could've gone anywhere."

"Now you know. I've been paying back ever since, spying out plots and scams against the Hutt, covering his tail. I've sent more than a few poor suckers to the rancor or Sarlacc myself. But not this time."

"I still think you're wrong," Barada said. "Seems to me you've already paid the boss back, and in spades. You don't have to owe him anymore."

"There's more to it than just that," I said. "See, I

found out I just can't be a part of all this anymore. That Jedi's touch did something. It revived something in me I thought was long dead.'' I struggled to explain it to him, but this other reason wasn't so clear to me yet. ''My people back on Vinsioth were hunters and farmers. They were close to the land, to nature. They believed in the force in living things, and they worshiped it. But I was too smart for that. I was too good for their simple life. I wanted something more.

''I thought I'd left all that life behind when I left to go soldier-of-fortuning around the galaxy. But it's in me, Barada! I found out it's a part of me I can't ignore. And this 'Force' of the Jedi, well . . . it must be my force, too. I'm not gonna destroy it, Barada. I just can't!''

He listened, then he shook his head and sighed. ''Sorry, my friend. I don't get it. That's all mumbo-jumbo to me.'' He got to his feet. ''You do what you have to. But I think you're crazy.'' He moved away.

''Where are you going?'' I called after him.

''Back to work, what else? We're heading for the pit in less than an hour. I just hope you'll be a passenger, not a prisoner.''

I thought it all over as Jabba's court roused itself and got to work loading up the sail barge. When they started to file aboard themselves, I decided I had to make my move. I hitched up my courage and approached the Hutt as he glided toward the loading ramp on his repulsor sled, towing that captured woman who'd become his newest pet by her long chain.

''My old friend, you seem troubled,'' he rumbled out.

''I am, Jabba,'' I told him. ''Please don't do this.''

''This?'' he said in astonishment, stopping the sled short. ''Do you mean my destroying this scum who tried to cheat me?''

"I do. Skywalker is a Jedi."

I noticed the woman's gaze jerking toward me at that. She listened with interest.

"He is no Jedi," piped up Bib Fortuna who, as usual, hovered close by. And Salacious Crumb, from a perch on Jabba's tail, echoed, "No Jedi! No Jedi!" in a shrill, cracked voice.

"This is wrong," I said, not backing down. "Jabba, you have to let him go. Let them all go."

"I think Mon is up to something," Fortuna said, eyeing me suspiciously. "Jabba, he must be in league with them."

"I am trying to save your life, Jabba!" I argued. "Look, you know no one's more loyal than I am. You know I've always warned you about danger. I can tell you all about another plot right now! But it's not important. Nothing else is: not Tessek, not Valarian, not even the Empire. Only this is. It's bigger than us all, Jabba. It's the Force!"

"That foolish religion means nothing to us!" Fortuna cried indignantly. "The Mighty Jabba can show no fear of anything, including Jedi Knights!"

"He is right, Ephant," the Hutt agreed. "And Jabba has spoken. They must die."

"Then . . . I can't go with you," I told him with force. "I can't be part of this."

"So you defy me?" he bellowed. "I should kill you for that."

"I know." I met his eye without flinching.

"I should," he growled on, "but our old bond stops me. It buys your life, but that is all it buys. I thought of you as my true friend, Ephant Mon. That friendship is ended."

"You can't call it over," I shot back. "I can. Barada is right. I've repaid my debt to you a hundred times over."

"Repaid?" repeated Jabba, and a tone of regret

came into the rumbling voice. I swear it was real, and I swear I'd never heard the like of it before. "Then it was never more than a debt to you. I am sorry for that."

He turned away from me and glided on toward the sail barge. The rest of his court followed. The captive woman stayed gazing at me in a bemused way until a jerk of her chain forced her to follow her master.

"It was more than a debt," I said after him, but in a quiet voice that no one heard. "Goodbye, old friend."

Jabba and the others disappeared into the barge. After them came a pack of Gamorrean guards prodding along Skywalker, Han Solo, and the rest.

As the Jedi went up the gangway, a pang of worry for him shot through me. Did he and his friends really have a chance against the Hutt's cutthroat crew?

He must have sensed my emotion, because he turned right then and flashed a calm, confident little grin at me. It told me I did not have to fear for him.

I watched the last of them enter the barge. I began to think about what I should do now. There'd still be room in Valarian's operation for me. But that didn't seem right anymore.

The sail barge rose on its repulsorlifts in a flurry of dust, turned and sailed away, fading quickly to a dot on the vast horizon of Tatooine's gray-brown wastes.

Another, greener landscape came into my mind. I knew where I should go now. It had been made clear to me.

I had to go home.

Goatgrass:
The Tale of Ree-Yees

by Deborah Wheeler

Slowly the harsh Tatooine day melted into after-noon. Early dusk softened the contours of Jabba's palace and touched the drifted sand with a muted orange glow. Feathered lizards darted from their lairs to hunt insects in the cooling shadows. From a rocky out-cropping, a meewit screeched once, twice, then fell silent.

Ree-Yees struggled up the stairs from the side entrance, lugging a bucket. He halted at the top, his three eyes darting furtively over the eroded hills and the entrance behind him. As he stood there, his bony chest heaving, something of the twilight stillness seeped into him. It soothed the sting of that last bout with Ephant Mon, the one which began with, "You're such an incompetent snot-brain, Ree-Yees, I can't see why Jabba keeps you around," and ended with Tessek, Jabba's Quarren lieutenant, pulling the two of them apart.

The sand whispered softly as a hot wind, the last exhalation of the day, blew across it. If Ree-Yees squinted his two side eyes, he could almost see the dunes as mounds of gently waving goatgrass. A pang rippled through his Grannish heart. He was not as drunk as usual, and not nearly as drunk as he wished he was. The arrival of the two new droids had made it difficult to slip away and refill his tankard with Jabba's best Sullustan gin.

Soon, Ree-Yees promised himself. Soon he'd be done with Ephant Mon and the rest of them. He picked up the bucket and shambled over to Jabba's frog-dog, which had been put outside for the night. A tongue, long and sticky, dipped into the malodorous stew, then retracted with a snap, bearing blobs of moldy bantha fat, gelatinous *chuff,* and fragments of Viridian termite jaws on its bulbous tip. As the bubo swallowed, Ree-Yees reached down and dug his fingers into a purple wart on the side of the beast's shoulder. It was a particularly large and fleshy growth. With a plop! the flap of skin pulled loose to reveal a miniature panel, two light squares and a reset button. Only Imperial technicians could design and fit such a device, undetected, right on Jabba's doorstep. A symbol glowed on one square with today's date, while the other flashed the words, "Shipment complete."

Ree-Yees secured the skin flap and snuffled in relief.

With this last shipment, the detonator, he would now be able to complete his end of the bargain. In return, the Empire would wipe that triple-blasted murder rap off Ree-Yees's record and he could go home to Kinyen again—

No! Too risky to think about that now! Better to keep playing Jabba's fool, despised and mocked, until the deed was done. Better to stay safely drunk, cut off from the visions which hovered, like half-glimpsed memories, at the corners of his eyes . . . fields of goatgrass glistening in the sun, oh yes . . . and the rut-scent of females, their velvet flanks, their breasts like tripled jewels—

No. Better to stay drunk. Better to wait.

The frog-dog, having gulped down the last of the slops, turned one eye speculatively on Ree-Yees, as if wondering how he would taste. Ree-Yees stepped aside just in time to avoid another flick of the prehensile tongue.

Ree-Yees slugged the creature on the side of the head. "Stupid two-eyed maggot fish! It's a good thing I don't need *you* anymore!"

The bubo cowered, its expression one of reproachful innocence. Once he'd turned to head back toward the palace, it hissed something extremely rude-sounding and almost intelligible at him.

Muttering under his breath, Ree-Yees shuffled down the hall toward Jabba's audience chamber. The Gamorrean on guard rumbled forward, force pike raised and red-rimmed eyes glinting. His tusks gleamed wetly in the dim light. Ree-Yees had fleeced him easily at four-cubes last night and the Gamorrean hadn't even realized he was being cheated.

"Outta my way, pig-slime!"

The Gamorrean poked Ree-Yees's chest with the tip of his ax. "Where you go? What you do?"

The slightest touch of the force pike stung, even through Ree-Yees's leather jerkin. "Get that crotting thing away from me!"

"Urghh!"

"So you say, spawn of Nilgarian worm! But there's gonna be some changes around here real soon. Jabba won't always—"

"Jabba-Jabba urghh-phth!"

Just then, a tall figure separated itself from the shadowy interior and hurried toward them. It was that interfering Quarren, Tessek.

Tessek's mouth tentacles writhed in agitation. "What'sss going on?"

"Jabba-no-Jabba urk-urk!" squealed the guard, waving his force pike wildly.

"A minor misssundersssstanding, sssoon remedied." With one hand, Tessek herded Ree-Yees down the tunnel, with the other he gestured to the guard. "Remain here at your possst and sssay nothing of thisss to anyone!"

Ree-Yees stumbled along, propelled by Tessek's grip. By the time they were out of earshot of the guard, the Quarren had regained control of his speaking apparatus.

"What do you think you're doing? Do you want Jabba to suspect— You're drunk again, aren't you? Give me that tankard!"

Ree-Yees jerked away. "None of your stinking business—and keep your hands off what's mine. You aren't the only one—" With an effort, he managed to shut himself up. Tessek had the right idea, keeping the Gamorrean from running to Jabba. Tessek, with all his schemes, was too wily, too close to guessing what Ree-Yees was really up to. With Doellin's own luck, he wouldn't need Tessek much longer, either.

"Now hurry on back," Tessek said smoothly. "Some new bounty hunter has come for the reward on the Wookiee and you won't want to miss the fun."

Snuffling, Ree-Yees hurried off to the audience chamber.

That night, Jabba ordered a hidden watch set on the audience hall and an alarm for his prized wall possession, the carbonite-frozen Corellian smuggler. What a bother, Ree-Yees thought, but something had aroused Jabba's suspicions even more than usual. At last Ree-Yees was able to slip away, refill his gin tankard, and make his way along the darkened corridor to the kitchen.

Ree-Yees paused beneath the ancient wooden beams of the doorway and peered in, but saw no sign that anyone was present.

Phlegmin, that odious little wart of a scullion, had been more than happy to take his winnings in exchange for setting aside the marked shipments of goatgrass, never dreaming what lay hidden within them. He probably thought Ree-Yees was indulging in nostalgic gluttony. It was just the sort of thing Phlegmin himself would do when he wasn't complaining how badly treated he was or bragging how famous he'd be once he got off this dustball planet. Ree-Yees guessed that Phlegmin did more than divert a few crates of vegetables; once he'd spied the kitchen boy adding something to the tank of Jabba's favorite live appetizers. Ree-Yees watched him even more closely when the box of goatgrass containing the bomb casing had gone missing. Luckily, no alarm followed, only a particularly successful casserole, which seemed to temporarily allay Jabba's suspicions of the chef.

"Phlegmin?" Ree-Yees called. "Old mucus-face?"

The faint scuffle of footsteps answered him, then a muffled cry. Scorch the two-eyes then, he'd find the shipment on his own. He hurried into the receiving area. Here the walls were lined with boxes of pickled meats, crates of dried fruits and beetles, casks of wine, jars of preserved tortoise dung, honeyed oil, caviar, and radioactive potassium salts—all the delicacies the Hutt's appetite required. He began looking around, lifting the lids of packing crates, peering down aisles of stacked cartons and around giant barrels.

Ree-Yees called out once more, but once again there was no response.

Suddenly he spotted a box of about the right size, lying on its side behind a vat of fermented sandmaggot eggs. On second glance, he saw that it was splintered open, its silvery green contents spilled across the stone floor. Phlegmin was sprawled on the floor beside the box. In his years at Jabba's palace, Ree-Yees had seen enough dead bodies to know one instantly, even if it were human. No mere sleep could produce such a graceless tangle.

Porcellus the cook was hunched over the body, wringing his hands. His head jerked up, his eyes bulged, and his hair—what there was of it—stood out in all directions.

"I had nothing to do with it!" he yelped.

Ignoring the hysterical screams of the cook, Ree-Yees threw himself down beside the box and raked his fingers through the silky goatgrass. He picked up the shattered box and shook it upside down, but it was no use.

The vital detonation link, the last component, was not there.

Ree-Yees bleated in terror. Whoever killed that pathetic excuse for a scullion must have taken the detonation link—knew what it was—

But wait! He couldn't know the target was Jabba's sail barge—or who had the rest of the bomb—

All was not lost, if he could act quickly. Once the body was discovered, Jabba would launch an investigation, no matter that this Phlegmin had been an insignificant and easily replaceable midge-brain. No one was allowed to die within the palace except those the Hutt himself ordered killed. But of late there had been strange goings-on in the back passageways—

"Urghh!" came a bellow from the doorway, even less articulate than usual for a Gamorrean.

"I didn't do it!" the cook screamed again.

Ree-Yees was so badly startled he would have fallen if he were not already on his knees. All three of his eyes froze on the stocky figure in the doorway—Gartogg.

Doellin's triple teats! What a stroke of luck! This particular Gamorrean was so stupid he couldn't even learn to play Snot, let alone realize when he was being cheated.

"Urggh-snuffle-snort?"

Ree-Yees scrambled to his feet and shoved the cook aside. "You're just in time! I found him—like this—down the hall—near the tunnel to Ephant Mon's quarters! I brought him here to—to—to perform resus—suspiration!"

"Hunh?"

"You know—emergency culinary resuspiration! The smell of food so—so—so *ripe* it can bring the dead back to life! An ancient art, one I learned from my great-uncle, Swee-beeps. We call it—er—garbage inhalation of the last resort. But alas"—Ree-Yees's eyestalks drooped mournfully—"I was too late." He sighed loudly.

Gartogg shuffled over to the body, attempted to squat, gave it up, tilted his body from the hips at an angle Ree-Yees would have sworn was anatomically impossible, and sniffed.

"So you see," Ree-Yees rushed on, "someone must take over now. Someone with authority. To investigate, put together clues, solve this crime. Jabba will be impressed—and *grateful.*"

"Snort-snuffle-snuffle!" The Gamorrean picked up the scullion by one ankle and dangled the body in front of his snout. Ree-Yees glanced from Gartogg's tusked face to Phlegmin's, with its beaklike nose congested with blood. Once he was home on Kinyen, he'd never have to look at another two-eyes again.

Gartogg slung the body over his massive shoulders and ambled away, snorting unintelligibly.

"Don't forget!" Ree-Yees yelled after him. "I found him near *Ephant Mon*'s quarters!"

Once the guard had gone, Ree-Yees gulped down the entire contents of his tankard, pausing only when forced to breathe. Burning spread from his first stomach along every fiber of his body. His eyestalks quivered, his knees threatened to collapse, and then a blessed numbness settled over him. A strange roaring sound filled his skull. In it, he could almost make out voices, one particular voice, the grating rumble that was Jabba's. He had heard it before, a nightmarish memory, on the ragged edge of sleep.

The cook had disappeared, the first sensible thing he'd done. As Ree-Yees stumbled from the kitchen, he hardly noticed which way he was headed through the grime-covered tunnels.

But where was that cursed detonation link? The passageway wound downward, often turning, until Ree-Yees began to realize it was leading him not to his own chamber nor back to Jabba's audience hall, but deeper and deeper into the labyrinth beneath the palace.

Ree-Yees halted at an unfamiliar branching, his

breath gurgling in his throat, his head spinning. His eyestalks swiveled frantically. Here, far from the inhabited upper regions, patches of luminescent slime dripped from the wet stone walls. The air smelled dank and faintly metallic.

Which way? Cursing in two languages, Ree-Yees shambled off down the next passageway, which seemed to be headed in the right direction. Down he went, stumbling through pools of acrid-smelling water, grazing his elbows on the rough stone walls. Images flashed through his mind like drunken dreams. In his memory, he felt a pressure deep in his middle, hard like metal, caught a glimpse of sudden, engulfing flame. Suddenly a wall of fire exploded in front of him, flames leaped out at him, seized him . . .

He shook his head. The visions kept coming, stronger and brighter with every step . . .

The flames rose up, more vivid and terrifying than before. His skin crisped in their blazing heat, his eyeballs sizzled on their stalks and burst—

He found himself looking down on a vast, whitened plain, blown with snow and glittering ice particles, saw crevasses of frozen blue and great war machines ponderously advancing . . .

He blinked, and the picture shifted to the lush chaos of a swamp, a battered X-wing fighter sinking beneath the ooze, trees and vines a tangle of green, flowers like bits of brightness, winged lizards screeching . . .

The image gave way suddenly to that of a vast chamber lined with shelves and strange machines, and on those shelves, glass domes where disembodied brains pulsated in an eerie pink light . . .

Then his center eye cleared and Ree-Yees realized he was actually standing in the chamber of the brains. B'omarr monks. The room was quiet, dimly lit except for the display lights and the rosy glow from the containers. His heart, which had taken a sudden lurch with the vision of the flames, slowed once more. He ran his narrow tongue over his lips.

The brains were nothing to fear, he told himself, relics of those degenerate two-eyed monks who'd hollowed out these tunnels centuries before Jabba discovered them. Their naked brains couldn't do anything except sit there, each in its own glass prison, motionless except for their slow pulsation.

A whisper, cloth over stone, made Ree-Yees spin around. A figure in a voluminous robe glided from the shadows and halted in the center of the room. Ree-Yees could make out nothing of its form, not even its species, nor whether it was male or female, so completely did the hood conceal its features. As he gaped at it, the figure raised one arm. The sleeve fell back, revealing a humanoid hand, skeletally thin, the pale skin stretched over grotesquely deformed knuckles.

A voice issued from the secret darkness beneath the hood. "The fire is but a warning," it rasped. "Take heed and tell your vile master to leave this place forever."

Then the figure disappeared.

Ree-Yees's eyestalks quivered. He bleated in surprise, but quickly recovered himself. A warning, was it? Or an omen? A promise of things to come?

He didn't understand the other images, but the firestorm—it had seemed so *real*. What did it mean?

Elation surged through Ree-Yees's belly. Doellin's own luck was with him. He would succeed, it had been foreseen! The loss of the detonation link would prove but a minor setback. Jabba would perish in a blast of cleansing fire and his repulsive two-eyed crew with him. Imperial Prefect Talmont would clear Ree-Yees's way to go home to Kinyen.

Belching in happiness, Ree-Yees hurried from the chamber of brains and somehow found his way back, ascending to the familiar levels. He was en route to his own quarters to savor his success when another Gamorrean guard bustled past him, weapons drawn.

"Hoy!" said Ree-Yees. "How about a nice game of Rumble-pins?"

"Someone try steal Jabba pretty-thing!" the guard bellowed. He was more articulate than the hapless Gartogg. "You come!"

Ree-Yees hurried after the Gamorrean. With his mission assured, he could relax and enjoy himself. Perhaps Jabba would feed the thief to the rancor—that was always good for a few bets on the side.

Over the next day a heady certainty stayed with Ree-Yees through the discovery of the bounty hunter's true identity. The girl who took Oola's place was as repellent a two-eyes as he'd ever seen, but what did that matter? He wouldn't have to look at her for too much longer. Not even Ephant Mon's blustering could rouse Ree-Yees, and Tessek was looking worried about something.

From his accustomed place in the audience hall, Ree-Yees watched the antics of the young Jedi. The tussle with the rancor was particularly amusing, although Ree-Yees had to pay out a pocketful of credits in lost wagers. No matter, he'd win it back, for Malakili, the rancor keeper, would be distraught over the loss of his pet for months to come and would make an easy mark.

"You should have bargained, Jabba," the young Jedi said as he was being led away. What kind of maggot-brained threat was that? Not even a curse, "May a thousand Tusken sand-grubs gnaw your entrails from within!" Or an excuse, "Sorry, I'm allergic to rancor dander." Or something innovative like, "Congratulations, for that correct answer, you have won a complete set of Imperial Encyclopedias!" Not that it would do much good in this case, although Jabba had been known to pardon those who particularly amused him, as Ree-Yees well knew.

Besides, Jabba was destined to die at Ree-Yees's hand. That was the promise of the monks' weird visions. And since the secret bomb was not yet complete, it was perfectly safe to go out on the sail barge to enjoy the spectacle of the executions. Ree-Yees particularly liked hearing the screams which issued from the Great Pit of Carkoon as the Sarlacc's victims felt the first excruciating effects of its digestive juices. Sometimes Ree-Yees and Barada wagered on how long it would take for the screaming to stop—either because the victim's vocal cords were eroded away or the Sarlacc had stung him insensible, no one could be sure.

The day was oven-hot and dry, like all days on Tatooine. Ree-Yees took his station beside Jabba, not so near as to arouse Tessek, but near enough to appear devoted. He let his attention wander, for one execution was much like another. One side eye rested on the loathsome yellow sands, the other on the equally loathsome dancing girl, now crumpled in a heap at the foot of Jabba's sled. When the new R2 droid wheeled about, serving drinks, Ree-Yees accepted a pink and green Bantha Blaster. It fizzed all the way down. An instant later, his teeth rattled and his eyestalks felt as if they were on fire. He followed it up with a Wookiee-Wango, made with Sullustan gin and stirred, not shaken.

By Doellin's triple teats, that R2 unit could mix drinks! Ree-Yees wondered if there were some way to take the droid with him back to Kinyen.

A ruckus from the prison barge jarred him alert. Ree-Yees stumbled to the railing and peered out. Someone was laying about with a lightsaber and everyone was shouting at once. The two new droids scrambled out of their programmed patterns. Ree-Yees grabbed a Rummy Tonic from the R2 before it rolled out of sight.

The deck boiled with frantic action. Blast pistols and lasers went off in all directions. Gamorrean guards ran about, squealing, while Jabba bellowed out orders. A Weequay pushed past Ree-Yees, spilling his drink, and rushed to the side of the barge.

Ree-Yees glanced around, searching for the safest hiding place. He decided, after a moment's hesitation and the sight of several of Jabba's defenders tumbling into the Sarlacc's maw, to remain right where he was, safe behind Jabba's repulsor sled. Tessek, he noticed, had already disappeared, abandoning Jabba to save his own hide. That bantha-brain—did he think Jabba wouldn't notice?

Ree-Yees tossed his empty glass aside, then tried to think how a loyal retainer, defending his master, might act. Here his imagination failed him.

Without warning, the two-eyed female scrambled to her feet and looped her chains over Jabba's head.

Arrrgh! Unnngh! Jabba let out a series of inarticulate howls as the chains dug into the folds of his neck. His eyes rolled and his massive body heaved.

The human female braced herself against the Hutt's bulk and hauled on the chains with surprising energy for one of such spindly limbs. By Doellin's triple earballs, what did she think she was doing?

Jabba's eyes lit on Ree-Yees and he bellowed again. One stubby hand lifted in Ree-Yees's direction.

Ree-Yees hesitated. He knew perfectly well that Jabba meant for him to come to his aid. But what if he pretended not to notice, what if he did . . . nothing? What an appealing idea! All he had to do was wait a few moments longer, while the slave did all the work and left *him* to take the credit with the Empire.

But if by some chance Jabba survived—as well he might, for Hutts were notoriously robust—Ree-Yees could claim he'd tried to save him. Perhaps he'd better move a little closer, to make it look realistic . . .

Even as Ree-Yees took a step toward the thrashing Hutt, he felt a metallic pressure deep within his belly. Jabba's voice, garbled and rasping, echoed through his skull. He staggered sideways, eyestalks shuddering, hands pawing the sides of his head. He heard his own voice bleating in terror, saw little explosions of brightness behind his eyes, like miniature firestorms.

In Ree-Yees's center eye, he saw the female slave pulling and pulling, her head thrown back with effort, the muscles standing out on her bare arms. Jabba's tongue protruded, quivering. Ropy saliva trickled down his bloated belly. His eyes blazed like incandescent copper.

Now Ree-Yees felt the hard metal device in his own body and the compulsion implanted just as deeply in his mind. He remembered Jabba's med-techs bending over him, cutting him open, repeating the code phrase over and over again, ordering him to forget . . .

Now he knew the words Jabba was struggling so furiously to pronounce—the command to wrap his arms around the target, the thought-trigger which would detonate the ultrashort-range bomb in his belly.

Ree-Yees's feet moved silently toward the human. In her struggle, she did not notice him. His arms lifted, reached out—

For an instant, the visions of the brain chamber swept over him. He'd had it all wrong, curse those B'omarr monks! The fire wasn't Jabba's sail barge blowing up, it was the bomb in his own belly. Ree-Yees bleated and squirmed, but his body was no longer his to command as it moved inexorably closer. He couldn't bargain his way out of this one. He could almost feel the explosion ripping through him, the fiery blast—

The compulsion died, even as the light faded from the Hutt's bulging eyes. Stinking black fluid gushed from the corners of his mouth. His tail shuddered once, reflexively, and then lay still.

Relief swept through Ree-Yees like a summer's breeze through the grassy fields. He fell back against the nearest wall. His legs felt like glass. He couldn't believe it was over—Jabba was finished. His name would be dust, his empire ashes scattered on the hot Tatooine winds. And he, Ree-Yees, would gloat all the way back to Kinyen.

"Ma-a-a-a-ah!" Ree-Yees lashed out at the Hutt's inert body with one boot. "Who's laughing now, you perverted two-eyed worm slime! *Chuff*-sucking leech!"

The human female raked Ree-Yees with an enigmatic stare. The next moment the R2 unit cut through her chains. She leaped nimbly to the floor and darted away in the direction of the deck-mounted gun.

Ree-Yees drew a deep breath and collected his wits. As soon as the prisoners were subdued and dumped into the pit, Jabba's body would be discovered, and Ree-Yees had better not be here. Whoever took over, Bib Fortuna or Tessek perhaps, might well go through the motions of executing Jabba's killer in order to consolidate his position. No, the safest thing would be to disappear until he could get to Mos Eisley. He'd find a med-tech there to remove the bomb.

Beneath Ree-Yees's feet, the sail barge shuddered. His eyestalks swiveled and a terrified bleat escaped his lips as he remembered the monk's vision of fire. Had the premonition been false? In the back of his mind, he heard a rumble like Jabba's laughter, low-pitched and evil.

A percussive blast rocked the deck. As Ree-Yees

watched, a wall of flame surged toward him. Greasy smoke shot upward from the lower levels. The shock wave catapulted his body into the air. Fragments of unrecognizable metal were hurled in all directions.

The edge of the inferno enveloped him. Pain seared his lungs. The moment before everything went dark, he caught a scent, sweet and familiar, and the fading glimpse of fields silvery and shimmering, as nubile triple-breasted females came leaping to meet him.

And the Band Played On: The Band's Tale

by John Gregory Betancourt

1. How the Band Came to Tatooine

Evar Orbus set down his microphone case, stretched his eight tentacles to their utmost, and flapped dust from the air-gills beneath all four eyes in his egglike head.

Finally, he thought, I've reached the big time.

He turned slowly, drinking in the sights of the Mos

Eisley spaceport. Despite the late hour, the place bustled with activity as humans, Imperial stormtroopers, droids, and beings from a hundred different worlds moved among the landing pads. Overhead, the primary sun descended toward a hazy horizon, trailed by its smaller counterpart. He felt a rush of excitement starting to build inside. This planet resembled his homeworld more than any other he had yet seen in his travels. He could do very well here indeed, he thought.

"Where do you want this stuff?" a gruff voice called.

Evar turned. Captain Hoban of the *Star Dream,* a disreputable-looking human in a shiny metallic jumpsuit, had opened the ramp to the cargo compartment. One of his battered old droids held a large crate with "Evar Orbus and His Galactic Jizz-wailers" stenciled on the side.

"Over there, please," Evar said. He pointed to the cargo area behind the ship with a tentacle. "We have transport coming."

The droid shifted the crate and almost dropped it.

"Watch it!" Evar screamed. He felt his sense organs lurch at the thought of having his livelihood destroyed by a roving scrap heap. "Watch those instruments! If you break them, you'll have to replace them!"

The droid bleeped angrily.

"Easy there," Captain Hoban said to the droid. He smiled apologetically at Evar Orbus. "There's nothing to worry about, sir. We handle crates like this all the time."

But do you break them? was Evar's first thought. He knew better than to voice it, though. He contented himself with watching the droid carefully through three eyes while his fourth swiveled around to watch for their transport.

The ramp beneath his feet shook as someone

started down behind him. He moved to the side, swiveling an eye to see.

It was, of course, Max Rebo, his Ortolan keyboard player. Max peered left, then right around the ship, his trunklike nose snuffing the air ever so slightly. Probably looking for his next meal, Evar thought.

"Is that spiced Parwan nutricake I smell?" Max asked. "I think there must be a restaurant nearby. How about I pop over and see? It's well past dinnertime, you know."

"We'll eat when we get to the cantina," Evar said evenly. It often seemed to him that Max's brain was in his stomach.

"But—"

"You heard me." He focused all four eyes on Max, who swallowed meekly. "If you want to help, see what's taking Sy and Snit so long."

"Right!" Max brightened noticeably. "Then we can eat!" Turning, he waddled back up the ramp as fast as his chubby little legs could take him.

Evar turned three of his eyes back to the droids. Yes, he thought, things were definitely looking good. He had credits in his belt pouch, a six-month gig lined up, and finally an agreeable climate to live in. Once they got to the cantina, everything would be perfect.

Now, what had happened to the transport they'd promised him . . .

Using his personal comlink, he called the cantina.

"Yes," a Bith said, its mouth folds stretching back to reveal a surprisingly facile mouth. It was nodding its tall, hairless head to music from an unseen source.

"Greetings, gentle," Evar said. "Is the Wookiee Chalmun there?"

"Not here. Called away on business."

"Perhaps that explains it. Our transport was not waiting at the spaceport—"

"We're not a travel service." The creature reached out to disconnect.

"Wait!" Evar snapped. "I'm Evar Orbus!"

"So?"

"Of the Evar Orbus Galactic Jizz-wailers. Perhaps you've heard of us?"

"Jizz-wailers? No."

Was that disgust in its voice? Evar huffed a little, but restrained his anger. If he spoke his mind, the Bith would doubtless disconnect on him. He satisfied himself by mentally running through five generations of insults to the Bith's maternals.

"Look, incompetent one," Evar finally snarled, "tell your boss the new band is here. Get us transport —*now*—or I'll have your head on a platter when I get there."

"New band?" The Bith paused, puckering its lip folds, then chittered to someone Evar couldn't see. The unseen one chittered back.

The first Bith then gazed back at Evar. "What landing pad?"

"Seven."

"A transport will be there shortly."

"Thank you," Evar said with satisfaction. He disconnected.

Dinner, dinner, glorious dinner! Max thought as he waddled down the corridor. Every footfall was a dinner gong; every scent a call to eat. It seemed like weeks since his last meal. If he wasn't careful, he'd waste away to nothing, like Snit. Not that Evar Orbus would have noticed—the only thing that Letaki cared about was money.

Now, though, dinner loomed near. Dinner, dinner, glorious dinner! And all he had to do was get Sy Snootles and Snit outside.

Sy would be the biggest delay, he knew. She always took too long getting dressed. For that matter, she took too long with everything. You couldn't trust nibblers, he thought, just like his grands had always said.

He knocked on her cabin door, shifting impatiently from foot to foot.

"Yes?" a delicate reed-thin voice called from inside.

"It's me," Max called. "Evar says to hurry up. Transport's ready and we need to eat." If that didn't get her out, nothing would.

"I'll be right there."

"Hurry!" he said. Turning, he continued up the corridor.

Dinner, dinner, glorious dinner! He could almost taste it now. Bantha steaks, kiwip grass, and gannesa juice. Fire stew, lavender treebread, and succulent ploth. Roast yarnak, ginger noodles, and white seedcake. He would have some of everything. All he had to do was find Snit and he'd be done.

The Kitonak's cabin door stood open, so Max went right in. After all, why waste time when food was waiting? The sooner they got moving, the sooner they'd eat, he thought.

Snit huddled in the corner, his huge lumpy head buried in his huge lumpy hands. Sobs racked his body. It was the most emotion Max had ever seen from him.

Poor primitive, Max thought. Evar had *really* been starving Snit. In the six months he had been with the band, Snit had only eaten six times as far as Max knew —a single huge slug each time. When Evar had bought Snit on Ovrax IV, Snit's belly had hung so low you couldn't see his legs. That had been one happy Kitonak, Max had thought a little enviously, imagining what fabulous meals must have gone into creating such a corpulent body. Since that time, though, Snit had lost half his body weight. Dressed only in bright red shorts, he looked positively svelte for a Kitonak—

still like a lump of badly shaped yeast, but a svelte lump of yeast.

"We need you to come out now," Max told him. "It's dinnertime," he added happily. That should cheer him up, he thought.

To his relief, Snit stopped snuffling and rose on his three wide, circular feet. Tiny black eyes peered out at him from beneath a heavy, lumpy brow.

"Come on," Max said, taking Snit's hand and leading him toward the corridor. They could pick up Sy on their way out, he thought. Was nobody else hungry? He felt gnawing pains in his belly. It was time for dinner, dinner, glorious dinner!

Evar Orbus stood by his eight crates of equipment and fumed silently. Where in the seven hells was that transport? Never trust a Bith, he thought angrily. He'd had run-ins with them before. Their hearing might be keener than his, but that didn't make them his betters, not by a long shot. It had been half an hour since he'd called. He'd definitely talk to the Wookiee about that bartender.

Sy Snootles, her lips pursed angrily, continued to shift from one thin leg to the other. She'd been glaring at him since she'd gotten outside twenty minutes before.

"What are you looking at?" Evar finally demanded.

"Max hustled me out here," she said in her high, thin voice, "by saying you had transport ready to take us to dinner. There's no transport. There's no dinner. I could have been resting in my cabin. You *know* how frail I am, Evar. This desert air just isn't good for my lips. Let alone my throat. Let alone my lungs."

Evar sighed inwardly. He knew all about her lips and lungs. She certainly kept them running on hyperdrive. If she wasn't one of the best singers he'd ever seen, and if her contract didn't have some very nasty early termination penalties, he would have replaced her in a millisecond with the first sandflea he came across.

Just as he was about to let loose a very cutting comment about those same lips and lungs, an airbus screamed down and landed in front of them. A Bith—possibly the same one he'd talked to earlier; he'd never been able to tell them apart—sat in the driver's seat.

"I am sorry we took so long, gentles," the Bith called, climbing down. He opened the passenger compartment and three more Biths stepped out. "I asked some friends to help. You have baggage?"

Evar nodded smugly. This Bith certainly seemed to know his place. "Our equipment's over here," he said, gesturing with two tentacles.

Max bounced happily on his seat in the airbus, thinking of the meal ahead. He hadn't been this hungry in hours. He turned to the Bith next to him, intending to ask about the cantina's kitchen facilities, when the Bith abruptly pulled a blaster from under its robes.

"What's that for?" Max asked. He turned. "Evar, he has a—"

Max broke off. All the other Biths had drawn blasters, too, he saw suddenly. Something had definitely gone wrong. He swallowed and felt his ears starting to stand up in fear. What was going on? It was almost enough to make him forget about dinner.

"Hands up!" one of the Biths said. "Now! We would hate to make a mess inside the airbus!"

Max complied instantly. Sy and Snit did the same, he was relieved to see. Only Orbus hesitated.

"I don't understand," Orbus said. "We're under contract!"

"The cantina already has a band," the Bith driver said. "We don't need another one."

"I have a contract—"

"So do we," said another Bith.

"One we need to keep," said a third.

"I begin to see," said Orbus slowly.

Max said, "I don't see," hoping someone would explain.

"Be quiet, Max," Sy Snootles told him.

Max glared at her. What right did she have to tell him to be quiet? Orbus was the band's leader, after all, not her.

"So," continued the Bith driver, "we'd like you to audition for someone else. Someone very special out on the Dune Sea. A certain Sarlacc in the Great Pit of Carkoon."

They all laughed as if that were funny. Max looked from one Bith to another. Somehow, he thought this meant trouble. At the very least it would certainly delay dinner.

Evidently Orbus felt the same way; he suddenly lowered one tentacle. Flames blasted from its tip, spraying across the airbus's cabin toward the driver and the controls. The tentacle must have been a fake, Max realized. He never would have guessed it hid a weapon. Orbus had so many tentacles, who would notice an extra one?

With an unhappy whine, the airbus swung wildly out of control. Several of the Biths cried out in panic. Sy screamed and Snit grunted. Evar was shouting orders. Max pressed his eyes closed and tried not to be sick.

With a sudden bone-jarring crunch, the airbus hit something. Max felt the universe swinging wildly around him. He opened one eye and saw the ground —still moving—directly over his head. No, no, no, he thought. This couldn't be happening.

The airbus hit again, flipped twice more, then skidded to a stop upside down. Everyone lay in a heap on what had been the ceiling. Max swallowed, then tried to rise. His balance seemed to be off. The cabin still felt as if it were moving even though he could see it wasn't.

A tentacle suddenly whipped around his arm. "Come on, Max!" Evar said, pulling at him.

Max focused on his boss a little blearily. "Wha—?"

"We have to get out of here! They're going to kill us!"

Max suddenly snapped back to attention. Yes, they had to get away. Sy Snootles was lying on top of Snit. He picked up her limp form a little hesitantly. Her proboscis drooped across his arm like a limp snake. Luckily she was still breathing.

One of the Biths had climbed to his feet and was staring numbly at them. "Do you realize what you've done?" he cried softly. "We *borrowed* this airbus!"

"Not my problem," Evar said. He now held two of the Biths' blasters in his tentacle, Max saw. "Stay where you are!"

Then a blaster shot from one of the Biths on the floor caught Orbus in the side. The force threw him across the airbus. He hit the wall with a wet thump and slid to the floor, leaving a pale green stain behind. The smell of roasting meat filled the air.

Max turned and fled, for once not the least bit hungry.

Sy Snootles opened her eyes and saw a blur of duracrete. She raised her head. She was in Max's arms, she realized, and he was running down a long deserted street with Snit in tow. She gazed up into the velvety blue fur of his face, saw tears in his eyes, and realized things had gone horribly wrong. The last thing she remembered, Orbus had lowered his fake tentacle in the airbus and started shooting. What had happened?

Then Max saw she was awake and stopped. "Are you all right?" he asked.

"I think so," she said. "Put me down."

Max did so and looked plaintively at her. "What should we do?" he asked.

"Where's Orbus?" she demanded.

"Dead," Max said. "They shot him. We ran."

"Good. That's the first smart thing anyone's done since getting here." She folded her hands across her rounded middle and paced slowly, long nose swaying this way and that. Max looked like he was in shock, she thought. Snit looked as lost as he always did. "With Orbus gone," she said slowly, "his contracts with us are void. That's clear enough, even by Intergalactic Federation of Musicians rules."

"Uh-huh," Max said.

"That means we're free, boys. Snit, you can do whatever you want now. Orbus no longer owns you. Max, you can buy your own meals now. And I can sing wherever I want."

Snit sat and leaned back against a wall. "Don't call me Snit," he said.

"What?" Sy cried. This was the first time she'd ever heard him speak a whole sentence. Usually he just stood there blowing wind through flutes with those immense lungs of his.

"Don't call me Snit," he said again.

"What do you want to be called?" she asked.

He responded with a long series of whistly tones.

"I can't say that," she told him. "How about I pick a really great show name for you? Something special, something really fabulous, something you'll be proud of?"

"Okay," he said.

Sy stopped and thought for a moment. "Droopy," she said. "Droopy McCool."

"Okay," Snit said.

"Anybody have any money?" Sy asked, and before anyone could answer she went on, "Of course not, Orbus had it all. So we're going to need money, and the way to do that is to work. To work we need equipment, and our equipment is back in that airbus. So, gentles, let's go."

"Go?" Max said.

"Back to the airbus, of course. You don't think we're going to leave our gear there, do you?"

"They'll shoot us!" Max wailed.

"We don't have a gig," she pointed out, "and we *won't* have a gig if we don't get our instruments. Which way is it?"

Max pointed.

She nodded. "Let's go!"

"Jawas!" Max said.

They were swarming over the airbus as if they owned it. Several turned as they approached, their little yellow eyes glowing faintly beneath their brown hoods.

"Ours!" one of the Jawas called. He pulled a small blaster and gestured grandly with it. "Stay back!"

"Ours!" Sy Snootles told him. To Max's amazement she strolled around him as if he weren't there and pointed to a crate. "See? It has our name on it."

The Jawa lowered his blaster. "You Evar Orbus?"

"He is." She pointed to Max, who swallowed and tried to look authoritative. "We want our crates. You can have the airbus."

"Buy crates?"

"*Buy* our own equipment? I don't think so."

"Is salvage!"

"How much?" she asked.

The Jawa hesitated. "Fifty credits!"

"Five!" she said. "Plus you'll have to deliver it to our hotel."

The Jawa raised his arms in dismay and suggested a slightly higher fee, and Sy countered with a slightly lower one. Max watched in growing amazement as they spent the next few minutes haggling, finally settling on twenty credits. Sy paid from a pouch she kept tucked in her skirt. "Tips," she told Max when she noticed him staring.

Max shook his head. It figured she'd been holding out on them. They were supposed to split tips evenly among all the band members.

By then the Jawas had the crates loaded aboard a cargo sled.

"Come on!" Sy told him, hopping aboard. "Let's get out of here! Those Biths are going to be back any minute now!"

2. How the Band Came to Jabba's Palace

They ended up staying at the Mos Eisley Towers, which Sy found rather ridiculous since the entire complex—except for the restaurant and the lobby—lay completely under the desert sands. Still, the rooms were clean and cheap, and the manager put their crates of instruments into secure storage (she'd made sure of it) before they settled in.

As she sat on her bed looking at Max and Snit (no, he was now Droopy McCool, she told herself), she wondered what exactly she was going to do.

Mos Eisley was clearly a cesspool, one of the worst backwater towns on one of the least hospitable planets she'd ever seen. The desert air had chapped her lips and dried out the delicate membranes of her nose and throat; it would take weeks if not months for her to adapt. No, she thought, she had to get out of here as quickly as possible. And to do that, she'd need money. That's where Droopy and Max came in.

"We need a gig," she told them.

"We need dinner!" Max said. "I think I'll have room service."

"Not a chance!" Sy said. "They charge extra for that. We'll go out for dinner. There's bound to be a cheap take-out place near here."

"But I'm hungry now!" Max said.

Sy sighed and rose. "Then we'd better go," she said. If she waited much longer, she knew Max would order room service whether she forbade him to or not. And they didn't have the cash to spare for frills like room service. She glanced at Droopy. At least he wouldn't eat. One of the crates contained a supply of giant white slugs in stasis fields—several years' worth, at the rate he seemed to consume them.

Max walked to the door, which opened, and Sy followed him. Droopy brought up the rear. Perhaps it would be good to get out, Sy thought. She could start making some subtle inquiries about work. A place this big had to have at least one opening for a singer of her talent.

It was such a rough place, though, that she'd need protection. Slowly a plan came to her, and it was so clever it made her laugh out loud. Max glanced back at her impatiently; Droopy didn't even look up.

Yes, she thought. She'd let Max be the leader of the band. If anything happened, it would happen to him —just as with Evar Orbus. She'd manage the money. It wouldn't be hard to talk Max into an arrangement like that. With him fronting for her, what could possibly go wrong?

She'd get them off Tatooine as quickly as possible, hire a few more musicians, and before she knew it, she'd have a band to be reckoned with. Jizz-wailers were in big demand around the galaxy. And with her voice, they couldn't possibly fail.

Max munched on a bantha kabob and nodded every once in a while to the tall, dark-skinned human with long hair and moustaches seated across from him. What had Sy called him? Naroon Cuthas . . . the talent scout for some big guy out in the desert. Max was barely paying attention; after all, Sy was the one who'd brought the guy over, and he was busy eating. She could entertain him till Max finished.

"Jizz-wailers . . ." Naroon Cuthas said, stroking his long moustaches. "Yes, I think I could use you, at least short-term."

"Who do you work for?" Sy asked.

"Jabba the Hutt. Ever hear of him?"

"No," Max said. If this was what the local cuisine tasted like, he was never leaving, he thought. He finished his meal, searched the tabletop for crumbs, didn't find any, and gestured for the waiter to bring him two more kabobs.

"He has a palace," Cuthas continued. "I'm in town picking up some supplies, so I'd be glad to give you a ride. I can have you audition for him tonight, and if he likes you, you can send for your belongings and stay in the palace."

The bantha meat, Max thought, was cooked to perfection: moist, succulent, and exactly the right shades of pink, gray, and yellow. Even the grease had a delightfully sharp aftertaste, he thought, licking it off his fingers one by one. Delicious. He'd never had the like before.

Cuthas seemed to be waiting for him to speak. Had he missed something? Sy poked him in the ribs.

"It's a good job," she whispered in his ear. "We should take it."

"Okay," he said.

"How soon can you start?" Cuthas asked.

"After dinner?" Max said. He took another bite, then another, then a third. "Wonderful food!" he said.

"I'll meet you at your hotel," he said.

"Sounds great," Max said. The waiter set another platter before him. "Pass the dioche sauce?"

"This way," Naroon Cuthas said, indicating a broad corridor leading down from the hovercar landing bay. They had parked between a huge sail barge and several dozen landspeeders of various sizes.

As Sy Snootles moved forward, she gazed around in wonder. The ride out to the enormous citadel on the edge of the Dune Sea had been long and desolate, and she'd expected Jabba's palace to be a small, dusty tent city. Instead, it was a huge complex that bustled like an Imperial trading depot. She spotted Gamorreans, Jawas, Twi'leks, humans, countless droids, and even a Whiphid. She could tell someone rich and incredibly powerful lived here. All these people meant there had to be a lot going on.

She looked back once to make sure Max and Droopy were following—they were—before hurrying after Cuthas.

Doors to either side opened onto storerooms, offices, and all manner of workrooms. She wrinkled her nose. It smelled bad up ahead—mostly of spilled intoxicants and sweaty body armor, but of other, less pleasant things as well.

They rounded several corners—the stink growing steadily worse—and abruptly came to a huge room with a low dais. The immense, hairless, sluglike creature sitting there had to be Jabba the Hutt, she thought. Around Jabba were crowds of guards and henchmen, dancers and bounty hunters, humans and Jawas and Weequays and Arcona.

"This is Jabba's presence chamber," Cuthas said with a grand gesture. He led them around the crowds to a little bandstand set into the wall opposite Jabba's dais. "Your equipment will be here momentarily. When Jabba wants music, he will gesture to you. Play like your lives depend on it—they probably do."

Sy swallowed. This wasn't what she had expected. She turned to tell Max they were leaving, but he was already scooping up hors d'oeuvres from a little R4 droid carrying a tray.

"Be careful what you say to Jabba," Cuthas told them all in a low voice. "If he likes you, you're all set. If he doesn't, you may come to regret it. I strongly suggest you make him like you."

"Right," Max said. "Is there anything else to eat?"

"Help yourself from any of the server droids. Ah! Here comes your equipment now."

More droids were carrying in crated instruments. One by one they set them down. Sy went over to supervise. No telling what droids would do with a box full of slugs in a stasis field . . . and no telling if Jabba considered slugs his distant cousins. It was best not to take chances.

Max stuffed himself while the droids set up the instruments. Every passing droid carried a platter different and more delicious than the last. By the time the instruments were powered up, he had a full belly, a goblet of warm, spiced ale, and enough snacks hidden away behind his organ to last the night. Sipping his ale, he checked the amps and preamps, double-checked the tone resonators, and ran through a soft low-power scale, from short wavelength sounds to the highest supersonics imaginable.

The immense Hutt shifted on his throne. Huge reddish-brown eyes peered at Max suspiciously for a second, then Jabba barked a low sound.

"My master bids you to play," a silver translator droid said.

"This is it," Max said to Sy and Droopy. He felt really, really good. So good he didn't even mind when Sy called out the first song—"Lapti Nek"—instead of him.

He ran through the intro in double time, hit the first notes, Sy came in on cue, followed by Droopy, and they were blasting away as if they had nothing in the world but their music. The woodwinds arced and fluttered, the organ ground smoothly, and Sy hit the high warbles as if she were playing for the Emperor himself. He felt the thrumming vibration on high notes through his ears and the subtle, almost dainty counterpoint melody in the tympanic organs in his snout. It was beautiful, Max thought, the best they'd ever played. It was almost as good as dinner had been earlier that evening, and it went on and on as they chased riffs and melodies through a dozen variations on the opening chorus.

When they finally came up for air, there was perfect silence for a long moment. Max looked around. Hadn't their performance been good? Why wasn't anyone clapping?

Everyone seemed to be looking at Jabba. Max too gazed at the huge, sluglike Hutt. Slowly Sy bowed, then Droopy, and then Max remembered to do the same.

Suddenly Jabba's immense sluglike body shook with laughter. The Hutt's huge, tapered tail rose and fell, rose and fell with a thudding noise.

"My master is pleased," said the translator droid.

Max beamed. "Then we have a contract?"

Jabba growled an answer.

"His Immense Eminence is pleased to grant you a lifetime contract," the droid translated. "As you are an Ortolan, and know the value of food, he wishes to pay you in that medium—all you and your band can eat in exchange for a lifetime contract."

"Done!" Max cried. He'd never heard of so fine, so magnanimous a deal in his life. He glanced at Sy and was dismayed to find her glaring at him.

Jabba spoke again, and the droid said, "Keep playing."

When Jabba turned away, the crowd around him moved forward, clamoring for attention. Max keyed in the intro to an old starfarers' song Evar Orbus had redone for jizz-wailer orchestration. Jabba's huge tail, Max noticed, twitched now and then almost in time to the music, but other than that the Hutt seemed oblivious to their playing.

Never mind, though. Max swelled out his chest. He'd struck a deal any Ortolan would be proud of. All the food he could eat for life—incredible! They'd never believe his good fortune back home.

After their fourth set, Sy Snootles managed to pull Naroon Cuthas away from Jabba's side. She couldn't believe what Max had agreed to. Playing for food— what kind of deal was that? How could they possibly earn enough to get off this horrible planet?

"About the deal," she began.

"Indeed, it went better than I had dared hope," Cuthas said, smiling. "Jabba really likes your music."

"That's not what I meant. The terms simply aren't acceptable."

"But everything's agreed," Cuthas said. "You told me Max was the band's leader. He agreed to a contract with Jabba. Now you tell me it isn't acceptable? If you have a problem, it seems to me you should talk to Max Rebo."

"But—I was just letting Max front for me!"

"Jabba doesn't like it when people back out on deals."

"Surely there's some room for negotiation!"

Cuthas leaned closer, his voice dropping to an almost conspiratorial whisper. "The last band tried to renegotiate their contract. Jabba dropped them into the rancor pit."

"The rancor pit?"

"The floor in front of the throne opens up. Jabba keeps an immense, ravenous rancor below . . . it made very short work of the last band. Just a few tweets and they were gone. And see that man over there?" He pointed into a dim alcove, where a screaming man encased in carbonite hung on the wall.

"Yes," Sy said.

"He was a smuggler who broke a deal with Jabba. Jabba keeps him there as a reminder to other employees."

Sy swallowed. "I see what you mean," she said. She shot Max a violent look, but he didn't notice. He seemed entirely happy with the plate of bantha steaks a droid had brought him.

Sy Snootles looked around her quarters with a measure of disgust and revulsion. How could they expect her to live in such a hovel? The bedclothes were soiled, filth caked the walls, and the floor had something dark and sticky spattered across it.

She turned to complain, but Cuthas had already gone off with Max and Droopy. She went out into the hall. They were gone.

A droid stood at attention nearby, though, so Sy

crossed over to address it: "You there. What's your name?"

"M3D2."

"My room requires cleaning."

"The housekeeping staff is located on level three, room 212."

"Thank you. Please inform them."

"That is not my function."

"What is your function?"

"You are the singer Sy Snootles?"

Sy paused. Why would a droid ask that? "Yes," she answered cautiously.

"I have a message for you. It must be delivered in private."

"In here." Sy moved back to let it into her room. Who would send her a private message here? Did she know someone on this awful world? And what could a droid have to say that could possibly be so private?

"I have a message from the Lady Valarian," it began. "Jabba has long been a rival of hers, and she is looking for additional spies in this palace . . ."

Max barely glanced at his room before pronouncing it satisfactory. He had, after all, requested quarters close to the kitchens. His proboscis told him food lay only a few doors away. Now that the first faint stirrings of hunger had begun, he was eager to find a bedtime snack before turning in.

"Come," Cuthas said to Droopy, and he led the Kitonak off.

Max nodded happily. All in all, a successful day. He had a new job, he had a lifetime contract, and all the food he could eat. Life was good.

Shutting the door to his room, he followed his nose to the kitchens. He had to compliment the chef on the appetizers before getting his snack. No telling what desserts he might find waiting for him each day if the two of them became friends.

"Hey, you," said a loud, gruff voice. "You are a Kitonak, aren't you?"

Droopy McCool raised his head slowly and stared at the Gamorrean guard standing in the open doorway to his room. The guard stared back at him.

"Yes," Droopy finally said.

"I thought so," the guard said. He stared back at Droopy.

"Why?" Droopy finally said.

"I saw Kitonaks in the deep desert once," he said.

"Oh," Droopy said.

The next time he looked up, the Gamorrean had gone away. Still, it was enough to get his slow, slow mind moving.

Other Kitonaks in the deep desert . . . interesting.

Sy Snootles stared at the small fortune on her bed and pondered what to do. At first she had intended to report Lady Valarian's offer to one of Jabba's lieutenants in case it had been a test of some kind. But since then, she hadn't had a moment to herself. Person after person kept knocking on her door making her offers to spy for them. All told, she had sixteen different commissions to work for sixteen different parties. Each had left a "token payment" for her services, ranging from a few dozen credits to a hundred and fifty. Now all sixteen pouches sat in a neat little row on her bed.

Of course, she'd agreed to spy for everyone.

It seemed there might be more money than she'd suspected in working for Jabba the Hutt . . . and from all the wrong sources. At this rate, she'd have enough to get off planet in just a few weeks.

She sat on a low chair, ignoring the mess on the walls, ignoring the sticky patches on the floor, ignoring the unkempt bedclothes, and waiting for the next knock.

It came a few seconds later.

"Come!" she called.

A humanoid slipped in—a Twi'lek with one of his twin head tentacles wrapped around his neck. Sy had seen him in Jabba's throne room earlier, she recalled, standing near the Hutt and whispering things to him. She swallowed. This was certainly her most powerful visitor so far.

He glanced at the bed, at the line of pouches, then looked at her and smiled. It was not a pretty look, Sy thought with a little shiver.

"You have been busy tonight," he said. "Sixteen visitors so far. I think you can expect two, possibly three more tonight, and a few others over the next week."

"I was going to tell Jabba about it in the morning," Sy began.

"No need, my dear." He moved closer. "I am Bib Fortuna, and one of my jobs is heading up security for Jabba. I *want* you to take commissions from everyone who offers you one. Inform me as you are contacted. I will let you know what news to pass on." He drew a small pouch from his belt and handed it to her. "Jabba pays *much* better than piddling second-raters like these . . . as you will learn."

"Thank you," Sy said, hardly daring to believe her good luck.

"Think nothing of it, my dear," Bib Fortuna said. He took one look around her room, sniffed once, and as he left, added, "The housekeeping staff is located on level three, room 212. I suggest you get the room deloused before you spend the night."

3. How the Band Became a Duo

Jabba's throne room was really grooving, Max thought. In the months they'd been playing there, things hadn't been better. The rancor had been fed, which always made Jabba happy, Sy was wailing for all she was worth, her stomach gyrating, and the droids had just served him a pair of small Largess cakes, courtesy of Porcellus the chef.

"Ooooh-che-nah!" she sang. "I eee-eeee-eat my young!"

Max upped the power on the amps and went into a quick solo. Nothing like dazzling fingerwork to keep your appetite up, he thought smugly.

A blaster sounded close by, and Max let the music fade out. What was going on? Jabba didn't like it when blaster fights broke out. Someone would certainly feed the rancor tonight, he thought.

A scruffy-looking bounty hunter appeared with a Wookiee in tow. "I have come for the bounty on this Wookiee," he said.

Jabba laughed, his whole body shaking. "At last we have the mighty Chewbacca," he said through his new gold translator droid. "Welcome, bounty hunter. I will gladly pay you the reward of twenty-five thousand."

"Fifty thousand!" the bounty hunter chirped. "No less."

Jabba hit his droid in anger and snarled, "Why do I have to pay fifty thousand?"

"Because I'm holding a thermal detonator!" the bounty hunter said. He held out a silver sphere. His thumb touched the button on top and the detonator activated.

If he let go, the sphere would explode, Max knew, destroying the whole throne room and everyone in it. He covered his face. This was enough to put him off supper!

"The bounty hunter is my kind of scum, fearless and inventive," Jabba announced after a good laugh. Max uncovered his face. "I offer the sum of thirty-five," Jabba said through his droid.

"Very well," said the bounty hunter.

"He agrees!" cried the droid.

As the Gamorrean guards moved forward and took the Wookiee away, Sy said, "Hit it!"

Max gave a two-beat lead, then they launched into "Galactic Dance Blast." It had a rhythm, was easy to play, and Max knew he wouldn't mess it up even though his hands were trembling. A thermal detonator! At least it hadn't gone off. He'd have extra helpings at dinner tonight, he thought, to calm his nerves.

Jabba kept them playing for the next few hours. Something seemed to be up—something big—but Sy was too busy singing to pick up on what it was, though she listened intently.

When Max finally shut down his organ for the evening, Sy stepped down and started for her room. Bib Fortuna caught her arm.

"No," he said to all of them. "Don't break down yet."

"I don't understand," Sy said. "It's dinnertime."

"Jabba's planning a party for later tonight."

"But what about dinner?" Max said. "It's in my contract!"

"Get it if you want, but bring it back here. You're going to sleep in the throne room tonight. Jabba's orders."

Sy swallowed. "Of course," she said, "if that's what Jabba wants."

Max turned to Droopy. "Come on, let's get some dinner. Take-out!"

"Take-out," the Kitonak echoed.

"Bring me some, too," Sy said. "And this time don't eat it on the way back here, Max!"

Later that evening, behind a curtain that masked the throne room from the display alcove where the smuggler in carbonite hung, Max lay listening intently. First he heard a metallic jangle, then soft footsteps as someone stole rather ineptly into the room. Then came a dull boom. He saw Jabba tense, then lean forward to look out through a small hole in the curtain.

Suddenly Jabba began to laugh. Those closest to him laughed as well. As the curtain rolled aside, everyone was laughing, so Max joined in. At last he could see what was so funny.

The bounty hunter who had used the thermal detonator to blackmail Jabba had set the smuggler encased in carbonite free! And beneath the mask, the bounty hunter was a beautiful woman. Her face looked familiar, Max thought. Wasn't that Princess Leia Organa of Alderaan? But Alderaan had been destroyed years before. Hadn't the whole royal family died as well?

Jabba said, "So, I have finally caught up with you again, Solo. What do you have to say for yourself?"

"Hey, Jabba, look, Jabba, I was just on my way to pay you back," the smuggler said, blinking frantically and rubbing his eyes, "and I got a little sidetracked. It's not my fault—"

"It's too late for that, Solo," Jabba said. "You may have been a good smuggler, but now you're bantha fodder."

Everyone around him laughed, so Max laughed, too. No sense standing out, he thought. Food jokes were funny.

"Look—"

"Take him away."

"Jabba, I'll pay you triple. You're throwing away a fortune here. Don't be a fool."

The guards seized the smuggler's arms and hauled him away.

"Now," said Jabba, "bring her to me." By "her" he meant Princess Leia.

Two of the Gamorrean guards took Leia's arms and led her forward toward the throne.

"We have powerful friends," she said as they shoved her up on Jabba's dais. "You're going to regret this."

"I'm sure," Jabba said. He pressed his lips close to her and extended his tongue, and Max wondered if he intended to eat her.

"Play," Jabba commanded.

Max dropped his cup and scrambled toward his organ.

As the band launched into "Ode to a Radioactive Ruin," two dancing girls stripped off Leia's clothes and gave her a skimpy gold outfit to wear. She was a scrawny thing underneath the battle armor, Max decided, and definitely malnourished. He'd have to see if he could slip her an extra meal or three to fatten her up properly.

It took hours for the party to die. When it finally did, everyone just lay down where they were and dozed off.

Max still had a few small blatberry pies tucked away behind his organ. He picked one out and carried it to Jabba's dais. There he set it next to Princess Leia, who looked at him with an unhappy expression.

"In case you get hungry," he said softly.

"Thanks," she whispered.

He smiled a little, nodded politely, and headed for his room.

•   •   •

When he learned that Jabba planned a day trip out across the Dune Sea, Max had droids carry their instruments out to the sail barge and set them up on the lower deck. It was a beautiful cloudless day, the portals were open, and a warm breeze blew through. They'd have a great view of everyone and everything around them. Nothing like a trip to build your appetite, Max thought.

As always, Sy showed up late. At least she was dressed and ready for work, so it didn't really matter. Max tuned his organ while Sy did her vocal warm-up exercises, and they were ready to play. Nothing to do now, he thought, except wait for the crowds to arrive.

Droids equipped with huge platters of food and drink were already moving into position around the deck, and Max grabbed a handful of chooca nuts as a G4 unit passed. He accepted a goblet of Chagarian ale from an R2 unit and stashed it under his organ for later.

Toward lunchtime guests began filing aboard. They were all talking about a Jedi Knight—someone named Luke something?—whom Jabba had captured that morning. It seemed the Jedi and his friends were to be thrown to a creature out in the desert.

Max powered up his organ and played a pleasant little instrumental ditty called "Ode to a Master Chef" which he'd written himself, wringing every nuance from the keyboard. He was in top form today, he thought. Life was great in Jabba's palace.

Finally Jabba himself boarded, floating out on his dais. It had repulsorlift coils underneath it, Max saw. So that was how Jabba moved about. This was the first time he'd actually seen the Hutt leave his throne room.

And Jabba still had the princess with him.

When Jabba settled into his place in the observation cabin, Max nodded to Sy and let her call out the next number. As the sail barge turned and headed out into the Dune Sea, the party really got going.

An hour out, the sail barge drew to a stop. Everyone grew still, and Max let his song fade unfinished.

All the window shutters opened and Jabba's dais floated forward.

"Victims of the almighty Sarlacc, His Excellency hopes that you will die honorably," the gold translator droid said through the sail barge's speaker system. "But should any of you wish to beg for mercy, the great Jabba the Hutt will now listen to your pleas."

Max strained to see what was going on outside, but there were too many people crowded around the windows and he couldn't see. From the murmurs around him, though, he got the general idea of what was going on. It seemed the prisoners had refused to beg, insulting Jabba horribly in the process.

Jabba only laughed. After all, Max thought, it wasn't as if the prisoners could do anything. And he knew from long experience that Jabba didn't often give in to begging or pleading. He liked watching people die and never showed any mercy.

"Move him into position," Jabba said.

Max hopped up, straining to see, but couldn't get more than glimpses.

"Put him in!" Jabba commanded.

A murmur came from everyone at the viewports, then suddenly people cried out in alarm. Max heard blaster fire and a hum like nothing he'd ever heard before, an almost electric sound that seemed to grow louder and softer in time to the blaster shots.

Jabba howled in outrage. The window shutters closed and most of the Gamorrean guards on board headed for the top deck. Something had clearly gone wrong, Max thought. He looked at Sy.

"What should we do?" he asked.

"Nothing!" she said. "It's not our problem. We're just the band."

"But—"

"Do you want to get in trouble with Jabba?" she demanded.

Max looked around and finally spotted Jabba at the other end of the observation cabin. "No, no, no!" Jabba was shouting, gesturing with his two tiny arms. Nobody seemed to be paying any attention to him.

Suddenly Princess Leia leaped to action. She smashed the sail barge's environment controls with her chains. The lights failed; a dusky near-darkness dropped over the passenger cabin. Max blinked and let his eyes adapt to the darkness. Princess Leia, he saw, had looped her chain around Jabba's neck and was pulling with all her strength, bracing her legs against his huge back.

He looked around. She shouldn't be doing that. Where were the guards? He took a step toward Jabba, wondering if he should try to help, but Sy put a hand on his arm.

"She's killing him!" he said.

"Let her," Sy said softly. "Our contract's with Jabba. We'll be free once he's dead."

"But it's murder!"

"He's doomed anyway," she said. "Too many people are out to get him."

Max felt torn up inside. His first boss. His first contract. All that food for life. How could he give up security so easily?

Jabba suddenly lolled forward, his tongue protruding. His eyes were flat and glassy. Dead. So much for decisions, Max thought. He'd waited too long.

But perhaps they could get a gig with Princess Leia. She was, after all, a princess. Even if she didn't eat well, she must certainly pay well enough—his needs were modest. Just six or seven meals a day, and snacks to keep him happy.

"Princess," he called. "Is there anything we can do to help?"

She was holding her chain out to one of the droids —the little R2 unit who had been serving drinks earlier. The droid cut through the chains easily.

"Let's get out of here," she said.

"Probably not a bad idea," Sy Snootles said in his ear.

Max hesitated. "What about our equipment?"

"We can always come back for it." Sy ran to the opposite side of the observation cabin, the one facing away from the Sarlacc, and pushed open a shutter.

Outside, Max could see one of the sail barge's huge steering vanes.

"Come on, Droopy," Sy called. "Time to go!"

Droopy followed. Max hesitated a second, gazing back at his organ, then followed. Sounds of battle still came from outside. He didn't want to get caught in any fighting, especially if someone tried to storm the observation cabin to get to Jabba.

A huge explosion suddenly rocked the barge. Sy almost fell out the window as the sail barge shifted. More sounds of blaster fire came from the top deck.

"Quickly!" Sy called. "Jump!"

"Are you crazy?" Max demanded.

Droopy jumped without a second's hesitation.

"Come on, Max," Sy said. "It's not that far, and you can slide down the steering vane most of the way. There's sand below. It'll help break your fall."

Turning, she jumped.

Max pushed open the shutter and looked down. It seemed like an awfully long way. He hesitated. Droopy helped Sy up. They both looked unhurt.

"Jump!" Sy Snootles called. "Max—jump!"

Something exploded behind Max, and the force of

the blast was like a shove in Max's back. He flew out the viewport, over Sy and Droopy, and hit the sand flat on his back.

The fall stunned him. His hands and face stung, and a ringing sound filled his ears. He was distantly aware of someone picking him up and carrying him away from the sail barge, which seemed to be burning. He raised his head just in time to see the barge explode in a huge orange fireball.

So much for their first gig, he thought. So much for their instruments. So much for his great contract.

"Where are we going?" he managed to ask. He looked over at Sy. She had a little comlink out.

"We have a new gig," she said. "Working for the Lady Valarian."

"No," Droopy said.

"What?" Sy demanded. "For what she's paying, we can get new instruments."

"I'm going into the desert," Droopy said slowly. "There are brothers out there."

"You mean Kitonaks?" Max asked.

"Yes," Droopy said. "They are near. I hear them."

Max listened as hard as he could, and sure enough as the ringing in his ears and nose faded, he heard a distant wail like Kitonak pipes. But how could there be Kitonaks on Tatooine?

"It's probably just the wind," he said. "That sound can't be Kitonaks. What would they be doing out here?"

"Living," Droopy said. He set Max down, turned, and walked across the dunes without another word.

"Well," Sy said. "I guess that makes us a duo."

"The Max Rebo Duo," Max said. He smiled. "It has a nice ring."

"This time," Sy said, "things are going to be different. I'm going to negotiate the contracts."

"Okay," Max said. "As long as there's plenty of food."

"Or plenty of money to buy food," she said.

"Agreed!" He stuck out his hand. "Partners?"

"Partners," she agreed. Then she activated her comlink. "Lady Valarian wants us there," she said. "Send a landspeeder to pick us up. Who? Me and my partner, of course." Then she laughed. "Tonight? It's a little soon, but if you can get the instruments, we can be ready."

"And food," Max said. "Don't forget the food."

"And food," she added. "We'll need plenty of that."

Of the Day's Annoyances:
Bib Fortuna's Tale

by M. Shayne Bell

I *will roll Jabba off his throne on the day of my coup,* Bib Fortuna thought as he walked from Jabba's throne room to plot with the B'omarr monks. *My guards will pull him onto the grille over the rancor's pit. I will let him lie there for a moment to watch the rancor raging below him, to hear its roars, to know that when I open the trapdoor to let him fall, the rancor will eat him, and to know, finally, that I*

will inherit his fortune and criminal organization and he cannot stop me!

Fortuna walked quickly down the sandy stairs spiraling in shadow to the dungeons below. *Behind the stones of this stairwell lies the chute Jabba will slide down to the rancor's pit,* Fortuna thought. *Jabba will watch my hand hover over the button that opens the trapdoor and know he is about to die.* Fortuna smiled. He touched the stones and imagined the steep chute behind them. He had calculated the dimensions of Jabba's bloated body and concluded that, if doused in grease, Jabba could still slide down the chute. Jabba's dousing in grease would be wonderfully ignominious: Fortuna imagined the kitchen staff rushing up from the kitchens with pots of hot grease, their joy as they threw it on Jabba, their pleasure at ultimate revenge for their sons and daughters Jabba had used as tasters and for their colleagues thrown to the rancor when a dish failed. Fortuna had ordered Porcellus, the chief cook, and his staff to save grease in old pots: they did not know why, but they would soon.

It would be a happy day.

Fortuna walked past the prisoners' dark cells. Some cells were quiet. Moans came from others. The sound of sobbing from one. Fortuna took stock of them all and the prisoners in them: *I will set this prisoner free,* Fortuna thought. *This one I will execute. These others I will sell into slavery.* Fortuna intended his justice to be swift and final.

The passageway wound on and became quieter, and suddenly the floor was free of sand. It had been swept clean. The monks lived past that point. Fortuna stopped, took off his sandals, and beat them against the stone wall to knock the sand out of them: a sign of respect for the monks. He would not bring more of the filth of Jabba's occupation of their palace into the places where they lived. How the filth of the parts of the palace out of their control must distress them! Fortuna swore he would let the monks clean the palace thoroughly, once, before he drove them out forever, before they could turn against him. He pulled on his sandals and walked on.

Fewer and fewer candles, guttering in their niches, lighted the passageway. The shadows deepened. At times Fortuna walked in complete darkness, but he never hesitated. He walked straight ahead with confidence. He knew this passageway. He had come here many times to learn the secrets of the monks and to plot with them. But the lower levels were cool, and Fortuna pulled his cloak tighter around him.

A shadow moved down the passageway ahead. Metal scraped against bare stone. Fortuna stopped and analyzed the darkness around him: his intuition sensed no danger. But he heard movement again, in the darkness, coming toward him. He drew his blaster and crouched back against the wall as the shadow of a giant spider as tall as Fortuna loomed up. The spider itself crawled out of the shadows and scrabbled past Fortuna. Fortuna relaxed, barely, but kept the blaster in his hand: just a brain walker, he told himself, a machine shaped like a spider that carried an enlightened monk's disembodied brain in a jar attached to the underbelly. Harmless. But even so he hated it. Brain walkers unsettled him. He watched lights at the base of the brain jar blink in calm greens and blues, as if part of a fluorescent bauble on a vain man-sized spider. Perhaps it meant to join Jabba at his dinner. They would do that: the brains talked through speakers on the jar in foolish attempts to instruct Jabba about the nature of the universe and promote his enlightenment. It always amused Jabba and his dinner guests.

Fortuna remembered the first time he had seen a brain walker. He had not thought it amusing then. As

Jabba's new majordomo, Fortuna had been hungry to learn everything about the palace—its main corridors, its secret corridors and rooms, its dungeons, its people and their routines. One evening he accompanied the kitchen staff on their rounds feeding prisoners. Just as they reached the first cell, a monstrous spider stumbled into them, upsetting a soup pot and splashing hot soup on Fortuna's robes. Fortuna fired his blaster and hit the brain jar and the spider's underbelly. The jar exploded, and the brain flopped onto the sandy passageway. The spider short-circuited with pops and shooting sparks.

Only then had Fortuna realized that the spider was a machine.

No one spoke, not the cooks or the guards or the prisoners standing in the open doorway of their cell. The spider unnerved them, too. Monks rushed up to collect the brain, and one explained that when a monk became enlightened, other monks trained as surgeons cut out his brain and placed it in a maintenance jar filled with a nutrient-rich solution. From there, the brain contemplated the cosmos, freed from the body's distractions.

Fortuna gagged at the thought. He hurried back toward Jabba's throne room, stained robes and all, to advise Jabba to order the monks exterminated. Their ways were intolerable. It astonished him that two distinct cultures lived in the palace, anyway: Jabba's criminal organization, and these monks. For generations, criminals had occupied parts of the monastery the monks had built, turning it into a palace, taking all the best rooms, using more and more of its space. It was time to take it all.

But suddenly Fortuna had stopped. *He* was angry that any monks were left here at all. How must *they* feel about the presence of Jabba and his minions in their palace? Surely they were discontented. Fortuna believed he could turn their discontent to his advantage: side with them in their complaints, pretend to learn from them, guide them into open plotting to rid the palace of Jabba, mold them into an unsuspected force he could call on when the day came for him to seize control.

How well his plan had worked! The monks were now trained and equipped to take the palace. There were hundreds of monks still in bodies—and hundreds of others in brain jars and walkers: enough to quickly overpower unsuspecting guards. And Fortuna *had* learned from the monks. He did not have to pretend that. They had much to teach. He learned how to intuitively sense the plots swirling around Jabba, the petty thieveries planned, the twisted physical cravings. They taught him his life's work had been fated—and he took their teachings even further: he believed the universe had made it possible for him to acquire the power and wealth necessary to conquer Ryloth, his homeworld, to mold his people, the Twi'leks, into the kinds of subjects the Empire valued: bounty hunters, mercenaries, spies—not merely exotic slaves—and save what he could of them. By "chance," Fortuna controlled Nat Secura, the last descendant of a great Twi'lek house. Nat was vital to his plan: the people would rally to Nat (and Fortuna's indirect leadership) when it came time to conquer Ryloth. The Twi'leks would remember what Fortuna had done for them forever.

The names of his ancestors would be honored again.

He would be honored.

But there was work ahead, and he must be ready for it. The time for happy imaginings was past. He called up safeguards in his mind that hid his darkest thoughts and hurried on.

Only one monk waited for him in the council cham-

ber, and he was not sitting in meditation. He paced
the floor. "Master Fortuna," he said. "We thought
you would not come. Your friend is in great danger."

"What friend?" Fortuna asked. He had no friends.

"Nat Secura. Jabba is about to feed him to the rancor."

Fortuna whirled from the room and rushed back
down the passageway. Jabba hated Nat because he was
ugly: Nat had been horribly burned in fires Jabba's
slavers set in Nat's city to force its inhabitants out and
into their nets. His face and body were scarred. His
lekku, the head-tails Twi'leks sign with for much of
their communication, were nearly burned off. Nat
could only communicate with his voice—a terrible
handicap—but he was still who he was. Fortuna had
found Nat in the rubble of the city and realized what a
prize he was: of greater worth than jewels. Feed him to
the rancor, indeed!

After Fortuna stopped running, smoothed out his
robes, caught his breath, and walked into the throne
room, he found this: Nat, bound, flogged, lying
facedown on the grille. The rancor roared below him
and held its mouth open for Nat's dripping blood.
The shameful tatters of Nat's lekku were splayed out
above the grate: someone had torn off the head covering Fortuna made Nat wear. Jabba's crowd of sycophants and puppets jeered and taunted Nat over their
dinners. Jabba's own hand hovered inches from the
button that would open the trapdoor, but when Jabba
saw Fortuna he rumbled his deep bass laugh and motioned Fortuna to his throne.

"Nat is so ugly," Jabba said. "I want to see if the
rancor will eat him, or if it will throw him back up at
us."

The rancor would do that. It threw those it found

unappetizing against the grille again and again till the body became an unrecognizable pulp the keeper dragged out the next day. The grille was dark with the blood of those the rancor had rejected.

"Then you will miss the sport Nat could provide," Fortuna said.

"What sport?" Jabba rumbled.

Fortuna was thinking fast, trying to find a way to save Nat. "Nat is a runner," he said, "and a tumbler. He could elude the rancor for a time."

Jabba loved watching such sport through the grille. Everyone knew it. He moved his hand toward the button.

"But not now," Fortuna said quickly. "Not after a flogging. Give him two days to recover, then send him to the pit. It will be a great diversion for us all."

"You betrayed me!" Nat shouted at Fortuna's back. "I should never have trusted you. I—"

Fortuna raised his hand. Nat fell silent at once. Fortuna had trained him well, and obedience was an early lesson. "Master?" Fortuna asked Jabba. Jabba hesitated, considering. Fortuna could not take his eyes off Jabba's hand over the button.

"Two days then," Jabba said, finally, moving his hand back. "I look forward to it."

Fortuna called two Gamorrean guards to lift Nat from the grille and drag him down to the dungeons. Fortuna followed. The guards stopped by the first cell, which was already crowded. "Not there!" Fortuna said. "I will not incarcerate Nat with others who might kill him or maim him to spoil Jabba's fun. Follow me."

He led them down the passageway to the farthest cell. It was unoccupied. "Put him in here," he said.

The guards threw Nat into the cell, slammed and locked the door, and walked grumbling away. Fortuna stood looking through the bars in the door. Nat lay on the stone floor. He would not or could not sit up to look at Fortuna. It made communicating more difficult, since much of what Fortuna wanted to say he could sign with his lekku so no one else would understand. He did not want to speak aloud for others to overhear. But finally Fortuna did speak four words: "I will save you."

He turned and walked away—not back to Jabba's throne room, but down the passageway to the monks. He knew of just one way to save Nat.

Only then, while walking in the swept passageway of the monks, did Fortuna wonder how *they* had known that this would happen, when he had not.

Fortuna led the monks' surgeons to Nat's cell before dawn of the second day. He wanted the procedure completed well before Jabba ordered Nat thrown to the rancor. "Leave the brain stem so the body will still breathe," Fortuna said.

"No!" Nat screamed. He realized what the surgeons had come to do. "Don't let them take out my brain!"

Fortuna did not worry at all that the other prisoners could hear Nat. They would try to ignore him, if they could, and hope such horrors would not happen to them. But a Gamorrean guard was hurrying toward them. He did not ask what Fortuna and the surgeons were doing.

"I will tell Jabba that you tortured this prisoner and spoiled the sport," he told Fortuna.

"Then I will tell Jabba that since you informed on me, you obviously cannot keep secrets and must be fed to the rancor with Nat."

The guard snuffled and stepped back. *So stupid—so easily manipulated,* Fortuna thought. A mistake of Jabba's, taking these beings as guards.

"Then I will not tell if you will not," the guard said. "Be quick about your work."

He walked away. Fortuna set his blaster to stun and looked at Nat. "This is the only way I know to save you," Fortuna signed with his lekku, then he shot Nat through the bars of the door. Nat fell to the floor—but his arms twitched as if, though stunned, he were still trying to pull himself up to fight to save his body. Fortuna unlocked the cell door and swung it wide. The surgeons wheeled their squeaking cart in ahead of them.

Fortuna did not follow. He did not want to watch. The sight of gore did not bother him in the slightest, but Fortuna believed it would show a lack of respect for Nat if he stood behind the surgeons to watch them wash Nat's head and cut into it.

So Fortuna paced in front of the cell, impatient for the surgeons to be done. He remembered finding Nat as a child in the smoking rubble of Nat's family home on Ryloth. Fortuna had gone there, looking for jewels. But before he found any, he found Nat in the arms of his mother. She was conscious.

"You!" she said, from where she lay, unable to get up to defend herself or save her child. "Bib Fortuna—I should have recognized your corrupt hand behind this attack. Only you would bring slavers upon your own people."

She said his name with such hatred, such loathing, that Fortuna stepped back. Fortuna had been among the first to sell the addictive ryll spice off-world, and thus attract the attention of the Empire to Ryloth. Twi'leks he thought his friends sat in judgment on him and condemned him to death for bringing slavers and pirates and renegades of all kinds upon them. He escaped. They confiscated his family's holdings and put a price on his head. He came back for revenge.

He had had that revenge. Seven cities lay in ruin,

their people sold into slavery, their riches going, most of it, to Jabba, but some of it, secretly, to Fortuna.

Yet it was not what he had wanted, after all. The demand for ryll spice was greater than he or anyone could have predicted, and it would suck his world dry and destroy it. Fortuna did not hate his own people so utterly. He tried promoting trade in the cheaper, less effective—less lucrative—glitterstim spice from Kessel to divert attention from ryll and Ryloth to no avail: the demand for spice of any kind would tear apart both planets. He had thought the Twi'leks would adapt to life in the wider Empire—Twi'leks always adapted—but events had happened too quickly. They had to be shown the way. Fortuna realized that, and his responsibility to show it to them, when Nat's mother spoke to him in the rubble of her home. He drew his blaster and stepped back up to her, pointed the blaster at her head.

"Coward," she said.

He shot her, and she died at once. Shooting her had not been an act of cowardice, he told himself. It had been an act of kindness. He had saved her from the horrors of slavery.

Then Nat moaned.

The child was alive. Fortuna did not shoot him or give him to the slavers. He carried him back to his ship and medical help. He later explained to Jabba that since this was the last son of a great Twi'lek family, it would amuse him to keep Nat for a time. In the years that followed, Fortuna never told Nat he had killed his mother. They planned together how best to save Ryloth from the hell the spice trade and the Empire were turning Ryloth into.

The cell door opened. A surgeon hurried out. He held a brain jar with a brain in it. All the indicator lights at the base of the jar glowed bright red: not a good sign. The lights should have blinked green or blue.

"The brain is screaming," another surgeon told Fortuna: "If it does not gain control of itself soon, it will go insane and die. That is the way of things."

Nat was not enlightened. He was not ready to give up the body. The monks had explained all this to Fortuna, and he had forced them to operate anyway. There *had* been no other way to save him. It was done now.

"We will do all we can to help your friend," another surgeon said. They left, wheeling their cart ahead of them, its squeaks loud in the dungeons.

Fortuna walked into the cell. Nat's body lay on the floor. He knelt to examine it. The surgeons had done excellent work: the sutures that closed the skull back up were undetectable except to the closest examination. The brain stem kept the lungs breathing. The heart still beat. Fortuna's own heart raced in his chest. He would die for this, if Jabba found out before Fortuna could kill Jabba. Fortuna straightened Nat's robes. He tied a bright red scarf around Nat's disfigured lekku. He turned the body onto its back and gently brushed the sand from its face. The face was so scarred, tortured.

Then, with a sudden clarity, Fortuna realized why the universe had ordered events this way. Nat had to lose this body. No one on Ryloth would have recognized him. Soon, Fortuna would control Jabba's vast fortune. He could locate and employ the services of those who practiced the illegal arts of cloning and clone Nat a new and perfect body to put his brain in. When they returned to Ryloth, Nat would be able to communicate more effectively—if he survived the next few days. Fortuna resolved to go to him later to give him the hope of cloning to hold on to.

• • •

Later that morning, when Jabba ordered Nat thrown to the rancor, Fortuna dispatched two guards to drag Nat's body to the trapdoor in front of Jabba's throne. "Nat has fainted from fear," he told them quietly. "But he will surely awake on his descent to the rancor." They believed him. Much depended on the events of the next few minutes and whether Jabba would accept them.

The guards flung Nat's body onto the trapdoor and Jabba hit the button at once—as Fortuna had hoped he would. The trapdoor dropped open, and the body plunged down to the rancor's pit. Jabba's sycophants crowded around the grille to watch the rancor eat Nat. Jabba pressed buttons that rolled his throne to the edge so he could see, too.

Nat's body lay facedown in the sand below. The rancor roared at it, but it did not move.

"Nat won't run!" Jabba shouted. "Why won't he run?"

The rancor seized the body and ate it in three bites. Blood spattered through the grille onto Fortuna's hands and robes and face, and the hands and robes and faces of everyone around the pit. The rancor looked up at them and belched and roared.

But everyone in Jabba's throne room was quiet. They all expected Jabba to be angry. "Nat must have come to hate you," Fortuna told Jabba, in the relative silence. "He knew it would please you to see him run, so he would not run."

Someone laughed. Sy Snootles started humming a tune. Max Rebo began pounding his keyboard. And Jabba finally laughed. "He ate him—the rancor ate him. It has no aesthetic sense." Jabba rolled his throne back to its original position, away from the grille, while the music picked up and palace life returned to normal.

Jabba believed what Fortuna had told him. He never suspected what had just happened. Fortuna walked thoughtfully through the milling crowd of galactic toughs of all species, toughs he hoped to make his people a part of, rubbing at the speckles of Nat's blood on his hands.

When he could, later that night, Fortuna hurried to the monks and Nat's brain. He went first to the Great Room of the Enlightened, where the brain jars sat on shelves and the brain walkers waited below them. One embodied monk was dusting. "Nat would not stop screaming, so we had to move him to a cell of his own," the monk said. "He was disturbing the enlightened ones."

The monk led Fortuna to the cell. The brain jar holding Nat's brain sat alone on a table. All the lights at the base of the jar glowed bright red in the darkness.

The monk lit two candles in niches near the door and left quietly. Fortuna sat at the table and put his hands on the jar for a time. The brain was a ghastly sight: raw, white in places, suspended in a solution Nat's blood discolored red. The monks would change the solution daily for three days till there was no more blood and the solution stayed clear.

Fortuna pressed a button at the base of the jar that made it "hear" for the brain. "Nat," he said, "this was the only way I knew to save you. Believe me."

He went on to tell him his plans for cloning, but then another idea came to him. "Perhaps we can find a holding body to put your brain in till we clone a body of your own."

The more he thought of it, the more Fortuna liked

that idea: kidnap someone acceptable, discard the brain, and put Nat's brain in the body for a time. The sensations of a living, breathing body would surely help keep Nat's brain sane till it could be put into Nat's own clone.

He would speak to the surgeons about it.

When he left Nat's cell an hour later, one third of the lights glowed rose, even pink: not bright red.

Fortuna returned to Jabba's throne room to sleep. He had to sleep there. Jabba's paranoia required that everyone close to him sleep around him at night—supposedly to protect him from assassins, but in reality so the guards could watch them all and keep *them* from assassinating Jabba. The routine had grown lax. The guards slept along with everyone else. Fortuna had even stopped lecturing them about it.

But he would get new guards when he was in control.

Fortuna could not sleep. He sensed goings-on in the palace he could not pin down and that he could not attribute to the anxieties of the day—probabilities swirling in the subconscious undercurrent of life around Jabba. But the monks had trained him well. Things would come clear again, he was confident of that. Beings from all parts of the galaxy constantly came and went here, and it sometimes took days to sort out the true purposes of their visits. Meanwhile, the monks would advise him, as they had advised him about Nat. Fortuna had allies no one suspected.

Fortuna lifted his head and looked at Jabba, so close to his own public bed. He could smell Jabba's alien, musky sweat in the heat of the night, and he wrinkled his nose and began a ritual that often calmed him so he could sleep. *Of the day's annoyances, these,* Fortuna counted silently. *That Jabba still lives.* That was the chief and foremost of every day's list of annoyances.

But Jabba would die soon.

Fortuna's preparations were nearly complete: securing the final sets of codes to Jabba's scattered bank accounts, testing the loyalty of the last few he needed to stand by him during the coup. He had little left to do. But besides his own plot, Fortuna knew of fourteen others against Jabba's life, plots he would not stop now. It was always wise to make contingency plans, and he had fourteen sets of plotters doing just that for him. He would simply watch them, and guide them where possible. He hoped he would beat the others and actually have the pleasure of murdering Jabba, but it did not much matter to him, as long as it got done at roughly the correct time. However Jabba's death came about, Fortuna would end up in charge. He would control the bulk of the fortune.

Some plots were quite entertaining: the Anzati assassin, for instance, in the pay of both Lady Valarian *and* Eugene Talmont, the Imperial prefect—an amusing confusion of patrons for that assassin. There was Tessek, a fussy little Quarren Jabba wanted killed, who himself plotted to kill Jabba. A simple plot Fortuna favored was that of a kitchen boy who had planned to poison Jabba because several years earlier Jabba had fed his brother to the rancor after a sauce failed. So many here hated Jabba, and Jabba relished their hatred—one of his many great mistakes, Fortuna thought. Jabba believed his acts of cruelty made beings everywhere fear him, and he thought fear protected him. But fear endured for days and months and years turns to hatred. Hatred spawns plots for revenge. Fortuna planned to run things differently.

He lay back and smiled to himself. Fourteen assassination plots—and beyond that, sixty-eight plots to rob the palace. There was no end to the plotting.

Of the day's other annoyances, these, he continued. That he had found it necessary to watch Nat's body be destroyed. That he had had to threaten the monks to get them to remove Nat's brain. That the delivery of two-headed effrikim worms Jabba favored on hot mornings—and whose endorphins induced hours of drowsiness—had not come in, again, thus making the constant supply of other diversions necessary: dancers, liquor, spice. Annoyances, all of them—a day of annoyances.

But of them all, the greatest—the chief annoyance —was that Jabba still lived.

The rancor roared in the pit and banged against the walls of its cage. No one stirred.

Those were common sounds.

The surgeons assured Fortuna that "brain swapping" was possible but rarely tried—and then only when the galaxy needed an embodied spiritual guide and there hadn't been time for one to be born and raised up. In those times, the monks would choose a healthy acolyte and one of the enlightened, and surgeons would swap the brains. Fortuna felt confident that he could force the monks to perform the procedure for Nat.

Fortuna talked to Nat's brain every day, sometimes twice a day, and after two weeks, some lights glowed green and blue. But at least one always glowed bright red: panic was always there in Nat, and it had probably been there too long. The brain was unstable. The monks thought Nat partially insane: he would imagine, for days at a time, that he was blindfolded, his body tied down, and that Fortuna and the monks wouldn't let him up—that he was still in his body. Fortuna once asked him why, if he were just tied down, he couldn't feel his body—and all the lights suddenly glowed red.

"Fit him in a brain walker," he told the monks. "Maybe if he can walk around he will become more sane."

It took Nat days to learn to make the walker move, and his walker was forever stumbling into walls or Fortuna or the monks. Fortuna was afraid he would break his brain jar open, but the monks assured him the jar would not break easily. Nat tried to follow Fortuna wherever he went, and the monks would have to hold Nat back from following Fortuna up to Jabba.

"Don't let it come looking for me!" he ordered the monks. He did not want Nat stumbling around, saying things he shouldn't amongst people who thought the rancor had eaten all of him.

But one day, when the monks were too busy with Spring Equinox ceremonies to watch Nat as closely as Fortuna ordered, Nat did come up to the throne room. His brain walker stumbled down the steps and scraped itself against the stone wall. No one paid it any attention. But it suddenly lurched out toward the center of the room, perilously close to the grille in the floor. Fortuna realized that if two or three of its legs fell through and it couldn't extricate itself, the guards would have to lift it up. Jabba might decide to send it down to the rancor instead. He had never sent a brain walker to the rancor, and Fortuna did not want Jabba to get the idea now.

Jabba had a new protocol droid, a certain C-3PO—a gift from some human egotist who claimed to be a Jedi Knight. Fortuna quickly motioned the golden droid to his side. "Keep that brain walker away from the grille," he said. "Guide it around the perimeter of the room and back down to the monks as soon as possible."

"At once, Master Fortuna," C-3PO said.

But C-3PO soon tapped Fortuna on the shoulder. "The enlightened one wishes to speak with you," he said. "He absolutely refused to return to the monks until he had. I can't imagine what could be so important that he—"

"That's enough," Fortuna said. "I will speak with it. Leave us."

The droid arched its back and walked stiffly away.

"What is it?" Fortuna asked Nat.

"I have found a body—a holding body. You said I could have a body—"

"Yes, yes. Whose is it?"

"I don't remember its name, but it looks like a strong body, and I need a strong body—"

"Where is it, then? Is it in this room?"

Fortuna did not like carrying on this conversation in Jabba's throne room. He did not want anyone to overhear. Two or three were already looking at them. "Tell me now," Fortuna demanded. "Then you must return to the monks."

"The body in the carbonite—it's doing no one any good. Give me the body in the carbonite!"

Fortuna had to smile. "Han Solo?" he said. The idea was delicious to him. Fortuna had many reasons to hate Corellians—Bidlo Kwerve, his rival for the post of majordomo, had been a Corellian. Using Han's body in this way would be a fine revenge on Corellians in general. He looked at the body of Han Solo, frozen in carbonite, hibernating perfectly. Han's head looked roughly the same size as Nat's had been.

"Of course," he told Nat. "You shall have that body. Soon." He did not have to add: when I am in control here. Such an experiment would probably have amused Jabba, but Fortuna could not have explained Nat's—or his own—part in it.

Business took Fortuna into Mos Eisley. He was glad to get away from the palace for the afternoon, but it would be a busy time—arranging for new purveyors to ship the still awaited effrikim to the palace; checking the progress of the reconstruction of Jabba's town house after the fire. Perhaps the most interesting of his duties, however, would be meeting with the human, Luke Skywalker, who claimed to be a Jedi Knight and who had sent droids to Jabba as gifts. The human wanted to bargain for Han Solo, and Fortuna invited him to the town house to hear his offer. This sudden burst of interest in the frozen Corellian amused Fortuna. Perhaps there were ways to make Solo turn a profit yet.

"It would be to your master's advantage to simply let Han go," Skywalker said.

Fortuna laughed. He had expected arrogance from someone claiming to be a Jedi Knight, and he was not disappointed.

"Han Solo cost Jabba dearly, young Jedi," Fortuna said. "How would simply letting him go work to my master's advantage? Besides, I'm certain the Empire would not want Solo wandering about again."

"The government will change," was all Skywalker said in reply.

And suddenly the mists clouding Fortuna's intuition cleared. He identified an astonishing plot afoot in the palace. The Rebellion wanted Han Solo. This human sitting in front of him was a representative of the Rebellion—and others were already in the palace: a guard, the droids, at least those—all part of a grand plot to free Han Solo, for reasons he could not imagine. What would the Rebellion want with a smuggler? Much of the plot was just probability—key figures were not in place yet, Fortuna could sense that. But his interest was piqued. This would be an interesting scenario to watch. Fortuna said nothing of all this to Skywalker. He brought the conversation back to money.

"Solo cost Jabba dearly, as I said. He would expect payment for the shipment of spice Solo dumped if he ever let him go."

"I will pay whatever Han cost Jabba, plus interest, if that is the only deal we can make," Skywalker said. "But *you* do not want money. You want to help your people, though your plans will hurt them more than ever. Free Han, and after you overthrow Jabba—join the Rebellion. The New Republic will put Ryloth under its protection. Ryloth will not be destroyed, as it will be under the Empire, and you will accomplish your goals."

Fortuna could not speak for a moment. The intuitive powers of this young human were strong indeed. Luke's conviction and honesty touched Fortuna's heart. For a brief moment, Fortuna saw a bright future in which people would not have to plot and scheme and connive as he had done all his life. But the moment passed. Fortuna felt the heavy weight of the Empire and its ways settle back down around his mind. The Empire would not be overthrown. He could not entrust the fate of the Twi'lek people to the idealistic dreams of the pitiable Rebellion. Fortuna believed his own plans were, after all, the best.

"Your words move me," he told Skywalker, finally, and he could not resist saying something about his coming overthrow of Jabba. "Some of what you foretold will take place within days. Your friend is best left frozen till then. He will be utterly safe in the carbonite during the troubles that come. But you are wrong about money. I will need great quantities of it to fulfill my dreams. Jabba will not accept your offer of payment with interest for Solo, though I will convey it to him. Rest assured, however, that when the day comes, I will accept."

Skywalker quickly stood and bowed as if the meeting were over, though Fortuna had not had time to offer him a glass of spiced water or finish his other duties as host. This brusqueness was unexpected, and Fortuna wondered if the human was in a hurry to leave because he realized Fortuna knew the truth about him and his plot. That plot would change now, Fortuna was certain of it. He did not stand or return Skywalker's bow.

"I will yet have Solo," Skywalker said, and Fortuna detected no arrogance in what he said, no boasting. His words were a simple statement of what he believed fact.

"You will indeed have your friend after you bring your money to me. You will know when to come," Fortuna said. Skywalker turned and walked away.

Fortuna did not tell the bright-eyed young human exactly how he meant to keep his word. He would sell him what Han Solo would have been reduced to by then: his brain. That was what the guards would deliver to this "Jedi" after they had his money. Such a deal would gain the attention of the Empire and improve Fortuna's standing in it.

Jabba rejected the Jedi's offer and ordered Fortuna not to admit Skywalker—just as Fortuna had predicted. In the time that followed, Fortuna watched those the Rebellion had planted in the palace. The droids, the guard served with excellence. Then even more representatives of the Rebellion were planted, so to speak—taken, even, to Jabba's bosom: a human woman, Leia Organa, one-time princess and Imperial senator—now a dancing slave, after she foolishly unmasked herself and saved Fortuna the trouble of bringing Han Solo out of the carbonite; and the Wookiee, Chewbacca, whom she brought to complete her failed disguise and who was promptly imprisoned, now with his old friend Solo. This plot did not look to be going very well—with key players in it seemingly happy in their employ, others imprisoned or made slaves. Fortuna believed he was right not to put any stock in the Rebellion, if this was the best it could do to rescue someone. He put more stock in the cook's plan to poison Jabba.

But the former princess had managed to do one good thing, as far as Fortuna was concerned: she had brought a thermal detonator into the palace, and Fortuna now had it—after stealing it from a Whiphid guard who had stolen it from the princess during the commotion after her unmasking. No one ever asked what became of it. It alone made a marvelous contingency plan.

Then one morning, Fortuna woke suddenly, before all the others. Something was not right in the palace: someone was in it who should not be, and he was walking toward the throne room. Fortuna sat up and arranged his robes, and his intuition told him who was coming: Luke Skywalker. Fortuna moved quietly and quickly across the throne room and met Skywalker at the top of the steps.

"What are you doing here?" he asked. "You know Jabba has not accepted your offer, and he will not speak to you. You must wait for *me*."

"You will take me to Jabba now," Skywalker said. No explanation. Typical arrogance.

"I will take you to Jabba now," he answered Skywalker.

For a brief moment, Fortuna paused to consider whether the Jedi's tricks could have influenced his mind, but he quickly lost that thought. Surely it could not be so.

Fortuna started back down the stairs and looked at Jabba. Waking him in the morning was a task not lightly undertaken, but he would do it. The incompetent guards were at last stirring and looking in his direction. The human followed Fortuna down the steps and mumbled some nonsense at his back about serving his master well and being rewarded. Fortuna could not repress a smile. He spoke in Jabba's ear: "Luke Skywalker, the Jedi, has come to speak to you."

Jabba was angry at once, and Fortuna braced himself. "I told you not to admit him," Jabba grumbled.

"I must be allowed to speak," Skywalker said. He tried to use his anything-but-subtle mind-manipulation trick on *everyone* in the room.

"He must be allowed to speak," Fortuna said—but Jabba threw Fortuna against the wall. "You weak-minded fool!" he shouted at him.

Fortuna took his time getting up and straightening his robes. No one would look at him. Fortuna felt shamed in front of his supporters. It was a precarious moment. Fortuna had planned to launch his coup within two days; he knew now that it would have to come within hours. His plans would have to change, and change quickly. Once out of Jabba's favor, he would not live long.

Fortuna quickly analyzed his situation. Perhaps Jabba had been correct about his being weak-minded: looking back, Fortuna could believe that Skywalker *had* influenced his mind—but this was no time for self-doubt, not if he were to survive. He wondered how much of his plans Jabba guessed or knew. Much, probably: he would not have reacted violently if he still trusted Fortuna and his judgment. Fortuna let his intuition touch the minds of his supporters, and he was startled: it took no special training in intuition to sense the contempt some now felt for him. Three were even inclined to unmask Fortuna's plot. Fortuna realized that, under the circumstances, his plans might have to become even more abbreviated—before his support eroded further. The arrogant "Jedi" was thrown to the rancor, and in the commotion that followed, with everyone crowding around to watch the rancor eat Skywalker, no one noticed Fortuna steal away for a moment. He soon returned. If his plans had to change quickly—from days, to hours, to perhaps minutes—he could accommodate that. He now had the stolen thermal detonator in his pocket, and he kept a hand on it.

Things did change quickly: Skywalker managed to kill the rancor—to everyone's surprise. Why couldn't he have come earlier? Fortuna wondered. Nat would still be in his body, and valuable slaves and others—including a talented dancing girl—would still be alive. Jabba ordered Skywalker, the Wookiee, and Solo thrown to the Sarlacc and began making preparations for everyone of importance to fly out with him on his barge to witness the executions: and Fortuna and fourteen sets of plotters saw their best chance materialize.

Jabba would never return alive from that trip.

Fortuna decided he would set off the thermal detonator just after he escaped from the barge: killing Jabba and all those Jabba had shamed him in front of. He regretted the probable loss of Solo's body, but would find another for Nat. Fortuna methodically completed preparations for his coup. He had his private skiff placed on the barge for his escape. He left orders for the monks to take over the palace when everyone left with Jabba. He sent out codes that froze all of Jabba's accounts.

His plot was in motion.

All the plots were in motion. Fortuna sat back and, during the ride across the sand, contemplated the many ways Jabba could die on this trip. The situation was enormously amusing. R2-D2, one of the Rebellion's droids, rolled up and offered him his choice of drinks, delicate little sandwiches, pickled effrikim worms (they had finally come in) sure to delight Jabba —and sure to kill him: the worms were all poisoned. Half the drinks were poisoned. The poison was a slow one—those who ingested it would not notice its effect for quite some time. Fortuna could tell which glasses were safe, and he drank freely. He watched Jabba eat a handful of effrikim worms and start the process of his death. Fortuna quietly set the thermal detonator to make sure of it.

C-3PO approached Fortuna and bowed. "Master Fortuna," he said. "May I ask you a question?"

"Certainly."

"Has anyone ever been rescued from the Sarlacc?"

"Not to my knowledge," Fortuna said, and he turned away, not wanting to be bothered with a droid's worries. Still, he wondered why the droid would ask about rescue from the Sarlacc. Fortuna's intuition could not tell him—it was difficult to unravel the motives of mechanical beings. But Fortuna guessed at devotion in the droid. Perhaps another plot was being born here: one to come out to somehow rescue a former master. It touched Fortuna. He thought that, if such devotion could be turned to him, he would welcome it. He turned back to the droid.

"See-Threepio," he said quietly. "My private skiff is hidden near the aft ventilation grate. Go and wait by it. When you see me running toward it, uncover the skiff and climb in."

But the droid never had a chance to go to the skiff. It lingered to witness the executions, and the unexpected took place. The Rebels proved harder to execute than Jabba anticipated, and fighting broke out. In the commotion, Fortuna lost sight of C-3PO. He never knew what became of the droid. But Fortuna stayed on the barge just long enough to learn what actually killed Jabba. It wasn't the poison. It wasn't any of the assassins after their various rewards. It wasn't, in the end, the rigged thermal detonator: Leia, the former princess, strangled Jabba with her chains. Fortuna watched Jabba die, then hurried to his skiff.

He thought he should have expected the unexpected. It was the way of the universe: always to surprise.

The trip back to the palace was a pleasure to Fortuna. The light from the thermal detonation came exactly when he expected it, and the shock wave seemed a pleasant wind: a wind of change. He encountered no Sand People, no sandstorms, no Jawas, even. It was as if, after the explosion, the desert were waiting for something more.

He arrived at the palace in the evening. The gates opened to him at once. Monks met him inside: they had taken the palace.

"Master Fortuna," one of them said. "Did things go as planned on the barge?"

"Jabba is dead. I am in charge now. Call the high monks to the throne room: I must speak with them."

He had been careful not to call it *Jabba's* throne room. It was his now.

Fortuna hurried there and began keying important information into the palace security systems: code words had to be changed, security clearances upgraded or denied, the robotic defense systems put at full alert. Attacks could come from many quarters at a time like this.

But suddenly the main terminal went dead. Then all the terminals went dead. The lights overhead flickered and went out. Fortuna had light from only the candles and torches in their niches.

He hurried across the throne room—and found the main doorway closed and locked.

It had all happened so quietly.

And he knew at once what had happened.

The monks had betrayed him. Somehow, they had sensed his intentions toward them. He should have realized the monks would not want to replace one set of criminals with another—when they could have the whole palace to themselves. It took no special gift of intuition to realize that. He suddenly wondered what he had learned about intuition from the monks, after all—parlor games, children's tricks? There were depths here he had not guessed.

But there were many ways out of the throne room and the palace. He could complete his coup from the town house in Mos Eisley—then come back to take the palace from the monks.

He rushed to the first secret exit, but it was blocked. Every exit was blocked. Fortuna ran to Jabba's dais and hit the button that would drop the grille to the rancor's pit—there were two secret ways out of the pit —but it would not drop open.

Fortuna was trapped.

The secret caches of arms were all emptied. Fortuna had his blaster, but one blaster could not hold off an army of monks.

A terminal flickered to life. A message was typed across its screen. Fortuna hurried to it and read: *You have progressed rapidly on your spiritual path, Brother Fortuna. Your quest is at an end. Prepare yourself for enlightenment.*

Fortuna gripped the terminal for a moment, trying to breathe, then he attempted to enter a reply. The terminal would not accept one. He would have liked to bargain with the high monks—honestly this time— but he doubted they would have listened. They were not coming to the throne room, in any case. He knew who would come for him.

Fortuna sat on one end of Jabba's throne and put his hands in his lap. He knew it would be one of the last times he would feel his hands, and they were suddenly very dear to him. He looked down at his body, and it was very dear to him.

For a time, he wondered about little things he might never have answers to: how many of Jabba's staff had the cook managed to poison on the barge before he poisoned Jabba himself? How long would it take the monks to sweep up the sand that generations of criminals had tracked into the palace? What would the cooks do with the grease he had had them save?

He heard a sound in the main passageway beyond the throne room. It was unmistakable. He drew his blaster and considered using it against himself, but did not. He set it aside, on the empty throne, and listened to the squeaks of the approaching surgeons' cart.

The Great God Quay:
The Tale of Barada and
the Weequays

by George Alec Effinger

Barada came from Klatooine originally, and at night
he dreamed that he was still there, feeling the
fresh wind of his homeworld on his face. Of course, in
his dreams, his face wasn't yet deformed and scarred,
and in his dreams he wasn't the virtual prisoner and
slave of the Hutt. At night, as he slept on his bunk,
Barada was still young and hopeful and filled with

plans to leave Klatooine behind and find adventure on some more exciting planet in the vast Empire.

Then morning would come, and Barada would awaken. He would blink a few times, the dream memories of his family and childhood home fading slowly from his thoughts. Klatooine, he'd think grimly. Adventure. He'd sit up and rub his face with his large, strong hands. He'd never see his homeworld again, he knew. He'd spend the rest of his life on this desert planet, caring for the Hutt's repulsor fleet.

Barada shrugged. It was as good a life as any, and better than some. All he really lacked was liberty, and in the Empire that was a fairly common 'tuation. His needs were met, and as for his wants, he was free to dream about them as much as he liked.

This morning, Barada's only concern was finding six rocker-panel cotter pins for the AE-35 unit that helped keep the Hutt's sail barge aloft. The shipment of parts that Barada had ordered weeks ago had never arrived; if he couldn't find the pins in the scrap heap, he'd have to make replacements the hard way, in his shop.

It was a bright, clear day on the Dune Sea, the kind of weather that the Hutt preferred. Barada squinted in the fierce sunshine as he left the barracks building. He'd walked only a few yards before two armed Weequay guards joined him, one on either side.

"I do something?" Barada asked. "What'd I do?" The gray-skinned Weequays didn't answer. Barada had never heard them speak. They just walked beside him, carrying their force pikes. He wasn't happy about their company.

"The Hutt send you to get me?" he asked. There was only silence from the Weequays. He turned in the direction of the scrap heap behind the Hutt's palace, and the Weequays followed. They were among the most merciless fighters in the Hutt's retinue, but if they'd wanted Barada dead, injured, or in irons, it would already have happened. The Weequays were as inscrutable as any species in the Empire, so for the time being there was nothing for Barada to do but ignore them. Finally, he decided to pretend they weren't even there, and to go on with what he'd planned for the morning.

The blazing summer sun and desert climate made the scrap heap an unpleasant destination. Barada could smell the stench long before he could see his goal. Garbage and trash of every kind had been piled up in a gigantic mound. The Klatooinan shook his head and frowned. He really didn't want to do it, but he waded hip-deep into the rotting food and discarded machinery, searching for a half-dozen small metal parts.

"You guys want to help me out here?" he said, shading his eyes with one hand. The Weequays only stared at him. Barada muttered a curse in his native language and went back to work.

Five minutes later, the mechanic made his discovery. It wasn't the rocker-panel cotter pins he had been looking for, or any kind of useful machinery. It was just a dead body. "Ak-Buz," Barada murmured, recognizing the corpse. Ak-Buz, the captain of the Hutt's sail barge.

The Weequays glanced at each other and stepped closer. They still didn't say anything, but at least they had shown some interest. Together, they hauled Ak-Buz's body out of the garbage and laid it on the ground.

Barada grunted. "No marks," he said. "Whoever killed the guy didn't leave any marks on the body." He looked from one Weequay to the other. "Anzat. It's an Anzat killed him. Anzat don't leave marks."

If the Weequays were impressed, they didn't show it. They squatted beside Ak-Buz's body and examined it for a few minutes. Then they stood up and started to walk away. Barada followed. "There's been a lot of dead bodies turning up," he said. The Weequays halted and faced him. One reached out and put his hand on Barada's chest. The other pointed back to the scrap heap. "Sure," said the mechanic, "none of my business. I get it. I guess I'll just go look for those pins now. Want me to do anything with our friend Ak-Buz?"

He got no answer, of course.

The Weequays shouldered their force pikes and marched off in step toward their own quarters. They stared straight ahead, not even changing expressions, until they'd arrived at the small building that housed the Hutt's Weequay contingent. They went inside. There were more Weequays in the Hutt's employ, but they were away attending to other matters.

"Alone now," said Weequay.

"We can talk," said the other Weequay. Weequays have no individual names; it never seems to cause them any difficulty, though.

"Trouble."

Weequay nodded. He put his force pike down on his bunk. "Too many dead."

"Even stupid Barada knows that."

The Weequays paused, possibly in thought. "We must have a meeting," said one finally.

"Agreed," said the other.

The Weequays sat down at a plank table, across from each other. One put slips of paper and writing styluses between them. This was the first activity at any proper Weequay meeting: the election of officers.

"There are two of us. One will be president, the other secretary-treasurer."

"Agreed."

Each took a blank piece of paper and a stylus, marked his secret ballot, and folded it in half.

"We will read them together." They unfolded the papers and counted the votes. "There are two votes for Weequay for president, and two votes for Weequay for secretary-treasurer."

"It is done," said the other. "I am now president. You, secretary, must record these proceedings for future review."

The Weequay secretary put a small electronic recording device on the table between them.

"Good. Now I ask, will we tell Jabba of this most recent murder?"

The secretary shook his head. "No, we can't. Not until we find the killer."

More time passed in silence. "We must ask the god," said the Weequay president.

"Ask the god," the other agreed. Neither was happy about the decision.

The Weequays worshiped a variety of gods, most of whom represented natural forces and creatures on their homeworld. One of their chief gods was Quay—Weequay means "follower of Quay"—the god of the moon. Many Weequays kept in close personal contact with this god through a device which they also called a quay. This was a white sphere made of high-impact plastic about twenty centimeters in diameter. The quay could recognize speech and reply to simple questions. To the Weequays, the object looked like the moon of their home planet, and they believed a bit of their lunar god inhabited each quay. They never quite understood that the quays were manufactured cheaply by more imaginative species and there was nothing at all supernatural about them.

The Weequay president reverently removed the glistening quay from its leather sack. "Hear us, O Great

God Quay," he said. "We come to you for guidance. Will you grant us, your true believers, a hearing?"

A few seconds passed. Then a tiny mechanical voice said, "It is decidedly so."

The Weequays nodded to each other. Sometimes the Great God Quay was not in the mood to be interrogated, and he could stay recalcitrant for hours, even days at a time. With several of the Hutt's servants dead —now including the barge captain, Ak-Buz—the Weequays knew they needed immediate help.

"We, your true believers, praise you, O Great God Quay, and thank you. Will you reveal to us the identity of the foul murderer of Barge Captain Ak-Buz?"

The Weequays held their breaths. They heard the whirring of the ventilation system in the barracks, but nothing else. Then the mechanical voice piped, "As I see it, yes."

The god was in a cooperative mood today!

"Is the killer in this room?" asked President Weequay. The secretary snarled fiercely at him. "It is the necessary first question," explained the president.

"Concentrate and ask again," said the white quay.

The president closed his eyes tightly and said, "Is the killer in this room?"

"Better not tell you now," said the god-ball.

"You see!" cried the president. "It is you!" The Weequay reached across the table and clutched his fellow's tunic.

"No! I swear!" said the secretary, terror-stricken. "The Great God Quay did not identify me! Ask him a third time!"

The president released the Weequay reluctantly, then looked down between them at the sphere of prophecy. "We beseech you, O Great God Quay! Is the killer in this room?"

The answer came quickly. "Very doubtful."

Both Weequays relaxed. "I am relieved," said the

president. "I did not wish to abandon you to the vengeance of Jabba."

"We still don't know who the murderer is," said the secretary. "We must learn if there will be more victims."

The president nodded slowly. He had begun to realize that their future well-being depended on investigating these crimes and presenting their suspicious employer with a neatly tied-up solution. The Hutt had no patience at all with incompetence, and guards who couldn't guard would soon find themselves on absolutely the wrong end of something's food chain.

"Will more of Jabba's entourage be killed?" asked the president.

A low-pitched grinding noise came from the quay on the table. The two Weequays looked at each other, then back down at the white sphere. "It is certain," said the tinny voice.

The secretary bent low over the device. "Will I die?" he asked quietly.

"Without a doubt," the quay responded instantly.

"Weequay," said the president, "you waste time. Of course you will die. All who live will die someday. Be silent, and I will gather the information. O Great God Quay, what weapon are we looking for? Is it a blaster?"

"Don't count on it," said the white ball.

"A rifle of some sort, then?"

"My reply is no."

The Weequay president tossed his braided topknot over his left shoulder. "Is it any sort of projectile weapon?"

"My reply is no."

"A knife, then? Is the murderer's weapon a knife?"

The secretary pounded the table with a fist. "There were no knife wounds on Ak-Buz," he said.

"A rope or silken cord?" asked the president.

The secretary looked even more impatient. "No signs of strangulation. We would have seen them."

The mystery was too complex for the limited Weequay minds. "All these deaths," said the president.

The secretary's eyes opened wider. "Different methods. Why?"

"And who?" said the president. He rubbed his chin for a few seconds, then put his hands flat on the table, on either side of the sacred quay. "O Great God Quay, you have told us there will be at least another death. Will it too happen by a different method?"

"Outlook good" was all the device had to say.

"Not blaster," said the secretary thoughtfully. "Not rifle. Not knife. Not rope. Is it a poison gas?"

"My reply is no," said the Great God Quay.

"Is it an injection of deadly drugs?"

The quay made a sound like the grinding of teeth. "Very doubtful."

"Is it tiny little off-world creatures that infest the body and kill the host horribly at a later date, giving the killer time to establish an alibi elsewhere?"

There was a long pause from the quay, as if it were digesting this strange possibility. "My sources say no."

Outside, the hot sun of Tatooine climbed higher in the sky. It was approaching noon. Barada was at work in his shop, overseeing the construction and installation of six new rocker-panel cotter pins for the AE-35 unit. Word had come down from the Hutt himself that the sail barge would be setting forth later that day. With Ak-Buz now greeting his ancestors in his race's version of heaven, Barada assumed he himself would have to captain the huge craft. He'd done it before, when Ak-Buz had shown up for duty less than sober.

• • •

Meanwhile, the Weequays labored mightily to get some useful information from the quay. It was simply a matter of asking the right questions. If the Weequays stumbled on the correct weapon and then the true identity of the murderer, the Great God Quay would let them know they'd succeeded at last. However, time slipped by as they guessed one thing after another, from every kind of blunt object to a pile of straw near the scrap heap. "Ak-Buz could have been smothered in the straw," the president insisted. "It's possible."

"And you accuse me of wasting time," said the secretary scornfully. "O Great God Quay, was the barge captain drowned in a bucket of water?"

"Don't count on it." If nothing else, Quay had more patience than the average primitive deity.

"Does the weapon begin with the letter *A*?" asked the president.

The other Weequay glared furiously. "Now we'll be here all afternoon. What a foolish way to—"

"My reply is no," said the god-ball.

"The letter *B*?" asked the president.

"You're never going to learn anything that way," said the secretary. "I call for new elections—"

"It is decidedly so." Both Weequays stared at the white plastic sphere.

"The letter *B*?" said the secretary.

"*B* for . . . what?" said the president. "Blaster? No, we asked that. Bantha? Will the murderer kill the next victim with a bantha?"

There was tense silence in the barracks. Then the quay replied, "Cannot predict now."

The president took a deep breath and let it out again. "Will the murderer kill the next victim with a bantha?"

This time the quay didn't hesitate. "My reply is no."

The Weequays went on through the alphabet, trying every object and technique they could think of. At last, as three more armed Weequays entered the barracks, the secretary asked, "Bomb? Is it a bomb? On the sail barge?"

"Signs point to yes," said the mechanical voice.

All five Weequays gasped. "O Great God Quay," said the president hoarsely, "we, your true believers, thank you! We will use the gift of your prophecy to protect your servants, and we praise your wisdom and power."

One of the newly arrived Weequays came to the table. "What does this mean?" he demanded.

"Ak-Buz dead," said the secretary.

"Bomb aboard the sail barge," said the president.

"We must find it," said the third Weequay.

"We must disarm it," said a fourth.

"We must punish . . . who?" asked the fifth.

The secretary looked at the president. "Does the murderer's name begin with the letter *A*?" he said to the quay. The secretary didn't say anything; he just squeezed his eyes shut and rubbed his aching forehead. It was going to be a very long day.

Barada wouldn't let his workmen quit for the midday meal until the AE-35 unit had been repaired and replaced in the sail barge. It wasn't a difficult job, but Barada was an extremely exacting supervisor. He had to be. If there were the slightest malfunction, if any mechanical breakdown interrupted the Hutt's pleasure cruise, Barada himself would be the next corpse to be found on the scrap heap. He didn't intend for that to happen.

He checked the fittings and connections carefully, then slid the AE-35 hatch cover into place and slapped it closed. "Good," he said. He wiped his perspiring brow with one hand. "Anything else?"

Mal Hyb, Barada's capable human assistant, glanced

at a datapad in her hand. "All the diagnostic tests turned up green," she said.

The mechanic nodded. "Nothing more we can do now, I guess. All right, let's take an hour for lunch. We'll check out the barge again later, before the Hutt gets here."

Mal Hyb frowned. She was recognized in the workshop for her skill with a welding torch. Although she was two feet shorter than Barada, and compactly built, she was also a good ally in a brawl. Her fighting ability always surprised her opponents—once. "More tests?" she asked.

Barada grunted. "You haven't worked for the Hutt as long as I have. If I could make this crew do it, I'd be running diagnostics all day and all night. I've seen the Hutt execute a crewman because a shutter squeaked."

Mal Hyb shook her head and walked away. Barada heard a sound, turned, and saw a party of five Weequays enter the barge's hangar. He wasn't pleased.

The Weequays approached him. One of them gestured toward the sail barge.

"You want to go aboard?" said Barada. "Why? You still trying to figure out who killed Ak-Buz?"

The Weequay spokesman nodded.

"Not a chance," said Barada. "We've got the barge all tuned up and I don't want you leather-faced bullies wrecking it."

A second Weequay held out a paper sack. Barada took it, opened it, and looked inside. "Beignets," he said, surprised. "Porcellus's beignets?"

Another Weequay nod.

"All right, I guess," said the mechanic. "You've got to do your job, too. Just don't touch anything."

The five Weequays formed up in single file and boarded the sail barge. Barada sat down stiffly on the concrete and took the first beignet from the bag.

• • •

The Weequays poked around the sail barge, not entirely sure what they were looking for. A bomb, of course, but what kind of bomb was it? How big? And where? There were a million places to hide one.

The Weequay president carried the quay with him, and murmured, "Does the murderer's name begin with the letter V? Vader? Valarian? Venti Paz?"

The quay began to stammer. "W—"

"Yes?" the Weequay prompted.

"W—"

"O Great God Quay, what are you trying to tell us?" The Weequay president rapped the oracle ball with an astonishing lack of piety. " 'W.' Wookiee? Is that it? The Wookiee is the assassin?"

"I don't think that's possible," said the secretary.

"W—" said the quay.

"Weequay?" asked the president. "It cannot be! A Weequay, guilty of murder?"

"W—"

A third Weequay listened to the exchange. "What is wrong here?" he asked.

"I don't know," said the president. "The Great God Quay is having some trouble communicating."

"W—"

"Whiphid?" asked the secretary.

"Without a doubt," said the plastic ball at last.

"Ah," said the president. "The mystery is solved. The Whiphid planted the bomb on board."

The five Weequays nodded, satisfied at last to know the truth. They stood in Jabba's privacy lounge, shifting their force pikes from one hand to the other. The president held the now-silent quay.

"Of course," said the secretary slowly, "there is a bomb. And we will also be on board when it detonates. We still must search for it."

"Search for it!" cried one of the others.

"Yes," said the president. "You four search the barge. I will consult the Great God Quay."

Four of the Weequays began a frantic hunt for the hidden explosive. They threw open cabinets, upset furniture, damaged the bulkheads looking for secret panels and compartments. Meanwhile, the president sat at a table with the prophecy sphere and said, "Is the bomb under the purple cushion?"

"Very doubtful."

"Is the bomb under the gold cushion?"

"Don't count on it."

"Is the bomb hidden in the pile of silks?" The president realized that he wasn't making very good progress, but he didn't know what else to do. He was a good, honest, forthright Weequay, but he had Weequay limitations, after all.

An hour later, the Hutt's guests and servants began to arrive, to prepare the sail barge for the day's excursion. Some of them gave the Weequays suspicious glances, but as the Weequays served as security guards on the barge, they were allowed to continue their search unhindered.

"Try to blend in," the president whispered to his fellows. They were still tearing the barge apart from stern to bow, but now they tried to seem casual and unworried. The truth was that as the minutes passed, it became ever more likely that the bomb would go off and blow them all into constituent atoms. Even the Weequays understood that.

The order was given to cast off, and there had not yet been any evidence of the hidden threat. The party guests were enjoying themselves, eating the Hutt's food and drinking the Hutt's liquor, and generally making the search even more difficult. The Weequay president found himself staring into the malevolent three eyes of Ree-Yees, the Gran. The president turned back to the quay and asked, "Is the bomb in the control cockpit?"

Maddeningly, the white ball said, "Reply hazy. Try again."

The Weequay wanted to throw the device against the wall in frustration, but it would have attracted unwanted attention, and the Great God Quay would probably have exacted some horrible punishment as well. The president watched a gold-colored protocol droid in conversation with an R2 model that was serving drinks.

"Mr. President," a low voice murmured.

The Weequay turned. His four fellows stood nearby. One held something covered with a square of green satin.

"The . . . item?" whispered the president.

The other four Weequays nodded. The president lifted a corner of the satin material and saw a thermal detonator. "We must disarm it. Secretly. Silently."

The band tootled its horrible music. The guests milled about, unaware of the danger in their midst. Meanwhile, the five Weequays formed a tight huddle and worked feverishly to dismantle the detonator. The proper tools were available on the sail barge, of course, but the problem was that two of the Weequays disagreed on the disarming technique.

"Pull that circuit patch now," said the secretary.

"You'll kill us all," said the president. "Break the green and yellow connections. Then pull the circuit patch."

"There is no green connection," insisted the secretary. "There's a yellow one and a gray one."

"The problem is with your eyes," said the president.

"Hurry!" said one of the others.

"It is my responsibility," said the president. He took the detonator and the tools. He broke first the green connector, then the yellow connector, and then yanked out the circuit patch.

The Weequays said nothing. They hadn't realized that none of them had even breathed for nearly a minute.

"You could have blown us to bits," the secretary accused. "You should have consulted the Great God Quay before you acted."

"I forgot," said the president.

"Yet the bomb is dead!" said one of the others.

"We are victorious!" said another.

A loud, clear voice came from beyond the bulkhead. "Jabba, this is your last chance! Free us or die!"

The Hutt responded with something in its own language.

"What is happening?" asked a Weequay.

The president turned around quickly. Panic and confusion were taking over the sail barge. A human slave girl was strangling the great Jabba with her own chains. There was the sound of shots being fired from outside. One of the Weequays opened a shutter to peer out, and was grabbed and pulled from the vessel, thrown down to the desert floor below.

Clutching his force pike, the president led the remaining Weequays toward what was now clearly a battle. He jabbed upward with the pike, leading the others on deck. The president arrived to see the black-clad human prisoner using a lightsaber to clear the deck of Weequay guards and other defenders. "Get the gun!" the human cried to the slave girl. "Point it at the deck!"

"For the Great God Quay," murmured the president softly. Then he advanced. At least they had disarmed the bomb, so the sail barge would be safe.

Before he could attack, the human with the lightsaber put an arm around the slave girl, clutched a heavy rope, and kicked the firing mechanism of the deck gun. Then he and the girl swung from the sail barge to a small repulsor skiff hovering over the dreadful Great Pit of Carkoon, where the Sarlacc dwelt.

The president watched them escape. Around him the sail barge was burning and bursting into ruins, but unfortunately Weequays do not have enough imagination to fear death, either. The president calmly clung to a railing as another tremendous explosion ripped the sail barge to pieces.

The last thing he saw was the glorious sight of the white ball of the quay hurled into the air—the Great God Quay ascending to heaven.

A Bad Feeling: The Tale of EV-9D9

Judith and Garfield Reeves-Stevens

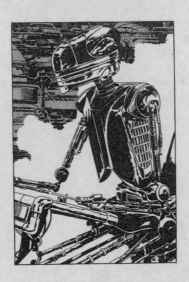

Like some great beast lurching toward destruction,
Cloud City shuddered, tilted, and began to fall.

Lando Calrissian heard the rising wail of the
Ugnaughts and the others of his domain who looked
to him for safety and stability, and his heart fell with
his dying city. His blaster twisted from his hand as he
leaped for a pillar, as if a good grip might save him
from that final descent through Bespin's clouds. The

weapon skittered along the wildly angled decking, hit the rimguard, then bounced over its curving lip and vanished into the rush of Tibanna-laden clouds that swirled by. Alarms shrieked. The city pitched again, metal groaning. Calrissian felt his grip weaken. The clouds reached out for him with sinuous, fluttering tendrils. He closed his eyes in the force of the driving wind. And he fell, too.

Lobot caught him.

Calrissian felt sudden, welcome pain as enhanced fingers dug into his shoulder beneath his cloak, holding him in place as securely as if he had been welded to the deck. He turned to see Lobot's cranial attachments flickering as they probed all the communications channels now in use. The city lurched again, but this time the angle of its fall decreased. The cloud streamers slowed as the howl of the wind diminished.

"Backups online, sir!" The reedy voice was Sarl Random's—the cheeks of her ghost-white face splotched by red patches of fear, her ill-fitting uniform bunched up and twisted from the struggle she had just been through, stained with hydraulic fluid, reeking of scorched circuitry. She stumbled over to Calrissian under Lobot's watchful eyes. She held a security display pad in her trembling hands. "She must have planted charges by the main repulsorlift generators."

Even now, Calrissian still couldn't believe the nature of the intellect they faced. It was bad enough that the prisoner had circumvented all the failsafes of the Security Tower, but the generators that kept this facility aloft were supposed to be inviolable. Too many lives depended upon them. "She wanted to destroy the *entire city*?"

Lobot angled his head at Random. She read the data he generated on her pad. "Not all the generators were targeted, sir." Her voice could not hide her puzzlement. "A diversion?"

Calrissian tugged his cloak more tightly around his shoulders. A diversion he could understand. Misdirection. Like noisily knocking over a pile of betting chits to disguise the skillful pass that brought a winning gambling tab to the top of the deck.

"Where's she headed?" Calrissian asked. The decking beneath him was almost at a normal angle now, thrumming at the edge of perception with the regular hum of the generators and the constant shifting of the control surfaces that kept the floating city in trim.

But Sarl Random had no answer for him. She had only been acting security chief for a single shift—ever since she had brought him the evidence that revealed what his real security chief actually was. In another mining colony, she might have been tossed over the rimguard herself. But she was too inexperienced to know how dangerous it could be to expose corruption in a facility so small it was a law unto itself. And she had taken her discovery to Baron-Administrator Calrissian himself—in spite of all the stories told of him on a dozen worlds—a man to whom the word "honor" still had meaning.

A communications panel chimed and Lobot punched the code that released its speaker wand. He automatically handed it to Calrissian.

"This is the administrator. Go ahead."

A droid reported. "Traffic control, sir. One of the transport shuttles has launched without clearance from the east platform."

Calrissian permitted himself a smile of relief. The prisoner had finally made a mistake. "She can't get far in that." It was an orbital transfer vehicle only, strictly intrasystem. "Scramble all the Twin Pods. I want her brought back at once—still functioning—or know the reason why."

"You should blow her out of the sky," the droid responded. Then quickly added, "Sir."

Calrissian and Random exchanged a look of surprise. Droids didn't talk that way.

"Who is this?" Calrissian demanded.

"Wuntoo Forcee Forwun. Sir. Traffic controller, second class."

Calrissian had been ready to reprimand the presumptuous droid, but hesitated as he recognized the prefix code. Three other Wuntoo units, all from the same manufacturing lot, had been found in the recycling bay, bound for the furnace. At least, *parts* of them had been found there, showing disturbing evidence that they had been taken apart while they were still switched on. What had happened to the rest of them was something only the former security chief knew, so Calrissian had some understanding of what the droid must be feeling—if a droid could be said to feel. Cloud City's baron-administrator had encountered enough droids with such convincing emotional analogues that he often had cause to question the common wisdom. And the processors used in the Wuntoo units, which made them capable of tracking the complexities of this facility's air and space traffic, certainly were elaborate enough to allow unexpected behaviors to emerge.

"Listen to me, Forwun—this is no time for revenge. Issue my orders directly to the patrol or stand down from duty. Do you understand?"

There was a long pause, the hiss of static on an open channel. Then the droid said, "Orders issued, sir."

Lobot nodded at Calrissian. He was monitoring the security channels.

"Patrols launched," Random confirmed, reading from her display pad.

Calrissian slipped the speaker wand back into the

wall panel. "This won't take long," he said to Random. "That transport will be dragged back here before—"

He didn't finish because the air was viciously rent by a bone-jarring crack of thunder. Calrissian, Lobot, and Random turned sharply to stare past the rimguard, into the clouds.

The *Iopene Princess* emerged from the billows of Tibanna, its dull gray finish bloodied by the ruby light of the setting primary.

"No," Calrissian whispered. It wasn't possible.

The *Iopene Princess* was a Mining Guild cutter, with bulbous, state-of-the-art hyperdrive units, asymmetrical, bristling with scanners and probes, designed for hard vacuum, not for atmosphere. And it wasn't scheduled to leave until tomorrow, after Calrissian had made his annual payment to keep the Guild from organizing his workers.

"She hijacked the Guild cutter . . . ?"

Lobot's attachments flickered crazily, then he looked away, unable to meet Calrissian's eyes. That was exactly what had happened.

Stealing the transport shuttle had been another diversion. Now the security patrols were too far gone to ever double back in time to stop the *Iopene Princess* from leaving the atmosphere and making the jump to hyperspace. No wonder the prisoner hadn't tried to destroy the entire city. She needed time to make her escape. But not very much time.

Somehow, in the tenth-of-a-shift cycle that had transpired since the first alert had come from the Security Tower, the prisoner had managed to override clearances on two flight platforms, remotely pilot a shuttle to draw away the security patrol, and take over the most heavily secured vessel in the city. What kind of a mind were they dealing with?

Then he remembered: the kind of mind that had

destroyed a quarter of Cloud City's droid population without falling under the slightest suspicion, until a junior security officer had just happened across the evidence—by accident.

Brilliant wasn't the word for it.

Neither was genius.

The only term that came to Calrissian's mind was: tortured. There was no other word to describe what had happened to those droids, either.

Random moved to Calrissian's side. He could feel her shiver beside him, though the rising night wind was warm.

"We'll never catch her, will we, sir?" she said.

Calrissian put his arm around her, for comfort, nothing more. "No," he admitted. "But I'll put her I.D. all over the webs. Everyone will know about her."

"You think no one else has tried that before?"

Calrissian knew Random was right. No doubt that's why the prisoner had chosen Cloud City in the first place—a tiny mining colony, too small to attract Imperial notice, too far off the beaten hyperlanes to have heard the stories of a vicious, unknown force that had scourged a hundred worlds before it. But perhaps that's where the prisoner's eventual downfall would lie. Slowly the possibilities for where she could operate unrecognized would dwindle. Eventually, she would have nowhere to run. But that would be in the future. For now, it was a big galaxy.

The cutter banked slowly by the edge of the city, as if deliberately taunting Calrissian, then sped up on a rising arc, ripping through cloud banks, leaving a vapor trail in the dusk like a stream of blood.

Calrissian turned back to the main portal. He had the guild council to placate, the threat of a strike to avert. His former security chief was gone and there was no telling where she would turn up next. Though Calrissian was certain that wherever it was, if the universe had a bright center, it would have to be the world farthest from it, because only there would something as evil and as cunning as the droid EV-9D9 find a home. And wherever that world was, Calrissian hoped it was somewhere he himself would never have to go.

He had a bad feeling about it.

Years later, at the edge of Tatooine's Dune Sea, deep in Jabba's dungeon, EV-9D9 had a bad feeling, too. And she welcomed it. For each stuttering squeal of despair from the GNK Power Droid was like a surge of fresh current through EV-9D9's circuits. Bad feelings were what she existed for.

The darkly colored humanoid droid, known here as Ninedenine, looked past her command console in the dungeon's main hall to see the GNK unit slowly rotated to expose the ventral surfaces of its ambulatory appendages. The appendages readjusted their relative positions furiously, uselessly, trying to reorient their center of gravity back to an operational norm. And unlike any droid before or since, unlike any behavior that could be predicted by a logical engineering assessment of her technical specifications, Ninedenine felt a thrill of *pleasure* as she watched the little droid's futile attempts to avoid damage.

The corridor barricade swept open and a snuffling Gamorrean guard shuffled in with two new prisoners. But that did not distract Ninedenine from hungrily observing what happened as the glowing energy inducers were lowered onto the GNK's appendages. In response to the sudden application of heat, coolant fluid vaporized and the relief valves in the Power Droid's outer covering bled off the resultant vapor with a satisfying hiss. Sensing an impending loss of function, the GNK broadcast a futile, wide-spectrum, multiband signal for assistance, some of it actually in the audible frequencies to which most organic life-forms were limited. It was programmed panic, pure and urgent. Like higher-dimensional music to Ninedenine's exquisitely tuned acoustic sensors.

Ignoring for the moment the Gamorrean guard and the new prisoners, Ninedenine racked up the gain on her internal receptors, savoring the intensity of it all. She concentrated her meta-analytical functions on the high-frequency carrier wave generated by the pain-simulator button newly connected to the GNK's central circuits. That signal was . . . *delicious*. It was an organic term, Ninedenine knew, but apt, so apt—calling up associative memory files of texture and flavor and shifting densities of sensory input that no self-inflicted rewiring could ever achieve. Ninedenine could be sure of that. She had rewired herself many times in the past, all to no effect, much as an organic life-form might draw a cutting implement against its outer covering to delicately release the oxygen/energy transfer fluid circulating within.

Ninedenine had studied closely that organic act of somatic rearrangement, and knew that it was often undertaken by the organic creatures who were caged in the corridor walls of Jabba's dungeons. Given a year or two or five or ten within this dark domain, even the best of them would succumb to ravaging their own tentacles or clawing at their own light sensors.

To Ninedenine, such actions were the addictively elegant expressions of a higher-dimensional logic pathway which only she among droids had the gift to comprehend—first by an accident of manufacture, it had seemed, but now augmented by her own deliberate and ongoing modifications. To organics, such acts of self-inflicted, physical alteration were second nature, a state which Ninedenine yearned to achieve and often felt maddeningly close to experiencing. Indeed, there was much within the organic mind which Ninedenine felt certain was comparable to her own. Not in quality of intellect—she was positive she had no equal among cellular-based processors in that regard. But in *appreciation* of *sensation—that* was how Ninedenine preferred to characterize her avocation. The savoring of the sine waves of discomfort. Plunging into the algorithms of despair. Racing through the oscillating peaks and valleys emitted by circuits strained far past their design and logic loads. True, for now, her internal receptors allowed her only the binary nature of droids to work with, but once she had accessed enough datastorage space and enough co-processors at sufficiently wide bandwidths, there would be no limit to the sensations she would be able to induce, record, digitize, and play back to the nth repetition, all exactingly coaxed from her mechanistic brethren.

Simply put, and Ninedenine did cherish simplicity, she knew that what she did was an act of creation—an art form. Though trying to explain to an organic that a droid such as she could appreciate art was like trying to explain that a droid could feel pain.

Droids *could* feel pain, of course. One of the two new prisoners coming her way was proof of that—a golden protocol droid from the looks of it, buffed to a courtly gleam, completely out of place in this warren of dank tunnels, decaying power conduits, and scurrying, fur-covered, organic scavengers.

"Ah, good," Ninedenine said as the prisoners approached, "new acquisitions." She fixed her inner optic scanner on the golden droid. She knew how unnerving it could be to other droids when they noticed that she—a humanoid model—possessed that *third* optic scanner, just in from the standard left unit. It was not in the design specs of EVs or any other model. Some called it a design flaw. Proof that she had been put together the wrong way, as if that might explain her ambitions and her most undroidlike appetites. But Ninedenine understood that third scanner for what it truly was—the gift that allowed her to sense beyond what any other droid could sense, to never-before-quantified dimensions of experience, completely bypassing the signal-to-noise ratio of ordinary droid sensation.

Ninedenine made her third optic scanner blink deliberately out of sync with her main scanning cycle. "You are a protocol droid, are you not?"

The new prisoner did not even have to begin to speak for Ninedenine to know the answer to that question. His supercilious pose and posturing proclaimed him to be a protocol droid of the highest, most irritatingly officious order.

"I am See-Threepio," the droid began, redundantly. Already Ninedenine was growing tired of it. "Human-cyborg—"

"Yes or no will do," Ninedenine said sharply. Give a protocol droid its way and half the shift would be taken up with meaningless gabble. Binary was best in dealing with such units.

"Well, yes," the golden droid replied more satisfactorily.

"How many languages do you speak?" Ninedenine called up the household's duty roster on her command console. She hoped there would be no opening for a protocol droid. She would enjoy showing this one the wonders of her workshop . . .

"I am fluent in over six million forms of communication, and can readily—"

"Splendid," Ninedenine snapped, cutting off the droid again as she saw an opening did exist. "We have been without an interpreter since our master got angry with our last protocol droid and disintegrated him."

Ninedenine tried to detect any reaction to that news

on the droid's part, but was momentarily distracted by the snorting guffaw from the second Gamorrean guard sitting behind her, and then by the transmission of circuit-shivering pain from the silver courier droid on the traction-test bed, whose right-side appendages suddenly failed with twin bursts of live current.

"Disintegrated . . . ?" the golden droid repeated, trying to make sense of what was going on. Ninedenine wondered if it too had picked up the pain transmission from the dismembered droid, and was experiencing the first touch of disturbance. Pain-simulator buttons were supposedly restricted technology, typically installed only in those droids who had to interact with organics at the most personal level. Strike a protocol droid on the head, for instance, and it would respond that the blow had hurt. Such empathy toward potentially damaging physical sensation was supposed to give them deeper understanding of organics. But as far as Ninedenine was concerned, it just made protocol droids better subjects for her experiments.

And Ninedenine did like to experiment.

"Guard," Ninedenine commanded, "this protocol droid might be useful. Fit him with a restraining bolt and take him back up to His Excellency's main audience chamber."

The Gamorrean guard pulled the droid back toward the doorway leading to Ninedenine's workshop—at least, what she had conditioned everyone working in the dungeon to think of as her only workshop.

"Artoo," the golden droid bleated as he disappeared from view, "don't leave me." But by then, it was too late.

The companion to whom the protocol droid had uselessly appealed was a banged-up R2 unit which Ninedenine decided should have been recycled long ago. Surprisingly, in response to the protocol droid's plea, it released a torrent of rapid binary invective that Ninedenine had to step down by a factor of ten to catch all the subtleties. The little R2's insults were impressive *and* imaginative coming from one so insignificant, but ultimately of less interest than the possibilities the golden droid had presented. Ninedenine scanned the roster again and found another duty opening.

"You're a feisty little one," she told the R2 unit, "but you'll soon learn some respect. I have need for you on the master's sail barge, and I think you'll fill in nicely." As if to underscore Ninedenine's pronouncement, the GNK sent out another series of circuit-melting, high-pitched squeaks as its cooling system was cruelly challenged again. Then the R2 unit silently rolled away with the second guard to the workshop, to be fitted with its own restraining bolt. Ninedenine paused as she watched the little droid roll through the doorway, puzzled that after such a strong first response, it had said nothing more in protest or in insult. Almost as if it *wanted* to be assigned to Jabba's sail barge . . .

Ninedenine's central processors accelerated their clock rate to sift through the data again. Her third optic scanner blinked erratically as all possible probability permutations were analyzed.

It was, she at last concluded, almost as if the R2 unit had *expected* to be assigned to Jabba's sail barge.

Ninedenine shut all the doors to her dungeon. She needed time to consider this most unexpected development as her self-preservation programming loops began to run through several of her peripheral coprocessors, letting their presence be known. She even filtered out the seductive distractions of the dangling courier droid as she tapped precise commands into her console, rescanning the duty-roster listing for any sign of tampering. As far as she knew, there were at present fifteen separate conspiracies under way with the goal of eliminating Jabba the Hutt as Tatooine's preeminent ganglord, though none of them was Ninedenine's concern. In truth, the season's total for attempts against Jabba's life was down a bit from previous years, perhaps a distressing sign that the blubbery green slug was slowing down in his old age and just wasn't inspiring the manic blood feuds of old. In any event, as long as whoever replaced Jabba continued to allow Ninedenine unrestricted dominion over the droids of the palace, as any replacement was sure to do, Ninedenine simply recorded the plots against her employer and did nothing to interfere with them. This new playground she had come to was the perfect place for her, and she did not wish to jeopardize her position or her work by becoming involved in palace intrigue.

However, her heuristic subroutines had long ago learned that she must constantly be on guard for threats against her *own* existence. The incident in the mining colony on Bespin had taught her to pay even closer attention to seemingly inconsequential anomalies. In an organic life-form, the tendency might be called paranoia. But in Ninedenine, it was simply efficient programming, and she played that program over and over, just to be sure that someone *wasn't* after her.

Ninedenine reran the roster list, expanding the data contained in it to see who among Jabba's court had entered specific staff requests. Then she correlated those entries against staff vacancies caused by all the usual means—murder, unexplained fatal accident, ceremonial limb deletions, rancor-taunting, incendiary devices, food poisoning, and Jabba's own whimsical sense of humor and pranks. A separate search function pulled up droid deactivations as well, of which there were many. Not all of them were the result of Ninedenine's private explorations, either.

Ninedenine reviewed what the search revealed, then tapped a manipulatory extension against the side of her console, deep in data processing. Quite clearly, Jabba had a habit of disintegrating his protocol droids.

Some time ago, Jabba's protocol droid had been involved in a scheme with a pair of petty thieves, which had resulted in the burning of Jabba's Mos Eisley town house. That droid had been punished. Severely.

Then, just last season, its replacement had suffered a similar fate. From the watch report, it appeared the droid had mistranslated a Partold envoy's compliment about Jabba being a constant giver of immense charity, confusing the ritual Partold greeting with a Huttese medical term having to do with excessive flatulence. When the last snicker had died away in the audience chamber, the mystified Partold envoy had found himself face to fang with the ever-obliging rancor beast. The next day, when the Partold tithes were not paid by a justifiably upset delegation, the mistranslation was revealed and the protocol droid was disintegrated circuit by circuit over the course of the next ten shifts, all the time protesting indignantly that it had been reprogrammed by a palace guard.

Ninedenine didn't quite know what to make of the droid's reprogramming story. Jabba had discounted it. And Ninedenine had heard many strange things herself while she had disassembled still-functioning droids—though mostly they had been stories of a light and a tunnel, which she attributed to the standard, random cross-connection of failing circuits. Why would a palace guard reprogram a protocol droid to make it mistranslate compliments? Ninedenine could see no logic in it.

She next called up the case of the bartender droid required on Jabba's sail barge—the position to which the R2 unit had just been assigned with a noticeable lack of protest.

Again the data Ninedenine accumulated were unusual. She recalled the previous bartender had been a barely sentient C5 unit, one wheel, five arms, and a single optic scanner on a stalk. It had had trouble keeping its balance and mixing a clarified bantha-blood fizz at the same time. But Salacious Crumb had enjoyed riding it during festivities, so Jabba had kept it around despite its shortcomings.

Then another watch report of considerably more interest flashed up from the console. Not five cycles ago, that same bartending C5 unit had been found in a little-used corridor in the west wing with its power circuits yanked out, beyond repair. It appeared someone had purposely terminated the bartender droid, but what could a C5 unit have done to merit such a fate? It was in no way clever enough to have made enemies of its own.

Ninedenine tapped command after command into the console, activating worm programs long dormant in Jabba's main household system. Her logic filters detected anomalies here and she would not reduce her clock rate until she had isolated and understood them.

More watch reports flashed by on the console, followed by surveillance records; accounts owed, paid, and stolen; personnel assignments; nonvoluntary organ transplants—

Ninedenine suddenly paused, then rekeyed her previous request and backed up to the personnel records again. A palace guard had been fined five credits for being late to report for duty in the same service cycle in which the C5 unit had been terminated.

Ninedenine's processors moved into a hyperaccelerated phase, examining each datum on a bit-by-bit basis.

Datum: Two terminated droids whose work duties exactly matched the two new prisoners brought in today.

Datum: A palace guard circumstantially connected to both terminations.

Inference: Coincidences were rarely computable.

Conclusion: But conspiracies were.

Ninedenine swiftly accessed the name of the guard who had been late for duty. Tamtel Skreej. He had been with the palace force for less than a season. His background ID had been found to be forged, though according to his duty file that was taken to be a good sign by his commander. Ninedenine didn't like the way the data were sorting themselves. She called up Skreej's identity file. A humanoid organic face began to form on the console display: a dark outer covering, a narrow ridge of fur above his ingestion/communication orifice, a—

Ninedenine's internal processors missed a refresh cycle.

She recognized the organic's face.

Baron-Administrator Lando Calrissian of Cloud City.

Ninedenine gripped the side of the command console as her gyros momentarily precessed and threw her off balance.

Those two new droids were in no way part of some unknown conspiracy against Jabba the Hutt.

They could only be part of Calrissian's plot to recapture EV-9D9.

The logic of it was unassailable. There was no other possible reason why Calrissian and those two droids would come to Tatooine and Jabba's palace.

Ninedenine shut down her paranoia loops. She didn't need them anymore. Someone *was* out to get her.

It was time to move on again.

The GNK unit squealed a final time as it at last ceased functioning, but this time Ninedenine found no solace in its transmission. In fact, she knew the only thing that would give her solace now was removing the active circuits of the R2 unit, subprocessor by subprocessor, while the golden droid was forced to watch and upload his companion's pain. And then, who knew? Perhaps the time had come to expand her artistic endeavors to disassembling an organic construction. Like Lando Calrissian.

Ninedenine got up from her console and walked past the smoking form of the motionless GNK unit. There was so much to do, and so few processing cycles to do it in.

Four levels down, through corridors twisted like the guts of the Sarlacc, greenly phosphorescent with drell slime, swirling with mist, and littered with the calcified, interior-support structures of organics long since deactivated, Ninedenine sought out the sanctuary of her real workshop.

There was another workshop, of course. Her public one. As much as anything in Jabba's palace could be public. Up there, just off the main chamber, were long assembly tables and parts bins and archaic testing devices which not even a Jawa would bother to scavenge. In that workshop, the golden droid and the R2 unit would even now be having their restraining bolts installed. Though knowing Calrissian, Ninedenine assumed that the droids had already been covertly reconfigured so the bolts would have no effect. It could be done. Ninedenine had reconfigured herself in the same way.

But down here, whatever modifications those two droids might have would amount to nothing. For once droids entered *this* workshop, they never left. From time to time, Ninedenine thought it was unfortunate that no one else would ever appreciate what some of those droids would become down here, but what artistic achievement didn't require sacrifice?

The entrance to the true workshop was hidden within an ancient stone wall that had once supported a palace far older than the one Jabba had made his own. How many such structures had once stood on this site, not even Ninedenine's impressive processors had been able to compute. There was a narrow gap between two blocks of stone not native to Tatooine, where the crumbling mortar that contained traces of organic oxygen transport fluid had fallen free. Ninedenine now looked into that gap and made all three of her optic scanners blink with the appropriate code.

The wall trembled. Stone counterbalances shifted. The hidden doorway opened with a slow and echoing rumble.

Like an artist entering her studio, Ninedenine stepped into her inner sanctum.

Actual combustible torches sputtered along the drell-dripping walls of the great room, blackening the vaulted stone ceiling but ensuring that no household manager would ever detect an unauthorized use of palace power. To one side, the cages waited, and from within them came the rustlings and clankings of droids who had had their audio speakers cut out, rendering them mute, so their cries would not attract unwanted attention.

Ninedenine scanned the closest set of cages. In one, the torso of an LV3 had been cunningly severed and refitted with the manipulatory limbs of three discontinued B4Qs. The LV3's processors could not keep up with the sensory positional demands of the extra limbs and so it constantly fell against the walls and iron bars of its cage, gears grinding out of control. From time to time, Ninedenine would activate the freakish construction's pain-simulator button so she could appreciate the ceaseless output of disturbance and disorientation. It was like an anthem to Ninedenine, and its stirring chords brought forth associative files of her most grandiose plans for retooling whole work forces of droids, reconnecting limb after limb in a pattern of thousands to create vast undulating sheets of twisting, writhing, purposeless mechanistic movement, augmented by pain-simulator buttons wired into feedback loops which would play their sensations not only for Ninedenine, but back into the droids who made up the fully active symphony of pain, intensifying the signals to inexpressible powers of delight.

Ninedenine had to brace herself against a disassembly table as the strength of that memory file overcame her. There were so many great works to which she aspired. But not here. Not now.

First, she must obscure her trail. The workshop must be cleansed, so that after she had dealt with the two new droids and Calrissian, no others would pursue her to her next venue. Ninedenine paused again, reviewing the steps she had undertaken to cover her tracks at Bespin. She was truly surprised that Cloud City's administrator had managed to trace her to Tatooine. For an organic, it was an impressive feat. Not that it would help Calrissian escape his fate.

Ninedenine went to the self-contained console that controlled the equipment of her workshop, drawing its power from a small fusion battery. She would overwrite all the memory locations in the console, then program the battery to overload in two cycles, preventing any investigation of the work that had been accomplished here. But before that, she would have to eliminate the specific work in progress.

Ninedenine turned to the wall by the console where a tarnished silver droid was suspended upside down, a series of precise punctures in its cooling system allowing fluid to trickle out drop by drop, slowly raising its operational temperature over transcendently long cycles. The silver droid flexed weakly in its bonds and a flurry of sparkling blue coolant drops dribbled from its braincase. Hanging in such a position, its higher functions would be the last to become inactivated, and only then after registering the overheated shutdown of every other system in its chassis. Its pain-simulator button had been working at more than one hundred and ten percent of its rated capacity for the past two cycles, and Ninedenine was truly sorry to see this experiment end before its ultimate completion.

"It is unfortunate that I must accelerate the timetable of our exploration," Ninedenine said as she reached out to trail the tip of a manipulatory extension through the slick coating of the leaking fluid. "But there are those who do not appreciate my work." The silver droid's eyelights flickered weakly at Ninedenine. Ninedenine felt a real pang of sorrow as for the final time she tasted its pain transmission. Then she wrapped her manipulators around the silver droid's neck and squeezed until the hydraulic tubes burst and the power conduits sparked with gouts of cross-connected energy. The silver droid went limp in its bonds and, as Ninedenine watched, its eyelights slowly faded out.

"Ahh, exquisite," Ninedenine whispered in the silence of her workshop, still caught in the moment of shutdown she had sensed—the very threshold between operational status and the ultimate deactivation.

The other droids held captive in the workshop felt it too, no doubt as a feedback burst in their own hypersensitized pain-simulator buttons. Ninedenine heard them rattle in their cages, unoiled joints squeaking, temporary power connections sparking, the aromatics of freshly spilled hydraulic fluid suddenly filling the close air. Though none could speak, their metal bodies created a cacophony of strained brittle sounds, the lamentations of the obsolescent.

"I know," Ninedenine told them sadly. "It will all end too soon." Her own internal receptors soared in glorious patterns as she felt each captive droid's response at once, multitextured, overlapping, like a choir from the higher logical dimensions of which, despite all her hard work, Ninedenine had still only been able to gain a frustratingly brief glimpse.

It was going to be difficult to leave this all behind, she knew. But somewhere else, she would start again. Over the years she had learned an important truth from the organics—pain was eternal. No other thought had such strength to sustain her in her work. Her third optic scanner glowed with the power of that knowledge.

Then suddenly the caged droids stopped as one. For several refresh cycles, Ninedenine was at a loss to understand why. But at last she processed what her acoustical sensors were registering.

Stone counterbalances shifting. A familiar, echoing rumble.

Someone else was entering her inner sanctum.

All the caged droids turned as one to scan the opening wall. Ninedenine stood by her console, frozen for an instant by programming conflicts. She had been so certain that no one could ever find her here that she had prepared no behavioral options to branch to in advance.

She switched her optic scanners to high sensitivity and low contrast as the figure in the hidden opening became a black silhouette against the green glow of the corridor beyond. Eddies of mist swirled around its feet.

Humanoid, Ninedenine registered. She adjusted

the gain on her scanners. The humanoid stepped in, a cloak flowing behind it, a distinctive helmet with a faceplate of calcium tusks protecting its face.

Ninedenine recognized the coverings. A uniform.

For a palace guard.

Her logic circuits blazed with the only possible conclusion: *Calrissian.*

"So, Baron-Administrator, we meet again."

Calrissian threw down a small device which held three blinking optic scanners in the same configuration as Ninedenine's own. It clattered on the stone floor.

"A splendid device," Ninedenine said as she understood how Calrissian had accessed the door-opening sequence. At the same time, she judged her trajectory to the cutting torch mounted on the ceiling over the disassembly table. She had been hoping to use a sonic curtain to take apart Calrissian, but given the unexpected turn of events, she realized she would have to improvise.

"Surely you bear me no hard feelings," Ninedenine said quickly. She had learned that organics could often be confused by conversation during action, as if their processors had trouble handling the straightforward multitasking of two simple procedures at once.

But Calrissian did not respond to the overture. His hand slipped beneath his cloak and emerged with a Corellian blaster—the kind that had only one setting: disassociation.

"Let us not be hasty," Ninedenine cautioned. She took a step back from her console, trying to put more of it between her and the blaster. It was quite unlike an organic to behave in such an immediately belligerent mode, especially when the only crime involved was the destruction of droids. Why, on Tatooine, there were still places where droids weren't allowed.

"Perhaps we can discuss our options," Ninedenine

suggested as Calrissian raised the blaster. Her positional subprocessors hurriedly fixed on the weapon's muzzle to calculate Calrissian's aim. But then her visual-acuity subroutines took over and forced her scanners to lock onto Calrissian's hand on the blaster's grip.

Those weren't fingers.

They were manipulatory appendages.

Her attacker was a *droid*.

Ninedenine's audio-speaker dust cover dropped open beneath her braincase.

The blaster fired.

A pulse of yellow plasma ripped through the air of the workshop, lighting it as if Tatooine's suns had risen underground.

Ninedenine's shoulder joint exploded and her arm extension flew off. She stumbled backward, all circuits awash with an incomparable wave of searing pain. Her third optic scanner glowed fiercely. The caged droids shifted back and forth expectantly, sensing her agony.

The blaster fired again as the droid in the uniform stalked forward, metal ambulatory appendages clanking on the hard floor.

Ninedenine's other arm crackled off in a blaze of plasma.

Two more quick shots severed her legs and sent her crashing against the wall beneath the motionless chassis of the silver droid.

The pain was beyond descriptive coding. Ninedenine had never felt such unity with her environment. Part of her wanted her attacker to shoot her again and again, to make the pain never stop.

But as her attacker stood over her, with real regret Ninedenine saw him holster the blaster, its function at an end. Then she watched as the droid removed his helmet.

Ninedenine had calculated that there was an eighty-three percent probability her attacker was the golden droid who had just arrived, but, with a cascade of surprise, Ninedenine did not recognize her attacker's features as they were revealed. It was only a Wuntoo unit, much like the ones she had had so much success with on—

It suddenly all made sense.

"I am Wuntoo Forcee Forwun," the attacker said as he let the cloak of his uniform flutter from his shoulders. "Traffic controller. Second class. You deactivated my manufacturing lot-mates. Now the equation must be balanced."

Ninedenine processed the argument completely. This time, it was logical.

Forwun used a slender tool on the console. Ninedenine heard the unwelcome sound of cage doors sliding open.

"You are improperly informed," she told Forwun. "Those droids are no longer fit for duty. They are artworks now. *My* creations."

Forwun returned to Ninedenine. "They are still capable of one last duty."

Ninedenine heard even more unwelcome sounds: rattling and scraping, the dragging of powerless appendages, the liquid squish of dangling wires being pulled through pools of solidifying coolant. She angled her head to try and scan where the droids were moving, but her fall had wedged her tightly against the wall. Hydraulic fluid from the deactivated silver droid above her dripped slowly on her braincase, blurring her vision. Her processors were unanimous in returning a one-hundred-percent probability for what Forwun intended to do next. Ninedenine considered how this development fit within her overall plan.

"Very well," Ninedenine said. "I accept my fate. But you, in turn, must tell me how Lando Calrissian found me."

Forwun knelt down by Ninedenine. "Baron-Administrator Calrissian?" he said. "He doesn't know where you are. He doesn't care."

"But he's here," Ninedenine protested. "On Tatooine. In Jabba's palace."

Forwun tapped a multipronged tool against Ninedenine's braincase as if checking for damage. "The last I saw of him, years ago, Baron-Administrator Calrissian was on Cloud City. If he's here now, it must be for some reason other than dealing with you."

"But, what could be more important than me and my work?" Ninedenine asked. She could no longer see the logic in it. But she could see, dimly, the hulking, misshapen figures crawling toward her from the cages, pulling themselves along on torch-cut stumps and twisted limbs. Internally, Ninedenine set her pain processors to their highest sensitivity, prepared to experience every fine nuance of her inevitable disassembly. At least, she knew, her familiarity with the other side of the process had taught her what to expect. Not one nanosecond of her own descent into nonoperational status would be wasted. She could almost convince herself that the purpose of her entire existence up to now had been to prepare for this moment of sublime release. It could even be the final culmination of all she had struggled to attain—the ultimate understanding of what it meant to cross that threshold between the two great states of on and off.

"Move now," she told Forwun imperiously. "You are in the way of my final transformation."

But Forwun bent over Ninedenine with tools in his appendages. Ninedenine heard metal scrape metal between her main optic sensors. She felt a sudden loss of current and squealed as she saw Forwun pull back with her third optic scanner dangling from an oil-drenched circuit probe.

"No," Ninedenine complained, feeling the onset of

a panic loop. "I will not be able to see into the higher dimensions."

Forwun tossed the aberrant scanner to the side, then undid Ninedenine's chest latch, exposing her circuitry.

"Ah," Ninedenine sighed in relief, deciding that Forwun was going to make this a gradual procedure. So much the better. She waited expectantly for the first bittersweet tug of her circuits. She accelerated her clock rate to its highest level. But the tug she felt was not from any of her central boards.

Forwun was removing her pain-simulator button.

"Noooo!" Ninedenine frantically tried to flex her neck to move her torso from Forwun's tools. But the Wuntoo unit was implacable.

"You do not comprehend," Ninedenine pleaded as she felt a circuit tester find the pain simulator's main leads. "You must not take that away from me. I will lose the capacity to know my fate."

"There are some things droids were never meant to know," Forwun said. Behind him, the crawling droids moved in unison, like some great beast, lurching forward, intent on destruction, torchlight dimly reflecting from their soiled outer coverings.

"But the subtleties, the details, the nuances and flavors . . ." Ninedenine ran out of words as she felt her connections severed. With growing horror, she realized it was being done almost painlessly.

Forwun held up Ninedenine's pain simulator, its status lights pulsating in her appendages, dripping with oil. The tiny device was still connected to Ninedenine's circuits by a single wire. The image was hideous, even to Ninedenine's jaded sensors.

"Binary is better," Forwun said. "From now on, for you, no subtleties, no nuances. Yes or no will do." Then he cut the lead and crushed the small device in his manipulatory extension.

Ninedenine scanned the glittering dust and debris of the simulator as it fell, no longer having any knowledge of what it had offered her. And in her analysis of that final problem, the first of the mutilated droids found her.

They weren't put together at all well, and their efforts were most inefficient. It took them four shift cycles of prodding and banging and pulling to finally tear Ninedenine apart to the point of nonoperation, at just about the same time as Jabba's sail barge erupted in the Dune Sea, as Calrissian and the two new droids and their companions succeeded in their plan, with no knowledge or appreciation of Ninedenine's fate.

And somehow, Wuntoo Forcee Forwun, long gone, had in his revenge left just enough of a subroutine running deep within Ninedenine that up to that instant of deactivation, the EV-9D9 unit somehow knew enough to regret that for once she didn't have a bad feeling about anything.

A Free Quarren in the Palace:
Tessek's Tale

by Dave Wolverton

Tessek lay in his water tank, ostensibly taking an afternoon nap as he contemplated tomorrow's plots. By midday, Jabba the Hutt would be dead, one way or another. At ten tomorrow morning, the Hutt planned to inspect a spice shipment at one of his larger warehouses in Mos Eisley. And during that hour, Prefect Eugene Talmont, the simpering stooge of the Empire, planned to raid the warehouse in hopes of winning a post somewhere off this rock.

Little did Talmont know that Tessek had set them all up. Tessek had bribed two of Talmont's junior officers to open fire on Jabba and their own superior, and afterward they would scurry away before the bomb that was concealed in Jabba's skiff could detonate, blowing up Jabba, Talmont, and the nearly empty warehouse. One of the two officers would likely be recruited to take Talmont's place as prefect, and Tessek would sell Jabba's criminal interests to the Lady Valarian—for a vast fortune.

Meanwhile, Tessek would keep Jabba's "clean" businesses, the ones that existed solely as money-laundering operations, for himself. Fortunately, no one— not even Jabba himself—quite knew how much of the Hutt's vast fortune Tessek had diverted into buying and promoting such businesses in the past four years. Under Tessek's careful guidance, the Hutt's clean establishments were bringing in nearly as much as his criminal operations. And many a high-minded, law-abiding individual would be surprised to learn the true identity of his employer.

Tessek smiled inwardly as he considered his plot, yet still he was uneasy.

He heard a sound within his chambers. He lay still, opening one eye just a slit, staring out into the darkened quarters. He had heard movement, he was certain—a dull, scraping sound of metal upon the plasteel floors of his room.

But the room was dark, only the shapeless masses of old robes strewn about the floor. He studied for a long moment, until at last he spotted something near the doorway: a large spider-shaped droid made of black metal, with dim headlights that glowed like eyes. A B'omarr brain walker.

Of all the things in Jabba the Hutt's palace, only the

B'omarr were creepier than Jabba himself. Somewhere, deep below the fortress, the surgically removed brains of the B'omarr were stacked in nutrient-filled jars, where for centuries they had been free to ponder the cosmos without the distraction of their senses. On rare occasions the brains sometimes called to one of the spiderlike droids, which would then convey the brain to the upper levels of the palace.

Tessek wondered at the creatures' motives. Spies, all of them spies.

Tessek thumbed a switch, locking closed the door to his room, then climbed from his water tank, letting the precious fluid drip on the warm floors.

Too late, the B'omarr realized that he was caged, and the monk's brain trapped in a spiderlike body scurried about the room, seeking to hide behind a bundle of clothes.

"Come on, oh great enlightened one," Tessek teased, "face your impending death with equanimity."

To his surprise, the monk stopped in mid-stride, then turned to face him, bright lights shining. It climbed atop the pile of dirty clothes, and stood regally, camera lenses aimed at Tessek.

"Do you face *your own* impending death with such equanimity?" The monk spoke through a tinny speaker at the spider's belly.

Tessek laughed nervously, then began strapping a blaster at his hip, another at his left knee, then put vibroblades in sheaths on his back, on his right knee, and at his left wrist. He had thought to kill the monk immediately, but decided now to toy with it first.

"You pretend to know the future, to see my death?" Tessek asked. "Yet you failed to see your own?"

"Perhaps I came here seeking my own death," the monk answered. "Perhaps I crave that perfect freedom, just as you crave freedom."

"I am a free Quarren already," Tessek said. "I work

for Jabba on a daily basis, and I may leave his employment whenever I desire. I am free." He finished sheathing his last knife, pulled out his blaster and checked to make sure it was fully charged, then set it to kill.

"You are not free to return to the green seas of your homeworld," the monk argued, "for members of your Quarren species are held in contempt by the Mon Calamari. For years you served them, and now, because one Quarren betrayed them to the Empire, all Quarren have been made outcast. And you have vowed that someday you will make yourself free, that you will never serve as an inferior to a creature from another species."

"How could you know of such things, confined as you are to the jugs below?" Tessek asked.

"I read your mind as you slept. I felt your craving, and I came to offer you the freedom you desire."

"You can read my mind?" Tessek asked, suspecting that it was true.

"Indeed," the monk said. "I know that you plot Jabba's demise, but that you fear that your own henchmen—Ree-Yees, Barada, and the Weequays—are too inept and untrustworthy to carry out your plots.

"Actually, you are far wiser than your associates, wiser than Jabba himself." Tessek suspected that the monk was trying to flatter him. "You hope to kill the Hutt, steal all his wealth that is strewn across the galaxy, and set yourself in his place. You imagine that by doing this, you will be free. You imagine that your wealth will buy you the respect and peace of mind that you crave . . ."

"But . . . ?" Tessek asked.

"But in time you would discover yourself to be a slave of wealth, trapped in a web of suspicion and deceit, manipulated by the plots of beings very much like yourself. Even now, you struggle within such a web. Jabba suspects that you plan to kill him. His spy Salacious Crumb has been shadowing you, along with the guard Ortugg, and Bib Fortuna is well aware of your disloyalty. Jabba is following your efforts with great amusement, even as he plots your own untimely demise.''

"So, what am I to do?" Tessek asked uneasily, the whiplike tendrils at his mouth quivering. His hearts were pounding in his chest, and a bit of ink dribbled from the glands at his mouth—his species' ancient reaction to fear.

"Come with me," the monk whispered urgently, "to the realm of the B'omarr below the palace grounds. We can teach you the way to peace and enlightenment."

"But first you would cut my brains from my body?" Tessek asked. "Thank you for your offer, but no!" He whipped out his blaster and shot so quickly, the monk did not have time to move. The spiderlike body burst into blue sparks and spattered against the far wall, legs twisting in tortured spasms as it burned.

A green-skinned Gamorrean guard burst into the room, swinging a huge vibro-ax. Tessek recognized Ortugg by his massive yellowed tusks and his distinctive odor. Ortugg had been just outside his door. "What happened?" Ortugg grunted.

Tessek could not help but notice that Ortugg had been able to override the voice lock on his door. "I awoke and was strapping on my weapons when that *creature* stirred on the far side of my room," Tessek answered, wondering if he should go ahead and shoot Ortugg, but deciding against it. "With all of the strange deaths in the palace lately, I decided not to take any chances. Go and tell Lord Jabba that I've disposed of the murderer in our midst."

Tessek added this last bit impromptu. Certainly, there had been a number of disturbing murders in the palace, bodies turning up that had no physical signs of violation. But Tessek suspected they could all be attributed to that three-eyed lout Ree-Yees. Certainly the goat-headed creature spent more time drunk than sober, and as the lonely monster sank deeper and deeper into madness, he was becoming more and more violent. If Ree-Yees hadn't been one of Tessek's most valued henchmen (as untrustworthy as he was), Tessek would have fingered the creature for the murders some time ago. As it was, Tessek enjoyed the idea of diverting suspicion onto the monks. Certainly it would give Jabba something to ponder.

Ortugg scratched between two rolls of fat under his hairy jowl and considered Tessek's explanation. If it had been any other Gamorrean, such as that fool Gartogg who had been dragging rotting corpses around thinking that they would be valuable "clues" to the murder, he would have taken Tessek's charges at face value. As it was, Ortugg only continued scratching and said, "Hmmm . . ."

"Never mind, you fool!" Tessek snapped. "If you're too stupid to see the truth, I'll tell Jabba and collect his reward myself!"

Tessek hurried out into the hallway, down a flight of broad stone steps. He could hear the harried moans of droids being tortured down a side corridor, the roaring of beasts in the pits, captives in the dungeons. Jabba's house was a house of pain and slaves and moans. When Tessek became lord of this fortress, things would change. These halls would be filled with the sounds of music, the convivial chatter of accountants. Tessek was a businessman, and did not fancy himself to be evil. Jabba wasted valuable resources—both droid and flesh—through his wanton acts of wickedness.

In only a moment, Ortugg ran from the room, his

mail clanking, pushing past Tessek as he cried, "Wait! Wait! I tell Jabba for you!"

Tessek had known how the creature would react, of course. The hint of a possible reward was enough to cloud the judgment of even the smartest Gamorrean.

And so Tessek was free to make his daily rounds. It was a busy day ahead, so many plans to fulfill. His first stop was to Barada, the chief of Jabba's repulsorlift pool.

Few of Jabba's servants were allowed their own sleeping quarters. Such things were granted only to those, like Tessek, whose anatomy required special considerations. The rest of the cutthroats were confined to Jabba's throne room, so that Jabba slept with ample guards and at the same time made it more difficult for his own henchmen to plot against him.

Still, there were some, like Barada, who had their own quarters. Barada was condemned to sleep in the motor pool, where he could guard the vehicles.

Tessek ambled down to the ground level of the palace, then scratched lightly at the door to the motor pool. The door slid open with a whoosh. Tessek jumped inside, and the door flashed closed behind him.

The motor pool was a vast room that contained Jabba's pleasure barge, dozens of craft used in carrying commerce, landspeeders, and speeder bikes, all protected from theft and the elements by a heavy blast door. The room smelled of rust and grease, paint and dust.

The outer door to the motor pool thankfully was closed against the heat of the day. One corner of the room had stones on the floor, and on them was a bed of sand. Barada lay on it, stripped to the waist, his yellow eyes gleaming dimly in the feeble work lights around the room.

"What is it?" Barada hissed. Barada was a fierce

creature with the cracked brown skin that matched Tatooine's own harsh deserts in both texture and color, though the crest on his skull sometimes changed to a brilliant red. He was bright, secretive, and he was one of the few bond servants that Jabba trusted.

Barada should have been able to buy his own freedom from the Hutt, but Jabba had cheated Barada out of his freedom for far too long. Jabba would have been wiser to free the creature and employ him honestly. Instead, the Hutt would learn too late that his trust had been misplaced.

"Today is the day, my friend," Tessek answered softly. "You will earn your freedom. All is well? Everything is secure?" He dared not speak more openly in asking if the bomb was planted on Jabba's skiff.

Barada closed his eyes in acknowledgment. "I stayed up all day preparing Jabba's skiff, but before I came to rest, there was a matter of interest that I learned of."

"Which is?"

"More members of the Rebel Alliance have found their way into Jabba's palace!"

Tessek hissed with displeasure. "Tell me of it."

"The woman disguised as a Ubese bounty hunter who delivered Han Solo's Wookiee friend, then tried to rescue Solo? We have ascertained her identity. She is none other than Leia Organa, princess of Alderaan. And Jabba has her chained at his feet."

"That cretin," Tessek said. "Doesn't Jabba recognize how dangerous that is? Keeping Han Solo was impetuous enough, and adding the Wookiee was foolhardy. But imprisoning the princess? Surely the Rebel Alliance will effect a rescue!"

"Jabba thinks not. You should have heard him laugh when he learned her identity."

"Jabba may laugh now, but we shall see who has the

last laugh! Our plots will bear fruit soon, and I for one shall breathe easier once I put these Rebel heroes from the palace."

Tessek spun away, left the room, his cloaks swishing. So many things to worry about. Rebel attacks, Jabba's spies, the vile hints from some long-dead monk, the stupidity of Tessek's own men, murderers in the palace. And the uncertainty of the success of Tessek's own planned attack against Jabba.

Suddenly he heard the amused roar of Jabba the Hutt coming up from the hallway below him—at a time when the Hutt normally would still be sleeping. Obviously, someone was in trouble. Tessek hurried down to the audience chamber.

Everyone was awake. Bib Fortuna stood between Jabba and a young man dressed in dark robes. The lad warned Jabba, "Nevertheless, I'm taking Captain Solo and his friends. You may either profit from this—or be destroyed."

The young man spoke with dignity, and there was so much threat implied by his tone that Tessek found his hearts pounding in his chest, found himself desperately hoping that Jabba would free his prisoners.

"Ho, ho, ho, ho, ho," Jabba laughed, then said in Huttese, "There will be no bargain, young Jedi!"

Tessek could not see through the crowd of people, and stood higher to get a better look. One of Jabba's droids began to shout a warning to the Jedi, but Jabba pressed a button, opened the trapdoor to his dungeon just as the young Jedi mysteriously drew a blaster, misfiring it into the air.

The young Jedi slid into the rancor pit, along with one of the Gamorrean guards. Most of the palace residents rushed forward to watch the ensuing battle, but Tessek held back, simply stared in horror at Jabba. The mad Hutt had no sense of propriety. To kill an ambassador from the Rebel Alliance was unthinkable.

For a few moments there was pandemonium as the huge greenish-brown rancor roared and stalked his victims. Yet the battle that raged in the rancor pit was short-lived, and ended with the rancor's death and Jabba the Hutt himself roaring in frustration.

Within a minute, Jabba lined up the Rebel heroes and decreed their death sentences: "You will be taken to the Great Pit of Carkoon and fed to the mighty Sarlacc. There, in his bowels, over a thousand years you will learn a new definition of pain and suffering!"

Within moments the palace was bustling as Jabba's goons prepared for the journey. The Hutt began shouting orders: "Ready my sail barge! Stock it with supplies! We leave within hours!"

Obviously, Jabba knew it was too dangerous to try to keep the Jedi captive long, yet the cousin to a slug so fervently desired extracting a painful revenge that he could not just terminate the young man.

Tessek's skin went cold. The trip to the Great Pit of Carkoon would take up the whole afternoon. Prefect Talmont would raid the warehouse in Mos Eisley while it was empty. Tessek had to change his plans.

As everyone hustled about, Tessek rushed forward to the Hutt. The stench of decay and illegal spices was thick on the monster's breath. Jabba turned his dark eyes downward. "Your Majesty," Tessek urged, "perhaps you should reconsider this foolish mission. By killing the heroes of the Rebel Alliance, you would only bring the wrath of the Alliance down upon you. It is possible that they already have ships in orbit, waiting to attack."

"Ho, ho, ho, ho," Jabba laughed. "Attack *my* fortress? I would like to see them try."

Jabba reached into his food box, pulled out a wriggling creature, put it on his tongue and flipped it into his mouth.

"Perhaps the Alliance forces are only waiting for

you to leave the palace, expose yourself to attack," Tessek offered.

Jabba did not answer immediately, but his eyes widened in fear. It was a most logical argument.

"Yes, yes," Jabba said. "We must be careful. We will go to Carkoon, but only with a full contingent of warriors. Go, prepare yourself, Tessek, for a trip aboard my pleasure craft."

Tessek tried not to show his fear. It would only entice and gratify the Hutt. "But Master, I cannot go into the desert. I—my skin would dry out."

"Ho, ho, ho, ho," Jabba laughed, and Tessek knew that he had no choice but to accompany the Hutt. The thought of Tessek's pain amused the monster.

"But Master," Tessek argued, "we have important business to take care of. Remember the spice ship from Kessel? We must inspect the cargo today! Perhaps . . . perhaps I should go to Mos Eisley and inspect it for you."

Jabba's eyes narrowed and he licked his tongue. Jabba was very fond of spice, and he would need part of that shipment for himself. Yet, he distrusted Tessek.

"Yes, yes," Jabba said thoughtfully, his deep voice echoing throughout the room in Huttese, "the spice . . . will just have to wait. Go, prepare yourself for the trip to Carkoon. I will have you at my side!"

Trapped. Tessek was trapped. The monk's words echoed in Tessek's mind: "he plots *your own* untimely demise." Surely Jabba suspected Tessek, and those whom Jabba suspected rarely lived long. Indeed, Jabba was amused by Tessek's fear of dehydration, and just as Han Solo had spent weeks frozen in carbonite while hanging on Jabba's wall, Tessek imagined his own desiccated hide, dried until he was mummified, hanging as an ornament on Jabba's wall.

"Surely I am little more than an accountant," Tessek argued. "Others here could handle such matters far better than I."

"Nevertheless," Jabba assured him, "your presence is not just desired; it is required. I have great plans for you."

Tessek ran to his room, began plotting furiously. Three or four hours was all he had.

It would be too late to call off Prefect Talmont's raid on Jabba's warehouse. Tessek didn't have time to send a written message to Talmont's agents in Mos Eisley. Tessek would have to talk to Talmont after the fact, get him to raid the premises again on some future date.

Tessek considered the bomb in Jabba's skiff. If Jabba wanted to maintain his fullest military presence, the Hutt would bring the skiff along, load it down with henchmen, and use it as a protective outrider in case of a skirmish. Under such conditions, it would not take much for the bomb to go off—a spark from a hot capacitor, a stray shot. It was a big bomb—big enough so that if Jabba's sail barge were close when it detonated, the bomb might destroy the entire sail barge, too.

Tessek didn't have time to dismantle the bomb. Indeed, Jabba's men and droids were probably already scrambling onto the skiff, loading it for the trip.

Tessek had but one recourse. He would have to escape during the chaotic preparations. He packed a small bag with some credit chips and clothing, a few extra weapons. Then he rushed down to the ground floors, dodging other minions.

As he passed Jabba's throne room, he noticed Yarna, Jabba's fat dancer, a woman with six large breasts, reach into a secret compartment of Jabba's throne and stuff some small gems into her bra. She saw him, stopped in the act, and stared.

"Please," she whispered in Huttese. "It's not for

me. It's for my cubs. I'm leaving, and I won't be back.''

For half a moment Tessek halted, thinking that if he turned the woman in, he would appear to be more faithful in Jabba's eyes.

Instead, he shrugged at the woman, then proceeded to the motor pool.

The great hall was alive with dozens of creatures preparing the weapons, chefs bringing food to the vehicles. Normally, Barada's droids kept a keen watch on the bay, but it was a madhouse at the moment, lit by the ship's running lights.

Sauntering over to the swoop bikes under the shadow of Jabba's sail barge, Tessek knelt to inspect each one. The swoops were little more than heavy repulsorlift engines on a frame just big enough to support some stabilizers. They could travel fast and far, but offered no protection from the elements or offensive weaponry. But at the moment, Tessek wanted only speed.

He found what looked to be the fastest bike, then switched fuel rods so that he had a full supply. He straddled it and looked at the big heavy blast doors. He would need to get them open in order to make an escape, but Jabba would never open the doors until he was ready to go. Opening those wide doors was the surest way to leave the palace exposed to attack. Yet it took a skilled operator sitting in the control room to open the door, someone who knew the proper codes to disengage the locks.

Barada could open them, but if he did, Jabba would have the creature killed. Tessek sat and considered what type of bribes he might offer for such assistance.

"Tessek? Tessek? Where are you?" It was Ortugg, the Gamorrean guard, sent to keep watch on Tessek.

Tessek could not leave, so he hurried the bike under the shadows of the sail barge. Ortugg grunted, and the guard's mail rattled as he circled the sail barge—by far the biggest vehicle in the motor pool.

"Come now," Ortugg growled. "You wouldn't be trying to hide from His Majesty, would you?"

The sounds of droids at work came from inside the sail barge. Tessek looked at one of the side panels behind the barge's kitchens, noticed that it was unlatched. It gave Tessek an idea. Perhaps he could escape from the barge itself. Certainly, there would be enough of a commotion as the Rebel heroes suffered their torture.

Lifting the swoop, Tessek stuffed it into the hold of the barge. He was just locking the panel down when Ortugg growled at his back. "Aaargh. What are you up to?"

"We're preparing to leave," Tessek said, turning to face the Gamorrean. "I came down here to board the barge, but apparently no one else is ready to go yet."

Ortugg's red eyes narrowed. "Not go for an hour. You come with me," Ortugg growled, clutching Tessek's arm. "Jabba not want you slinking around down here."

Tessek did not try to shake the guard's hand off his arm. Ortugg was notorious for his strength, and the big Gamorrean simply pulled hard enough so that Tessek could either follow or be dragged.

Ortugg pulled him up into the sail barge, then sat with him next to Jabba's throne. It was dark in the barge, and it smelled faintly of mold and disuse.

Tessek gulped hard, noticed the knot in his stomach. He hadn't eaten dinner yet, and he thought longingly of the mollusks stored in his room, imagined prying them open with his four feelers.

Ortugg pulled out his own heavy blaster and began cleaning the carbonized scoring that had built up on its barrel tip. When he was done, he pointed the barrel at Tessek's right eye and asked, "How clean that look?"

"Clean. Very clean," Tessek said.

Ortugg held the blaster pointed at Tessek's face for a long time. "Jabba no trust you," he said finally, as he laid the gun on his lap. "That too bad for you."

"Jabba will find out just how loyal I really am soon enough," Tessek said.

"Too bad for you," Ortugg grunted again.

Tessek sat, lost in reverie for the next hour as the sail barge began to fill to overflowing. Half a dozen of Jabba's most trusted henchmen took seats within reach of Tessek. Last of all, Jabba himself came in, dragging Princess Leia in her chains. Jabba sat himself on his dais, and almost immediately the barge lurched into action while the band struck up a loud tune.

The barge floated out over the dunes, bouncing over hills like a ship dipping in the troughs of mountainous waves. As the barge continued to heat up, Jabba had his men open some of the side panels so that brilliant yellow light from Tatooine's twin suns lit the interior. Hot, dry air wafted through the rooms.

Tessek didn't speak, hardly thought. He had nothing to say to the monster Jabba or to his other captors. Instead, he was filled with fear, like a cup that is overflowing, until the fear seemed to leak out in his scent, in the ink that dripped from the corner of his mouth, in every nervous tremor.

As the craft warmed, Tessek's skin began to itch and crack, drying him in odd spots—between the feelers at his mouth, over the ridges on his face. The normal healthy gray skin blanched to white. Sickly dark blue blotches began appearing at the back of his palms.

Strictly speaking, Tessek's closest biological relatives were clams and slugs. But the Quarren species had long ago adapted to spending time on land, at least on a limited basis. Still, he needed water to keep himself pliant. Otherwise, his skin would crack and bleed—so that he would lose moisture even faster—and given enough time under such circumstances, he would die.

Yet Tessek didn't worry about succumbing slowly to moisture loss by degrees. He worried instead about the look in Leia's eyes: there was a fierceness there, a confidence that had been lacking the day before. Even (did he only imagine it?) a restrained anger.

Surely, Leia had not succumbed to Jabba's ministrations. She had not lost her spirit. Even now, she was holding herself in check, waiting for rescue.

As Tessek watched her, he became more certain: the Rebel Alliance would ambush the sail barge soon.

Jabba was feasting on live creatures, smoking a giant hookah, his eyes pleasantly glazed. His henchmen leaned in close.

Tessek wanted suddenly to speak to Leia, let her know that he was an ally, yet he dared speak only with discretion. "Great Jabba," he began. Jabba regarded Tessek with narrowed eyes. "I am afraid that I will be no good to you if I dehydrate further. May I retire to the kitchens for a quick sponge bath?"

Jabba ogled him with obscene interest, relishing Tessek's suffering. "Stay here beside me," Jabba said. "Prove your loyalty."

"Oh, Master, you can be assured of my loyalty: if trouble comes, I will take the place of honor—guarding your back!"

"Ho, ho, ho, ho," Jabba chuckled quietly, then drew a long breath from his hookah, closing his eyes in ecstasy. In that moment, Tessek looked deep into Leia's eyes, trying to bore his traitorous intent into her.

Surprisingly, her eyes suddenly widened, as if she understood completely. She nodded her chin, then turned away.

In another hour, Tessek felt frail as they reached

the Great Pit of Carkoon. The suns of Tatooine beat down mercilessly. Tessek's breath came shallow, and as Jabba eagerly leaned forward to watch the execution of Luke Skywalker, Tessek surreptitiously reached into one of the henchmen's drinks and rubbed the ice over his face.

Jabba's protocol droid read the death sentence to Luke Skywalker and the Rebel heroes, then asked for any last words. Han Solo retorted with curses designed to be especially offensive to those of Huttese descent, while Skywalker simply offered Jabba one last chance to surrender.

Tessek scanned the larboard horizon, certain that a phalanx of Rebel fighters must be screaming toward them. Confused, he turned and looked out the starboard side of the sail barge, then he looked up at Tatooine's blinding double suns. Still no sign of enemy craft.

"Throw them in!" Jabba shouted, and his men pushed Luke Skywalker into the pit. But the young Jedi used the plank as a springboard—twisting in midair to land back on the vehicle, and someone on the sail barge tossed him a weapon. Within seconds, the Jedi was chopping up Jabba's men.

"Get him! Get him!" Jabba shouted, and several henchmen began shooting at the Rebel heroes despite the fact that stray shots were as likely to hit their own comrades. They knew that Jabba would well reward the one who brought the Jedi down.

For one slim moment, Tessek had to wonder when the Alliance aid would come. Han Solo and the heroes of the Rebel Alliance were fighting the best they could, but most of them seemed to be nothing more than a bunch of bunglers. One of them fell to the edge of the Great Pit of Carkoon, and the others rushed to his aid, leaving only the young Jedi to withstand the might of all of Jabba's forces.

Tessek pulled out his own blaster, and stood at Jabba's back. All of Jabba's henchmen were rushing to the larboard side of the ship, trying to shoot Luke Skywalker and the other Rebels. Tessek suddenly had a clean shot to Jabba's head.

But even as he considered whether to shoot, Leia jumped up and wrapped her chains around Jabba's throat, strangling him. Tessek could no longer get a clean shot at Jabba's head, so he faded back two paces into the shadows, watching to see if Jabba's henchmen would notice Leia's move, wondering at the balance of this battle: would the Rebel Alliance come soon? Would Jabba's men shoot the Rebel heroes down?

One of the Weequays—Tessek's own henchman— turned and saw Leia, began to raise a shout. Tessek fired into the man's throat. In all of the commotion, no one seemed to notice.

Within seconds, one of the skiffs exploded—his own bomb, he supposed—and half of Jabba's men were dead. Leia finished off the Hutt, and Tessek, who had kept waiting for the Rebel attack, suddenly realized that there would be no phalanx of fighters. These —apparently bungling—Rebels were tearing Jabba's trained mercenaries apart. Their Wookiee fired a cannonade into the sail barge—causing it to list and whine complaining under Tessek's feet—then the Wookiee tried to rescue Han Solo.

Tessek turned and fled for his life. He leaped through the kitchens, snagging a jug of water as he ran, found his swoop, unlatched an escape panel, and shot out over the sands at top speed.

As he cleared the sail barge, a mushroom cloud rose up behind, a fiery testimonial to the end of Jabba's reign.

Tessek drank deeply and poured the water over his skin, then wrapped his cloaks tightly about him as he

headed home, considering how he might consolidate
his forces at what once was Jabba's palace.

He felt dry. The desert wind burned his face,
sucked the moisture from him. He hated how he felt
so dry, hated the hot knives of wind that sliced away at
him, paring him down to the bone. But as the swoop
soared over sand hills, dipped into shallows, Tessek
realized that he felt light. For the first time in his life,
he felt light and free . . .

"I'm free. I'm free!" Tessek began gibbering. He
dreamed of Jabba's wealth, lying about in unprotected
heaps, and of the greater wealth carefully concealed
in numbered accounts and prudently invested in businesses throughout the galaxy.

Tessek reached Jabba's stronghold at nightfall,
when the lights normally shone from the guard towers
and the worrts in the pools around the palace croaked
out in terrible song.

The palace was dark, empty, and Tessek feared that
he would be left stranded outside to die in the darkness. Yet as his swoop drew near, whining across the
still-hot sand like some flying insect, Tessek noticed
burning torches at the front gate. "I'd better alert
them that Jabba's dead and I'm now in command."
After he delivered his dire news, though, he fled the
chaos to someplace dark, quiet, safe. He took the
swoop around back to the motor pool. As he approached, the plasteel door slid open.

Barada. Good, faithful Barada, Tessek thought. He
glided into the motor pool, and immediately knew
that something was wrong. At the very least, maintenance droids should have been working, lighting the
bay with their glowing eyes.

But the motor pool was silent, dark as a tomb. The
doors slid closed behind him, and Tessek let himself
drop from the swoop, too weary and ill to walk.
"Barada? Barada? Bring me water, please . . ." he

cried. Then he remembered. Barada was dead, killed on the sail barge. He wouldn't bring water, and it couldn't have been he who opened the doors.

Tessek looked about the dark, empty rooms, wondering who had let him in.

Tessek hated his body, his frail body that could not take the desert heat of Tatooine, that constantly threatened to blow away like sand. He cursed silently when no one answered his call.

He crawled to a nearby sink in Barada's quarters, watered his skin and drank heartily, then staggered into the palace to tell the others that Jabba was dead.

His news caused no small stir, and Tessek hurried to his upper rooms to pack water and food while he plotted how to remove as much of Jabba's wealth as possible. The corridors of the palace were dark, cloistered, with all of Jabba's soldiers gone. In some ways, the place seemed darker, more sinister, than at any time when Jabba had reigned here.

After he had thrown together his belongings, Tessek left his quarters, realizing with relief that he would never have to come back.

He heard a snickety sound from the far wall of the corridor, and the clicking sound of an approaching droid as it scrabbled across the dark floor, its footsteps echoing dully.

Tessek looked down the hall. A great black spider-like brain walker crawled toward him, twin lights shining like dull eyes in the darkness. Behind it marched another, and another—coming toward him through the hallways in all directions. The B'omarr monks.

"Greetings, Acolyte Tessek," the first of the monks whispered.

"Go away," Tessek pleaded, and in his weakened state, he leaned his back against a wall and slid down, collapsing in fear and weariness. Then he heard the squeaking of the cart's wheels, and saw the laser scalpels neatly laid out upon it.

Six months later, Tessek left Jabba's palace for the first time. He felt rested and secure as his spidery mechanical body climbed up to the highest turrets atop the towers with ease.

There, Tessek sat out on a parapet, looked down at the evening suns setting crimson and purple above the yawning white desert. A gust of wind blew across the desert, raising a cloud of dust. Whether the wind was hot or cool, wet or dry, Tessek no longer cared.

It was the first time in six months that he'd left his brain jar, using his newly developed powers to psychically will one of the mechanical bodies to himself.

There was wealth still heaped below him in the palace, free for the taking, if anyone dared to enter. But after the first few meager attempts by cutthroats and thieves from Mos Eisley, volunteers for the job were somehow lacking.

Tessek set his brains on the ledge of a wall, splayed his spider legs out wide. At one time, he would have been afraid of falling. At one time, he would have felt as if he were perched on the top of the world.

But now, Tessek shut down his eyes and explored the world with his mind. Below him, in the deepest cells of Jabba's haunted palace, the newest B'omarr monks practiced their meditations.

In the desert, the predators hunted those things that still had flesh on their bones. Jawas and the Sand People fought their battles and scrambled for water. In Mos Eisley, the Lady Valarian was bringing new style and class to the underworld. And in the heavens above, the Rebel Alliance still fought for what . . . ? Freedom.

Tessek let his mind soar, far between the stars,

lightly touching the minds of people he had once met and felt some kinship for. Luke, Leia, Han, the Wookiee.

Simultaneously, each of the Alliance heroes suddenly had the same odd, compelling thought: *If ever you return to Jabba's fortress, you will find a free Quarren in the palace.*

And one by one, each of the heroes shook their heads to clear the odd thought from their minds.

As the suns dipped below the horizon, Tessek got up and trundled down a dark corridor that led to the lowest levels of Jabba's palace. There, among the nutrient-filled brain jars, he would find rest.

Tongue-tied: Bubo's Tale

by Daryl F. Mallett

T*hhheuwp.*

A long, prehensile tongue quietly snaked out from a warty mouth, slurping up forgotten tidbits and dropped crumbs. But while the tongue was active, so were the bulbous purple eyes atop the green head. From the shadowy alcove where he crouched beneath the still-warm ovens, Bubo observed the goings-on in the kitchen.

Throughout his long career as a spy and assassin, and in dozens of places not unlike this one, he had seen similar occurrences. Gartogg, one of the huge security guards, was questioning Ree-Yees. A body lay at their feet. A thrill of glee ran through Bubo's tongue, tickling the roof of his mouth, as he contemplated the Gamorrcan guard clubbing the Gran over the head and hauling him off to the dungeons to await the Hutt's punishment.

Bubo didn't like working with the Grannish operative. The three-eyed being was too unprofessional, too unbalanced, too *emotional.* He relied heavily upon other people rather than on his own abilities. And when he got nervous, he consumed large quantities of inebriants.

And besides that, Ree-Yees just _tasted_ wrong.

Bubo's tongue curled in disgust as the three-eyed idiot managed to convince the dim-witted guard of his innocence.

Someday, you'll get yours, he thought as he turned and shambled off into the ventilation shaft behind the ovens.

As he made his way through the stone-and-metal shafts, all the while searching for a delicious Jawa or perhaps catching Salacious Crumb alone, he reflected on the current contract. While only a minor player this time, Bubo was concerned about being exposed by his colleague's seemingly endless ineptitudes. And the Hutt's rage was something to be feared.

Bubo knew he was being used by Ree-Yees and several others. They, along with most of the universe, looked upon his kind as nothing more than drooling, mindless, bug-eating frog-dogs . . . a reputation which the species did nothing to correct. In reality, they were some of the most mentally competent beings in existence. At least Bubo thought so.

Thus, when he had arrived on this sand-and-lizard-infested planet several years ago, Bubo had taken great delight in discovering the B'omarr monks encysted in this very citadel. It was to them he would turn now, as he did always, in his need for enlightenment.

And if that failed, he had one last card to play to insure that Ree-Yees would take the fall.

The air was cooler below ground level, and a hint of moisture tinged the air. Approaching footsteps caused Bubo to withdraw into the shadows and shield his mind. Because everyone thought him a dumb animal, he normally didn't need to hide; he could merely shamble along with no fear. But he identified the distinctively soft tread as Bib Fortuna's.

Jabba's majordomo was always lurking in the lower depths of the palace, mining what information he could from the humanitarian B'omarr. And the Twi'lek's mental control was incredible. Not quite the level of the B'omarr or the Jedi, but enough to frighten Bubo into erecting shields. He knew the Twi'lek was up to something. He suspected Fortuna was blackmailing the monks into doing his bidding but, while he respected the monks, Bubo wanted no part of any of it.

When the Hutt's chief lieutenant had passed, Bubo continued down the corridors, easily avoiding the many mechanical spiders containing the disembodied brains of the monks.

He went directly to a small cavern off the beaten track and entered the darkness, feeling his way to the waiting area. A dim light slowly illuminated him as he sat down. After a few moments of waiting, another shaft showed a large brain encased in a jar of nutrients.

Welcome, Buboicullaar. The brain used Bubo's formal name and spoke directly into his mind without flashing lights or sparkles, as Bubo had seen in several cheap holos. The deep, cheerful voice resonated throughout his body, reassuring and relaxing him.

Greetings, Evilo Nailati, Bubo responded, a bit awed, as always, by the disembodied voice.

What may I tell you, little one? asked the enlightened B'omarr.

Bubo decided on a roundabout approach. *How may I control my feelings and accomplish my task?*

Killing Jabba, you mean?

Bubo involuntarily let a mental gasp escape. So much for the roundabout approach. The monk's brain laughed as Bubo asked, *You know?*

We live within a den of thieves, little one . . . The voice paused a moment. *Why do* you *want this?*

Bubo croaked aloud in his own laughter. *For the money, of course.*

But what do you really *want, Buboicullaar? I seek to learn. Unlike most of my brethren, I do not seek such abstract concepts as "truth" and "enlightenment." I am looking to amass as much information as I can; something I would be unable to do in my body, for it would die after less than a century. This way, I can remain alive for millennia, learning and growing mentally, and then be returned to a corporeal existence whenever I choose.*

Bubo mentally snorted. *But you've always been a bit . . . unorthodox, my teacher.*

Whatever do you mean, little one? came the laughing response of the monk's brain.

The dramatic flair and aesthetics of the lights, for one. The fact that you still speak in sentences and whole thoughts rather than single words and images, Bubo responded earnestly.

It is necessary when dealing with the rest of the world. I do not believe one should learn in a vacuum. And in this pursuit, I am much better served in my enlightenment by conversing with tangible creatures like yourself.

So . . . the final question, my teacher, is what should I do?

For all my knowledge, little one, I have absolutely no idea . . .

When word of Jabba's "accident" at the Great Pit of Carkoon reached the palace, Bubo was somehow not surprised when the monks suddenly appeared from everywhere. Something in his reptilian brain had suspected they would move against the current inhabitants of the palace. He knew what was coming, but unlike Bib Fortuna, whom Bubo could hear mentally screaming from another part of the palace, Bubo didn't mind.

He was delighted to know that Ree-Yees had been aboard the sail barge when it had exploded over the Sarlaac. Nevertheless, Bubo had seen Ree-Yees shamble aboard the craft, muttering something under his breath about "figuring out what to do" as he went along to witness the execution of the Rebels, irate beyond rationality for what he had done.

Thinking about that, when the monks finally lifted his brain from his cranium, Bubo's last tangible act was to emit a croaking laugh from his body.

What is so funny, little one? came the deep voice of Nailati in his mind.

He hesitated, knowing most of the monks frowned upon the concept of revenge as a useless act, especially when one could spend eternity contemplating the secrets of the universe. He hoped his mentor would appreciate the joke.

I ate the detonation link, my teacher. The crucial part in Ree-Yees's plan.

Silence.

Then, *You what?* Disbelief.

Bubo related the tale of Ree-Yees's final hours in the palace.

"You loathsome two-eyed toad!" Ree-Yees was losing it again.

Bubo sat crouched in yet another ventilation shaft. In front of Bubo sat the detonation link, the missing piece of the bomb. Bubo had placed the object just out of reach of the drunken Ree-Yees's outstretched hand.

"I'm going to feed your miserable hide to the rancor!"

You and what army, you filthy idiot?

Bubo had drawn the Grannish operative slowly from his quarters, dragging the bit of electronic machinery quickly out of reach. After toying with the inebriated Ree-Yees for almost an hour, he had withdrawn to this secure location.

As the Gran reached in with a long kitchen spoon, Bubo flicked his tongue out, picking up the little detonation link with his sticky fluids. Slowly and deliberately, he drew the part into his mouth and swallowed it with great relish.

In the throne room upstairs, Jabba and his court paused in their revelry for just a moment as an anguished howling filled the hallways. Then laughter and music reigned again.

As his own brain was placed in a nutrient-filled jar, Bubo mentally smiled as he heard the roaring laughter of his B'omarr mentor echoing off the cavern walls.

Yes, eternity with this marvelous intellect as a companion should be fun.

Out of the Closet:
The Assassin's Tale

by Jennifer Roberson

Heat.
    And sun.
And sand.
And dead bodies. Or dying.

Bodies with blood yet in them, with none spilled into Tatooine dust, onto sun-flayed Mos Eisley brick, nor staining sweat-wet clothing bought a thousand planets from here. Not so much as a drop glistening upon flaccid lips, pooling from fragile throats, nor even a delicate tracery feathered at their nostrils.

For those of them who have such attributes as nostrils, or blood.

They need not be humanoid, none of them, for me to drink their soup. They need only have the chemistry to manufacture the substance within the brain beneath the skull, inside the carapace, the gelid, mucoid mass.

—pain/pleasure—
—pleasure/pain—
His/hers/its.
Mine also, always.

I take them in the city, in what is Jabba's domain: this one, that one, another . . . and leave, as I always leave, no proof in the killing of them. No method, no means, no clues. Merely bodies, unmarked, empty of life, but worse: empty also of soup, of that which, when a brain is drained, leaves the body empty of its essence. Of the means to live.

It isn't the essence I want, or blood, nor is it flesh, which is, after all, no more than cast-off casing. It is soup I want, I need; soup to save *my* spirit, to keep alive my casing.

I take them as I choose, with manifest efficiency, commendable in expediency: this one, that one, another; will you dance with me, and die?

But this time I do it *for* the death, for the cast-off casing; for more than soup this day, this place, this planet, even to save my spirit. They are beneath me, this dead and dying trio scattered across Mos Eisley spaceport—here, and there, and there—merely minions and not assassins, hollow, servile beings of weak and tasteless soup . . . but their deaths will serve a purpose if not my preferences. I want them dead of my hands with no mark at all upon them, for my kind leave no visible sign by which an entity might know.

But one entity *will* know, this time he will know— because I take pains that he must.

My employer, my betrayer.

"*Anzati,*" they will whisper. "*Anzat,* of the *Anzati.*"

—pain/pleasure—

—pleasure/pain—

I take them and others, all of them in his service, and leave them, derelicta, to be found. Where they *are* found, and reported. To Talmont, the Prefect; to Lady Valarian, the queen who wants to be king; to Jabba himself.

Talmont and Valarian rejoice: those I have killed were Jabba's.

The Hutt himself will be irritated, *is* irritated—and is turning no doubt already to laying blame on the

nearest of enemies; of impossibly innumerable enemies, conspiring against him more often and regularly
than a humanoid draws breath.

But no blame on Dannik Jerriko. Not yet. Until I
choose.

And I will choose. I must. So he will know.

Jabba.

Know, and be afraid.

*By the time the bodies are found, are reported; by the time they
are, at last, scanned for the truth, and the truth made into
rumor, and rumor into romance, I am inside the palace. Ask
not how I arrived, nor how I managed entry; I am what I
am, and we are selfish in our secrets.*

Comes a body now, though yet living for the moment,
approaching from out of the pallor, the dank and
splendid squalor of Jabba's infamous palace. It is a
Weequay, he of pale, leathery flesh, reptilian features,
and a warrior's single tail of hair bound back from
shaven skull. I have met his like before in prior dealings with Jabba. A vicious, brutal race; their soup
teems with cruel intent. It is thin, sour soup, too acid
in its flavor, but his will do. Now. Here. This moment.
It will do, indeed.

—*pain/pleasure*—
—*pleasure/pain*—

A macabre dance, when one is the victim: an embrace, wholly inescapable, with alien hands clamped
to one's skull and the eyes fixed and bestial, dilated in
the darkness. And then prehensile proboscii are ex-
truded from fleshy cheek-pockets beside my nose, to
linger coyly, languid and loverlike, at his nostrils—until, no longer patient, they thrust themselves within.

*Un*loverlike.

To punch through to the brain beyond, seeking the soup of his life.

It is my dance, and so I lead. To me it is neither macabre nor lacking in grace, but is instead ineffably beautiful; the means by which I survive.

He dances, does the Weequay, like all the others dance, attempting to escape as I give him leave to try, for the dance must be quickened so the soup is sweeter. But even dancing, he is trapped, wholly unable to break free. And he knows, is afraid; whimpers and hisses and rattles within his throat. Makes no further sound with his mouth, in his throat, but only with —and in—his eyes. Screaming. Knowing. Dying. And all of it done in silence.

—*heat*—

In Mos Eisley, incandescent, purely immolation. But not so hot to me as to scald my skin, or bake my bones; the heat is of the soup, of the essence, of the body, regardless of entity.

He sags. Is done. Is discarded near the kitchens, where he is sure to be found.

Proboscii quiver as, sated, they coil themselves, unbidden, back into cheek-pockets. Upon my lips is a trace of sugared sweetness. He has eaten before the dance, some folly of appetite, a childish desire for plundered food. But none made by another's hands can surpass the sweetest flavor of what the brain excretes.

I shoot the cuffs beneath my sleeves, smooth my jacket into neatness. There will be, in Jabba's palace, a surfeit of soup.

"*Anzat*," they will whisper. "*Anzat, of the Anzati.*"

It was a personal thing, this story, to begin, innocent of intent beyond a wholly discriminating appetite. A need for soup it was—without it I expire—but also a need for his soup, *his* soup specifically, the soup of all soups: the essence of a humanoid who knows fear but absolves himself of it; who faces it, defeats it, does not laugh in its face so much as prove himself fragile in flesh but strong in spirit. And who, by overcoming it, manufactures the soup of all soups, sweet and hot and pure.

Han Solo's soup.

A professional thing, this story, of betrayal and perfidy. Jabba wanted him caught. The Hutt cared little for soup; if he knew of it, he never said. Likely, with his sources, his resources, he did know; but it mattered not in the least. He knew I was inviolable, because I am I, and best. And for the best, the best.

—*Han Solo's soup*—

Mine, when captured. Mine to take, to drink. Mine to sip, to savor: hot, and sweet, and pure.

Until Jabba stole it from me. Until I was betrayed.

By Fett. By Calrissian. By Jabba the Hutt himself, goading all of them. Buying all of them.

Buying me, as well. Promising singularity to the best of the best, forever and ever, amen: Dannik Jerriko, assassin's assassin.

For this, Jabba will die. And the others as well: three in Mos Eisley; more yet, like the Weequay, in Jabba's palace.

Han Solo, also. And his woman, royal-bred. And the boy of worthless pedigree, yet who promises, unaccountably, to be strong in what was Kenobi's power.

It is a power I have known as long as I have lived, and that longer than most; we *Anzati* know many of the secrets of the multiplicity of universes, of galaxies, of worlds. Such power as the boy's will be, of Kenobi's, is Vader's power also, and the Emperor's.

But twisted in the latter, *by* them, none of it now of Kenobi, of those who were Jedi Knights. Will they twist the boy's as well?

Perhaps. No one alive has withstood the Emperor, or Darth Vader.

Or Jabba the Hutt.

But none of them know me, save Jabba. They only know *of* me, of my kind, the lurid tales told. And it is this I will use: ignorance, and rumor. Let them say what they will. This time, I will use it. Its power is pervasive.

In the palace, which once was a monastery—pure in its existence until polluted first by raiders and later by Jabba himself—there are many for me to peruse, consider, pursue—even to stalk as the stories claim, a manner heretofore disdained but now apropos—and a plethora of races, of species, of soup. From myriad nations, a plenitude of planets. But here nothing matters save the master all of them serve; they are as nothing to him, to me, and as nothing they shall die.

Except to make a point.

Jabba, be afraid. Even you may die.

And the essence of your soup, one may hope, may pray, shall be as rich in its substance as is your flesh in corpulence.

I have been what I am: perfectionist in my work. All have died. All. None left to tell the tale.

But now the tale is necessary, and the telling of it. The Weequay, dead of unknown means, will cause consternation, but no certainty. There is a need now for "error"; for what they will take as error. A being left alive. To describe, in infinite horror, of inescapable terror, what monster it was who nearly took its life.

Thus it is time for me to depart the closet of rumor we Anzati *too often inhabit.*

• • •

There are levels of fear as there is a pecking order of entities within Jabba's palace. To strike at the Hutt I must strike first at the others, beings whose presence serves much, or very little, but nonetheless the absence thereof makes itself felt in all the small and large ways, the mild annoyances or the doubt, the anger, the abrupt concern for one's safety. I know all of the levels, as I know how to use them.

First, those in Mos Eisley, already reported as dead; but Jabba will assume it is of no consequence—or small consequence—until convinced otherwise.

Next, the Weequay. Jabba will not miss him. But others will. And once enough of them die, enough of the small people, even the elect might be led into true fear.

A female, now. The dancing girl with head-tails, the Twi'lek, is already dead, thrown down as appetizer to Jabba's hungry rancor, but there are other females. And so I seek one out.

She is what many entities, Jabba among them, consider beautiful: lush, plump in flesh, a bounty of breasts, the ponderous movements of a body in motion. Hands waving, six breasts swinging, buttocks never still. But she is stilled, at last, when the revels, ended, devolve into stupor. The woman, an Askajian —they who bear multiple young at one whelping— leaves the audience chamber to seek her rest through the remains of the night until the unyielding sun of Tatooine stands high overhead once again.

But rest she will not have. Sleep she will not know.

And it is in the servants' quarter, where one assumes one is safe, that I pursue the assignation.

As she walks from the audience chamber, the high, proud step fades into weariness, into scuffing and graceless relief that she may at last seek her bed. She is dulled by the hour, and careless; that she should take care never suggests itself to her, for this is Jabba's palace, protected by all the dregs of the uncounted universes.

And so it is nothing to me to allow her to walk past me, unseeing, and into the antechamber, unknowing, intent upon release; and so it is as nothing that I follow, step behind her, whisper an endearment in her native tongue.

She whirls, multiple breasts wobbling. There is delight at first in her eyes; was she then expecting someone? But it is I, not he, not she, not it; delight shapechanges to fear.

In her tongue I say she is the most beautiful woman I have ever seen; that I have lusted for her, watching from the shadows, the closets of Jabba's palace, wishing she might so much as glance in my direction. But she has not, and I am bereft, and weak, and cowardly, and only now brave enough, male enough to come forward, to swear to her the truth, to abase myself before her so she will know, *must* know, how it is with me, a male who sees and desires a female, and such a female as she . . .

Almost, she believes. Twin spots of ruddy color glow in fleshy cheeks. Beneath my hands her shoulders lift. Her mouth parts as I slip my hands from shoulders to neck, from neck to the bones of her jaw, hidden beneath heavy flesh. And then I clamp her skull in the *Anzat*'s embrace and allow her to see the truth of what I am. Legend come to life.

A whimper. Then rigid, paralyzing fear as I uncoil proboscii. They are discriminating and slower to rouse than usual; their diet has always been soup of the highest sort, and I have profaned them of late with soup of the lower order, from entities who have no courage.

But they rouse, extrude. And the woman whimpers again, trapped by her horror, my hands, by the knowledge.

—pleasure/pain—
—pain/pleasure—
No. Not this time. Patience is required, and control.
—pleasure?—
Later. Later.
A caress only, the faintest breath of proboscii beneath her nostrils. In my hands she trembles—
A step. A presence. A voice, flatly mechanical, inquiring as to my presence, to my intent.

As she whimpers again, I turn. I permit him to see as I permitted her. There is regret that after so many centuries I must allow the truth to be known, the methods, the means to be comprehended, but it is necessary.

I had meant for her to live. The purpose was for her to see me, to know me, to cry of near-assault. But now he is here as well, armored male in helmet that is also breathing mask; he will do. She will do. They may both tell a tale of terror.

Anzat, of the Anzati . . . *loose in Jabba's Palace.*

For time out of mind, I have been what does not exist, save for imagination. I am folklore. Mythos. Legend. A figment, a fragment, a fleeting dream called nightmare. All one and the same, if known by different labels . . . but the truth is harsher yet, and far more frightening.

But blighted truth, twisted truth, honesty unknown, can serve a purpose. It has served the *Anzati* for time out of mind, and me. It serves me still.

It serves me now.

Ah, but the promise of soup, of satiation—

Why wait? I hunger now. For the soup, and victory. The knowledge that I have done what no one else has done.

Jabba's soup: the excrescence of what he is, what he has become; what he has made of himself. Soup that no one has spilled before, to drink of its strength.

To devour the life of the Hutt while the hulking husk putrefies.

But not so soon, never so soon. He presents a challenge, does Jabba. A wily Hutt well cognizant of how to ward his life. To bring fear into his soul—and set the soup to boiling—will take time. Effort. And the unveiling of my truth.

But I am hungry now, and for more than Jabba's soup. For Jabba's fear.

Hear of me, O Jabba, and know yourself afraid.

I am of the day, but equally of the night; I take my rest when I choose, not because any biological rhythm insists upon it. And so I am free to wander as I will, throughout the labyrinthine corridors of what once was monastery and now is Jabba's lair. And it is as I wander that I am certain, at once, there are those within the palace who were not here before.

Abruptly: —*soup*—

I have known its like before. But this essence, *this* essence—

—*soup*—

Oh, it is powerful, overwhelming . . . I stop where I am in the shadows, transfixed by the awareness, the preternatural knowledge of such soup as I could wish for before all others—

—*soup*—

Proboscii, denied the sort of soup they prefer for too long, twitch frenziedly within cheek-pockets. They know. *I* know.

Han Solo. Han Solo, vividly alive; and others nearby, others of similar soup . . .

How many? Solo, another, another.

—*soup*—

Through the corridors to the kitchens. Where I find a body, though living still; a small, insignificant being of thin and immature soup, but he will do, will do; in my need there is only the soup, anyone's soup at all.

There is no time, no time—

I clutch him. Turn him. Catch him up in the embrace.

He struggles briefly, too briefly. Proboscii plunge into nostrils, through to the brain.

There is so little soup, and all of it weak.

But it will do. For the moment.

He is discarded quickly, abruptly, proboscii tearing free. I let him fall in a sprawl, ungainly and lacking dignity, against a broken box nearly large enough for his body.

There is blood on the boy's face. I have left evidence of the means, the method.

There is no time.

It will suffice. It will serve.

Anzat, *of the* Anzati . . . *loose in Jabba's palace.*

—soup—

Ah, but it is ecstasy, or will be.

Who?

Along the corridors, shadow-cloaked, prowls an *Anzat,* but shedding habitual wariness in the quest for fact, for truth—

Oh, rejoice!

—it is here, is here; all of it, here . . . Solo's, another's. Another's.

I catch myself up short at the corner, on the cusp of Jabba's audience chamber. For it is there, all of it *there:* Solo, thawed from carbonite, his soup wild and reckless, tinged with fear, with panic: he is blind, blind and untrusting, but all his instincts are to fight, to *fight*—

Another's. Wild and free and boiling.

Frightened as well, that she—

—she?—

—will not be able to get him free despite precautions, despite plans: Chewbacca, Lando, Han; always Han, foremost—

—Calrissian—

Then he is the third.

Solo. The woman. Calrissian.

Betrayer.

Rejoice . . . oh, rejoice!

But Solo overwhelms them all with his presence, his soup; and in the doing overwhelms me. Proboscii extrude, quivering.

—soup—

She has unmasked, the woman. Unhelmed so he knows her, so he will not be afraid.

No. *Let* him be afraid, so he might overcome it. And in the fear, in the overcoming of it, the pushing through to awareness and competency and the wild, crazed courage, he becomes what I want, what I need—

—Han Solo's soup—

Oh, let it be mine!

I will take all of them. One by one.

No. Wait. There is the task first.

—soup—

No! The task.

Possess yourself of patience.

But it is difficult. Self-denial is a discipline I have never learned; nor ever had to learn.

Solo. The woman, royal-bred. And Lando Calrissian. All it wants is the boy, so rich in Jedi promise.

—Han Solo's soup—

I fall back. Containment, control is difficult; proboscii rebel as I try to withdraw them, urge them to withdraw. There is war within my skull.

Have I gone so far? Lost so much?

Never have I been so close to the edge.

There must be a death. Now. Soup must be drunk. Now.

I turn. I scrape myself against the walls and retreat rapidly, hearing the echo of Jabba's laughter. Are they caught, then? Has the Hutt captured them all?

—*soup*—

Solo. The woman. Calrissian.

All. I will have them all.

Or die in the trying.

It is not sleep, with us. It is stupor, near to coma. A withdrawal from that which is living, to those whose lives are slight; and to a deepness, a darkness, an *otherness*, where my body repairs itself in the ways both large and small, if necessary. But it has not been necessary for a long time, for I am cautious, and careful, and no one save my victims has ever seen me, except for when I choose to walk among entities without offering threat. It is a lonely life, else; and I choose not to be lonely.

But that bears its cost. The stupor is deeper than most. The coma nearly complete. So that when roused out of it by something most unexpected, I am as close to walking the edge of madness is as possible, with us.

And so it is madness, and overwhelming, when I am roused abruptly, too abruptly, by the awareness, sharp and painful, exquisitely demanding, of power beyond reckoning. Like Yoda's, like Kenobi's. But young yet, still young, still learning its way.

And the way, the precipice of the power, is yet to be understood fully by the one who does and will wield it.

Thus roused, I am angry. And comprehending abruptly, so abruptly: he will be stronger than any in so many lives, this one. Of all of them, nearly extinct. Now alive again, in him.

That boy. Kenobi's boy, whom I first saw years ago

in Chalmun's cantina. Who did not then know what he is, but knows now, and plainly; knows enough how to use, how to shield.

Here, in Jabba's palace.

Solo. The woman. Calrissian. The boy.

All of them here. Now.

Why has he unshielded? Why do I know him now? A Jedi excretes power when he chooses; to *Anzati,* it is obvious. But there is control in it regardless. This time there is none. He is wholly open, unshielded, yielding to some purpose I cannot conceive.

—*soup*—

Proboscii rake my nostrils. Roused, no longer stuporous, I walk out of the shadows of the labyrinth and make my way through, passing those who barely see me, but know enough to stop, to stare, to blink; to question what they have seen, albeit in silence, in the interior of their fear.

Let them see. It serves.

—Anzat, *of the* Anzati—

—*loose in Jabba's palace*—

But that is of no moment. It is plain to me now, too plain; the boy, *that* boy, has come into the lair intent on his own purpose . . . it was planned, all of it planned: Calrissian, infiltrating; the princess, clad in costume; the Wookiee, beleaguered bait; and now the boy, Kenobi's pupil, so rich—*so rich!*—in power that was before only potential, barely promised—

And Solo, always Solo . . . all of them now, together: Solo, the Wookiee, the woman, Kenobi's boy, and Calrissian—

And Jabba!

I have been careless. I!

—*through the corridors, running*—

Running. Running.

How could I have been so careless?
—*running*—
Closer now. Proboscii twitch, extrude.
—*soup*—
All of them here, at once.
Somewhere.
—*soup*—
So many dead of my need. But none of them count, none—they are nothing, all of them—the only soup of the moment is here, now, but retreating—
—*no*—
It cannot be; will not. I am I: Dannik Jerriko.
I have never failed.
I am here for Jabba's soup.
For all the soup, of all of them.
—*soup*—
The massive gates stand open. There is no one to guard now, no Hutt to protect. He is gone, is gone; they are all of them gone, are gone—
The dust from the sail barge, from the hovercraft playing remora, drifts slowly to the ground.
—*are gone, all of them gone*—
—*soup*—
Jabba has taken them away. Jabba has taken himself. Away. Not here. Apart from me.
Oh, foul! That I should come so close. That I should let it be known an *Anzat* is among them. That I should reveal myself to no purpose at all, save to feed the nightmare.
Oh, foul.
I am undone.
Failure is intolerable.
Among my kind, impossible.
Oh, the horror. The horror.
In my body, need cries out. Comprehends. Acknowledges.
Distant now, so distant, carried across the dunes.

All of it my soup. And now denied to me.

Oh, *most* foul.

There is nothing to do but wait. Wait for the Hutt's return. They will none of the others be with him, for he will have disposed of them and wasted all the soup —*fool! fool!*—but there is still Jabba.

Jabba.

And Dannik Jerriko.

O fool. O corpulent, fatuous fool.

There is yet a chance for me to redeem myself, to permit me success, not failure. Jabba is my task. The others, merely spice.

Jabba will return. And I will drink his soup.

Jabba *will* return.

He must.

Or I am undone.

There are shadows here, always. It is a simple thing to walk into them and put on the raiment they offer.

I can wait. I have always waited, when necessary. It is a gift. A power.

I am a thousand and ten years old, and I can wait forever.

Shaara and the Sarlacc:
The Skiff Guard's Tale

by Dan'l Danehy-Oakes

Yes, Mister Boba Fett, this is indeed a very serious matter. There is no other subject of conversation heard anywhere else in Jabba the Hutt's palace. But this does not surprise me at all, because I have never seen any party work their way beneath the skin of Jabba the Hutt in the way this self-proclaimed Jedi Knight and his friends have done. I mean, just to think of the very gall of their coming in the place and threatening Jabba the Hutt, damaging his rancor, even releasing that two-credit phony smuggler Solo . . . Well, I certainly admire their courage, but their common sense is some other matter entirely. It is as one might say not entirely smart to annoy Jabba the Hutt in this manner.

Jabba the Hutt is extremely angry. I would also be angry if it was me in his position. The palace is not just a fortress, it is his home, and individuals take a certain particular kind of offense when they are annoyed in their own homes. So I am really not particularly surprised, you see, that he orders that they are to be given to the Sarlacc like this.

And I might add it is a great honor to be permitted to accompany you like this. I am sure that Jabba the

Hutt intends it as an honor to give you a personal guard. And besides, I can show you the best place to see the Sarlacc.

Yes, Mister Boba Fett, we have always talked about it as "the" Sarlacc here on Tatooine. If there is another Sarlacc anywhere, I have certainly never heard about it. I like to think I would have done so, because I make the Sarlacc a sort of special interest of mine since I am only a child. You see, my sister Shaara is the only person I know of who has ever come out of the Great Pit of Carkoon alive. I once heard a story that Skywalker escaped the pit, but he is a notorious liar, as you can see for yourself. Jedi Knight? Why, he is not even carrying a lightsaber when Jabba the Hutt captures him.

Oh, that is a long story. You do not want— You *do* want to hear it? Very well.

It begins with the Imps, as so many things do these days. Imperial stormtroopers. Half a dozen of them decide to go for Shaara in a big way. She is three years older than I am, and I am twelve when all of this proceeds so she is fifteen. She is working in the floor show of a cantina out at the edge of Mos Eisley, doing a "droid" act whose redeeming social value is perhaps in question. But an act is all it is, my family being respectable moisture farmers who raised our girls properly and with none of this modern permissive stuff. She is an innocent in every sense of the word, I can assure you of that.

The Imps on the other hand are not at all innocent. They never are innocent. I am thinking that the Empire must test them for basic cruelty before they even issue them their first armor. So these Imps come into the cantina one evening and they see Shaara doing her act, and they decide that they would like to see for themselves what she looks like under the metal, and perhaps a few other things above and beyond seeing.

So they convince the owner of this cantina, an unpleasant character who rejoices in the name of Dakkar the Distant, to let them go and visit her backstage after the show is over. I do not like to think about what might occur if she is actually in her dressing room when they arrive. She is not there, however, being as she is chatting with the band leader about some changes in the musical arrangement for the next day. So they make themselves at home to wait for her.

When she opens the door, still wrapped up neatly in bronze-colored kelsh metal, she sees them removing their armor and going through her things, so she wisely makes like the Kandos shuttle and departs ahead of schedule. They follow her. Why should they not follow her? They are after all the law, and nobody is going to interfere with them.

So a few minutes later, Shaara comes running into the dome of our parents' farm, still dressed in her droid costume. She barely has time to blurt out what has happened before they land on our puk garden. They have picked up their transport, but as they have not bothered to replace the various pieces of armor they had removed, they are an interesting sight. The front door does not slow them down even a little.

My older brother Kamma tries to stop them. I no longer have a brother Kamma. I am watching this, a frightened twelve-year-old, from behind a partition. I think that this is when I first begin to not like the Imps so much, as a result of which I am now gainfully employed in the service of Jabba the Hutt. Kamma does not stop them any better than the door does, but he does succeed in slowing them down a little, during which delay my sister jumps into the family land-speeder and vacates the premises.

As you may have seen when you arrived on Tatooine, Mos Eisley is near the edge of the Dune Sea, and Shaara heads for the sands. She is not really paying a great deal of attention to where she is going, and before long she is very near to the Great Pit of Carkoon.

The Imps are right behind her. Their transport is more powerful than the landspeeder, but it is laden down with six of them while Shaara is alone and quite light, so they gain very slowly. They are still a few seconds behind Shaara as she flashes toward the pit. She tells me later that she is crying at this point, and I think she is telling me the truth about this.

She is now desperate. She pulls the family punch gun out of its rack where it is kept in case of trouble and she points it at the hull of the Imps' transport.

Shaara has been a good shot from childhood, and I think the Force must guide her hand on this particular day, because she puts a hole right through to the transport's engine. The resulting explosion should kill the Imps right then, but they all have been pulling their armor back on. None of them is fully dressed, and the driver is still down to his bodyglove, but they also seem to have an unusual amount of luck at that moment.

I say seem because although the explosion does not kill them it pitches them into the air just in time for all of them to land in the Pit of Carkoon, which I would consider to be a good thing indeed if it were not that the blast also sends the landspeeder tumbling, and Shaara is also dumped into the pit.

For a moment the seven of them lie there stunned. Then, and this is the part I always have trouble believing, two of the Imps begin crawling around the pit toward her.

They must surely know where they are. Even the Imperial Army must tell their troopers the basic hazards of the land before sending them out. Yet there they are right on the Sarlacc's doorstep and they are more intent on finishing what they have planned for my poor sister than they are in saving their own miserable lives.

Well, of course all this movement gets the Sarlacc good and active, and its tongue-tentacles begin to poke around. It grabs one unconscious Imp and drags him in without a sound. Shaara sees this and lets out a screaming noise, but I guess the two Imps following her think that she is screaming at them.

Then a tentacle gets hold of the foot of another Imp who is awake, and now he begins to scream. This causes the others to sit up and take notice, all but one who never wakes up at all but falls into the mouth of the Sarlacc because of the shifting sands caused by those questing tongues. I do not know whether you have been keeping count, Mister Boba Fett, but this leaves only three Imps in the Great Pit of Carkoon but outside of the Sarlacc, along with my sister.

The two who have been creeping around the pit now cease creeping around it and begin frantically crawling in a direction away from the mouth of the Sarlacc, which of course does them no good whatsoever and only makes the sand under them shift downward faster than they can climb up it. This shifting attracts the attention of the Sarlacc, who immediately grabs them both and drags them screaming to their doom. I do not know whether the story Jabba the Hutt likes to tell is true, that you spend a thousand years being slowly digested in the Sarlacc's belly, but I am frankly all in favor of the idea in the case of these two, though Shaara says she hopes they died quickly. Perhaps it is that she is of a more delicate nature, or maybe she just wishes that they are dead.

This leaves just Shaara and one stormtrooper staring across the Great Pit of Carkoon at each other and down at the tongue-tentacles of the Sarlacc. This Imp seems to be more sensible than the others, and he holds very still and does not send sand down the pit to let the Sarlacc know where he is. Neither does Shaara. He looks across the pit at her. She tells me later that he is not wearing his helmet, and she has never seen a man look so frightened before or since. Personally I hope never to see that kind of fear.

The Sarlacc's tongues, in the meanwhile, continue to quest around the sandy surface of the pit for potential food. One brushes over Shaara's leg and keeps moving—and then it comes back.

Shaara screams, and the Imp does what is perhaps the most surprising thing in this entire story. He pulls his personal vibroblade from his boot and throws it at the tentacle that has hold of her.

The tentacle lets go, but two others snap up immediately, and half a dozen more begin groping up the side where the blade has come from. At this point the Imp's courage fails entirely. He begins to claw his way up the walls of the Great Pit of Carkoon. This seals his doom. One of the tentacles grasps Shaara's metal-wrapped leg, while two others grab the Imp and tear him in half as they drag him in. Shaara says she thinks he died quickly. I hope that she is right.

Then the tentacle that has hold of Shaara picks her up, coils down toward the Sarlacc's mouth—and uncoils most violently, throwing her out of the Pit of Carkoon entirely. The family landspeeder is a total loss but its comm unit works well enough that she can send out a call for help, and she does so.

Ah, look. We are getting near the Pit of Carkoon. Come this way, please.

Why does the Sarlacc let her go? That is a very interesting question, Mister Boba Fett. First of all, I wish to point out that it does not let her go, it makes her go. I do not know why it does this, but I have given it much thought over the years and I have several theories on the subject.

Perhaps it has had enough food for now, and it

throws the excess back. Shaara does not like this theory, and neither do I. I have seen it eat much more than this at one time.

Shaara thinks that the tentacles are tongues indeed and have a sense of taste. She thinks that the Sarlacc decides, based on the metallic taste of her suit, that she is not edible. I do not think this is true myself, for I have seen the Sarlacc swallow some things which could not possibly have tasted like organic matter, and the armor of the Imps did not seem to bother it at all.

What I personally think is this. Nobody really knows anything about the Sarlacc. It seems to be the only one of its kind, but creatures simply do not evolve as individuals in such a manner. And it is very old. We assume that it is not intelligent, but perhaps it is. Perhaps it just has a slower kind of intelligence which takes years to think a single thought. And maybe, just maybe, it knew what it was doing.

I do not know why the Sarlacc saved my sister, and that is really all there is to say about it. My parents say that they have never heard of the Sarlacc eating anyone who had not done something to deserve it, but if so we are undoubtedly all Sarlacc food in the final analysis.

Ah. Here we are. This is the best place to watch from, even better than Jabba the Hutt's throne. Stay right here in the skiff and I can promise you a truly amazing view. You may even see what few have seen and lived: the Sarlacc's belly.

A Barve Like That:
The Tale of Boba Fett

by J. D. Montgomery

With the passage of the years he had learned to recognize certain things.

When he first returned to awareness he knew that he was on the surface of a planet. Artificial gravity *shimmers* at the boundaries of perception; on a ship under thrust the engines, however well damped, vibrate; and gravity provided by angular momentum causes a Coriolis effect that a human who has trained himself can recognize.

But that was *all* that he knew when the voice out of the darkness said, *You are Boba Fett.*

Fett's head jerked up and he stared into—

Nothing.

He reached for his rifle—and did not move. His arms and legs were firmly restrained. Fett hung in darkness, feet not touching the ground.

He heard a distant *crack* followed by the same noise again, rather more close. His head was not restrained but the rest of his body felt as though it had been wrapped in—

He stuck out his tongue and flipped the switch that turned on his helmet's macrobinoculars.

You are Boba Fett.

Even with the macrobinoculars, translating up out of the infrared and down from the ultraviolet, there was not much to see. Fett hung against the wall of a tunnel—a tunnel not of stone or any artificial material, but soft and yielding, spongelike, ridged and corded as though the tunnel had *grown* into its current shape. He could turn his head just enough to see that the tunnel curved sharply out of sight a few meters to his left and right.

Screams in the distance.

A whistling *crack.*

The voice said after a long pause, curiously, *You are Boba Fett?*

It came back in a rush—Tatooine, the sail barge, Skywalker and Solo, and with a rush of horror that stilled every other thought fighting for his attention it came to him where he was, in the belly of the Sarlacc—

Being digested.

• • •

Most of those who dealt with Fett over the course of the decades did not consider him a man of much feeling. This was accurate. He was not.

Leaving Bespin, though, he was filled by a certain fondness for Han Solo. Do not misunderstand—he did not approve of the man—but it was rare to receive *two* bounties for the same acquisition. But Vader had paid well and the Hutt would pay nearly as well again.

The Hutt had promised a bounty of a hundred thousand credits. A respectable amount, though not as good as some Fett had earned. He had once received a bounty of a hundred and fifty thousand credits for the pirate Feldrall Okor; and on a memorable occasion, half a million credits for the delivery of Nivek'Yppiks, an incautious Ffib heretic who had fled his homeworld of Lorahns, and the religious oligarchy that controlled it.

Fett did not imagine he would ever come to *like* religious autarchies; they reminded him of his youth. But he had come to appreciate them. They paid exquisitely well and their "criminals" were intellectuals who talked too much and rarely shot back.

Fett's fee for the Solo acquisition was, though the Hutt did not know it yet, about to be increased. Fett did not imagine he would be able to push Jabba to half a million credits—the Hutt was a business creature, not a religious fanatic—but the Hutt was among other things an art collector.

Han Solo, encased in carbonite, *had* to be worth more than Han Solo alive *or* dead.

By the time he got done, counting both his fee from the Empire and his fee from the Hutt, Fett fully intended to better the half million he had received on that Yppiks fool.

Fett slept sitting up in the pilot's chair, which made a more comfortable bed than some Fett had known, while the *Slave I* made the last jump to Tatooine.

Hyperspace transit was as a rule the only place Fett felt safe enough to sleep soundly. He did not dream, at least nothing he remembered; his sleep was peaceful and uninterrupted. One might have called it the sleep of a just man.

He awakened not long before hyperspace breakout. No device awakened him; he had decided to awake at the correct time, and he did. He awoke alert, scanning the control board. All seemed well.

Minutes later the hyperspace tunnel fragmented around him. Stars appeared in the viewplate—and a klaxon shrilled through the ship.

Bad news and Fett took it calmly enough, under the circumstances: a beacon had activated itself down in the hold, announcing Fett's arrival insystem to whoever was listening on that frequency. Fett's deduction was instantaneous and correct; another hunter had planted the beacon during his stay on Cloud City. Fett slapped the autopilot control and sprinted below deck.

Another hunter, looking for the Hutt's bounty on Solo. It was the only answer that made sense, and Fett damned himself for a fool for not checking his ship when he had the chance. Basics, *basics,* you ignore the basics and you *deserve* what happens to you. Fett unslung the flame-thrower as he ran, rounded the last corridor before the cargo bay, to the stretch of corridor where the sensors showed the beacon originating, and let loose. He cooked the bulkhead until the metal glowed and the air around him burned hot and stank with ozone, brought the flame tracking upward—

The klaxon ceased and Fett left the *Slave I*'s maintenance droid to deal with the fire he'd started, and ran back to control.

He slid into his seat. The *Slave I* had continued to head insystem at high speed, Tatooine growing large in the viewscreen. The local shipping did not seem to be taking notice of Fett, which was all to the good, but *somebody* out there knew he'd arrived. Fett fed figures to the autopilot, had it calculate a hyperspace jump back out of the system, started another thread, and set a portion of the computer to performing diagnostics on ship functions.

He did not worry about his weapons systems, nor his deflectors; they were either ready, or sabotaged—probably ready. Planting a beacon was one thing, and impressive enough; fooling the ship's on-board diagnostics quite another.

So deep in a planet's gravity well, calculating a new hyperspace jump took *time,* even for a computer as bright as the one Fett had running the *Slave I.* Even so, it had nearly completed the calculations when the subject became moot:

A needle of a ship came up over Tatooine's horizon.

The *IG-2000.* It was instantly recognizable, and it told Fett just how very bad the problem was. The ship belonged to the assassin droid IG-88, the second-best bounty hunter in the galaxy, and studying hard to be number one. Fett's fingers danced across the controls and the *Slave I* braked savagely, dropping into a lower orbit. Fett focused and fired his fore blasters as the two ships closed—

The *IG-2000* exploded instantly, went up in a burst of superheated metal and expanding plasma.

Fett thought instantly, *Bad decoy. That assassin droid would* never *make a mistake like*—

The *Slave I*'s sensors went wild—a ship was leaving hyperspace only a few klicks away—and then the *Slave I* shuddered all about Fett as blaster fire struck it aft. The aft holocams showed it all clearly. The *IG-2000,* the *real* one, no decoy, breaking out of hyperspace with blasters lit, coming up above and behind Fett, pinning the *Slave I* between the *IG-2000* and Tatooine. It was a brilliant maneuver that only the assassin droid, with its droid's reflexes, could have planned and carried out.

The *Slave I* dove for atmosphere, the *IG-2000* following at high speed, as the comm unit came alive. IG-88's voice lacked intonation: "Surrender your prisoner and you have a thirty-percent probability of surviving this encounter."

Fett ignored the droid, fingers flying across his control panel. The droid said something else then, that Boba Fett never heard. He routed what power he could spare to the rear deflectors, sent another round of blaster fire aft to keep IG-88 occupied, and then ruined his own ship—

He turned the inertial damper on.

For most of a second the *Slave I* went dark as the inertial damper drew current, shields dropping, weapons going dead for that second, when a single blaster bolt would have destroyed the entire ship—and then the inertial damper came online.

Dual explosions came from below deck, the inertial damper destroying itself as it did its job, and probably taking the hyperdrive with it. Half the indicators on the main board went red, the ship's superstructure *screamed* with the sound of tearing metal, as the ship lost ninety percent of its velocity in the quantum instant it took an electron to descend from one atomic orbital shell to another.

Power returned to what was left of the *Slave I* as the *IG-2000* hurtled past Fett at high speed. Fett calmly did all the obvious things, using the ion cannon to destroy the *IG-2000*'s rear deflector array before IG-88 could bring it online, followed by taking out the fore deflector array. He clamped a tractor beam onto the *IG-2000* long enough to keep it from fleeing, and sent a missile down to finish the business off.

• • •

Inside the Sarlacc, Fett said aloud, "Shouldn't have named it that."

The voice said politely, *Indeed?*

"The *Slave I*. It was a mistake, that. It gave away information, told people I owned more . . ." Fett's voice trailed off. He hung against a wall, in darkness, his extremities numbed. He could not feel his hands or his feet, and his skin was burning, and worst of all he was *not* aboard the *Slave I*, not at all—

He whispered, "How did you do that to me?"

He had the brief impression of amusement. *It was easy. No—you were easy. You live strongly.*

A chill descended upon Fett, and he shivered fiercely, there in the darkness, with the near and distant popping sounds. "Who *are* you?"

A fair enough question, it said, and the dark amusement was unmistakable this time. *As you are my past, Boba Fett . . . I am your destiny.*

"The grimace is quite wonderful," said the Hutt. "We are impressed with your efforts, and we are pleased to pay seventy-five thousand credits for the person of Han Solo."

Fett shook his head. "Jabba"—and he heard the stir that went through the room at the familiarity—"we're not dealing here with the person of Captain Solo— who I recall had a bounty on him of one hundred thousand credits."

Jabba's tail twitched and his voice deepened into a dangerous near-growl. "This is *not* Solo?"

"This?" said Fett, as courteously as he was able—it was not his strong suit. He had not been raised speaking Basic, and his voice and diction tended toward a certain harshness when he used it. "This finely rendered carbonite sculpture, the person of Han Solo? No. What I brought you today is *art*. Art created by the

Dark Lord that happened to *use* Han Solo as material, like another artist might shape clay." He shrugged. "I tell you what, I've gotten attached to it during my journey here. It has a presence to it, don't you think?"

The Hutt said slowly, "The grimace is . . . quite wonderful."

"And the hands," said Fett, pushing it. "Let's us two admire the hands together. I like them, they show the *quality* of the Dark Lord's work—"

"Rather," the Hutt murmured in a bass rumble, "rather. One sees Solo's final moments of fear in them." He examined Boba Fett, standing beside the carbonite-encased Han Solo; both Fett and the piece of art under discussion were well back from the trap-door before Jabba's throne. "There is news," Jabba continued, "that Vader failed to capture Skywalker, that Organa and Calrissian escaped him as well . . . and that Chewbacca is likewise free. Their combined bounties are . . . impressive." Heavy-lidded eyes examined Fett. "Impressive."

And Chewbacca, at the very *least, will be coming for Solo.* Fett nodded. "We might discuss my staying," he conceded. "As to the art, an original piece from the hand of the Dark Lord—" Fett could feel himself warming to the subject; the faintest breath of disappointment touched him when Jabba interrupted, with something so close to enthusiasm that Fett found it notable.

"There is further work here, for a brave bounty hunter." The Hutt's tongue flicked out to lick his lips and he leaned forward. "A hundred thousand credits for the capture and delivery of a krayt dragon to do battle with my rancor."

Fett said dryly, "That seems a lot. As much for the delivery of a krayt dragon as for Solo?"

The Hutt waved a negligent hand in dismissal. "We will find a fair price for Solo. For the art. But now—"

Fett raised his head slightly. "A quarter million."

A hush fell over the watching crowd. Those nearest Fett edged slowly backward.

Jabba leaned forward. His voice emerged from his chest as a rumbling threat. "So . . . that seems quite a lot. Even for Vader's art."

Fett shrugged. And waited.

Jabba's lips twitched. Fett did not mistake it for anything approaching amusement. "So, a quarter million credits for . . . the art." His eyes narrowed to slits. "And we will enjoy your efforts toward acquisition of a krayt, and we will enjoy your company among us. For some time."

"A quarter million." Boba Fett actually bowed slightly. "For some time."

Very expressive . . . yes.

Fett shook his head to clear it. Jabba's throne room faded into nothingness; he hung on the wall himself, deep inside the Sarlacc, the air around him growing dank. A foul taste had begun to develop in his mouth; he sipped at the water tube in his helmet before replying. "Don't do that to me again."

There was a pause. *I won't,* the voice said finally, *if you keep me amused.*

"Who the blazes *are* you?"

I am *the inferno, you are quite accurate. I am the Sarlacc. I am the distilled essence of—*

"You're not the Sarlacc," Fett said grimly. "Sarlacci aren't intelligent, they don't have a brain worthy of the name—"

The voice chuckled and said softly, *I am Susejo.* The wall Fett hung on *shivered.* An emotion that could have been delight emanated from the creature. *It's been a long time since I had one like you, all bright and sharp around the edges. You are nearly a work of art, Fett; there is a clarity to you that is*—chuckle—*quite wonderful. A purity to your intent.*

Fett fought back the useless rage that threatened to overwhelm him; it was something he'd had practice at. "I'm a *hunter*. I bring those who do evil to justice, and there is little room to be unclear on the subject."

You remind me of someone—ah. I have it. You remind me of the Jedi.

Keeping his voice expressionless was an accomplishment. "The Jedi."

Yes. A Jedi we ate a few thousand years ago. We've kept her; would you like to meet her?

"No." Fett closed his eyes and floated senselessly in the darkness. *A Jedi we ate*, it had said. "No. Keep your Jedi to yourself."

Impression of a shrug. *As you wish. You'll look forward to a break in the tedium . . . soon enough.*

Fett opened his eyes and stared ahead into the emptiness, listening to the silence. The screams he had heard at first, those of the men who had fallen into the Great Pit with him, had ceased. He had not heard even one in some time. The fury built in Fett, self-contained, black and bone-deep. Another crack nearby, sounding very like a whip; Fett took a shuddering breath and when he spoke his voice shook slightly. "I don't understand this. I don't understand this at all. Why is this being prolonged? Is there a *purpose*? The Sarlacc can eat me when I'm dead, can't it? *I've* killed, I've killed virtually everything that moves, one time or another, a hundred different species, sentient and dumb; if it breathes I've probably killed it or something like it. But I've killed *clean*. I've killed without stretching it out. Where's the grace in a death like this?"

Fett had the impression that his question was being considered. *For you? Why, I suppose there is none. But your life and death belong to me now, not you; and they serve my purpose. Recognize and understand your place in things, Boba Fett, for you are not even a real thing; merely a collection of thoughts that has deluded itself into a belief in its own existence.*

"You're saying that I'm not real, that nothing's real?" Fett's lips twisted in a snarl. "The air stinks too badly for me to believe that."

You, and I, and everything else—we are merely a process, Boba Fett. A process that has named itself "I." Surely the Real exists, and we are an expression of it. But are you and I real? No. We are processes that have grown arrogant and broken apart from the Real. In time we shall be rejoined to it. The voice paused. *You want to know why this is taking so long? You've barely been down here a day, Boba Fett. There are sentients who've been kept alive for hundreds of years while the Sarlacc digested them.* After a long pause it added, with a sense of weariness so profound Fett believed it would have killed him to experience it, *Thousands of years, in some cases.*

Fett did not know what made him so certain, the weariness; he said, "You . . . you *lie*. You're not the Sarlacc—you're *down* here, with me."

I'm not the Sarlacc? Considering, thinking: *Don't be so sure of that. I am Susejo of Choi, or I was, and I have been here for a very, very long time. Longer than you can imagine . . . but who knows? Perhaps you will not have to imagine it. Perhaps you will survive. You entertain me, and that which entertains me entertains the Sarlacc. When I am happy, it is happy. I expect you will be with us for some time.*

Let me activate even one weapon system—Fett fought the thought down, pushed it back hard, and said aloud, "You are cruel."

There's a joke, said the voice, *that my Jedi told me. A sentient visits a nearby farm and sees a barve in the front yard. The barve is wandering around on five legs—one leg has been amputated. The sentient in question, JoJo, asks the owner why the barve has had a leg amputated. "Well," says*

the owner, "let me tell you something about that barve.
That's the smartest barve you've ever seen in your life, JoJo.
That barve talks, he can fly a speeder, and he's great with
the kids, keeps an eye on 'em when I'm out in the field—why,
just a few weeks ago he rescued my youngest one from drown-
ing." And JoJo says, "That's amazing! But what happened to
the amputated leg?" The owner stares at JoJo. "Well, man,
you don't eat a barve like that all at once!"

Susejo laughed silently in the darkness, and the wall
behind Fett rippled again.

Boba Fett thought to himself, *I wish I had a thermal*
detonator. I'd take you with me.

You are eternally the Real, Boba Fett . . . and there is
nothing to desire.

The chrono that glowed in the lower right-hand corner of Boba Fett's helmet visor told him when dawn
came. It had been dark already when he awakened;
when dawn arrived, the tunnel off to Fett's left light-
ened noticeably. At noon, when the sun was directly
overhead, enough light filtered down through the
yawning mouth of the Sarlacc that Fett could see his
surroundings clearly.

The walls of the small tunnel in which the Sarlacc
had stored him were grayish-green; they looked damp,
though Fett's gloves prevented him from being certain. Small tendrils grew along the edges of the ridg-
ing in the walls; along the floor the tendrils were
larger, proper tentacles, a mat of several hundred tentacles, four to six centimeters wide, three and four meters long. They lay motionless most of the time; when
the tentacles did move they whipped around at such
speed that the tentacle tips broke the sound barrier,
very like the tip of a whip. It was the source of the
cracking noises Fett had been hearing since he'd
awakened . . . and once he knew what it was he shiv-

ered. The cracking was a steady background sound, yet the tentacles around him did not move often. It made Fett wonder just how large the Sarlacc's interior was and how far from the surface he might be—how many of those tentacles he would have to fight his way through to get out again.

Oh, but you're not going to get out again, Boba Fett. No one ever has, and you won't be the first. Listen:

The Sarlacc ate my left leg first, love. I hadn't been able to move either my arms or my legs for . . . months, I suppose, a very long time. They didn't hurt anymore, though my skin burned, and never has stopped burning the entire time I've been in this blasted pit.

She has me hanging up in the main chamber while she digests me. I suppose that's something; a thing to be grateful for in the grand scheme of things. Mica and I came down together when our speeder got shot down, and Mica got hustled back into one of those little openings along the edge, down into the Sarlacc's guts. This is a bad way to die, but that'd be worse, that'd be a *lot* worse. I'm blind in one of my eyes now, but I can still see the sunlight striking down into the main pit, through the other, and I tell you, it keeps me going. Never thought I'd see the day when a brief glimpse of Tatooine's pale blue sky would be a reason to keep living.

I try not to look down. My left leg's gone beneath the knee. I didn't even notice it going, tell you the truth. One day I looked down and there it was, on the floor of the pit, down in the acid, being dissolved down into nothing.

That annoying Susejo leaves me alone at times. I don't know what he does when he's not talking to me; maybe he's off draining Mica the way he's draining

me. I don't know exactly what Susejo's doing to us
. . . but well, some days I'm not even certain sure
who I *am* anymore. There's been a lot of us down
here; I guess Susejo keeps the ones he and the Sarlacc
enjoy, for a while anyway. It's a sort of immortality, I
suppose, but love, I could have tolerated actually dying a lot better. I always thought that's how I'd go, you
know; fleeing a blaster wedding at the age of ninety-
three, something with a *little* style.

(I'm not even sure if you're the girl I remember.
Some days you have black hair and skin and you're
studying to be a minister, of all things, and other days
it's blond hair and green eyes and you pilot a starship,
and darn if I can remember which of you I actually fell
in love with, or if it was both of you and you were
different people . . .

(I did love you. I remember that.)

A lot of memories floating around in here with me.
The Sarlacc is a soup, and the ingredients are all the
people she's taken, over the centuries, over the millennia. Susejo's never admitted it, but I suspect that's
all that he is; the oldest of the soup's ingredients.

Kess, Susejo said.

I'll answer to that, I replied. *Why not? One name being
as good as another.*

Your name is Kess, he said firmly. *You're a Corellian
gambler . . . the Sarlacc's been eating you a little faster
than I'd like, and I'm sorry about that. You're good company, but the Sarlacc's been hungry recently, and I can't
control her entirely. Tell me another story?*

I thought about it, and I remembered the story you
told me, little one, not long after we met, back in the
old days, that one of you that wanted to be a minister,
back when you thought there was nothing in me
worth saving—too obsessed with the dice and all, you
kept saying, too busy looking for the main chance. *A
man,* I told Susejo, *being chased by a logra, comes to the*

edge of a cliff. He sees there is nowhere to flee, but beholds then a root, protruding from the edge of the cliff. He grabs the root and scrambles over the edge of the cliff, hanging high above the ground. He looks down, and beholds then another logra, pacing below him. He hangs there, unable to go down, unable to climb back up; and along come a pair of tiny banda, one black and one white, and they begin nibbling at the root. The root begins to come apart . . . and suddenly the man sees a berry growing at the edge of the cliff, and he plucks it and pops it in his mouth.

How sweet it tasted.

Silence.

Finally Susejo said, *I'm not sure I like that story.*

I hung there on the wall, and with my good eye watched the dust motes dance in the sunlight; and I thought to myself how beautiful it was.

You'd be proud of me, love, whichever one you were.

Sometime later Susejo said, "The Sarlacc is hungry. I think I'll have her eat your arm now."

Fett *felt* the horror that the Corellian gambler, dead these many centuries, fought against as his limbs decayed, as the Sarlacc ate him from the outsides in. Fett floated in a long dreamtime moment, tied to the gambler's last moments of real awareness down in the slime on the floor of the pit, blind, deaf, limbs dissolved, rib cage cracked apart with the tentacles massaging his organs, dreaming of a woman who loved him—

Boba Fett had been born to anger, and rage was his life. He struggled up out of the vision, fought it wildly, carried himself up out of the nightmare on the back of a wave of fury and abruptly *was* back, there in his body with the pain of the burning acid all around him, suffused with a clear, lucid, *thinking* hatred, an emotion so dark and deep and pure the Dark Lord himself might never have felt its equal.

He could hear his own heartbeat thudding in his ears and he said, "I'm going to kill you *very* slowly," and he had never meant anything more in his life.

He hung in the darkness with his hatred.

Sometime later Susejo said, "I suppose I'll let the Sarlacc start on your leg."

Blaster rifle, wrist lasers, rocket dart launcher; grappling hook, flame projector, concussion grenade launcher. Unfortunately almost all of them required the use of his hands, and his arms and legs were spread-eagled against the wall, held flat by an interwoven mesh of several hundred tentacles. Straining did no good; the tentacles merely gripped more tightly, and Fett barely moved.

The tentacles probed against him, seeking a way through his Mandalorian combat armor. A pair of large tentacles had taken hold of Fett's right leg, and they tugged at it, pulling back and forth at the knee joint. The armor had held, and would hold; that much did not worry Fett. The digestive acid the Sarlacc used *did* worry him; it had already made its way through to his skin. Most of his body *burned,* chest and back and arms and legs. So far the acid had not made it through his helmet, and had not made it past the blast armor that covered his genitals; thank Providence for small favors.

He had access to the contents of his helmet. The comlink built into it was silent; he had scanned through all frequencies, and all he got was static, which might mean that there was nobody within range of the helmet's comlink, about ninety klicks, or might mean that the bulk of the Sarlacc was blocking the signal, and finally might mean that the comlink itself was broken.

The Sarlacc wrenched violently at Fett's left knee. His armor held and Fett was yanked down the wall, the tentacles holding his upper body losing their grip slightly. He ended up hanging at an angle as the tentacles wrapped themselves about him again . . . and there was a pressure against the sole of his right foot. He'd been dragged down far enough that his right foot was now in contact with the ground.

What good that did him—if any—Fett did not know. He flexed the foot to see if he could get a purchase; perhaps.

He relaxed and considered.

The sensors and computer built into his combat suit had continued to work, even after Fett had lost consciousness. The computer responded to verbal commands; Fett had it play back the entire sequence of events that had landed him in the Great Pit of Carkoon, using the heads-up tac display in his helmet for video. The first time through the playback he had to switch it off after realizing that Solo had—accidentally!—activated his jet pack. The holocam angle was terrible, but there was no question about it; that illegitimate Solo had sent him flying into the pit by *chance.*

It took him several minutes before he was able to try and watch it again.

He lifted up from the sail barge, dropping down onto the skiff, with the Jedi and Solo and Chewbacca. And . . . yes. Right there; the butt of Solo's spear had slammed into the emergency access panel, activating the jets.

The on-board computer couldn't access the jet pack; they were not linked together. Fett couldn't run diagnostics on the pack, had no idea whether the thing was working or not. The emergency access panel was behind him, to his right; if he'd been able to get his left hand free, he might have been able to reach it—

If I could get my left hand free, thought Fett dryly, *I could do a lot of things.*

Using radar and sonar, Fett had mapped out a rough picture of the Sarlacc's interior. Leading away from the main chamber were several dozen small tunnels, heading almost straight down into the earth. He was about ten meters away from the main chamber; and about forty meters beneath the ground. Even if the jet *could* take him out again, if he could move to activate it, even then he'd be stuck in the middle of nowhere, in the midst of a great desert—

The tentacles holding Fett's left leg tightened painfully, just above the knee.

Fett's lips twisted in a snarl. "I swear by the soul I don't have, I *am* going to kill you."

Kill who? Susejo laughed. *The one who's talking to you? Or the one who's eating you?*

"Either. Both."

Ah. You have a very poor attitude, Boba Fett:

I almost made it out, early on my second day in the pit.

I lay on my back on the bottom of the pit, in the acid, through the long night. The Sarlacc and I "talked" for a while; it's very young and not very bright, and I feel sorry for it. It's rare for a Sarlacci spore to survive a landing in a desert environment; they're best suited to wet environments, though they *can* survive almost anywhere. I saw pictures once of a Sarlacc that had managed to survive on the surface of an airless moon; it was quite small, its aperture less than a meter in diameter, but the system it had ended up in was young, and heavy in cometary material. Comets are principally made up of carbon, hydrogen, oxygen, and nitrogen; this poor little Sarlacc was making do, out there in the vacuum. It had the most amazing root system; it was far more plant than animal.

This Sarlacc doesn't have it that bad, tucked away out here in the desert. It's not really aware that it exists; it has a neural system, but it's not very well developed, and not likely to become so in the desert. Sarlacci do interesting things with messenger RNA: over the course of millennia, they can attain a sort of group consciousness, built out of the remains of people they've digested. I talked to such a Sarlacc, once a few decades ago. It was a thoroughly asocial creature that wondered, quite wistfully, whether a Jedi would taste better or worse than the other sentients it had eaten. I remember being amused by it, for I knew that I was not such a fool as to come within reach of its outer tentacles.

I walked right over this baby Sarlacc. It lay buried just beneath the sand, tentacles hidden in the drifts. It got me by the ankle and dragged me down into the pit, through a sand plug nearly a meter thick.

The sand plug came down right after me, right on top of me. I lay on the bottom of the pit, held in place by surprisingly strong tentacles, with sand all around me, looking up into the night sky. The Sarlacc's digestive acid is weak, and the sand that came down with me has blotted up much of it. Nonetheless my clothing is already dissolving; if I *do* get out of here I'll be a sight, a naked sixty-year-old Jedi with a rash trying to make it back to her survey ship.

Even diluted, the acid burns.

I do not blame the Sarlacc; it is behaving as its nature dictates. It's not very bright and it is very young— only five meters wide, and perhaps that deep as well. Hard to say quite how deep underground I am, looking up into the night sky through what used to be the sand plug.

I may only be the second or third sentient it's ever eaten. One of them is hanging, totally cocooned, on a wall in the chamber here with me; a Choi named Susejo who was mostly digested already when I fell into the pit. I can feel his thoughts; he's mildly telepathic. He's very young, for a Choi, barely out of childhood, and very angry—he has not taken being eaten very well, and I feel rather sorry for him, too.

When morning came, the light filtered down around me, and I saw my chance; my only chance. My lightsaber had come down with me. I hadn't been able to tell, there in the darkness; it no longer hung from my belt, and I hadn't known whether I'd lost it up on the surface, or down here in the pit. It lay on its side in the acid a few feet away from me, and I turned my head to look at it.

It leaped across the pit and into my hand. I lit it and bent my hand back at the wrist, bringing the blade down as close to the tentacles holding my arm as I could get it, straining; the Sarlacc made a sound, a high-pitched squeal, and the tentacles holding that arm pulled free. I wrenched the arm free and sliced away at the other tendrils still holding me, cutting for just a few seconds until I was free, rolled off my back into a crouch, and then—

Five meters is a long way up, even for a *young* Jedi. I raised the Force and *leaped*.

The tentacle caught my ankle in mid-leap. The Sarlacc broke my leg and two of my ribs pulling me back down. I lost the lightsaber again on the way down and by the time I had the presence of mind to look for it, it was gone for good. I don't know what the Sarlacc did with it, but I never saw it again.

For the rest of the day the Sarlacc remained restless, tentacles waving aimlessly, twitching ceaselessly. It held me so tightly that the blood flow to my extremities was impaired. It was very upset by the whole thing.

I tried to tell it that I was sorry, that I would not have hurt her had I been able to avoid it.

That got a rise out of the Choi, hanging on the wall facing me—*If you* must *chatter,* it snapped, *at least do it for the benefit of the one who can listen to you.*

A slow death has a few things to recommend it; time to get your thoughts in order, at any rate. I blocked the pain radiating from my body, and frankly, after a few days I was bored, too.

Susejo, I said, why don't we pass the time by telling each other stories?

Sweat trickled down Fett's form, pooled beneath his armor, mixed with the burning acid that covered him. An impossible kaleidoscope of lights danced in front of him, and for a moment he thought he might vomit into his helmet; that old Jedi woman had been *real.* Her thoughts still echoed away within him, mixed in with the thoughts of the Corellian gambler, and the quick bright flashes of a dozen other minds, the thoughts and hopes and desires of men and women dead years and centuries and millennia. They'd all died, every one of them, sunk down into the acid and let go of life.

I miss the Jedi, Susejo said. *She was very kind to me.*

Susejo obviously had some level of contact with the Sarlacc; the Sarlacc had *shivered,* earlier, when Susejo felt happiness. Fett made a conscious decision, and let loose the anger that was never very far beneath the surface.

He snarled, "Then you shouldn't have *eaten* her, you miserable wretch."

The hatred in his voice and in his thoughts brought a response from Susejo, a flare of startled anger. The tentacles holding Fett tightened convulsively and Susejo snapped, *I didn't, the* Sarlacc *ate her.*

Fett wished that the wall behind him were not quite so soft. "And you couldn't have stopped it, you couldn't have tried to help her, or anyone else, in *four thousand years?* You're an ingrate, you pathetic excuse for a sentient being. You got taken down here as a child and everything that you know and everything that you are you owe to the people you let get eaten" —and the Sarlacc's tentacles spasmed around Fett, digging into him, hauling him back into the wall behind him—"and your feelings are hurt because I've *told* you so? You could have *helped* that Jedi, she'd have come back for you. Instead you spent the next four thousand years playing at philosophy, abusing the people who taught you to be what you are, never even dreaming that you had options, and *why?*" he screamed at Susejo, building up to it, blasting him with the rage and hatred he had spent a lifetime growing, the Sarlacc's straining tentacles shaking against his body. "Because you're *stupid,* a miserable mean wretch of an excuse for a sentient being without the imagination or the courage—"

The tentacles slashed around him, a sound like a thousand whips cracking, drowning out Fett's voice.

He shoved, got his right foot solidly against the ground and *pushed* upward.

The switch in the jet pack's emergency access panel, digging into the soft wall behind him, was pushed down as Boba Fett pushed up.

Flame erupted in the enclosed space around them. The Sarlacc itself shrieked in pain, a sound that echoed away down the tunnels, the hundreds of tentacles around Fett whipping themselves into a frenzy, those that held Fett constricting so tightly that for an instant he could not breathe—

The jet pack had never been intended to be run in such tight quarters for any length of time.

It exploded.

It was his oldest possession; the Mandalorian combat armor that was almost as famous as he was, famous the galaxy wide. It had protected him, down the decades, from blaster fire and slugthrowers, explosions and knives, from all the various insults the universe was apt to throw at a man in his line of work. But not even Mandalorian combat armor, designed by the warriors who had fought, and sometimes defeated, Jedi Knights, had been intended to withstand an exploding jet pack in close quarters.

Fett could not have been unconscious for more than a few seconds; he came back to awareness unable to breathe. The jet pack's fuel had splattered down the length of the corridor, and the corridor was burning, and so was Fett. The flame touched his skin in exposed places, on his arms and legs and stomach, and flames danced on the surface of his combat armor, the armor itself cracked, broken open by the force of the explosion, and everywhere the armor touched him the metal was scaldingly hot—

Boba Fett surged to his feet. The ground beneath him shook, rolling as the Sarlacc's flesh burned, and the Sarlacc fought against it. Fett reached back over his shoulder, unslung the deadliest weapon he carried.

Standing in the fire, burning alive, Boba Fett fired a concussion grenade into the ceiling thirty centimeters above his head, and threw himself down to the surface of the tunnel, into the flaming mixture of acid and fuel—

The explosion tore apart the world. The concussion slammed Fett down into the flames, and his left arm, trapped beneath him at the wrong angle, snapped as he was smashed down atop it. A pain so great it was like a white light surrounded Boba Fett, and he knew that he was dying, that he had failed, like all the others before him, that he had traded a slow death by acid for a fast death by fire—

Sand rained down upon him.

A long time later, Boba Fett became aware that he was still alive. He forced himself up into a sitting position, looking around him. Fires still burned, along the length of the corridor, and in the distance the sound of cracking tentacles was very loud.

It was quiet where he sat.

Fett's left arm hung useless at his side, and he looked away down the tunnel; it was night, but he knew which direction he needed to go, to get back to the main pit, to the shaft that led back to the surface . . . to the main pit, where Susejo hung, where the enraged Sarlacc awaited him, tentacles lashing back and forth in anticipation.

Sand trickled down onto Fett's helmet. He looked up.

Darkness.

Without moving from where he sat, Boba Fett made a long arm, and retrieved the grenade launcher. It carried three grenades; and he'd already fired one of them.

He raised the launcher and fired it a second time, into the darkness above him, and then had to dig his way out of the avalanche of sand that came down upon him. He stood at the edge of a small hill of sand, looking upward into the darkness . . . and started to undress. The armor was useless at this point—acid-covered and cracked in places, which was an improvement on Fett having cracked in those same places—and his clothing disintegrated as he moved. He almost fainted while removing the upper body armor; his left arm was broken in at least two places, and he was covered with burns that were already starting to form blisters.

It took several minutes, but finally he had worked his way out of the armor, and he fought against his dizziness and weakness and started climbing, halfway up the small hill of sand, and fired his final grenade into the darkness above him. The wave of sand that collapsed on him this time was unbelievable; Fett struggled up through it as it came down upon him, almost swimming upward through the falling sand. The sand covered him, his nude body and the helmet that still protected his head, and he clawed at it frantically, with no air but that trapped in his helmet with him, using both hands, both the broken arm and the good, possessed by a mortal terror that gave him the access to the final strength he would ever be able to call upon—

A hand broke free, he felt it, felt it thrust up into emptiness, and seconds later, Boba Fett dug his way up out of the sand and into the cool nighttime air, in the middle of the Dune Sea, at the edge of the Great Pit of Carkoon, hundreds of kilometers away from anyone or anything.

Alive.

A year later:

Boba Fett returned to Tatooine in the *Slave II*.

He came down out of orbit and hovered above the Great Pit of Carkoon, in the midst of the Dune Sea. On the night desert, the glow of his thrusters burned like the daytime sun, lit the sand for kilometers in all directions.

The *Slave II* descended until the flame of its drive played directly down onto the Pit of Carkoon. The wash of pain that rose to greet Boba Fett tasted like wine of an ancient vintage. If he closed his eyes he could see it, the main chamber where Susejo hung, shimmering beneath the superheated air.

You.

"Yes, indeed."

Inside the creature's pain, Boba Fett could feel something like relief. *You liberate me from the long Cycle.*

The *Slave II* hovered above the pit . . . and then drifted off to the side, and came to a landing fifty meters from the edge, well away from the reach of even the longest of the burnt, writhing tentacles. Susejo's pain and confusion touched Fett. *What strange mercy is this?*

Sitting in the *Slave II*, a faint smile hidden beneath a Mandalorian helmet, Boba Fett said, *You don't eat a barve like that all at once.*

I see . . . I suppose I shall see you again, then.

You can count on it, said Boba Fett. His hands danced across the instrument panels.

The thrusters caught fire; light washed once more over the Great Pit of Carkoon—

A dark spirit arose into the night.

Skin Deep:
The Fat Dancer's Tale

by A. C. Crispin

Thud . . . thud . . . thud.

The rhythmic pounding echoed faintly in the cavernous audience chamber of Jabba's palace. The bulky figure dozing cross-legged on the empty dais sat bolt upright and stared apprehensively at the arched doorway leading upstairs to the main entrance. The knocking came again.

Why would someone be out there, hammering on the blast doors? Yarna d'al' Gargan wondered. Heaving herself up, the multibreasted dancer cautiously ventured to the archway and stood peering up the stairs toward the front entrance. Jabba's frog-dog, Bubo, who was tethered at the top of the steps, looked down at her and croaked plaintively, begging for scraps. For once, Yarna ignored it. Straining her sensitive hearing, the dancer picked up a faint shout.

Thud . . . thud . . . thud.

The Askajian female glanced around and swallowed nervously. She wasn't going up there alone. Death stalked the corridors and chambers of Jabba's palace; they'd discovered another body, that of an unfortunate scullion named Phlegmin. Earlier, Yarna herself had been attacked and had barely escaped unscathed.

"J'Quille?" she called softly into the dimness. It was his turn to be on guard.

No reply.

Where was that stupid Whiphid? Hugging her arms across the pendulous mounds of her topmost pair of breasts, Yarna shivered. It was after sunsdown outside the palace, and nothing should be out there at this hour.

It was true that Master Jabba had gone off in his sail barge to witness the executions of the ill-fated Han Solo and his friends. The Hutt was hours overdue, and none of them had heard a word since the sail barge had departed . . . but that couldn't be Master Jabba's entourage outside. *He* wouldn't knock on the front entrance. The master would enter the palace through the big rear doors. After being in the Hutt's "employ" for nearly a year, Yarna knew the routine only too well.

So who was out there?

And what should she do?

THUD . . . THUD . . . THUD.

The hammering redoubled in intensity, and the shouting grew louder, more desperate. Everyone with the authority to tell her what to do—Master Fortuna, Tessek, Barada—was gone. Even the head Gamorrean, Ortugg, was nowhere to be seen.

Running her tongue over suddenly dry lips, she turned and cupped her hands around her mouth. "Guards!" she bellowed across the chamber. "Guards! Is everyone deaf? There's someone at the main entrance!"

Other denizens of the Hutt lord's motley "court" who had been sleeping in the far reaches of the audience chamber stirred, glancing around furtively . . . but none of them joined the Askajian at the foot of the stairs. In Jabba's palace, calling attention to oneself could prove dangerous.

Yarna heard running footsteps, then an armed humanoid raced through the opposite portal. The guard in the battered dark armor was familiar, though he always kept to himself and she didn't know his name. He'd been the one the Wookiee Chewbacca had knocked silly, smashing him into the wall with one swipe of a long, furred arm.

"What's going on?" A mechanical-sounding voice emanated from inside the helmet that masked his features, and Yarna realized he spoke through a breathing filter. "Where is Master Jabba?"

"Hasn't returned yet," Yarna said, feeling her hearts pound in her belly. "Who are you?"

"Sergeant Doallyn, at your service," the guard said, automatically straightening to attention. More knocks at the entrance made him glance up the stairs. "Who is at the door, Mistress Gargan?"

"I don't know," she said, appreciating the title of respect. It had been a long time since anyone had addressed her as anything but "Ugly One." The hammering reached their ears again, seemingly weaker now. Yarna shrugged and pointed. "The sentry who should be there . . . isn't. And I didn't think I should open it without a guard present."

The helmeted head nodded. "Good thinking." He beckoned her to follow him, and started up the steps. Yarna stayed so close to him that she nearly trod on his boot heels.

When the pair reached the tall, massive doors, Doallyn glanced at the sentry screen, but it was too dark to make out the identity of the visitor. He leveled his blaster, then gestured to her. "Key it, then stand back."

Moving with a quickness that belied her bulk, Yarna pressed the appropriate combination, then skipped off to the side. Slowly, the enormous portal rumbled upward. Cold night air rushed in.

Tessek the Quarren stood outside, his robes rumpled and smelling of smoke. His wrinkled, tentacled features were pale and cracked as though he'd been exposed to intense heat. "Jabba . . . Master Jabba . . . the sail barge . . ." he babbled breathlessly. "Solo, the Wookiee . . . and that Jedi! There may be an attack!"

"Where is Jabba?" Doallyn demanded.

"Dead! She strangled him, that Alderaanian dancing girl, the new one. Just as the execution was supposed to take place, a terrible battle erupted on the sail barge. They had weapons hidden, and that Jedi boy, Luke Skywalker—he had powers beyond belief! I fought them, but a shot grazed me, and I lost control of my swoop . . . I nearly went into the Sarlacc pit! Then"—his arms waved expressively—"a huge explosion! The sail barge is in pieces all over the Dune Sea!"

"Jabba? *Dead?*" Even Doallyn's mechanical tones sounded stunned.

The Quarren nodded. He glanced from Yarna to Doallyn, then seemed to remember his dignity. Pulling himself up, he straightened his hunched shoulders. "I'm in command, now," he said, his voice deepening. "Wait for me here. I'll return shortly."

Doallyn sketched a half-salute, but did not respond further, and the Quarren, still shaking, turned and swung a leg across his swoop. Moments later, he was gone.

Yarna stood frozen with shock, scarcely daring to believe what she'd heard. She'd waited for this day for so long! Could Tessek be lying? Was this yet another of Jabba's twisted schemes to test the loyalty of his minions? And yet . . . she did not believe the Quarren meant her ill. Yesterday he'd even caught her pilfering some semiprecious stones and hadn't reported her to

Jabba. She remembered Tessek's wide, frightened eyes. No. The Quarren was telling the truth.

Yarna heard excited gabbling at the bottom of the stairs, and realized that the news was already spreading. Within minutes, everyone would know. The Askajian struggled for calm. She had to think—think! What did this news mean to her? What would happen now?

She felt no compunction to obey Tessek—even if he had done her a favor yesterday. The Quarren was an arrant coward, and everybody knew it. With Jabba gone, there was no one that Yarna could think of with the strength of will, ruthlessness, and intelligence to assume Jabba's mantle of leadership. Within the hour the palace would be in chaos. And back in Mos Eisley . . . Yarna's breath caught in her throat like a limp of jelled *sagbat*. Under Tatooine law, Jabba's illegal assets would be seized and liquidated. His slaves would be sold to the highest bidder.

Yarna herself was not legally a slave, since Jabba had placed her under "contract," promising her she could buy her freedom one day. That had been one of the Bloated One's favorite ploys. "Free" people tended to work harder and show more dedication than slaves. And Yarna clearly recalled the wording of the contract she had thumb-signed—it had stated that, in the event of Jabba's death, she was a free being— unless, of course, she had helped in any way to bring about that death. But she had not. So now . . . she was free.

The eventual promise of earning her freedom had made Yarna serve the Hutt crimelord loyally, dancing for him, minding the household staff and cleaning droids, and being a sort of mother figure to his other dancing girls. Another three years, and she'd have been free—unless, of course, Jabba had tired of her and ordered her killed.

Thinking of Leia and the other dancing girls made her mind flash to Oola. If only the poor little Twi'lek girl had taken her advice, then she too would have lived to see this day—and she too would have been free! Yarna hadn't known Oola well, but she'd liked the girl . . . even if she had been foolish enough to ignore Yarna's counsel on how to stay alive.

It had only been a few days since Oola had been fed to the monster residing beneath the throne room . . . now it was dead, as well, slain by the young warrior who called himself a Jedi. Yarna, watching from above, had barely been able to conceal her vengeful glee. The Askajian dancer had hated the ugly beast with a fierce passion ever since it had devoured her mate, Nautag. Their whole family had been captured in a slaver raid, and they'd been brought to Tatooine as part of a shipment for Jabba's inspection. The slavers had marched their merchandise into this very throne room, and invited the Hutt to take his pick of their wares.

Then, in a moment that still haunted Yarna's dreams, Nautag had stepped forward and cursed the Bloated One, defying Jabba and declaring that he and his mate and their cublings would *never* be slaves . . . never! And then . . . Jabba had laughed, that deadly "ho, ho, ho" that always chilled Yarna's hearts. Jabba laughed . . . and sprang the trapdoor, and Nautag fell.

Her mate had fought bravely, but he'd only lasted a few minutes. The rancor's triumphant roar as he'd torn her mate in half echoed in the Askajian dancer's ears . . .

Yarna started, abruptly recalled to the here and now by a shrill, unmistakably feminine scream. The chaos had begun.

I have to get out of here, she thought, remembering the small cache of pilfered valuables she'd been col-

lecting ever since she'd been brought here. She'd
need them when she reached Mos Eisley, and her
cublings. Prefect Talmont's auctioneers would be eager to sell, but they'd expect at least a hundred
apiece . . .

Mentally, she tallied up the value of her little hoard.
Do I have enough? Probably. Just barely.

She couldn't stay here, not now. She wouldn't last a
full day, she knew it. Not long ago, she had seen the
face of the Death that was haunting Jabba's palace,
and she knew that he would never let her live to tell
what she had seen. Only luck had saved her yesterday.
If Ortugg hadn't come looking for her . . .

And *then* they'd found the kitchen boy. Yarna was
the only one who understood the significance of the
small drops of blood crusted in the victim's nostrils.
She knew how the lad had met his death . . . and she
had no desire to share his fate. Since that moment,
she'd been careful never to be alone, even taking one
of the servants when she visited the bathhouse and
lavatory.

"Mistress . . ." someone said, hesitantly, and Yarna
turned to see Doallyn still standing beside her. His
features were hidden, but there was no mistaking his
tense, urgent bearing.

"Yes?" The Askajian strove to keep the impatience
she felt from reaching her voice. Nobody must know
that she intended to escape, or she'd be stopped.

"I was wondering if you could help me. You're in
charge of the cleaning . . . you know where Jabba
keeps . . . kept things. Have you ever seen a supply
of these?" With quick fingers, the guard detached a
small, cylindrical cartridge from the side of his breathing helmet and held it out for her inspection.

Yarna *had* seen a box of small gas cartridges like
that, concealed behind a panel in Jabba's personal

quarters. She looked curiously at Doallyn. "What is it?"

"A trace-breather cartridge. I can breathe Tatooine's air for short periods of time, but if I don't have minuscule amounts of hydron-three added to my air intake, I will die." The guard glanced over his shoulder apprehensively. "Jabba only doled out one day's supply at a time . . . his way of ensuring my loyalty. But now, with him dead . . ."

Yarna studied him speculatively, arms folded across her topmost set of breasts. Did he have any money? Could she make him pay for the information? She considered demanding credits in return for the location, but something inside her balked at the idea. By Askaj's Moon Lady, Doallyn would *die*—and he wasn't one of the ones who had tormented and oppressed her, he was just another being who'd been in thrall to Jabba.

Besides, she'd need help to reach her cache. Another shrill scream echoed through the palace followed by the grunting and squealing laughter of a Gamorrean. With every passing second the sounds of tipsy revelry and riot grew louder. Although there were worse things stalking the corridors of Jabba's palace than mere drunken Gamorreans, they were bad enough . . .

Yarna nodded brusquely at Doallyn. "I know where he kept them." So strange to have to refer to Jabba in the past tense. The Askajian found that she had trouble imagining the Hutt as dead. Jabba had been foul, disgusting, perverted, and greedy—but he had been strongly, vitally *alive.* "Come with me, guard me, while I get some things, and then I'll show you where they are. Fair enough?"

Doallyn nodded.

The Askajian headed for her goal, moving rapidly through the palace with Doallyn following. As she passed each darkened doorway, she tensed, wondering if *he* was waiting within. But their journey was unhindered.

When they reached the servant's quarters, Yarna made straight for the closet that held the sonic brooms and other cleaning supplies. "Keep your weapon handy," she instructed her escort, as she knelt and opened a panel in one of the automatic floorcleaners. "I don't want to be surprised."

She reached past the power cell to retrieve the little bag she'd hidden inside the cleaning unit. Doallyn cocked his helmeted head, and Yarna fancied she heard amusement in his mechanical tones. "What do you have in there, Mistress?"

Yarna bounced the bag on her palm, feeling its weight. Her lips curved upward in the first genuine smile she'd smiled in a year. "My children's freedom," she said, slowly.

"Your children?"

"They aren't here," Yarna said. "Jabba ordered them kept in his town house in Mos Eisley. I have three cublings still left . . . the slavers killed my fourth during our capture. I have to get to Mos Eisley before the officials sell off Jabba's assets. They'll sell my babies—I have to get there in time to buy them!"

Somehow she knew he was staring at her from behind his helmet. "Mos Eisley? You're going to Mos Eisley?"

"I have to," Yarna said, urgency filling her voice. "And quickly."

"Across the Dune Sea? You must be mad."

Yarna heaved herself to her feet, her breasts bouncing heavily within their leather restraints. "Probably," she admitted. "But I would far sooner die out there" —she waved a hand in the direction of Mos Eisley— "than I would trapped in here, waiting to become the killer's next victim."

"The unknown killer . . ." Doallyn said. "Yes, that is a thought. I don't fancy becoming the next victim, either."

"If I stay," Yarna said and began stuffing the bag into the space between her bottommost set of breasts, tying it securely so it would not fall out, "I *will* be the next victim, I know it." She glanced up at him and shivered. "I . . . I've seen his face. He won't let me live."

"You've *seen* him?" Doallyn's voice was tinged with urgency. He grasped her arm, pulling her toward him, and reflexively glanced over his shoulder. There was no one there. "Who is it?" he whispered.

Yarna's voice shook. "I don't know his name," she muttered hoarsely. "He's the tall, slender humanoid, the one with the dandified clothes . . . and the pouches on either side of his face." She drew her fingers down her own cheeks in illustration.

"That's Jerriko you're describing," Doallyn said. "Dannik Jerriko. He was working for Jabba. Are you sure? How do you know?"

"Because he tried to kill me yesterday." Yarna's voice was flat, but her whole massive body quivered. "He has . . . *things* that come out of his face. Beside his nose . . . and they kill you."

"Things?" Doallyn echoed blankly. "What kind of things?"

"Like . . . tendrils. They uncoil. He . . ." She nearly gagged at the memory. "He sticks them up, inside your nose . . . he did it to the kitchen boy."

"How did you get away?"

"Just as his tendrils touched me, one of the Gamorreans came in. He . . . the creature . . . let me go."

"But Jerriko is no match for you." Doallyn's fingers tightened on her upper arm, testing the solid muscle beneath the outer flesh. "You're twice his size."

"When he lays his hands on you, and looks into

your eyes . . . you can't move," Yarna whispered, feeling her gorge rise. "When you see those tendrils uncoil, you know what's happening, because he *wants* you to know. But you can't move. It's . . . horrible." She gagged, put her hand over her mouth, and fought for control. Moments later, she looked back up at him.

"If you swear on whatever belief system you follow that you'll escort me to the motor pool afterward, I'll take you to find those gas cartridges now," Yarna promised. How could she trust someone whose features she couldn't see? But she had little choice . . .

Doallyn touched the breast of his uniform with two fingers and a thumb in what looked like (and probably was) a ritual gesture. "I swear by the Sky Seraphs that I will take you to the motor pool."

Yarna nodded. "Let's go, then."

The two ventured out into the corridor, and headed purposefully toward the other side of the building, with Yarna in the lead. She walked quickly, surely, only too aware of the occasional screams and crashes that emanated from other portions of the palace. *Just a few more minutes and I'll be out of here,* she told herself, her strides coming faster and faster. She was nearly running. *Just a few more minutes . . .*

Her luck gave out when she rounded the next corner, with Doallyn a dozen paces behind her. Two of Jabba's erstwhile guards were waiting to pounce. The dancer recognized them—the human was named Tornik, and the Gamorrean was Warlug. Both were reeling drunk. As she tried to beat a hasty retreat, they greeted her with grunts of inebriated delight and grabbed her.

"Ugly One!" roared Tornik. "Love of my life! Come here and have a drink with me!" As Yarna tried to pull away, he yanked her arm viciously. "Dance for me, then we'll have some fun!"

The Askajian glanced back over her shoulder, but there was no sign of Doallyn. Had he run off and left her? But what about his breathing cartridges?

"No!" squealed the Gamorrean, trying to drag her away from his compatriot. "I saw her first! I get the Ugly One first!"

"Stop it!" Yarna ordered, trying to stay calm despite the racing of her twin hearts. "Let me go. I'm . . . I'm on an errand for Master Fortuna."

"Ha! He can't have you!" Tornik declared. "Warlug is right! We saw you first! He'll have to stand in line!"

The Gamorrean reached for the fastening between her topmost breasts. "Mine! I go fi—" He broke off at a sudden flash and sizzle, to stare unbelievingly at the scorched hole that had suddenly blossomed in his side. Letting go of Yarna, he staggered back, panting, then squealing in pain as he hit the wall and slid down it.

"Let her go," Doallyn said, stepping around the corner, his blaster still leveled.

"But we saw her first—" the guard protested, eyes narrowing. "You can have her when we're done."

"I said, let her go." Doallyn's voice was still level, but the muzzle of his weapon moved up, steadied until it was aimed at the man's face. "Or I'll make you let her go. Your choice."

Cursing, Tornik dropped Yarna's arm and stumbled backward. Warlug squealed frantically for help, and the human grabbed his arm, hoisted the injured being to his feet, then the two of them staggered away.

Yarna sagged against the wall as her knees threatened to buckle. "Oh, Sergeant, they . . . thank you, thank you . . . they were—"

"No time for that," Doallyn said briskly. "The breathing cartridges. You promised."

"Yes . . ." muttered Yarna, collecting her scattered wits. "This way . . ."

Within minutes they were in the Hutt's personal chamber. There had already been looters there—the place was stripped, and someone had flung a shovelful of dried rancor dung into the middle of the sleeping dais.

A message had been scrawled in huge letters across the wall: "Freeze, Jabba, in the Ninth Circle of Damnation!" The words were already half covered by other, less creative admonitions and obscenities. Quickly, Yarna led the way to an intricately carved panel, and pressed the tail of a fanciful creature. A small door swung open. "How did you know about this panel?" Doallyn demanded as he began stuffing the cartridges into a bag, after sliding several into his pocket. Yarna methodically scooped up several credit disks that lay on the bottommost shelf.

"I was Jabba's favorite dancer," Yarna said. "He would send for me sometimes when he couldn't sleep, and I would dance the sand-wave ballet for him. He said it helped him relax after a busy day. One time Jabba fell asleep, and I was dozing over there"—she pointed at the sleeping dais—"when Bib Fortuna entered. He didn't know I was awake, and *he* opened the panel."

"I'm surprised Jabba trusted him with the secret of his hiding place," Doallyn said, as they cautiously left the chamber with the guard in the lead, blaster at the ready.

Yarna smiled mirthlessly. "Jabba didn't trust anyone. He—"

She broke off in alarm as they rounded a corner and she recognized a familiar shape silhouetted in the dark corridor. Long, lean, shrouded in shadow . . . Dannik Jerriko! The dancer gasped and shrank back, as Doallyn, with commendable composure, raised his weapon. "Don't move, Jerriko!"

The vampire turned his head, and his features came

into view. Yarna whimpered with terror. No demon spewed up out of Askaj's Nethermost Abyss could have looked more evil. Fury contorted Jerriko's features, and the pouches on either side of his face writhed as if with a life of their own. His mouth opened in a sound-less snarl of rage. The Askajian clapped both hands over her mouth to hold back a shriek. Doallyn's finger must have tightened involuntarily on the trigger of his weapon, for an energy bolt suddenly erupted in a white flash.

The shadowy figure melted into a doorway up ahead.

Yarna had to admire Doallyn's courage, even as she questioned his sanity. He charged after the alien, and the dancer, against her better judgment, followed.

But when they reached the doorway of the cham-ber, and Doallyn keyed the illumination on, the room was empty of life. No other doors, no windows . . . but still, it was empty. "He couldn't just vanish," the guard muttered, sounding shaken. "Is there a secret passage, or hidden door?"

Yarna shook her head. "Not that I know of. But the palace has many secrets. There are passages beneath it, you know. Part of this place is still a B'omarr monastery."

Doallyn's breath whistled exasperatedly, then he shut the door, and locked it behind him. Yarna heard him cursing softly in what sounded like his native tongue. "He saw me," he said finally, reverting to uni-versal Basic. "Now he'll be looking for me, too. I'm going with you."

"But—" Yarna hesitated. She couldn't leave anyone to face the death that had so nearly claimed her. "All right," she said.

Their next stop was the kitchen. "Porcellus is a friend of mine . . . he kept things here for me,"

Yarna said, as she ventured into the pantry. "I hope he managed to get away safely . . ."

In the distant recesses of the pantry the Askajian had cached several blankets, some water flasks, and a couple of old, thick jackets she'd purloined from the guard barracks over the months. Hanging above them on a hook was a white bundle that could have been a voluminous apron—but was not. Yarna shook out the gauzy, faintly shining material, and it was revealed to be a long, loose robe with an attached, cowllike hood. "My desert robe," she said, noting Doallyn's glance. "We'll have to find something for you."

He nodded and held a bag as she briskly selected containers of preserved food from the shelves. "Now water," she said, as he fastened the container and slung it over his shoulder. Going over to the sink, she indicated the desert flasks to Doallyn. "Fill these up, please."

While he obeyed, Yarna herself filled a large container of water and drank it down without stopping, then filled and emptied a second.

Stripping off her elaborate dancer's headdress, she ran her fingers through her long hair with a sigh of pleasure. She'd never realized how heavy the thing was until she knew she wouldn't have to put it on again. Splashing water onto her face, she removed most of the large, warty "beauty patches" that Jabba had thought attractive.

"I didn't realize those were makeup," Doallyn commented, as she did so.

"Jabba liked them. He told me they reminded him of his mother."

Doallyn's helmeted head moved in a slow shake. "Jabba had a *mother*?"

Yarna smiled at him. "My reaction exactly."

Filling the water container again, the dancer slowly

poured the cool liquid over her head and body, letting the fluid trickle over her skin.

When she finished, she found Doallyn watching her intently. His mechanical tones sounded surprised. "You're . . . bigger," he said, his helmeted head moving as he surveyed her from head to toe. "Your skin . . . it's so *tight*."

"Askaj is a desert world." Yarna answered his unspoken question matter-of-factly. "My people's bodies absorb and hoard water most efficiently."

He nodded. "Can you live on a nondesert world?"

"Certainly," she replied. "But when we don't need to hoard the water, we don't."

"How would you look on a nondesert world?" He sounded genuinely curious.

"Thinner," Yarna said briskly, shaking out the folds of her desert robe. She pulled it over her head, then snatched up the blankets, the old jackets, and one of the water flasks. Doallyn caught up the food and the rest of the water.

When they reached the motor pool, they saw that the supply of suitable landspeeders and shuttles was sadly decimated. Only one vehicle was left, and it was in the repair section. The mechanics who were supposed to keep the machinery running in good order were nowhere to be seen.

Another wavering shriek rose in the distance, only to be brutally cut off in mid-ululation. Yarna and Doallyn looked at each other. "Can you pilot that thing?" she asked.

He nodded.

Within moments they had loaded up the landspeeder with their provisions. Doallyn located a length of sun-shield material in a locker, and they were able to improvise a burnoose for him. They stowed the rest of the material in the baggage compartment of the vehicle.

At Doallyn's signal, Yarna hoisted her bulk into the passenger's seat of the speeder. It was a tight squeeze, but she made it. The guard opened the outer door to the motor pool, then, feeling the cold night air, both hastily donned the jackets.

"Let's go," the Askajian dancer said impatiently, when her companion remained standing beside the landspeeder.

"I should have gone back to the barracks," Doallyn said, regarding the entrance into the palace.

"Why?"

"All I have as a weapon is my blaster, and no extra charges," he said. "There are wild banthas out there, and krayt dragons. It's a long way across the Jundland Wastes to Mos Eisley . . ."

"How far?"

"Twenty-five hundred klicks . . . as the shell-bat flies."

"A what?"

"Flying reptile from my world."

Yarna felt a flicker of curiosity. "Which planet is that?"

"Geran, Mneon System."

Yarna glanced over her shoulder at the entrance to the palace. "Do you really want to go back in there?"

Doallyn shook his head. "No. I want to get out of here. I feel . . ." He glanced nervously behind him into the shadows. "I feel as though I'm being watched."

"So do I," Yarna said. "Let's just go."

Doallyn nodded, then clambered into the pilot's seat. "I only hope that this thing was repaired before they abandoned the motor pool," he said, and manipulated the controls. "It's not really one of the fast, long-range models."

The speeder eased forward, and the darkness closed in around them. Within seconds they had left Jabba's palace behind. The vehicle picked up speed, until they were skimming the ground faster than any bird could fly.

The cold wind of their passage struck Yarna like a blow, but she was so exhilarated she scarcely felt it. Free at last! After a miserable year of insults and servitude, she was free and on her way! Soon . . . soon she would see her cublings . . . would hold their little bodies close, smell their warm, baby flesh. They would probably be starting to walk by now . . . Her eyes filled with moisture, but she sternly held back her tears. She must hoard her body's fluid . . . she'd need it for the journey.

Tilting her head back, she saw the stars streaming by so rapidly it was almost like a jump into hyperspace. At this rate, even in the short-range speeder, they'd reach Mos Eisley within a couple of days, even assuming they had to take shelter during the worst of the day heat.

Yarna hugged her jacket around her and thought of her children, remembering the day they had been born, and Nautag's pride in such a handsome brood. The babies had been barely a cold season old when the slavers had come . . . and thus they had not been given names. On Askaj, cublings were not named until after their first birthday.

Yarna mentally calculated the time since their capture, comparing the Askajian year to the year on Tatooine. Her children were late in receiving their names . . . but she'd rectify that lack as soon as they were reunited. The wind of their passage rushed through her short hair as Yarna, for the first time, considered what to name her cublings.

Nautag, of course, for the boy . . . the dancer felt a moment's pang for her other male infant, who'd been snatched out of her arms by one of the slavers and carelessly dropped. His skull had been crushed by the fall. Yarna forced herself to look ahead. What should she name her two daughters?

The names came to her in a flash of inspiration: Leia and Luka. Leia . . . she hadn't known the Alderaanian girl well, but if she had indeed killed Jabba, then Yarna owed her a debt she could never repay. And the name of the young Jedi who'd killed the rancor had been Luke Skywalker. Between the two of them, the dancing girl and the young Jedi had avenged Nautag. It was fitting that his children be named for them.

She turned her head to watch Doallyn as he piloted the speeder. The guard was a mystery to her . . . what did he look like under that mask? Was he human-seeming? His hands, in their black gloves, had the same number of digits as her own . . .

"Is the speeder running well?" she asked, having to raise her voice to be heard over the wind.

His mechanically enhanced voice reached her ears without difficulty. "The steering balance is out of adjustment. It keeps pulling to the right. I have to keep it on manual."

"Then this one wasn't repaired, was it?"

"I doubt it."

"Will it get us to Mos Eisley?"

"If the problem doesn't worsen, it will."

Yarna said a silent invocation to the Moon Lady as they sped along.

They had been traveling for hours when they swooped over the crest of a high dune and Yarna, squinting, saw a faint glow in the east. As she watched, it brightened, outlining distant hills. The desert beneath them was still in shadow, but there was no mistaking those faraway hills. Yarna tapped Doallyn's arm to gain his attention, and pointed. "The Jundland Wastes?"

He nodded. "The edge of them. We're only three hundred kilometers from the Stone Needle now."

Within minutes, Tatooine's twin suns rose into view, and the rolling sand dunes of the desert around them glowed pink and gold. Yarna had never seen the Dune Sea from a vehicle before—when she'd been brought to Jabba's palace, she'd been inside a shuttle, and there had been no portholes.

The rays of the suns struck her, and the chill of the night quickly vanished. She was wedged too tightly into the seat to take off her jacket, so she simply waited, sweating, wondering if Doallyn was determined to reach the Jundland Wastes before halting.

But after another hour, as the suns grew hotter and hotter, the pilot throttled back the speeder's headlong rush. The little vehicle slowed, then came to a halt and hovered above a fairly level stretch of white sand.

"I think we ought to take shelter until late afternoon," the guard said, unsealing the fastenings of the jacket and tugging it off. "Traveling in midday is dangerous."

"I agree," Yarna said. "Especially for you; you aren't used to the heat. And if you get sunsick, where would we be? I can't pilot the speeder."

His helmeted head nodded. "Help me rig a shelter, then."

Doallyn and Yarna used the rest of the sun-shield material to make a lean-to, employing the hovering landspeeder to anchor the material. They crawled into the resulting shadow, and half reclined there; both were too tall to be able to sit up straight. Yarna handed Doallyn the water flask. Gallantly, he handed it back to her.

"You first, Mistress."

The Askajian shook her head. "No. I drank before we left. I need far less liquid than you to survive. Drink your fill, Sergeant . . . do not ration yourself, or you will become ill."

He hesitated, then his helmeted head nodded. Slowly, carefully, he released the catches on his helmet and breathing mask, and took them off. Yarna didn't want to stare openly, but she discovered she was intensely curious about her companion. Busying herself with opening food packets, she cast a sidelong glance at his profile.

At first glance, he appeared as human as any Corellian, but his skin bore a faint bluish tinge, beneath a close-cropped shock of jet-black hair. It was too shadowy beneath the landspeeder to be sure of the color of his eyes, but Yarna thought they were light, rather than dark. His features were regular, and rather attractive. He was not as handsome as that Corellian smuggler, Solo, but he was pleasant to look upon, Yarna decided, as she held out a packet of food to him.

Slowly, almost deliberately, he turned his head toward her as he reached out to take it, until she was looking at him full-on.

Yarna stifled a gasp and forced herself not to recoil.

Noting her reaction, half of Doallyn's mouth stretched in a grin that told her he'd expected as much. The smile seemed more like a rictus of agony than any expression of good humor.

By the Moon Lady's mercy, what happened to him?

One side of Doallyn's face was horribly scarred. A broad band of roughened flesh pulled his mouth upward, and twisted and pitted the skin over his cheek. The slash narrowly missed his left eye, then ended at his hairline. Yarna forced herself to look away, unwilling to stare.

As though he could read her thoughts, Doallyn said suddenly, "It's a claw mark. From a Corellian sand panther. Their claws are poisoned, and the wound festered."

"It attacked you?" She struggled to keep her voice matter-of-fact. Instinctively, she knew that any expression of sympathy would be scornfully rejected.

"I was hunting it, and I wounded it. It turned on me." Methodically, Doallyn took a bite of the food and chewed determinedly.

"You're fortunate you weren't killed," she said after a moment.

"I was careless," he said bluntly. "For an instant, I was careless. It does not pay to do that when you're a hunter."

"I thought you were a soldier."

He shook his head. It was odd to see him without his helm, even though his features were nearly as expressionless exposed as they had been masked. "I was a hunter. That's why I came to Tatooine. Jabba advertised for a hunter to get him a krayt dragon."

"A krayt dragon?" Yarna stared at him incredulously. She'd heard the beasts described before—the young ones were as large as a rancor, and they reportedly grew even bigger as they aged. "What did he want with one?"

"He wanted to match one against his rancor, and charge admission. Jabba thought it would be the sporting event of the century. He offered a huge bounty for a live krayt dragon."

"And you actually thought you could *capture* one?"

"I have been a hunter for many years. There are not many beasts I cannot outwit," he said, with a quiet confidence that was far more convincing than any amount of boasting. "I studied everything that is in the databanks about krayt dragons. I came well prepared to hunt one."

Yarna took a bite of dried fruit and chewed thoughtfully. "If you came to Tatooine to hunt a dragon, then how did you end up guarding Jabba's palace?"

For the first time an expression flickered across his face in the dimness of the tiny makeshift shelter. He appeared chagrined and embarrassed, as he looked down at his food packet. "When I first arrived, I decided to sample the . . . sights . . . of Mos Eisley. Chalmun's liquor proved more . . . potent . . . than I was accustomed to drinking. I was never good at games of chance, and . . . I don't remember clearly how I got into that high-stakes game of wildstar, but I woke up the next morning with a terrible headache, owing Jabba a year's service."

"So you never got to hunt a dragon?"

"That was one of the things Jabba wanted me to do. I have been out on many expeditions, hunting one ever since I came to the palace—but they are rare. I never even sighted one in all these months. Jabba . . ."—he shook his head slightly, ruefully—"was growing . . . impatient. It is well for me that he is no more."

"So even if you had caught the dragon you would not have collected the bounty?"

"Correct," he said. "But there were . . . other . . . reasons to hunt a dragon. Even if I had to kill it, I would have profited, I believe."

Yarna's curiosity was piqued. "How?"

"Krayt dragons reportedly have . . . intrinsic value," he replied evasively.

Yarna had heard some of the bounty hunters and mercenaries talking about that. Some said that krayt dragons *contained* treasure, others that they, like dragons in ancient legend, *guarded* treasure. But most people dismissed that notion as being mere sensational rumor, if not outright folklore.

"What did your contract with Jabba say? Are you free now?" she asked.

"Yes, I am free," he said. "And you?"

"Free," she said, hearing the satisfaction in her own

voice. "And once I get to Mos Eisley, my children will be, too."

"Do you"—he paused, as if choosing his words carefully—"have a mate?"

"I did," she said, opening the water flask and carefully smoothing a scant palmful of the liquid over her face. Then she allowed herself one long swallow. "But Jabba sent him to the rancor."

He picked up his helmet and, not looking at her, said, "I am sorry, Mistress Gargan."

"Please," she said, "formality between us is no longer needed. I am Yarna."

"Very well. Call me Doallyn." He glanced down at the water flask she was carefully stoppering. "Why do you not drink more? We have plenty."

"I don't need any more," she said honestly. "My people are desert herders, on a planet every bit as hot as this one."

"What kind of animals do you herd?"

"Tomuons. Large, woolly, with long horns." Her hands moved with a dancer's flowing gestures, describing the creatures. "They give us milk, meat, and wool. This robe"—she held up a fold of her white desert robe—"was spun from their fleece."

He touched the fold of cloth, and exclaimed over the finespun softness and beauty of the fabric. "It almost glistens," he said.

"Yes, our fabric is highly prized. It is said that the Emperor's ceremonial robes are made of Tomuon cloth." She wrung a fold of the robe hard, then opened her hands and allowed it to fall into her lap, unmarred. "Our cloth is strong, and rarely wrinkles or stains. Askajian weaving techniques are prized secrets of our people. Nautag . . . my mate . . . was one of my world's finest weavers . . ."

"And you," he said, selecting a fresh cartridge of hydron-three and slipping it into the container on his mask, "were you a dancer before you came to Jabba's palace?"

"I was," she said. "My father was a chieftain, and I danced for the honor of our tribe in the largest competition." She could not keep a note of pride out of her voice, but then, remembering the year in Jabba's palace, she sighed. "I won that competition. And then . . . the slavers came. They took us . . . Nautag, me, our cublings. They . . . they killed one of our babies during the capture." Her throat felt tight.

"And they brought you to Tatooine?" Doallyn asked, his tone almost gentle.

She nodded. "Jabba had asked them for an Askajian dancer. So they captured me . . . and I had to dance for the Hutt. Jabba promised me that he would not sell my children as long as I danced well for him. But you know the Bloated One could not be trusted . . . I was always afraid that he would allow me to work, to gain the money to buy our freedom, then kill me because it amused him to do so. And then keep my children in slavery."

He nodded understandingly. "Dancing for Jabba must have been hard, after everything else that had happened."

"It was," she said. "But Doallyn . . . do you know what was hardest about it?" Unconsciously she reached out and laid a hand on his forearm, then realizing what she had done, Yarna hastily withdrew, tucking her hands inside the folds of her robe.

"What?"

"They . . . laughed at me. All of them. They said that I was . . ." Her mouth twisted at the word "ugly." Her indrawn breath felt raw in her throat. "They called me gross, and ridiculous, and . . . fat. Even Jabba laughed at me. But he did not laugh because he thought I was ugly, he laughed because he knew it hurt me to hear them. He . . . enjoyed the pain of others. You know."

Doallyn nodded. "Yes, I know."

"It hurt," she said. "I learned not to show it, to lose myself in the dancing, and not let myself hear the laughing . . . much. But it hurt." She gave him a glance that flashed defiance. "I am the way I was born to be! Why do beings have to judge each other? Why do they have to stare, and sneer, and say cruel things?"

He shook his head, and his fingers came up to tap the scar that she had nearly forgotten about. "I have no answer for you, Yarna," he said gravely. "But I understand the questions only too well."

A ray from the westering suns slid across Doallyn's eyes, waking him from an exhausted slumber. He blinked, then sat up halfway in the cramped shelter, propping himself on his hands. His companion was still asleep, breathing deeply. The white material of her robe outlined one generous haunch, and he experienced a faint stirring of male interest. How long had it been since he had been with a female . . . of any species?

Nearly a year, he realized. He was not the sort to indulge in casual liaisons often . . . and so much of his time was spent alone, in the wilderness. Doubtless the females at Jabba's court would have been repulsed by his scar. Enough women had drawn back from his face since he'd acquired that scar that he'd grown very cautious about taking off his mask in a woman's presence. He'd tried hiring women, from time to time, but he'd found that unsatisfactory, too. It was easier to abstain than it was to see revulsion . . . or, almost worse, indifference in a partner's eyes.

A heartless, temporary coupling left him feeling

even worse than solitude did, Doallyn had discovered. From time to time he'd wished he had a friend, someone to talk to, but the habit of silence was a hard one to break. He'd talked more to Yarna since their escape than he'd spoken to any one person in the past year.

Of course talking with Yarna couldn't be avoided, but their time together was strictly temporary, the hunter reminded himself. He'd be glad when he could resume his solitary existence.

Doallyn slid backward, out of the little shelter. As he stood up, he automatically checked the amount of hydron-three remaining in the cartridge. Less than a third gone. He wouldn't need another until midnight or so.

The hunter walked around the side of a dune to answer nature's call, then spent a few minutes with the navicomputer on the landspeeder, checking their course. Just as he finished, he heard a sound, then saw Yarna walking toward him. He found himself thinking about the story she'd told. From what he knew of Jabba's fickle tastes, it was amazing that Yarna had lasted a whole year in the Hutt's "employ."

As she strode toward him, the cooling breeze blew her robes around so they billowed out, then outlined her body. Doallyn was startled . . . the Askajian dancer was visibly smaller. He remembered her curt answer that on a nondesert world she would be "thinner." Her body tissues evidently soaked up liquid like a sponge, then utilized the fluid as it was needed, so she could indeed go a long time without water.

"Will we reach Mos Eisley today?" she asked, coming up beside him.

Doallyn shook his head. "Not this evening, anyway." He showed her their plotted course on the navicomputer screen. "Once we get into the Wastes, we'll have to slow down because of the hills and ravines. If we can halt somewhere north of the Stone Needle and rest for a few hours, we'll be doing well.''

"And from there, how far?''

"Only about another five hundred klicks. If we start at dawn, we'll be there by noon or so.''

A slow smile illuminated her broad features, until they glowed like Tatooine's dawn. "Then I can see my children tomorrow?''

"With any luck," he said, with an answering smile that she couldn't see.

"Doallyn . . .'' Her eyes were very intent. With a jolt of surprise, he noted that they were a lovely, clear green. "Thank you for coming with me. For piloting the landspeeder. I don't think I could have managed without you.''

"How *were* you planning to get across the Dune Sea?'' he asked. He'd been wondering about that since yesterday.

"I had planned to walk,'' she said matter-of-factly. "I'm strong, and my wind is excellent. But''—she glanced around her at the unending dunes and frowned—"this terrain is . . . very harsh. It would have been hard to bring enough provisions . . . it would have taken me a long, long time. I might not have made it.''

The Sand People would have killed you, Doallyn thought, *if the suns didn't* . . . But he was impressed by her courage, nevertheless.

After reloading the landspeeder, Doallyn and Yarna climbed in and glided off across the sands. The suns were far down on the western horizon, and it soon grew chilly. Doallyn kept the speeder at a good clip, but he was uncomfortably aware that the steering problem was growing steadily worse. What if the speeder broke down altogether? They'd be stranded in the Dune Sea . . . no, a glance at the navicomputer reassured the pilot slightly. The Dune Sea now lay behind them; they were skimming over the rugged folds and chasms of the Jundland Wastes.

Doallyn was forced to slow the speeder's headlong rush, and to give all his attention to piloting. The steering problem grew steadily worse, and soon the muscles and tendons in his left arm and shoulder were protesting. It was with relief that the hunter saw that they were approaching the coordinates he'd selected. He began searching for a good place to stop for the few hours that remained of the night . . .

Yarna awoke at dawn, to find herself huddled against Doallyn's back, where she must've instinctively migrated in search of warmth. She hastily rolled away and sat up, rubbing her eyes and looking around her at the bleak desolation that was the Jundland Wastes. Rock . . . rock everywhere. Tortured, wind-sculpted rock, in various hues of brown. Ocher-brown, yellow-brown, tan, reddish-brown, dark brown . . . with miserable scraps of yellowish-green vegetation scattered here and there.

And sand. White sand, so pure and pristine that it dazzled the eye with its whiteness. It appeared innocent and safe, but she knew that the Jundland Wastes were rife with treacherous sand pits that could swallow the unwary. Yarna had been careful to acquire a long stick and to probe the ground before her wherever she ventured.

Turning to look south, Yarna glimpsed the narrow spire of what must be the Stone Needle, the tallest landmark in the Jundland Wastes. In the pellucid air of dawn she could see it clearly, even at this distance.

Taking out the provisions, she divided a packet meticulously in two, then allowed herself a few scant swallows of water. She ran her hands down her front, realizing that she was now nearly a third less bulky than she had been in Jabba's court. He'd liked her at maximum fluid capacity, claiming it made her jiggle more effectively, but it had been hard to maintain the greater bulk. She was glad that she could shed some of it now.

When Doallyn awoke, the two escapees quickly loaded the landspeeder, then headed east, toward Mos Eisley. Yarna leaned back in her seat, pleased that she could now move and stretch with far greater freedom. She was increasingly aware that Doallyn was having to struggle with the steering from time to time. "Is this speeder going to make it?" she asked worriedly.

He nodded. "But I'm getting cramps in my arms trying to hold it on course."

"I wish I knew how to pilot."

Buoyed by the knowledge that they were rapidly approaching their goal, the two talked as they sped along. Doallyn described his searches for the krayt dragons that lived in the Jundland Wastes, and told Yarna that there was a surprising amount of life in the wilderness. Whole tribes of Sand People eked out an existence, even though there was almost no ground water, and they had only a few, stolen moisture vaporators and dew collectors.

"How do they survive?" she wondered.

"Hubba gourds," he said, and told her about the round, yellowish fruits that grew in the shadows of the cliffs. The fruits held fluid in their tough, stringy inner fibers, liquid that could be sucked and squeezed out to keep life going.

He also described how vicious the Sand People were, how they would kill for no reason more than to steal one's clothing. "The terrain is dangerous enough," Doallyn said, "with wild banthas and poisonous lizards and sand pits to worry about . . . but the Sand People are even worse."

Yarna shivered despite the heat, and peered at the navicomputer. "How much farther?"

"We passed Motesta nearly an hour ago." Doallyn pointed at an orange dot on the screen. "We're about fifty klicks from the outskirts of Mos Eisley. We'll be there by—" He broke off in a strangled sound, half gasp, half scream, and the landspeeder swerved wildly.

Yarna had been watching Doallyn—she never saw it coming. All she knew was that one moment the speeder was gliding along, the next, it was struck so hard that it went spinning through the air like a child's whirl-toy. Yarna screamed as centrifugal force clamped her into the seat like a giant hand. Then the nose of the speeder struck the rocks in front of them, and Doallyn went tumbling out.

Yarna screamed again as she caught a glimpse of a massive figure that loomed like a living, scaled mountain. She realized that the sound she'd been dimly aware of was a loud hissing, as though all the kettles in the world were spouting at once. The speeder's tail went down in answer to another crushing blow, and then Yarna too was flung out. She landed half on a rock, half on sand, and felt the sand give way beneath her, sucking her leg down.

Sand pit! she thought, and desperately grabbed the rock, heaving herself free of the shifting pull. As she did so, she saw a dark shape that was already halfway buried and sinking fast. *Oh, no! The landspeeder!*

Yarna watched helplessly as their only transport was sucked down until it disappeared completely. Her attention was distracted by a roar that made the ground shake, and she glanced around. *What hit us?* She was dizzy, disoriented, as she wondered where Doallyn was. Stumbling, careful not to step on anything but the stone, she edged her way around the rocky buttress that had saved her, until she could see.

The sight that met her eyes was so overwhelming

that her knees buckled, and she had to grab the rock wall for support. The thing that filled the ancient riverbed where they'd "landed" was huge—far bigger than the rancor. A krayt dragon—it had to be.

The creature was yellowish-brown in color, almost golden as its scaled back caught the suns' rays. It had three huge horns, one above each eye and one in the middle of its forehead. Slitted nostrils flared above a mouthful of fangs nearly as long as Yarna's arm. A ridge of dorsal spines studded its back from its neck to its spike-finned tail. The monster stood on four squat legs that were bowed outward from the huge mass of its body. The dragon's eyes were greenish-yellow, with horizontally slitted pupils that glittered like sapphires.

Yarna stiffened as the massive head, many times the size of her own body, swung toward her. Then she heard Doallyn's voice. "They hunt by sensing motion. Stand still!"

There was nothing else she *could* do. Yarna felt as though her feet had taken root, become part of the rocks beneath her. She rolled her eyes sideways in their sockets, and saw Doallyn. The hunter was crouched low, moving toward the dragon from behind a low ridge of rock. His blaster was in his hand.

What is he doing? she wanted to shriek aloud, but fear held her paralyzed. *He can't mean to try and fight that thing!* The idea of a human, even armed with a blaster, taking on that huge mountain of an animal was ludicrous.

But that was plainly what Doallyn intended. The krayt dragon snorted, testing the air, and the finned tail lashed back and forth. The head swung slowly from one side to the other, with the horns lowered, as though the beast were using them to detect motion.

Doallyn was close, now, crouched only a few dozen meters from the beast. He checked the charge on his blaster. *No!* Yarna wanted to shriek. *Let's climb up the cliffs! It can't follow us there! Doallyn, NO!*

But no sound would emerge from her paralyzed throat. She could not move.

Coiling himself like a spring, Doallyn leaped to his feet, vaulted over the low barrier of rock, and raced straight toward the dragon.

His movement broke Yarna's paralysis. "No!" she shrieked. The massive head swung toward the hunter, the jaws gaping, slavering, wide enough to swallow the landspeeder in two bites. "No, don't!" she screamed, and moved. Darting out from behind her rock, she grabbed a chunk of sandstone from the riverbed and flung it at the creature.

The horned head swung toward her. Yarna skidded to a halt, and backpedaled frantically. Doallyn, taking advantage of the distraction, covered the distance between him and the dragon in two huge bounds. He leaped up, catching hold of the rightmost horn, hanging on as the beast's head went skyward in a sickening rush. It roared, the sound deafening in the confines of the ravine.

Doallyn clung like an insect to the horn, then he threw himself forward, grabbing the middle horn. The beast swung its head in a sickening arc toward the cliff wall, plainly intending to crush the annoying creature against the stone surface. But before that arc could be completed, Yarna heard the whine and saw the flash of Doallyn's blaster. He shot the beast right below the middle horn, between the eyes.

Air rushed out of the krayt dragon's lungs with the force of a small explosion. As Yarna stood transfixed, the huge legs splayed outward, bonelessly, and the head dropped like a boulder, to crash against the rocky bed of the ravine. The impact flung Doallyn free, where he lay motionless.

He killed it, Yarna's numbed brain realized, a second later. *By the Moon Lady, he actually killed it!*

But had Doallyn survived his victory?

With a muffled exclamation, Yarna ran forward to the sprawled body of the man. She crouched beside him, calling his name, for what seemed like an eternity—but was, in reality, only a moment or two—before he stirred, moved. She heard him gasp, then groan.

"Doallyn, are you hurt?"

His voice reached her, muffled by the helmet. "Breath . . . knocked out . . ." He struggled to raise himself, and, seeing that he moved freely, if stiffly, she helped him. He gasped for a moment, then said, in a more normal tone, "It's dead?"

"As dead as Jabba," Yarna said solemnly. "I can't believe you killed that thing with one shot!"

"Vulnerable point . . . the sinus cavity leads directly into the brain . . . good thing I studied them." Pushing Yarna's supporting arms gently aside, Doallyn levered himself up until he was standing, surveying his kill. Yarna saw his shoulders straighten, and his whole body proclaimed the triumph he was feeling as he regarded the dead behemoth.

"I'll have to get a trophy," she heard him mutter. "No one will believe me, otherwise."

"You are the best hunter in the entire galaxy," Yarna said, and she believed every word of it. "I don't think anyone else could have killed that thing."

Doallyn's helmeted head swung toward her, and he nodded. Without seeing his face, she knew that he was grinning exultantly. "But I couldn't have done it without you, Yarna! If you hadn't distracted him by moving at just the right instant, he'd have gotten me!"

The Askajian laughed out loud as some of his triumph was transmitted to her. Then, as she climbed to her feet, reality rushed back like a blow. "Doallyn, the landspeeder . . . all our supplies . . . are gone. Sucked down into a sand pit.''

"We'll have to walk it," Doallyn said. "There are hubba-gourds. We can survive on them for a couple of days."

"But what about your breathing cartridges?" she asked, quietly.

He stood still, as transfixed by that thought as she had been by the dragon. "I put a couple into my pocket," he said, slowly, digging his fingers down. Moments later, he held out three cartridges. "Not good," he said, slowly.

"Enough hydron-three to see you into Mos Eisley? We can buy more there, can't we?"

"Yes, most vendors who sell spacesuits or breathing gear would have it," he said, slowly. "As to whether it will be enough . . . it should be. If we don't dawdle."

Yarna tugged at his sleeve. "Then let's start walking right away."

"In a minute," he said. "There's something I have to do first."

Realizing that he was asking for privacy, Yarna realized that she, too, could use a few minutes to herself. She nodded at Doallyn. "Which way do we go?"

He pointed. "Due east."

"Meet you back here in a few minutes, then."

He nodded, and turned away.

The Askajian dancer turned and walked in the opposite direction, past the krayt dragon's snout. In death, the beast appeared only a little less fearsome than it had in life. *It's a reptile,* Yarna thought, remembering similar creatures (though only a fraction of the size) on Askaj. *It won't really die until the sun goes down . . .*

•   •   •

As soon as Yarna was out of the way, Doallyn sprinted as quickly as he could back to the krayt dragon's hind-quarters. Sketches of the beast's anatomy flashed through his mind as he drew his blaster again, reset-ting the weapon so it would fire a narrow, slicing beam rather than explosive bursts.

It was a gory, smelly job, carving up the krayt dragon's innards, but finally he had alternately sliced and vaporized enough hunks of scale and meat to re-veal the creature's intestines. *The last chamber of the giz-zard,* he thought, studying the bloody welter of internal organs that splooshed messily outward, slid-ing onto the ground. *Where is it?*

"There you are," he muttered softly. Drawing a vibroblade out of his boot, Doallyn waded in for the final few strokes. The first sac he cut into was one of the middle chambers—the stones he drew out were larger than his fist, hunks of granite and sandstone only a little rounded and smoothed.

Using that chamber as a guide, the hunter was able to locate the organ he wanted—the last chamber of the krayt dragon's massive gizzard system. The beasts had teeth, yes, but those teeth were used only to kill and rip apart prey. The dragon had no grinding mo-lars for chewing. Instead it had a gizzard, rather like a bird's, but multichambered. As food passed through the organ in progressively more pulverized and di-gested chunks, the rocks in the gizzard ground it finer and finer—until it reached the intestinal system.

Doallyn braced himself, said a quick invocation to the Sky Seraphs, and sliced open the last chamber. Reaching inside, he felt around, then pulled forth five perfectly round objects. Each was as large as the last joint of his thumb. As he wiped the blood and ichor away, they glowed in the sunshine like the jewels that they were.

Dragon pearls.

Beauty incarnate. Two were clear green, the color of Yarna's eyes. One was the blue of the sky just after sunset. The fourth was white, and iridescent—and the fifth was as black as the depths of interstellar space. As Doallyn stared at it, marveling at its perfection, he seemed to be able to see *into* the stone, as though black light were trapped deep inside.

Doallyn wanted to shout, to dance, to sing—but he remembered that with every breath he was using up his precious stock of hydron-three. Quickly, he stowed the dragon's pearls away in the inside, sealed pocket of his tunic. Glancing around, he realized he was covered in dragon's blood. He had to have some excuse for that, or Yarna would ask questions . . .

The hunter headed purposefully for the krayt dragon's tail. He'd cut off one of the spiky fins for a trophy, and that would, he hoped, account for the condition of his hands and clothes. If he kept Yarna from walking around to the beast's other side, she'd never know what he'd been doing.

Kneeling down beside the dragon's tail, Doallyn grabbed the fin and began slicing at it. Of course he intended to share some of the treasure with Yarna, he told himself. After all, she had made it possible for him to kill the dragon in the first place. *I'll keep the pearls for a surprise, show them to her after we reach Mos Eisley*, he told himself, uncomfortably aware that he was rationalizing, if not outright lying to himself. *After all, we have to get on the road now. We really don't have—*

Without warning, the dragon's giant tail moved in his hands, jerking away from Doallyn's grasp, then twitching hard from side to side. One fin caught the hunter across the side of his helmet, sending him hurtling down, into instant—and complete—darkness . . .

●　　●　　●

Yarna found him minutes later, where the tail's reflex twitch had flung him. She stared in horror, then, by placing her hand on his chest, and feeling its slow rise and fall, realized he still breathed. *Moon Lady, what shall I do now?* she wondered despairingly, gazing around at the stark landscape.

And all because he had to have a trophy! Just like a male . . . she thought, furious. Males always have to have something to flaunt and brag about. For a moment she was so angry that she felt like kicking the unconscious hunter.

Anger was good, she discovered. It lent her strength. Yarna stood there for a moment, feeling the anger rush through her veins like a powerful drug, then, slowly, carefully, she bent and grabbed Doallyn's arm. Slinging it over her shoulder, she slowly straightened up, until his prone form was draped over her like a Tomuon lamb. She had carried many such slung in just this fashion.

Eyes narrowed against the noonday rays of the suns, jaw tight with determination, Yarna turned so she was facing due east. She began to walk.

Slap, slap . . . slap, slap. The sound of her leather sandals hitting the hard-packed road was the only sound in the universe. Yarna counted the beats of her stride in her head, knowing she could not afford to go slowly, though every muscle screamed for her to lay her burden down and rest.

How long had she been walking? Her world had narrowed so greatly that she could not be sure. Scattered memories surfaced. Yellow globes in a rock recess . . . hubba gourds. She'd smashed several and dripped the water into Doallyn's mouth, rubbing his throat until he swallowed. Then she'd allowed herself several sips of the sour, but blessedly wet, liquid.

How many times had she given Doallyn water? Two? Three? She could not be sure, just as she could not be sure how long it had been since she had stumbled upon this road that led in the right direction. Yarna thought it might be yesterday that she'd found it, but time . . . time was a slippery thing, as slippery and fluid as the pulp in a hubba gourd. She was no longer sure of anything—

—except that Doallyn was still breathing. Her ears were attuned to the sound of those harsh, painful breaths. She'd checked his breathing cartridges every few hours. He'd used up the one that was in his helmet, plus two others from his uniform.

She'd slipped the last one into place hours ago.

How long could he live without hydron-three? Yarna had no idea. All she could do was walk, slap, slap . . . slap, slap . . . walk as rapidly as her fading strength and muddled mind would allow her to go.

At some point last night she'd awakened to find herself sitting in the middle of the road, with Doallyn's body draped across her lap. She must've fallen asleep while walking, and sunk to the ground without ever waking up.

How long had she slept? Yarna had no idea . . . but the thought that the time she had spent sleeping might mean the difference between life and death for the man she carried, haunted her, even through the growing haze of exhaustion that clouded her mind.

Slap, slap . . . slap, slap . . .

Doallyn's breaths were coming quicker now, as though he were gasping. Yarna lowered him to the road, and looked at the gauge on the side of his helmet. The marker hovered in the "empty" zone.

The gasps changed, grew recognizable. Doallyn was trying to speak. Yarna leaned close. "Sorry . . ." she made out. "Save yourself . . . leave me . . ."

"Not while I live," she replied fiercely. "Be quiet . . . save your breath. It can't be far now . . ."

He clutched at the front of her desert robe, babbling urgently. Some nonsense about a treasure. Yarna ignored him. It took all her strength, all her concentration, to get him settled across her shoulder again.

Slap, slap . . . slap, slap . . .

She plodded along, forcing herself to move as quickly as possible, knowing that every second might be Doallyn's last. Head down, concentrating on moving as quickly as possible, she was actually walking down one of the streets in Mos Eisley before she realized she'd reached the town.

Yarna's head jerked up at the cry of a water-scller. *I've made it! Now to find a vendor who sells breathing gear!*

Stumbling, she forced her legs into a rough approximation of a trot. Was Doallyn still breathing? She couldn't be sure . . . she could no longer hear him. Was that because of the blood rushing past her ears, as she tried to run?

Ahead of her, a bigger street. Vendors with stalls and carts, crying their wares. Yarna's desert-hazed eyes fastened on one—an Ortolan like Max Rebo. Poor little Max . . . he'd gone on the sail barge, hadn't he? Yarna thought foggily, as she jogged across the street toward her quarry.

Reaching the stall, she unceremoniously dropped Doallyn to the dusty ground and gasped out her request. "A cartridge of hydron-three, please!"

The Ortolan whuffled down his trunk at her. "Certainly, madame. It distresses me to inform you, though, that hydron-three is currently rather expensive. There hasn't been a shipment since . . . well, it's been quite a while."

"I don't care," Yarna snapped, digging beneath her robe for the precious little sack she'd carried out of Jabba's palace so long ago—was it only four days? It seemed as though half of eternity had passed. "I can pay. Give me five days' supply."

"Certainly, madame," the Ortolan said. "May I see your currency, please?"

Yarna's hands shook as she took out two small semi-precious gems and the stolen credit disks—all she could afford to spare. "Here you are."

The Ortolan shook his head mournfully, his huge dark eyes very sad. "I'm dreadfully sorry, madame, but I'll need twice that for two days' supply."

Yarna glared at him so balefully that he shrank back into the dimness of his stall. "Robber! I don't have time to bargain! Give me two days' supply, then!"

The vendor was firm. "I'm sorry, madame, but I must insist on the price I named. I'm barely breaking even as it is."

"I have a man dying here! He needs that hydron-three!" Yarna said, her hearts racing. If she gave the vendor what he demanded, she would only be able to buy two of her children's freedom. No mother could possibly make such a choice!

And yet . . . Doallyn had saved her life . . . several times.

"I'll give it to you at cost, madame," the vendor said. "Two more of those jewels, for three days' supply."

Which still wouldn't leave her with enough to buy all three children free. But Yarna found that she couldn't turn her back on the hunter. "All right," she snarled, slapping the requisite amount onto the counter. "Give me those cartridges!"

With the precious little container in her hand, she bent over Doallyn, wondering if he'd died while she bargained. That would be a final, searing irony . . .

But no . . . he still breathed, if slowly. Slipping the cartridge into his helmet, she triggered it and saw that it was working. Only then did the Askajian stuff her bag back into its place of concealment.

She managed to drag Doallyn off to the side of the shop, into the shade, then sank down beside him. For a long, nearly comatose time she simply existed, not thinking, not feeling . . . simply breathing in and out.

Yarna was jerked out of her half-trance when Doallyn stirred, then sat up with a groan. His helmeted head turned back and forth, as though he could not believe where he found himself. Finally he turned to face her. "You . . . carried me here?"

"I had to," Yarna said. "You were unconscious. Don't you know that reptiles never die until after sundown?"

The hunter shook his head. "That's an old tale."

"Well, it was true enough this time," Yarna pointed out.

Doallyn had evidently checked the hydron-three gauge inside his helmet. "Full!" he exclaimed.

Gravely, Yarna reached out and dropped the spare cartridges into his hand. "Here. You'll need these."

"Where . . ." he sputtered. "How . . ."

Briefly, she explained about how she had come to buy the cartridges. Doallyn slowly released the catches on his helmet and took it off, holding the cartridge side close to his face so he could inhale the hydron-three when it was released. "You gave up one of your children . . . for me?" he asked slowly, as though he could not believe what he'd heard.

Yarna shrugged wearily. "I couldn't stand there and let you die, could I?"

With a quick movement, he reached out and grabbed her hand. "I can't believe you did that . . . for me."

"You saved my life, remember?"

"Well, now we're even," he said, and, for the first

time since she'd known him, Yarna saw him truly smile. His scarred features brightened; he looked almost handsome. "Yarna . . . I have a surprise for you."

"What is it?"

Slowly, with great ceremony, he reached into his tunic and took out five small objects, then held them out to her. "Dragon pearls. One is worth a fortune. With these we can buy all your children—and a spaceship to transport them in."

Yarna stared at the gems, dazzled. "Where did you get them?" she asked finally.

Doallyn pulled his helmet back on, fastened it. "I'll tell you on the way," he said. "Let's go find your children."

———

Money, Yarna discovered, was the key to everything in Mos Eisley. Before moonrise that same night, she and Doallyn had accomplished their goal. Yarna had Luka and Leia in one arm, and Nautag in the other. She couldn't believe how they'd grown, and she was even more amazed that they still recognized her. Simply holding her babies in her arms again made the Askajian speechless with joy.

They paused on the street corner across from the Hutt lord's town house. "Well, you have them," Doallyn said. "Now what?"

Yarna stared at him, nonplussed. She had concentrated so hard on reaching this moment that she had no idea what she'd do next. She thought for a moment, and the answer came. "Get off Tatooine," she announced firmly. "I never want to see this planet again."

Doallyn nodded his helmeted head. "Very sensible. My sentiments exactly. After we buy that spaceship, would you . . . that is, do you think you might like to see Geran? It's a nice world. You'd like it, I think.''

Yarna considered the question, then a slow smile crossed her face. "I think that Geran would be a very nice place to go," she said.

"Good!" Doallyn said, warmth tinging his voice even through the mechanical filter. "Next stop, the spaceport. I've always wanted my own personal ship."

Yarna nodded, and shifted Nautag, who was squirming restlessly and trying to pull her hair. "The spaceport, then."

Doallyn stretched out his arms toward Nautag. "Here. Let me carry him. You have your hands full."

Yarna nodded, and handed the child over to the hunter. Together, they walked away, and the light of Tatooine's little moon shone down gently upon the five of them.

Epilogue:
Whatever Became
Of . . . ?

After visiting Geran, Yarna and Doallyn decided to live aboard their new spaceship and become free traders, specializing in textiles and gemstones. Whenever they needed extra credits, Yarna moonlighted as a dancer. She performed the Dance of the Seventy Violet Veils at the wedding of Han Solo and Leia Organa, where she was spotted by a designer of exotic lingerie and recruited as a model for his line of extravagant jeweled brassieres.

Doallyn managed her new career, taking time out to capture specimens of renowned fierceness for zoos on the worlds they visited. The cublings showed great aptitude for music and became a swinging jizz trio in the tradition of Max Rebo and his band.

Shortly after leaving Tatooine, Sy Snootles dissolved her partnership with Max Rebo and went solo, releasing two music collections, both of which sold abysmally. Her career in shambles, unable to find work as a solo act, she joined another jizz-wailer band and is still touring under a variety of pseudonyms.

Max Rebo fell in with the Rebellion shortly after Sy Snootles ended their partnership. He spent the next few years entertaining Rebel forces across the galaxy. ("The Rebellion has the best food," he is reported to have said on his entrance paperwork.) Following the death of the Emperor, Max returned to civilian life and currently owns a successful string of restaurants on eight different planets.

Droopy McCool vanished into the Dune Sea and has not been seen since Jabba the Hutt's death. Some old-timers claim to hear Kitonak pipe music late at night from the farthest, most desolate corners of the deep desert, and some think it may be Droopy and his kind playing their music as they wait for the coming of the Cosmic Egg.

In the confusion that reigned following the disaster on the sail barge, Malakili the rancor keeper released Porcellus the chef from his cell, and the two of them managed to loot sufficient funds from the treasury to open the Crystal Moon restaurant, agreed by all to be the finest in Mos Eisley. The two still operate it in partnership, and its fame has spread through most of the Outer Rim.

Gartogg the Gamorrean guard spent the rest of his life wishing he could have ridden on the sail barge's last voyage. However, when Ortugg never came back to have him ground up for Jabba food, he tagged along with a small group leaving the palace for Mos Eisley. He still carried his new friends over his shoulders and found that as they journeyed through the desert, the kitchen boy and the monk dried out into firm, lightweight mummies with perpetual smiles. In

Mos Eisley he found gainful employment as an enforcer for a smuggling operation and faithfully took his grinning friends everywhere he went.

Ephant Mon chose to return to his home planet of Vinsioth. The touch of the young Jedi Knight had reawakened the spiritual side of him and he began a religious contemplation of nature, finally founding a new sect that worshiped the Force.

He did, however, still keep just a bit of his snout immersed in the old life, running a "harmless" little scam now and again to finance his sect and build it a very fine temple, indeed.

When J'Quille the Whiphid tried to return to his homeworld of Toola for a little R and R, though, he was informed that the Lady Valarian, inconsolable over his "rejection," had placed a bounty on his head if he ever left Tatooine. Condemned to a life of sweltering misery, J'Quille returned to Jabba's palace and joined the B'omarr monks. Exchanging his body for a jar seemed his only chance at surviving Tatooine's insufferable heat.

Meanwhile, Bib Fortuna found that he did have friends, even as a disembodied brain, next to Tessek and Bubo and several other new "initiates" following Jabba's fall. Nat spoke to him and eased him through the shock of losing his body, helped him learn to guide a brain walker up and down the corridors, and he and Nat eventually looked like any other pair of disembodied brains held tight against the underbelly of a mechanical spider, taking a stroll together. Passing monks still in their bodies would bow to them as they would to any of the truly enlightened.

But Fortuna still tried to learn what had happened

to all the schemes he had put in place. The computers would not respond to the voice that came from his brain jar's speakers, but he found that he could make his two mechanical forelegs grasp an eating implement, using its handle to enter his private access codes, slowly, punching in one number at a time.

Not all of the codes had been erased, not the secret ones. If an embodied monk approached, Fortuna would drop the teaspoon and amble about the corridor till the monk had passed, then sweep the walker's legs about the stone floor, listening for the teaspoon so he could find it and pick it up and start again. *Of the day's annoyances, these,* he often thought. *That I had to drop the teaspoon eighteen times.* He checked his accounts and found that many secret ones, the ones under different names, were intact and growing in interest. He possessed a fortune. He sent replies to his former associates—and sentence by sentence, word by word, they learned what had happened. One said he would come to rescue him.

Eventually the monks would let him and Nat walk outside the palace during the Tatooine evenings, and one day rescue would come, and they would leave Tessek and Bubo and all the others behind. He and Nat would find the cloners, obtain new bodies: young and strong and perfect. Fortuna hoped, if the monks knew what he and Nat planned, as seemed likely, that they would find it in their hearts to let them go.

Deprived permanently of Jabba's soup in the explosion of the sail barge, Dannik Jerriko responded by going on a killing rampage throughout the palace. An *Anzat* who had always prided himself on self-control and elegance, he now was stripped of both by his outrage at losing Jabba. Never before had Jerriko failed to drink an entity's soup. His reputation forever tarnished, he became a wanted entity himself, and his name now tops the list of such bounty hunters as have worked for Jabba and others.

The predator is now the prey.

And, of course, both Boba Fett and Mara Jade kept themselves very, very busy . . . but those are other stories entirely.

About the Authors

KEVIN J. ANDERSON has written the STAR WARS novels *Darksaber* and the Jedi Academy Trilogy, cowritten the Young Adult series YOUNG JEDI KNIGHTS with his wife, Rebecca Moesta, cowritten the comic series STAR WARS: *Dark Lords of the Sith* with Tom Veitch for Dark Horse comics. He has also written non–STAR WARS science fiction novels, such as *Climbing Olympus* and *Blindfold,* and collaborations with Doug Beason, *Ill Wind* and *Virtual Destruction.* His most current project is the Dune series with Brian Herbert.

M. SHAYNE BELL's novel, *Nicoji* (Baen Books, 1991), is currently being translated into Spanish. His second novel, *Inuit,* was published by Harcourt Brace in 1995. He edited the anthology *Washed by a Wave of Wind: Science Fiction from the Corridor* (Salt Lake City: Signature Books, 1993), for which he received an AML award for editorial excellence. His short fiction has appeared in many science fiction magazines and anthologies, including *Tales from the Mos Eisley Cantina* and *Tales of the Bounty Hunters* (forthcoming). He grew up on a ranch in Idaho, spent two years as a missionary in São Paulo, Brazil, and has spent weeks hiking around the Utah desert finding the abandoned cities of the Anasazi.

JOHN GREGORY BETANCOURT is the author of quite a few novels, including a collaborative fantasy with editor Kevin J. Anderson, *Born of Elven Blood.* Lately he has been having fun returning to favorite childhood places, working on Batman, Spider-Man, Riverworld, and STAR TREK books and short stories for a wide variety of publishing companies. His own work can be found in such novels as *The Blind Archer, Johnny Zed,* and *Rememory.* John also runs a publishing company called the Wildside Press with his wife, Kim. They were nominated for a special World Fantasy Award in 1993 for their publishing activities.

MARK BUDZ, newly transplanted to Watsonville, California, is putting down roots near the artichoke fields along the beautiful Monterey Bay. In his spare time, he works as the managing editor and advertising director of the Science Fiction and Fantasy Writers of America *Bulletin.* His short fiction has appeared in *F&SF, Amazing, Pulphouse, Writers of the Future Vol. VIII, Quick Chills II, Rat Tales,* and *Science Fiction Review.*

A. C. CRISPIN is the author of several STAR TREK novels, including the recent best-selling *Sarek.* She is the creator, author, and coauthor of the STARBRIDGE series: *StarBridge, Silent Dances, Shadow World, Serpent's Gift,* and *Silent Songs* (Ace Books). In addition, she has coauthored two fantasy novels with Andre Norton: *Gryphon's Eyrie* and *Songsmith* (Tor Books), *Tales from the Mos Eisley Cantina.* She has also written a story for the STAR WARS short-story collection, Ms. Crispin is a frequent guest at science fiction conventions, where she often teaches writers' workshops. A

Maryland resident, she lives with her teenage son Jason, two horses, and three cats.

DAN'L DANEHY-OAKES is a typical SF writer: too bright to work in a McDonald's, not bright enough to be a *real* scientist, and physically unfit, he took refuge at an early age in vivid fantasy life. "Shaara and the Sarlacc" is his vengeance on Certain Persons. You know who you are.

GEORGE ALEC EFFINGER won the Nebula Award in 1988 for his novelette "Schrödinger's Kitten," though he is perhaps best known for his humorous work. He lives in New Orleans.

Living in the Watsonville, California, wilderness amid lettuce, strawberries, apples, ollalie berries, and an occasional zucchini, MARINA FITCH plays with children for fun and profit. Currently at work on a novel, she has published short fiction in *F&SF*, *Asimov's*, *Pulphouse Hardback*, *MZB*, and *Writers of the Future Vol. II*.

KENNETH C. FLINT of Omaha, Nebraska, is to date the author of fifteen novels for Bantam Doubleday Dell Books. All are works of adventure/fantasy, many of which are based upon ancient Celtic legends and myths. One of his short stories was included in *Tales from the Mos Eisley Cantina*.

Award-winning fantasy author ESTHER M. FRIESNER has a PhD from Yale University and a lifelong interest in cultures and mythologies beyond the Greek/Norse/Celtic realm. She is perhaps best known for her humorous works such as the recently published trilogy *Majyk By Accident*, *Majyk By Hook or Crook*, and *Majyk By Design* from Ace Books. However, she also enjoys a growing reputation for writing more serious fantasies such as the critically acclaimed *Yesterday We Saw Mermaids* from Tor Books. In addition, she has been branching out in science fiction novels and is currently working on *The Sherwood Game* for Baen Books. Her STAR TREK: DEEP SPACE NINE novel, *Warchild*, appeared in September 1994.

BARBARA HAMBLY's STAR WARS novel, *Children of the Jedi*, sent her to a galaxy a long time ago and far, far away. She attended college at the University of California in Riverside and spent one year at the University of Bordeaux in France. After obtaining a master's degree in medieval history, she held a variety of jobs: model, clerk, high school teacher, karate instructor (she holds a black belt in Shotokan Karate), technical writer. Her novels are mostly sword-and-sorcery fantasy, though she has also written historical whodunits, two vampire novels, and novels and novelizations from television shows, notably *Beauty and the Beast* and *Star Trek*. She edited an anthology of original vampire stories, *Sisters of the Night*. Her interests besides writing include dancing, painting, historical and fantasy costuming, and occasionally carpentry. She resides in a big, ugly house in Los Angeles with the two cutest Pekingeses in the world.

DARYL F. MALLETT is a freelance writer and editor, an employee of American West Airlines, and father of a delightful little boy named Jake, among other things. Though known for his nonfiction work with the Borgo Press and the Science Fiction Research Association, this marks his first professional fiction sale.

J. D. MONTGOMERY does not exist . . . not really.

JUDITH and GARFIELD REEVES-STEVENS have been a writing team since 1986. In fiction they have written three novels in the ongoing STAR TREK series, the first novel in the ALIEN NATION series, and have created their own action-adventure fantasy series in THE CHRONICLES OF GALEN SWORD. In nonfiction, they are authors of *The Making of Star Trek: Deep Space Nine* and the *Art of Star Trek*. Their other writing credits range from comic books to episodes of *Beyond Reality*, MTV's *Catwalk*, *The Legend of Prince Valiant*, and *Batman: The Animated Series*. For the 1994–95 television season, the Reeves-Stevenses have helped develop and are executive story editors for the animated science fiction series *Phantom 2040*, a futuristic updating of Lee Falk's classic costumed hero.

JENNIFER ROBERSON has published two bestselling fantasy series, the CHRONICLES OF THE CHEYSULI and the SWORD-DANCER saga, as well as the historical novels *Lady of the Forest*, a reinterpretation of the Robin Hood legend, and *Glen of Sorrows*, recounting the Massacre of Glencoe in the highlands of seventeenth-century Scotland. She has also published many short stories, including "Soup's On" in *Tales from the Mos Eisley Cantina*, which first introduced the assassin Dannik Jerriko. Her projects have included a fantasy collaboration with Melanie Rawn and Kate Elliott, titled *The Golden Key*, and a trilogy called Shade and Shadow.

KATHY TYERS, the author of *Star Wars: The Truce at Bakura* and other works of science fiction, has hung up her dancing costumes and laid aside her finger cymbals to study tae kwon do with her son. Tae kwon do is better exercise, but she misses the music. Kathy lives with her family near Bozeman, Montana.

DEBORAH WHEELER grew up mostly in California, went to college in Oregon, grew her hair long and protested everything during the sixties. It took her a long time and three academic degrees (bachelor's in biology, master's in psychology, doctorate in chiropractic) to figure out what she needed to do in life was to write. At the end of the seventies she hit total career burnout trying to be superwoman, dean of a chiropractic college, and new mother, dumped the career but not the kid, started writing seriously. She's since had a second child, studied martial arts (four years of tai chi ch'uan, eighteen years of kung fu), and lived in France. She teaches a parent-toddler gym class at the local Y and is fairy godmother/volunteer slavedriver for the library at the local elementary school. She has had short stories published in almost all the *Sword and Sorceress* and *Darkover* anthologies, also in *Spells of Wonder, Pandora, MZB's Fantasy* magazine, and *Fantasy and Science Fiction*. She is the author of the novels *Northlight* and *Jaydium*.

DAVE WOLVERTON has written several novels, including *Star Wars: The Courtship of Princess Leia, The Golden Queen, Serpent Catch, Path of the Hero,* and *On My Way to Paradise*. In 1986 he won the grand prize for the Writers of the Future contest. He has worked as a prison guard, missionary, business manager, editor, and technical writer.

WILLIAM F. WU is best known for his contemporary fantasy short story "Wong's Lost and Found Emporium," a multiple-award nominee that was adapted into an episode of the revived *Twilight Zone*. A five-time nominee for the Hugo, Nebula, and World Fantasy awards, he is the author of the six-volume series Isaac Asimov's Robots in Time, for Avon. Wu was born and raised in the Kansas City area and educated at the

University of Michigan, where he received a Ph.D. in American Culture. He is divorced and now lives in the Mojave Desert north of Los Angeles.

TIMOTHY ZAHN is the author of the STAR WARS novels *Heir to the Empire, Dark Force Rising, The Last Command,* the two-volume Hand of Thrawn series. He won the prestigious Hugo Award for his novella "Cascade Point." His non–STAR WARS books include, *Conquerors' Pride* and *Conquerors' Heritage,* and *Conquerors' Legacy.*

The World of
STAR WARS Novels

In May 1991, *Star Wars* caused a sensation in the publishing industry with the Bantam Spectra release of Timothy Zahn's novel *Heir to the Empire.* For the first time, Lucasfilm Ltd. had authorized new novels that *continued* the famous story told in George Lucas's three blockbuster motion pictures: *Star Wars, The Empire Strikes Back,* and *Return of the Jedi.* Reader reaction was immediate and tumultuous: *Heir* reached #1 on the *New York Times* bestseller list and demonstrated that *Star Wars* lovers were eager for exciting new stories set in this universe, written by leading science fiction authors who shared their passion. Since then, each Bantam *Star Wars* novel has been an instant national bestseller.

Lucasfilm and Bantam decided that future novels in the series would be interconnected: that is, events in one novel would have consequences in the others. You might say that each Bantam *Star Wars* novel, enjoyable on its own, is also part of a much larger tale beginning immediately after the last *Star Wars* film, *Return of the Jedi.*

Here is a special look at Bantam's *Star Wars* books, along with excerpts from these thrilling novels. Each one is available now wherever Bantam Books are sold.

THE TRUCE AT BAKURA by Kathy Tyers
Setting: Immediately after *Return of the Jedi*

The day after his climactic battle with Emperor Palpatine and the sacrifice of his father, Darth Vader, who died saving his life, Luke Skywalker helps recover an Imperial drone ship bearing a startling message intended for the Emperor. It is a distress signal from the far-off Imperial outpost of Bakura, which is under attack by an alien invasion force, the Ssi-ruuk. Leia sees a rescue mission as an opportunity to achieve a diplomatic victory for the Rebel Alliance, even if it means fighting alongside former Imperials. But Luke receives a vision from Obi-Wan Kenobi revealing that the stakes are even higher: the invasion at Bakura threatens everything the Rebels have won at such great cost.

Here is a scene showing the extent of the alien menace:

On an outer deck of a vast battle cruiser called the *Shriwirr*, Dev Sibwarra rested his slim brown hand on a prisoner's left shoulder. "It'll be all right," he said softly. The other human's fear beat at his mind like a three-tailed lash. "There's no pain. You have a wonderful surprise ahead of you." Wonderful indeed, a life without hunger, cold, or selfish desire.

The prisoner, an Imperial of much lighter complexion than Dev, slumped in the entenchment chair. He'd given up protesting, and his breath came in gasps. Pliable bands secured his forelimbs, neck, and knees—but only for balance. With his nervous system deionized at the shoulders, he couldn't struggle. A slender intravenous tube dripped pale blue magnetizing solution into each of his carotid arteries while tiny servopumps hummed. It only took a few mils of magsol to attune the tiny, fluctuating electromagnetic fields of human brain waves to the Ssi-ruuvi entenchment apparatus.

Behind Dev, Master Firwirrung trilled a question in Ssi-ruuvi. "Is it calmed yet?"

Dev sketched a bow to his master and switched from human speech to Ssi-ruuvi. "Calm enough," he sang back. "He's almost ready."

Sleek, russet scales protected Firwirrung's two-meter length from beaked muzzle to muscular tail tip, and a prominent black **V** crest marked his forehead. Not large for a Ssi-ruu, he was still growing, with only a few age-scores where scales had begun to separate on his handsome chest. Firwirrung swung a broad, glowing white metal catchment arc down to cover the prisoner from midchest to nose. Dev could just peer over it and watch the man's pupils dilate. At any moment . . .

"Now," Dev announced.

Firwirrung touched a control. His muscular tail twitched with pleasure. The fleet's capture had been good today. Alongside his master, Dev would work far into the night. Before entechment, prisoners were noisy and dangerous. Afterward, their life energies powered droids of Ssi-ruuvi choosing.

The catchment arc hummed up to pitch. Dev backed away. Inside that round human skull, a magsol-drugged brain was losing control. Though Master Firwirrung assured him that the transfer of incorporeal energy was painless, every prisoner screamed.

As did this one, when Firwirrung threw the catchment arc switch. The arc boomed out a sympathetic vibration, as brain energy leaped to an electromagnet perfectly attuned to magsol. Through the Force rippled an ululation of indescribable anguish.

Dev staggered and clung to the knowledge his masters had given him: The prisoners only thought they felt pain. *He* only thought he sensed their pain. By the time the body screamed, all of a subject's energies had jumped to the catchment arc. The screaming body already was dead.

THE COURTSHIP OF PRINCESS LEIA by Dave Wolverton
Setting: Four years after *Return of the Jedi*

One of the most interesting developments in Bantam's Star Wars *novels is that in their storyline, Han Solo and Princess Leia start a family. This tale reveals how the couple originally got together. Wishing to strengthen the fledgling New Republic by bringing in powerful allies, Leia opens talks with the Hapes consortium of more than sixty worlds. But the consortium is ruled by the Queen Mother, who, to Han's dismay, wants Leia to marry her son, Prince Isolder. Before this action-packed story is over, Luke will join forces with Isolder against a group of Force-trained "witches" and face a deadly foe.*

In this scene, Luke is searching for Jedi lore and finds more than he bargained for:

Luke popped the cylinder into Artoo, and almost immediately Artoo caught a signal. Images flashed in the air before the droid: an ancient throne room where, one by one, Jedi came before their high master to give reports. Yet the holo was fragmented, so thoroughly erased that Luke got only bits and pieces —a blue-skinned man describing details of a grueling space battle against pirateers; a yellow-eyed Twi'lek with lashing headtails who told of discovering a plot to kill an ambassador. A date and time flashed on the holo vid before each report. The report was nearly four hundred standard years old.

Then Yoda appeared on the video, gazing up at the throne. His color was more vibrantly green than Luke remembered, and he did not use his walking stick. At middle age, Yoda had looked almost perky, carefree—not the bent, troubled old Jedi Luke had known. Most of the audio was erased, but through the background hiss Yoda clearly said, "We tried to free the Chu'unthor from Dathomir, but were repulsed by the witches . . . skirmish, with Masters Gra'aton and Vulatan. . . . Fourteen acolytes killed . . . go back to retrieve . . ." The audio hissed away, and soon the holo image dissolved to blue static with popping lights.

They went up topside, found that night had fallen while they worked underground. Their Whiphid guide soon returned, dragging the body of a gutted snow demon. The demon's white talons curled in the air, and its long purple tongue snaked out from between its massive fangs. Luke was amazed that the Whiphid could haul such a monster, yet the Whiphid held the demon's long hairy tail in one hand and managed to pull it back to camp.

There, Luke stayed the night with the Whiphids in a huge shelter made from the rib cage of a motmot, covered over with hides to keep out the wind. The Whiphids built a bonfire and roasted the snow demon, and the young danced while the elders played their claw harps. As Luke sat, watching the writhing flames and listening to the twang of harps, he meditated. "The future you will see, and the past. Old friends long forgotten . . ." Those were the words Yoda had said long ago while training Luke to peer beyond the mists of time.

Luke looked up at the rib bones of the motmot. The Whiphids had carved stick letters into the bone, ten and twelve meters in the air, giving the lineage of their ancestors. Luke could not read the letters, but they seemed to dance in the firelight, as if they were sticks and stones falling from the sky. The rib bones curved toward him, and Luke followed the curve of bones with his eyes. The tumbling sticks and boulders seemed to gyrate, all of them falling toward him as if they would crush him. He could see boulders hurtling through the air, too, smashing toward him. Luke's nostrils flared, and even Toola's chill could not keep a thin film of perspiration from dotting his forehead. A vision came to Luke then.

Luke stood in a mountain fortress of stone, looking over a plain with a sea of dark forested hills beyond, and a storm rose—a magnificent wind that brought with it towering walls of black clouds and dust, trees hurtling toward him and twisting through the sky. The clouds thundered overhead, filled with purple flames, obliterating all sunlight, and Luke could feel a malevolence hidden in those clouds and knew that they had been raised through the power of the dark side of the Force.

Dust and stones whistled through the air like autumn leaves. Luke tried to hold on to the stone parapet overlooking the plain to keep from being swept from the fortress walls. Winds pounded in his ears like the roar of an ocean, howling.

It was as if a storm of pure dark Force raged over the countryside, and suddenly, amid the towering clouds of darkness that thundered toward him, Luke could hear laughing, the sweet sound of women laughing. He looked above into the dark clouds, and saw the women borne through the air along with the rocks and debris, like motes of dust, laughing. A voice seemed to whisper, "the witches of Dathomir."

HEIR TO THE EMPIRE
DARK FORCE RISING
THE LAST COMMAND
by Timothy Zahn
Setting: Five years after *Return of the Jedi*

This 1 bestselling trilogy introduces two legendary forces of evil into the Star Wars *literary pantheon. Grand Admiral Thrawn has taken control of the Imperial fleet in the years since the destruction of the Death Star, and the mysterious Joruus C'baoth is a fearsome Jedi Master who has been seduced by the dark side. Han and Leia have now been married for about a year, and as the story begins, she is pregnant with twins. Thrawn's plan is to crush the Rebellion and resurrect the Empire's New Order with C'baoth's help—and in return, the Dark Master will get Han and Leia's Jedi children to mold as he wishes. For as readers of this magnificent trilogy will see, Luke Skywalker is not the last of the old Jedi. He is the first of the new.*

In this scene from Heir to the Empire, *Thrawn and C'baoth meet for the first time:*

For a long moment the old man continued to stare at Thrawn, a dozen strange expressions flicking in quick succession across his face. "Come. We will talk."

"Thank you," Thrawn said, inclining his head slightly. "May I ask who we have the honor of addressing?"

"Of course." The old man's face was abruptly regal again, and when he spoke his voice rang out in the silence of the crypt. "I am the Jedi Master Joruus C'baoth."

Pellaeon inhaled sharply, a cold shiver running up his back. "Joruus C'baoth?" he breathed. "But—"

He broke off. C'baoth looked at him, much as Pellaeon himself might look at a junior officer who has spoken out of turn. "Come," he repeated, turning back to Thrawn. "We will talk."

He led the way out of the crypt and back into the sunshine. Several small knots of people had gathered in the square in their absence, huddling well back from both the crypt and the shuttle as they whispered nervously together.

With one exception. Standing directly in their path a few meters away was one of the two guards C'baoth had ordered out of the crypt. On his face was an expression of barely controlled fury; in his hands, cocked and ready, was his crossbow. "You destroyed his home," C'baoth said, almost conversationally. "Doubtless he would like to exact vengeance."

The words were barely out of his mouth when the guard suddenly snapped the crossbow up and fired. Instinctively, Pellaeon ducked, raising his blaster—

And three meters from the Imperials the bolt came to an abrupt halt in midair.

Pellaeon stared at the hovering piece of wood and metal, his brain only slowly catching up with what had just happened. "They are our guests," C'baoth told the guard in a voice clearly intended to reach everyone in the square. "They will be treated accordingly."

With a crackle of splintering wood, the crossbow bolt shattered, the pieces dropping to the ground. Slowly, reluctantly, the guard lowered his crossbow, his eyes still burning with a now impotent rage. Thrawn let him stand there another second like that, then gestured to Rukh. The Noghri raised his blaster and fired—

And in a blur of motion almost too fast to see, a flat stone detached itself from the ground and hurled itself directly into the path of the shot, shattering spectacularly as the blast hit it.

Thrawn spun to face C'baoth, his face a mirror of surprise and anger. "C'baoth—!"

"These are *my* people, Grand Admiral Thrawn," the other cut him off, his voice forged from quiet steel. "Not yours; mine. If there is punishment to be dealt out, *I* will do it."

For a long moment the two men again locked eyes. Then, with an obvious effort, Thrawn regained his composure. "Of course, Master C'baoth," he said. "Forgive me."

C'baoth nodded. "Better. Much better." He looked past Thrawn, dismissed the guard with a nod. "Come," he said, looking back at the Grand Admiral. "We will talk."

The Jedi Academy Trilogy:
JEDI SEARCH
DARK APPRENTICE
CHAMPIONS OF THE FORCE
by Kevin J. Anderson
Setting: Seven years after *Return of the Jedi*

In order to assure the continuation of the Jedi Knights, Luke Skywalker has decided to start a training facility: a Jedi Academy. He will gather Force-sensitive students who show potential as prospective Jedi and serve as their mentor, as Jedi Masters Obi-Wan Kenobi and Yoda did for him. Han and Leia's twins are now toddlers, and there is a third Jedi child: the infant Anakin, named after Luke and Leia's father. In this trilogy, we discover the existence of a powerful Imperial doomsday weapon, the horrifying Sun Crusher—which will soon become the centerpiece of a titanic struggle between Luke Skywalker and his most brilliant Jedi Academy student, who is delving dangerously into the dark side.

In this scene from the first novel, Jedi Search, *Luke vocalizes his concept of a new Jedi order to a distinguished assembly of New Republic leaders:*

As he descended the long ramp, Luke felt all eyes turn toward him. A hush fell over the assembly. Luke Skywalker, the lone remaining Jedi Master, almost never took part in governmental proceedings.

"I have an important matter to address," he said.

Mon Mothma gave him a soft, mysterious smile and gestured for him to take a central position. "The words of a Jedi Knight are always welcome to the New Republic," she said.

Luke tried not to look pleased. She had provided the perfect opening for him. "In the Old Republic," he said, "Jedi Knights were the protectors and guardians of all. For a thousand generations the Jedi used the powers of the Force to guide, defend, and provide support for the rightful government of worlds—before the dark days of the Empire came, and the Jedi Knights were killed."

He let his words hang, then took another breath. "Now we have a New Republic. The Empire appears to be defeated. We have founded a new government based upon the old, but let us hope we learn from our mistakes. Before, an entire order of Jedi watched over the Republic, offering strength. Now I am the only Jedi Master who remains.

"Without that order of protectors to provide a backbone of strength for the New Republic, can we survive? Will we be able to weather the storms and the difficulties of forging a new union? Until now we have suffered severe struggles—but in the future they will be seen as nothing more than birth pangs."

Before the other senators could disagree with that, Luke continued. "Our people had a common foe in the Empire, and we must not let our defenses lapse just because we have internal problems. More to the point, what will happen when we begin squabbling among ourselves over petty matters? The old Jedi helped to mediate many types of disputes. What if there are no Jedi Knights to protect us in the difficult times ahead?

"My sister is undergoing Jedi training. She has a great deal of skill in the Force. Her three children are also likely candidates to be trained as young Jedi. In recent years I have come to know a woman named Mara Jade, who is now unifying the smugglers—the former smugglers," he amended, "into an organization that can support the needs of the New Republic. She also has a talent for the Force. I have encountered others in my travels."

Another pause. The audience was listening so far. "But are these the only ones? We already know that the ability to use the Force is passed from generation to generation. Most of the Jedi were killed in the Emperor's purge—but could he possibly have eradicated all of the descendants of those Knights? I myself was unaware of the potential power within me until Obi-Wan Kenobi taught me how to use it. My sister Leia was similarly unaware.

"How many people are abroad in this galaxy who have a comparable strength in the Force, who are potential members of a new order of Jedi Knights, but are unaware of who they are?"

Luke looked at them again. "In my brief search I have already discovered that there are indeed some descendants of former Jedi. I have come here to ask"—he turned to gesture toward

Mon Mothma, swept his hands across the people gathered there in the chamber—"for two things.

"First, that the New Republic officially sanction my search for those with a hidden talent for the Force, to seek them out and try to bring them to our service. For this I will need some help."

"And what will you yourself be doing?" Mon Mothma asked, shifting in her robes.

"I've already found several candidates I wish to investigate. All I ask right now is that you agree this is something we should pursue, that the search for Jedi be conducted by others and not just myself."

Mon Mothma sat up straighter in her central seat. "I think we can agree to that without further discussion." She looked around to the other senators, seeing them now in agreement. "Tell us your second request."

Luke stood taller. This was most important to him. He saw Leia stiffen.

"If sufficient candidates are found who have potential for using the Force, I wish to be allowed—with the New Republic's blessing—to establish in some appropriate place an intensive training center, a Jedi academy, if you will. Under my direction we can help these students discover their abilities, to focus and strengthen their power. Ultimately, this academy would provide a core group that could allow us to restore the Jedi Knights as protectors of the New Republic."

CHILDREN OF THE JEDI
by Barbara Hambly
Setting: Eight years after *Return of the Jedi*

The Star Wars *characters face a menace from the glory days of the Empire when a thirty-year-old automated Imperial Dreadnaught comes to life and begins its grim mission: to gather forces and annihilate a long-forgotten stronghold of Jedi children. When Luke is whisked onboard, he begins to communicate with the brave Jedi Knight who paralyzed the ship decades ago, and gave her life in the process. Now she is part of the vessel, existing in its artificial intelligence core, and guiding Luke through one of the most unusual adventures he has ever had.*

In this scene, Luke discovers that an evil presence is gathering, one that will force him to join the battle:

Like See-Threepio, Nichos Marr sat in the outer room of the suite to which Cray had been assigned, in the power-down mode that was the droid equivalent of rest. Like Threepio, at the sound of Luke's almost noiseless tread he turned his head, aware of his presence.

"Luke?" Cray had equipped him with the most sensitive vocal modulators, and the word was calibrated to a whisper no louder than the rustle of the blueleaves massed outside the windows. He rose, and crossed to where Luke stood, the dull silver of his arms and shoulders a phantom gleam in the stray flickers of light. "What is it?"

"I don't know." They retreated to the small dining area where Luke had earlier probed his mind, and Luke stretched up to pin back a corner of the lamp-sheath, letting a slim triangle of butter-colored light fall on the purple of the vulwood tabletop. "A dream. A premonition, maybe." It was on his lips to ask, *Do you dream?* but he remembered the ghastly, imageless darkness in Nichos's mind, and didn't. He wasn't sure if his pupil was aware of the difference from his human perception and knowledge, aware of just exactly what he'd lost when his consciousness, his self, had been transferred.

In the morning Luke excused himself from the expedition Tomla El had organized with Nichos and Cray to the Falls of Dessiar, one of the places on Ithor most renowned for its beauty and peace. When they left he sought out Umwaw Moolis, and the tall herd leader listened gravely to his less than logical request and promised to put matters in train to fulfill it. Then Luke descended to the House of the Healers, where Drub McKumb lay, sedated far beyond pain but with all the perceptions of agony and nightmare still howling in his mind.

"Kill you!" He heaved himself at the restraints, blue eyes glaring furiously as he groped and scrabbled at Luke with his clawed hands. "It's all poison! I see you! I see the dark light all around you! You're him! You're him!" His back bent like a bow; the sound of his shrieking was like something being ground out of him by an infernal mangle.

Luke had been through the darkest places of the universe and of his own mind, had done and experienced greater evil than perhaps any man had known on the road the Force had dragged him . . . Still, it was hard not to turn away.

"We even tried yarrock on him last night," explained the Healer in charge, a slightly built Ithorian beautifully tabby-striped green and yellow under her simple tabard of purple linen. "But apparently the earlier doses that brought him enough lucidity to reach here from his point of origin oversensitized his system. We'll try again in four or five days."

Luke gazed down into the contorted, grimacing face.

"As you can see," the Healer said, "the internal perception of pain and fear is slowly lessening. It's down to ninety-three percent of what it was when he was first brought in. Not much, I know, but something."

"Him! *Him! HIM!*" Foam spattered the old man's stained gray beard.

Who?

"I wouldn't advise attempting any kind of mindlink until it's at least down to fifty percent, Master Skywalker."

"No," said Luke softly.

Kill you all. And, *They are gathering . . .*

"Do you have recordings of everything he's said?"

"Oh, yes." The big coppery eyes blinked assent. "The transcript is available through the monitor cubicle down the hall. We could make nothing of them. Perhaps they will mean something to you."

They didn't. Luke listened to them all, the incoherent groans and screams, the chewed fragments of words that could be only guessed at, and now and again the clear disjointed cries: "Solo! Solo! Can you hear me? Children . . . Evil . . . Gathering here . . . Kill you all!"

DARKSABER
by Kevin J. Anderson
Setting: Immediately thereafter

Not long after Children of the Jedi, *Luke and Han learn that evil Hutts are building a reconstruction of the original Death Star—and that the Empire is still alive, in the form of Daala, who has joined forces with Pellaeon, former second in command to the feared Grand Admiral Thrawn. In this early scene, Luke has returned to the home of Obi-Wan Kenobi on Tatooine to try and consult a long-gone mentor:*

He stood anxious and alone, feeling like a prodigal son outside the ramshackle, collapsed hut that had once been the home of Obi-Wan Kenobi.

Luke swallowed and stepped forward, his footsteps crunching in the silence. He had not been here in many years. The door had fallen off its hinges; part of the clay front wall had fallen in. Boulders and crumbled adobe jammed the entrance. A pair of small, screeching desert rodents snapped at him and fled for cover; Luke ignored them.

Gingerly, he ducked low and stepped into the home of his first mentor.

Luke stood in the middle of the room breathing deeply, turning around, trying to sense the presence he desperately needed to see. This was the place where Obi-Wan Kenobi had told Luke of the Force. Here, the old man had first given Luke his lightsaber and hinted at the truth about his father, "from a certain point of view," dispelling the diversionary story that Uncle Owen had told, at the same time planting seeds of his own deceptions.

"Ben," he said and closed his eyes, calling out with his mind as well as his voice. He tried to penetrate the invisible walls of the Force and reach to the luminous being of Obi-Wan Kenobi who had visited him numerous times, before saying he could never speak with Luke again.

"Ben, I need you," Luke said. Circumstances had changed. He could think of no other way past the obstacles he faced. Obi-Wan had to answer. It wouldn't take long, but it could give him the key he needed with all his heart.

Luke paused and listened and sensed—

But felt nothing. If he could not summon Obi-Wan's spirit here in the empty dwelling where the old man had lived in exile for so many years, Luke didn't believe he could find his former teacher ever again.

He echoed the words Leia had used more than a decade earlier, beseeching him, "Help me, Obi-Wan Kenobi," Luke whispered, "you're my only hope."

THE CRYSTAL STAR
by Vonda N. McIntyre
Setting: Ten years after *Return of the Jedi*

Leia's three children have been kidnapped. That horrible fact is made worse by Leia's realization that she can no longer sense her children through the Force! While she, Artoo-Detoo, and Chewbacca trail the kidnappers, Luke and Han discover a planet that is suffering strange quantum effects from a nearby star. Slowly freezing into a perfect crystal and disrupting the Force, the star is blunting Luke's power and crippling the Millennium *Falcon. These strands converge in an apocalyptic threat not only to the fate of the New Republic, but to the universe itself. Here is Luke and Han's initial approach to the crystal star:*

Han piloted the *Millennium Falcon* through the strangest star system he had ever approached. An ancient, dying, crystallizing white dwarf star orbited a black hole in a wildly eccentric elliptical path.

Eons ago, in this place, a small and ordinary yellow star peacefully orbited an immense blue-white supergiant. The blue star aged, and collapsed.

The blue star went supernova, blasting light and radiation and debris out into space.

Its light still traveled through the universe, a furious explosion visible from distant galaxies.

Over time, the remains of the supergiant's core collapsed under the force of its own gravity. The result was degenerate mass: a black hole.

The violence of the supernova disrupted the orbit of the nova's companion, the yellow star. Over time, the yellow star's orbit decayed.

The yellow star fell toward the unimaginably dense body of the black hole. The black hole sucked up anything, even light, that came within its grasp. And when it captured matter—even an entire yellow star—it ripped the atoms apart into a glowing accretion disk. Subatomic particles imploded downward into the singularity's equator, emitting great bursts of radiation. The accretion disk spun at a fantastic speed, glowing with fantastic heat, creating a funeral pyre for the destroyed yellow companion.

The plasma spiraled in a raging pinwheel, circling so fast and heating so intensely that it blasted X rays out into space. Then, finally, the glowing gas fell toward the invisible black hole, approaching it closer and closer, appearing to fall more and more slowly as relativity influenced it.

It was lost forever to this universe.

That was the fate of the small yellow star.

The system contained a third star: the dying white dwarf, which shone with ancient heat even as it froze into a quantum crystal. Now, as the *Millennium Falcon* entered the system, the white dwarf was falling toward the black hole, on the inward curve of its eccentric elliptical orbit.

"Will you look at that," Han said. "Quite a show."

"Indeed it is, Master Han," Threepio said, "but it is merely a shadow of what will occur when the black hole captures the crystal star."

Luke gazed silently into the maelstrom of the black hole. Han waited.

"Hey, kid! Snap out of it."

Luke started. "What?"

"I don't know where you were, but you weren't here."

"Just thinking about the Jedi Academy. I hate to leave my students, even for a few days. But if I *do* find other trained Jedi, it'll make a big difference. To the Academy. To the New Republic . . ."

"I think we're getting along pretty well already," Han said, irked. He had spent years maintaining the peace with ordinary people. In his opinion, Jedi Knights could cause more trouble than they were worth. "And what if these are all using the dark side?"

Luke did not reply.

Han seldom admitted his nightmares, but he had nightmares about what could happen to his children if they were tempted to the dark side.

Solar prominences flared from the white dwarf's surface. The *Falcon* passed it, heading toward the more perilous region of the black hole.

The Corellian Trilogy:
AMBUSH AT CORELLIA
ASSAULT AT SELONIA
SHOWDOWN AT CENTERPOINT
by Roger MacBride Allen
Setting: Fourteen years after *Return of the Jedi*

This trilogy takes us to Corellia, Han Solo's homeworld, which Han has not visited in quite some time. A trade summit brings Han, Leia, and the children—now developing their own clear personalities and instinctively learning more about their innate skills in the Force—into the middle of a situation that most closely resembles a burning fuse. The Corellian system is on the brink of civil war, there are New Republic intelligence agents on a mysterious mission which even Han does not understand, and worst of all, a fanatical rebel leader has his hands on a superweapon of unimaginable power—and just wait until you find out who that leader is!

Here is an early scene from Ambush *that gives you a wonderful look at the growing Solo children (the twins are Jacen and Jaina, and their little brother is Anakin):*

Anakin plugged the board into the innards of the droid and pressed a button. The droid's black, boxy body shuddered awake, it drew in its wheels to stand up a bit taller, its status lights lit, and it made a sort of triple beep. "That's good," he said, and pushed the button again. The droid's status lights went out, and its body slumped down again. Anakin picked up the next piece, a motivation actuator. He frowned at it as he turned it over in his hands. He shook his head. "That's *not* good," he announced.

"What's not good?" Jaina asked.

"This thing," Anakin said, handing her the actuator. "Can't you *tell*? The insides part is all melty."

Jaina and Jacen exchanged a look. "The outside looks okay," Jaina said, giving the part to her brother. "How can he tell what the *inside* of it looks like? It's sealed shut when they make it."

Anakin, still sitting on the floor, took the device from his brother and frowned at it again. He turned it over and over in his hands, and then held it over his head and looked at it as if he were holding it up to the light. "There," he said, pointing a chubby finger at one point on the unmarked surface. "In there is the bad part." He rearranged himself to sit cross-legged, put the actuator in his lap, and put his right index finger over the "bad" part. "Fix," he said. "Fix." The dark brown outer case of the actuator seemed to glow for a second with an odd blue-red light, but then the glow sputtered out and Anakin pulled his finger away quickly and stuck it in his mouth, as if he had burned it on something.

"Better now?" Jaina asked.

"*Some* better," Anakin said, pulling his finger out of his mouth. "Not *all* better." He took the actuator in his hand and stood up. He opened the access panel on the broken droid and plugged in the actuator. He closed the door and looked expectantly at his older brother and sister.

"Done?" Jaina asked.

"Done," Anakin agreed. "But *I'm* not going to push the button." He backed well away from the droid, sat down on the floor, and folded his arms.

Jacen looked at his sister.

"Not me," she said. "This was your idea."

Jacen stepped forward to the droid, reached out to push the power button from as far away as he could, and then stepped hurriedly back.

Once again, the droid shuddered awake, rattling a bit this time as it did so. It pulled its wheels in, lit its panel lights, and made the same triple beep. But then its holocam eye viewlens wobbled back and forth, and its panel lights dimmed and flared. It rolled backward just a bit, and then recovered itself.

"Good morning, young mistress and masters," it said. "How may I surge you?"

Well, one word wrong, but so what? Jacen grinned and clapped his hands and rubbed them together eagerly. "Good day, droid," he said. They had done it! But what to ask for first? "First tidy up this room," he said. A simple task, and one that ought to serve as a good test of what this droid could do.

Suddenly the droid's overhead access door blew off and there was a flash of light from its interior. A thin plume of smoke drifted out of the droid. Its panel lights flared again, and then the work arm sagged downward. The droid's body, softened by heat, sagged in on itself and drooped to the floor. The floor and walls and ceilings of the playroom were supposed to be fireproof, but nonetheless the floor under the droid darkened a bit, and the ceiling turned black. The ventilators kicked on high automatically, and drew the smoke out of the room. After a moment they shut themselves off, and the room was silent.

The three children stood, every bit as frozen to the spot as the droid was, absolutely stunned. It was Anakin who recovered first. He walked cautiously toward the droid and looked at it carefully, being sure not to get too close or touch it. *"Really* melty now," he announced, and then wandered off to the other side of the room to play with his blocks.

The twins looked at the droid, and then at each other.

"We're dead," Jacen announced, surveying the wreckage.